'A comp [illegible] al and tragedy that will have you turning the pages until the early hours'

Grazia

'The writing is so vivid that we became completely lost in the Tide family's world – this one's going to go far'

Good Housekeeping

'A compelling tale of grief and forgiveness' *Woman & Home*

'The Tides in Hannah Richell's forceful debut are a family . . . the revelations of what happened, and the burden of guilt the Tides carry, are powerfully evoked in a classy melodrama with very well-realised characters. Once you start reading, you'll be hooked' *Reader's Digest*

'This confident debut novel is a dark but compelling read. The characters are so believable your heart will ache for their pain, and you'll be driven to ask yourself the question could you forgive and forget?' *Candis*

'This novel flits between past and present, and dangles a just-out-of-reach secret that will have you frantically turning pages to reveal the shocking final truth'

Weightwatchers Magazine

'Moving between the past and present it's a gripping story of troubled young women' *Star*

Hannah Richell was born in Kent and spent her early childhood in Buckinghamshire and Canada. After several years working in book publishing, she emigrated to Australia in 2005. She now lives with her husband and two young children in Sydney and returns to the UK as often as possible to spend time with family and savour the green grass of home. *Secrets of the Tides* is her debut novel.

SECRETS
of the
TIDES

Hannah Richell

An Orion paperback

First published in Great Britain in 2012
by Orion
This paperback edition published in 2012
by Orion Books Ltd,
Orion House, 5 Upper St Martin's Lane
London WC2H 9EA

An Hachette UK company

A CIP catalogue record for this book is available from the British Library.

Typeset at The Spartan Press Ltd,
Lymington, Hants

Printed and bound in Great Britain by
Clays Ltd, St Ives plc

The Orion Publishing Group's policy is to use papers that are natural, renewable and recyclable products and made from wood grown in sustainable forests. The logging and manufacturing processes are expected to conform to the environmental regulations of the country of origin.

www.orionbooks.co.uk

For M, J & G

Fever of the heart and brain,
Sorrow, pestilence, and pain,
Moans of anguish, maniac laughter,
All the evils that hereafter
Shall afflict and vex mankind,
All into the air have risen
From the chambers of their prison;
Only Hope remains behind.

From 'The Masque of Pandora'
HENRY WADSWORTH LONGFELLOW

PROLOGUE

A half-empty train rattles through fields and farmland towards the grey concrete sprawl of the city. There is a young woman huddled in the farthest corner of the last carriage. Her hair is like a veil, hiding her tears. In her pocket is an antique brooch. Her fingers brush the cold arc of it before flipping it over and over in time to the rhythmic clatter of wheels on track. When she can resist no longer, she releases the clasp and stabs the pin deep into the flesh of her palm.

It's agony, but she won't stop. She presses the needle deeper still, until warm blood streams down her wrist and splashes crimson onto the carriage floor.

Finally, the train jerks and slows. Brakes squeal.

As they reach their destination she pushes the bloodied brooch deep into her coat pocket, grabs her bag and then drops down onto the platform.

People dart about her. Two women shriek and embrace. A tall man in a turban races for the ticket barriers. A spotty teenager hops from foot to foot, gazing up at the departures board as he shovels crisps into his mouth. Everything around her seems to buzz and hum while she just stands there on the platform, a single fixed point, breathing deeply.

Signs for the Underground point one way but she ignores them, hefting her bag onto her shoulder and making for the street exit. She strikes out across a busy pedestrian crossing and turns left for the bridge. Big Ben looms in the distance; it is three minutes to twelve.

She walks with purpose; she knows where she is going and what has to be done. But then she sees the river, and the sight of it, a shifting black mass carving its way through the city, makes her shudder. Whenever she's imagined this moment the water has been grey and flat, not dark and viscous like seeping oil. But it doesn't matter now. There is no going back.

She stops halfway across the bridge and leans her rucksack up against the wall. Then, with a quick glance about her, she scoots up and over the barrier until she is clinging to the other side of the balustrade.

The toes of her trainers balance precariously on the concrete ledge. She grips the wall, wincing as her bleeding palm scrapes the stone, and then twists so that she is facing the water below. The wind blows her hair, whipping it across her face and stinging her eyes until hot tears form. She blinks them back.

'Hey!' She hears a cry behind her. 'Hey, what are you doing?'

She is out of time.

She locks her gaze on a sea of grey buildings on the far horizon and, with a final breath, lets go of the balustrade. Then she is falling, falling, falling.

Any breath left in her body is punched out by the ice-cold water. She fights the urge to kick and struggle, instead surrendering herself to the inky blackness, letting the weight of her clothes take her stone-like towards the bottom.

By the time Big Ben chimes midday she is gone, lost to the murky depths below.

DORA

Present Day

It is late when Dora arrives home. She lets herself in through the heavy metal door of the old button factory and climbs the three flights of stairs to her flat. It's cold and gloomy in the stairwell but as her key turns in the door she hears music playing and the welcoming sound of saucepans and cutlery clattering from deep within the kitchen.

'Babe, I'm back,' she calls out, slipping off her killer shoes and kicking them into an ever-growing pile of footwear by the front door. A wet nose and huge brown eyes appear from behind the shabby leather sofa, followed by a long wagging tail. 'Hello, Gormley,' she says, giving the dog an affectionate pat on the rump. 'Busy day?'

Dan's chocolate brown Labrador wags his tail again, yawns and slinks back into the lounge.

'Don't come into the kitchen,' she hears Dan yell. 'I'm cooking . . . something experimental . . . very Blumenthal . . . you're going to love it.'

Dora smiles; they both know Dan doesn't cook. She rifles through the post on the table by the door – nothing but bills. 'I didn't think we had any food?' she asks suspiciously.

'Er . . . we didn't. Oh shit!' There's the sound of something smashing.

'You went shopping?'

'Sort of. Just don't come in yet, it's nearly ready.'

Dora walks into the living space, a large, white, open-plan

area flanked by floor-to-ceiling windows on opposite sides. As she moves through she starts at a movement out of the corner of her eye, but calms as she realises it's just her own pale reflection in the windows; she's feeling jumpy. Obediently she remains in the room, switching on a couple of lamps, returning a few of Dan's splayed art books back to the shelves next to the television. Gormley is already curled up on his bed next to the sofa, one lazy eye tracking her movements. Dora looks around her, wondering when it will ever really feel like *their* place. It's been six months and they've barely scratched the surface of the enormous project they took on. The exposed brick walls have been painted white and the floorboards sanded and polished. It's clean and spacious, but it feels a little like an exhibition space waiting to be filled. They just haven't had the time to turn it into a home; it's been one thing after another.

'Right, you can come in now,' she hears Dan shout.

Dora pushes the door to the kitchen; it sticks momentarily on the torn lino until she gives it a firm shove with her shoulder and it flies open with a bang.

Dan is standing by the wonky trestle table currently masquerading as their kitchen table. He indicates with a flourish two steaming bowls of tomato soup and a plate of buttered white sliced bread. She can see the open soup tin on the counter behind him. She walks across and puts her arms around his neck, kissing his stubbly chin.

'That's the nicest thing I've seen all day.'

'That bad, huh? How did the presentation go?'

Dora shrugs. 'Hard to tell; the clients weren't giving much away.'

'But your boss was pleased?'

'I think so. He'll be more pleased if we sign them. It would be a real coup for the agency – good for me too,' she adds, 'as I'd be on the account.'

Dan releases her from his big embrace and ushers her to the table. 'Come on, let's eat before it gets cold.'

Dora seats herself at the table and reaches for a slice of bread. 'Thanks for this.'

'It's nothing, really.' He pushes a mug of tea towards her. 'Are you OK? You look a little pale.'

'I'm fine; it's just been a really long day. I'm tired.'

He looks at her with concern. 'You're working too hard.'

'I'm fine,' she says again, with a shrug. 'Anyway, how was *your* day?' she asks, steering the conversation away from her. 'Did you get much done?'

It's as if someone has switched a light on in Dan's face. 'It was terrific. I had a huge breakthrough. I know exactly what my next piece is going to be. And Kate Grimshaw rang me back to confirm her order for three of the sculptures from my showcase, so I'm certainly going to be busy over the next few months.'

'That's great!' Dora raises her mug and he clinks his against it. 'Really, it's wonderful news.' They both know Dan has been waiting for inspiration to strike. His last set of bronze sculptures showed at a tiny London gallery and were picked up by a noted art collector, but since then he's been struggling with the pressures of following up with something better. Dora knows he's been privately agonising over the delay, so it's a relief to hear he has, at last, found inspiration. 'Do you want to tell me about the new piece?'

Dan shakes his head. 'Sorry, not this one. It's a surprise.'

'Intriguing. I take it the back room is out of bounds for now then?'

'Yes, and it's a studio, remember, not a back room?'

She smiles down into her bowl and they fall into a comfortable silence, slurping at their soup until they are both staring down at empty dishes.

'I'll wash up,' she offers.

'Just a minute, I got you these,' he says, holding out two brown capsules in the palm of his hand.

'What are they?' she asks, prodding them with suspicion. 'They look like horse tranquillizers.'

'Vitamins. Mrs Singh at the corner shop says you should start taking them.' He beams up at her and Dora takes them from his outstretched hand, placing them next to her empty bowl.

'Thanks,' she says, wondering how many people he has already blabbed the news to. They really do need to talk, she realises. Not now though, not when he's so happy about his work. It can wait.

She wakes later that night to the sound of rain drumming on the roof above their bed and Dan scuttling around the room in a panic.

'Do you need a hand?' she asks, propping herself up on one elbow in the darkness.

'No, stay there where it's warm. I'm fine.' She hears him trip over a saucepan and the sound of water splashing across the floor. 'Effing useless roof.'

She smiles in the darkness and listens as he artfully re-arranges the carefully cultivated collection of bowls and pans until the sound of water dripping on tin begins to mingle with the noise of the rain outside.

'It will be summer soon,' she tries cheerfully.

'Hmmm . . .' is all he says, which worries her. He is usually the optimistic one. The agent that showed them around the crumbling old factory had proudly declared the space a 'New York-style loft apartment' but they had all known it was marketing flannel. Really they were standing in the dingy and dilapidated top floor of an old East End factory. It had potential, and could provide Dan with the work space he needed to create his intricate bronze sculptures, but it was still a long way away from the beautiful, contemporary, open plan area Dora had mentally transformed it into when they had first looked around. The reality was harder to live with, and ever since they had bought the old place it has been Dan who has jollied her through her worries about rotten floor-boards, leaky plumbing and holes in the roof.

'Come back to bed. We'll deal with it in the morning,' she tries.

'We've been saying that for six months.'

'I know. But we will, OK?'

Dan gives up and dives under the covers, rubbing his cold feet against hers until she yelps. 'Sorry, you're just so lovely and warm.'

She turns her back on him and nestles into the reassuring curve of his body. They are two proverbial spoons. His arms slide around her waist and his hands, rough and strong, come to rest on her stomach. She can feel his breath slow against her neck and realises he is already drifting off. She envies him his ability to fall asleep so easily: the sleep of the innocent. She hasn't been able to sleep like that for a very long time and now that she is awake, her mind is suddenly buzzing.

First she is reliving the Sunrise Cereals pitch at work; she remembers her part in the performance. She had thought it went well, but now, lying there in the darkness, listening to the rain, she starts to wonder. She knows if she starts to stew on it she will be awake for hours so instead she tries to concentrate on relaxing her toes. Isn't that what those self-help books say to do when you can't sleep? Start at your toes and work your way up your legs, relaxing each part of your body in turn. By the time you get to your nose you're guaranteed to be asleep. She's sure she's heard that somewhere.

But she has only reached her knees, which prove very difficult to focus on, let alone relax, when Dora feels a cold, creeping panic trickling up from her guts. It's been the same thing the last few nights; a chilling grip on her insides and the sudden, overwhelming sensation of the breath being squeezed from her body, as if something heavy is lying on top of her, crushing her into the mattress. Dora's heart begins to thud wildly in her ribcage.

'Dan?' she says into the darkness.

There is no answer but the drumming of the rain and the loud beat of her heart.

'Dan, are you awake?' She nudges him.

'Mmmmm . . .' he groans. 'No.'

'We need to talk.' She can't bear to lie there alone a second longer.

Dan's arms tighten around her waist. 'Go to sleep. We'll sort the roof in the morning.'

'It's not the roof I want to talk about.' She swallows down the acid taste in her mouth. 'It's the . . . the baby.'

She can feel his arms stiffen slightly and his breath pause momentarily against her neck. 'What about the baby?' he murmurs.

'I think we need to talk about it.'

'Right now?'

'Yes.'

Dan raises himself up on one elbow in the dark and looks at her. 'What's up?'

She takes a deep breath and tries to control her trembling limbs. 'It's like we're just drifting along, out of control, letting life wash over us. I think we should decide whether we actually want this or not. It's such a huge responsibility, having a baby. What I mean is, how can we even think about raising a child when we don't even have a dry place to live?' Dora can hear the hysterical edge in her voice.

Dan is quiet for a moment. 'We'll get the flat sorted. Don't worry. These new commissions will help the cash flow. Now it's spring we can get the roof fixed, and then we'll do the damp in the kitchen and the bathroom. Then it's just the cosmetic stuff.' He stifles a yawn. 'We always knew this place was going to be a long-term project. I thought you were up for it?'

'I was, I mean, I *am*,' she corrects. 'This isn't about the flat. Not really. I mean, it is, but it's more than that.' She swallows. 'Don't you ever wonder if you're ready to be a parent?'

Silence fills the room.

'I'm not sure', she continues in a small voice, 'if I want to be a mother. It's such a responsibility. We wouldn't be a couple any more. We'd be . . . a family.'

Dan sighs. 'I'm sure every new parent feels this way, Dora. It's perfectly natural. I know it wasn't planned,' he gives another yawn, 'but it's exciting, don't you think? A family.' He pauses for a moment. 'That sounds good to me.'

Dora shifts slightly in his arms, turning to stare at the emptiness above their heads. Things for Dan are always so simple. He sees things in black and white. That's what she loves about him. But her life isn't black and white. It's shades of grey, like a storm-cloud oil painting hanging above a fire-place. How could a man like Dan, a man with nothing but lightness in his heart and an optimistic view of the world understand what she feels?

'Dora, is this about your family? About . . . well, you know?'

She nods in the darkness but cannot speak.

'I know it was terrible. I know, from the little you've talked about, that you still live with it. Believe me, Dora, I want to understand, I really do.'

She lies very still.

'But this is a chance for you to move on, don't you see?' She can feel his grip tighten around her waist and his hands stroke her stomach with gentle, reassuring movements. 'It's a new life . . . a new start . . . us and our baby. We'll be our very own family. Don't you want that?'

Dora doesn't know what to say. Of course she wants a life with Dan. She loves him and their life together in London. He is her rock. And yet, at the same time, she is utterly paralysed. Years have passed and she still feels like the same girl she was all those years ago. Nothing has changed, not really. How can she even consider the enormous responsibility of mother-hood . . . of being responsible for another human being when she has proved so catastrophically irresponsible in the past? And how can she contemplate starting a family of her own when the one she grew up in – the one she adored and thought would be there for her for ever – has been torn apart so completely? The truth is that she doesn't believe she deserves a family of her own. She doesn't deserve a fresh start with Dan. She doesn't deserve happiness. But how can she tell him that?

'Go to sleep,' Dan murmurs into her neck. 'Everything always seems worse at night. We'll talk tomorrow.' His grip loosens on her slightly and she can tell that she is losing him to sleep again. 'You'll feel better in the morning,' he whispers.

'Night,' she says, before turning in his arms to gaze into the blackness of the bedroom. Dan is wrong. She knows she won't feel better in the morning. She has spent the last ten years willing each morning to be better . . . to feel better. And each morning she awakens to the sickening knowledge that she is to blame for the disintegration of her family. She feels, sometimes, as though they've all abandoned her, as though she's been cut loose and left to drift through life on her own. But then she remembers that it is her fault they have been scattered like the floating debris from a shipwreck. She feels the guilt of it like a deep, throbbing pain.

As Dan begins to snore gently, Dora closes her eyes. She wants sleep to claim her too, but she knows it is a long way off. Instead, she lets her mind wander down the pathways of her past. Slowly, it drifts down a wide, tree-lined drive. She can almost hear the wind rushing through the tall sycamores and smell the salt carried on the breeze. She rounds a corner and there it is, a rambling old farmhouse standing high upon the Dorset cliffs, its whitewashed walls gleaming like a beacon in the sunshine. As she draws closer she sees the tangle of ivy creeping up its exterior, curling around the eaves of the grey slate roof. She drifts closer still and sees the solid oak front door, bleached with weather and age. In her mind's eye she pushes on the door, the smooth wood familiar under her fingers, and enters a hallway, cool and dark and haunted with the footsteps of a generation of Tides. She walks past an open door, ignoring the elegant dark-haired woman bent over a desk of books and papers. She turns away from the sound of giggles echoing down the creaking staircase and passes a handsome, fair-haired man seated in the drawing room peering at the newspaper spread across his lap. She ignores the lure of the house, instead making for the conservatory where the scent of roses and lilac wafts enticingly through the open doors. Drifting through, she wanders down the sprawling lawn towards the siren's song of the sea, crashing far away onto the cliffs below.

As she reaches a twisted old cherry tree down in the orchard she turns and studies the house, gazing up at the wide sash windows. She stares at them, searching for answers deep within their shadows, but the glass is blackened by the glare of the sun.

Clifftops. The house she once called home.

Dan shifts and sighs in his sleep and as Dora moves her hands onto her still-flat belly and contemplates her future, she suddenly understands. She cannot hide any longer. She must return to Clifftops. She must return to face her past.

HELEN

Sixteen Years Earlier

Helen stood in the hallway and surveyed the ever-growing pile of suitcases, bags, shoes and coats. It would be just fine by her if someone decided to cancel Easter. The packing was bad enough. There were the piles of washing to sort through, a fridge to clear, the airing cupboard to dig around in for long-lost beach towels, and then the challenge of squashing everything into the groaning boot of the car. Add to that the fact that Richard was still sitting in the study on a last-minute work phone call while the girls drifted about the house in aimless slow motion and it was enough to make Helen want to scream at someone, long and loud.

She entered the kitchen to empty the bin and found Dora, sitting at the kitchen table, gazing dreamily into the garden over her bowl of cereal.

'You're not *still* eating those cornflakes are you?' she asked, as she wrestled with the overflowing bin bag.

'Uh-huh.'

'Well hurry up,' she said, finally freeing the bag from its holder and tying it off. 'I need to get the dishwasher on.'

Dora nodded and raised a token spoonful of cereal to her lips. Satisfied, Helen left the room and went to find Cassie. She'd assumed she was upstairs packing but when she finally came upon her, she found her eldest daughter sprawled across her bed, half dressed and reading a paperback while she sucked lazily on the ends of her hair. It was the final straw.

'I thought I told you we had to be on the road by ten?' Helen yelled. 'We're going to get stuck in traffic.' She looked around at Cassie's messy room in exasperation. 'And didn't I ask you to tidy this up last night? You haven't even *started* to pack!'

'Relax, Mum. It'll take me five minutes. I really don't know what the big deal is. It's just a week at Grandma and Granddad's. You and Dad are acting like we're going on some polar expedition!'

Sarcasm, that was new. Helen saw Cassie's eyes flick back to the book in her hands and had to resist the urge to fly across the room and hurl it out of the bedroom window. Instead she took a deep breath and counted to three. At eleven years old Cassie was a bright girl and she already knew how to push her buttons.

'Well, I'm not going to ask you again,' Helen warned as she left the room. It was a weak parting shot, but she couldn't think of anything better to threaten her with; they couldn't exactly leave her behind, attractive as the thought was.

She closed the door on Cassie and retreated down the corridor to her own bedroom. A battered old suitcase lay open on the bed. She still needed to decide whether to pack a dress or another pair of trousers. Trousers would be more practical, but she knew her mother-in-law expected them all to make an effort on Easter Sunday. Helen eyed a green silk dress hanging in the wardrobe, then a pair of black cords, before caving in and placing the dress on top of the growing pile of clothes. She could at least *attempt* to keep the peace with Daphne this year.

'That's nice, have I seen it before?' Richard asked, entering the room and glancing at the dress now lying on top of the open suitcase.

Helen rolled her eyes. 'Only about a million times.'

'Oh . . . well it's lovely. Are we nearly ready to go?'

Helen bristled. *She* wasn't the one who had been on the phone all morning. 'The girls are still dawdling,' she said, struggling with the zipper on the suitcase until Richard came across and leaned heavily on it for her, 'but we should be on the road in half an hour or so.' It was optimistic, but secretly she didn't mind the delay. She really wasn't in any great hurry to get down to Dorset and start the week of polite chitchat, country walks and sedate cups of tea with Richard's parents. She knew it was a Tide family tradition, everyone together at the big house for Easter, and she knew how much Richard loved taking her and the girls to his childhood home, but she longed to spend the holidays quietly at home, just once; a bit of shopping, some reading, pottering around the kitchen, maybe even some gardening. Still, there was no point dreaming; it would never happen. When it came to family traditions, Daphne Tide always got her way.

'Mum's very excited about our visit,' said Richard, as if reading her mind. 'Apparently she's been baking all week. And Dad's thinking about taking the girls sailing.'

'Lovely,' said Helen, forcing herself to return her husband's smile. She would go along with it, as she always did, for the rest of them. It was only a week at Clifftops, after all.

Forty-five minutes later, after a final sweep of the house, a reshuffling of the boot and a last minute panic over Dora's missing swimming costume, the Tide family locked up their north London terrace and clambered into the car. Miraculously, they made it all the way to Winchester before the first sounds of bickering broke out in the back seat.

'It's not fair,' whined Dora, 'I never get to choose the music.' Helen could see her wielding a new boy band album in the rear-view mirror.

'That's because you've got rubbish taste,' said Cassie.

'I have not.'

'Have too.'

'Your turn to referee,' Richard muttered under his breath as he indicated and overtook yet another caravan creeping its way west for Easter.

Helen twisted round in the passenger seat and regarded each of her daughters in turn. Cassie was hunched in the far corner of the back seat, her head turned towards the window, her face obscured by a curtain of blond hair. She was stubborn and Helen already knew she wouldn't look at her. She turned instead to regard Dora, who stared up at her with imploring green eyes from beneath her wonky home-cut fringe. Helen sighed. 'Will you two settle down? Your father's trying to concentrate on the road.'

'But it's my turn to choose . . .' Dora's cheeks blushed red.

'If you girls don't stop squabbling there'll be no music at all.'

'B-b-but . . .' Dora fell silent under her mother's glare and Helen turned back to the front.

'You OK, love?' Richard lifted a hand from the steering wheel and placed it on her arm.

'Uh-huh,' she nodded, watching an endless ribbon of cats' eyes speed towards them. She was getting one of her headaches, and frankly she'd have preferred a bit of peace and quiet to the relentless thud of pop music; still, it was definitely preferable to one of Cassie's tantrums. She sighed quietly to herself; in twelve years the trip had never got any easier.

She could still remember the very first time she had travelled with Richard to Clifftops. It had been a bleak day in March, the sky so thick with cloud it made you wonder whether the sun would ever really shine again. She'd sat in the car nervously plaiting and replaiting the leather fringe on her handbag as Richard drummed percussion on the steering wheel with his fingers and they'd sped ever closer to the house he had grown up in and the parents she would soon, should everything go to plan, be calling her in-laws.

'They're going to love you,' he reassured her. 'Almost as much as I do.'

'And the baby?' she asked, stroking her barely-there bump protectively.

Richard's glance followed her hands before returning to the road. 'Let me handle that. It'll be fine. Trust me.'

And she had, implicitly, which was strange because they'd only really known each other a matter of months. Helen had been in her final year of university, studying as a Classics undergraduate. Richard – a little older – was finishing up five years of his Architecture degree to start a placement at his father's firm. They'd met, predictably, where most students did: in the pub. And they had hit it off right away.

Richard was tall and fair-haired with cornflower-blue eyes, broad shoulders and the sort of grown-up confidence that comes from being a beloved only child. Helen had noticed him watching her from across the bar. She'd gambled and smiled back at him and he told her later that it was that first smile that had got him, hook, line and sinker. Love at first sight, that's what he called it. He'd made his way over to their table and introduced himself. She'd liked the way he did it, straightforward and honest, no corny chat-up lines, no leering and winking at his friends. Right from the word go he had seemed good and honest and kind. And if what little experience she'd had with men up until then had taught her anything, it was that those qualities were very rare indeed.

They'd dated for a few weeks and it had been fun. He'd taken her to rugby matches and offered her his coat as she'd shivered in the stands. He booked tables at romantic candlelit restaurants and gave her a crash course in architecture by escorting her around the city pointing out the buildings and styles he particularly admired. They'd argued bitterly over politics and could never seem to find a film they both wanted to see, but all was forgotten when they fell into bed together at the end of the night, their differences seeming to ignite a passion that was best served in bed. Dating Richard was a new experience for Helen; he seemed far more grown-up than previous boyfriends, more attentive and self-assured. Even when she had discovered, with stomach-clenching terror, that she was pregnant, he'd been a rock. She could tell from the pallor of his face and the slight tremble in his hands that it was a shock, yet right from the off he'd said all the right things. It was her decision to make. He would support her, no matter what. And, once she'd decided to keep the baby, his proposal had followed just a week later, a beautiful antique diamond ring winking up at her from across the table of a local Italian restaurant.

'It's the right thing to do, Helen. Let's give this baby the best start we can. Let's create a life together. You and me.'

Helen hadn't been sure at first. It was scary enough deciding whether to keep the baby. Motherhood was one thing . . . did she really need to be a wife too? 'Lots of people have children these days and don't get married,' she'd said. 'We can be one of those terribly modern couples who—'

'No, Helen,' he'd insisted, 'I love you. If we're going to have a child, let's at least do it right.'

'Where will we live? What will we do for money? I was going to travel . . . get a job . . .'

'I've got some savings. My family . . . well . . . we're comfortable. We'll manage. We'll have this baby and then you can start your career when the baby's a bit older. It's not a life sentence, you know,' he'd tried to joke. 'You don't have to give up everything, Helen.' He had been so reassuring. He'd slipped the ring onto her finger with a broad grin and almost immediately begun to discuss the arrangements for a trip down to Dorset to meet his parents, leaving Helen with nothing to do but stare disbelievingly at the large jewel sparkling extravagantly on her ring finger. It was romantic. It was terrifying. And it was clear that life would never be the same again.

They'd driven straight to the beach, that very first time, so they could stretch their legs after the long journey. Richard had been hoping for a romantic walk along the shore, but the lead-coloured sea lashed against the pebbles, and a bitter wind raged at them, tearing at their coats. They stumbled and shivered their way along the shoreline until they both admitted defeat and hurried back to the car, heads bowed.

'Well, that was a great success,' joked Richard, fiddling with the car heater. 'There's nowhere quite like England in the spring, is there?'

Helen laughed, despite her nerves, and put one hand on his warm knee.

He drove them back through the sleepy seaside hamlet of Summertown, past tiny candy-coloured cottages and down treacherous, twisting lanes until at last they passed through a set of discreet wrought-iron gates and up a long and winding driveway. The car tyres crunched loudly on gravel as they sped past the wind-whipped sycamores lining the route up to the house.

'There she is!' Richard exclaimed, pointing to a large stone building looming in the distance. 'There's Clifftops. There's my home.'

Helen could still remember how her breath had caught in her throat. She wasn't exactly sure what she'd been expecting, but it certainly wasn't the beautiful old house that had darted in and out of view between the branches of the windswept trees. It was a wonderful nineteenth-century farmhouse, perfectly proportioned and spread across the promontory in an attractive L-shape, as if it had tired of the sea's buffeting embrace and turned one shoulder away from it. Much of the whitewashed exterior was adorned with trailing ivy which wrapped its way across the front of the house and all around the wide sash windows, and in the very centre stood a carved stone arch which framed an ancient oak front door, worn smooth over the years. The house was lit up from within, a warm orange light radiating from every visible window while at either end of the slate roof a chimney sent promising plumes of dove-grey smoke curling up into the darkening sky. Down the hillside Helen could just make out a long, sprawling lawn leading off to a gated fruit orchard, beyond which lay the white-capped wash of the sea. She knew, without even stepping one foot inside the house, that the views would be spectacular. The house alone was heart-stoppingly lovely, a picture-book farmhouse the likes of which Helen had only read about in children's stories, but it was made all the more dramatic by its isolated position on the windswept bluff overlooking Lyme Bay. To Helen it screamed of romantic, windswept trysts and secret smugglers' encounters.

'You could have told me you were lord of the bloody manor!' she cried, cringing inwardly at the thought of her parents' cramped suburban semi.

'It's not *that* big,' Richard laughed. 'It's deceptive from this angle.'

'Huh!' she snorted.

He reached across and gave her hand a reassuring squeeze but as they approached the house seemed to sprawl further and further across the promontory, rising up proudly against the skyline.

'I can see how it got its name,' she managed finally in a small voice, suddenly terrified at the prospect of meeting his parents and of spending two days in such daunting surroundings.

Thankfully, the reception inside the house had proved warmer than down on the beach. Daphne and Alfred Tide were delighted to see their son, and the initial introductions with Helen had seemed to go well. Helen thought Richard's father was charming. Alfred was an older version of his son; tall, broad-shouldered with silver hair, an easy smile and the same clear blue eyes as Richard. He pumped Helen's hand up and down enthusiastically as she walked through the oak front door and gave Richard a cheeky, approving wink when he thought she wasn't looking. Helen then turned to Daphne, Richard's mother, and knew with just one look that the attractive, grey-haired lady standing before her would prove more difficult to impress. She had a strong, serious face, steely grey eyes and the sort of posture that suggested years of Swiss finishing school. She wore a smart blue woollen dress and a string of pearls around her neck and Helen, standing next to her in the best dress she owned, felt cheap and shabby by comparison. Daphne's welcome had been warm enough but Helen could feel the woman's cool, appraising gaze sweep over her as she turned to answer more of Alfred's exuberant questions; it was the predatory gaze of a mother scrutinising her son's partner for signs of weakness or future heartbreak.

They'd taken afternoon tea in the drawing room in front of a roaring log fire that crackled and spat in the large stone hearth. 'A little indulgent, perhaps,' Alfred had half apologised as they'd settled themselves on the faded chintz sofas, 'but it's such a chilly day out there I thought a nice fire would be just the ticket.'

Helen had smiled and held her hands out to the flames, grateful for the warmth emanating from the grate as the four adults settled into the required social niceties. They covered Richard and Helen's drive down to Dorset, Daphne's new appliquéd cushion covers and the wild weather outside before Richard cleared his throat and told them he had a little announcement. Helen tensed and tried to ignore the worried glance Daphne threw Alfred.

He'd started with the good news. 'Helen and I have decided to get married.'

'Well,' exclaimed Daphne, 'my goodness. What a surprise!' Then after a pause, 'My goodness . . .' she repeated, fiddling with the single strand of pearls around her neck. She seemed to run out of words and looked across at her husband for help. Alfred began to clear his throat but Richard interjected before he could speak.

'Helen's pregnant.'

Alfred seemed to check himself at the news of the baby. He looked back at his wife helplessly.

'We know it's all happening rather fast,' admitted Richard, looking from his mother to his father, and then back to his mother, 'and it's going to take a little time for you both to get used to the idea, but all you really need to know is that we love each other, we want to have this baby, and we've decided to get married this summer.'

The silence stretched on and on until, at last, Daphne found her voice. 'Well, my darling, you're right; this is all happening *very* fast. Goodness. Perhaps we should all have a little drink. What do you say, Alfie dear?'

Grateful for something to do, Alfred leapt into action. 'Yes, yes, of course, Daffy. Jolly good idea. Whisky? Sherry? Or perhaps we should open a bottle of bubbly? I think we've got some in the cellar . . .'

'I'd like a sherry,' Daphne replied quickly, clearly not quite ready to celebrate. 'And I should think a little sherry would do Helen the world of good too,' she added, with a meaningful nod. 'You look a little peaky, my dear.'

It seemed rude to say she didn't drink sherry so Helen consented with a small nod.

Alfred left at a near-run, seeming to take an age bringing the decanter and glasses through from the dining room, and as Daphne sat smoothing the pleats on her skirt, Helen glanced about, drinking in the casual elegance of the drawing room. The furnishings were pretty and worn, faded floral fabrics and threadbare Persian rugs lending the room a cosy, lived-in feel. Next to an old carriage clock stood a vase of early spring flowers trailing petals across the mantelpiece. A pale cashmere shawl lay strewn across an ornate ottoman. Here and there were oddities and antiques: an old barometer hanging upon one wall; tarnished silver picture frames scattered across a table; eclectic lamps and paintings drawing the eye; while nearest the door stood a sunken leather Chesterfield chair, a hint of stuffing bursting forth from one tatty arm. It was all very chic – perhaps a little busy for Helen's personal taste, a little overdone – yet there was no denying that the overall effect was one of timeless good taste and style.

'Do sit down, dear,' Daphne urged Richard who was pacing

nervously by the French doors. He obeyed, sitting next to Helen and taking her hand in his. She could feel a slick of sweat on his palm and they both started as a log fell in the grate, sending sparks spiralling up the chimney.

Eventually Alfred returned, to the relief of them all. He passed around the glasses before offering up a half-hearted toast.

'To the happy couple.'

They drank in silence.

'So,' Daphne tried brightly. 'Tell us a bit about yourself, Helen.'

The afternoon had limped slowly towards evening and the four adults had shared an uncomfortable meal in the rather grand wood-panelled dining room, seated at a large mahogany table set with linen, silverware and two enormous candlesticks which cast an intimate, flickering golden glow all around them. As Daphne served the meat and passed vegetables around the table and Richard began to talk through their plans, Helen watched a stream of molten wax as it trickled down one of the candlesticks and form a gluey pool on the starched white tablecloth.

'It makes sense for us to move to London as soon as possible. We'll look for a flat before I start work at the firm.' He reached across and gave Helen's hand an affectionate squeeze. 'It's all very exciting.'

'Yes, and of course Helen can settle you in to your new home. It will be good for her to have a little project while she waits for the baby to arrive,' agreed Daphne.

Helen raised one sardonic eyebrow at Richard, but he missed the gesture, turning instead to reach for the wine.

'Of course you must talk to Edmund,' suggested Daphne. 'He has places dotted all over London. I'm sure he would love to help you out, Richard. Why don't you give him a ring?' Seeing Helen's curious glance, she turned to her and explained, 'Edmund's my brother . . . Richard's uncle. He's a lovely man, very kind, and he dotes on Richard.'

Helen nodded politely as she chewed carefully on a green bean; privately she wondered what sort of family just happened to have 'places dotted all over London'. Sitting here in his family home next to his parents, Richard suddenly seemed even more self-assured and grown-up. She couldn't help but compare the way he acted with Alfred and Daphne to how she felt when she returned to visit her own parents; it didn't matter how hard she tried, she always felt more like a petulant teenager than a grown woman.

As the conversation moved along without her, Helen stole covert glances around the grand old room. Along one wall hung a collection of paintings, still lifes and landscapes shimmering seductively in the candlelight. There was a mahogany sideboard, its surface cluttered with an array of items including an elegant silver champagne bucket that looked like it could use a good polish, a dusty old crystal decanter, a hand-carved wooden bowl overflowing with lemons, and a rather beautiful porcelain vase depicting two young women standing beneath the swaying fronds of a weeping willow. The artful chaos of the room contrasted wildly with her parents' own sterile dining room, with its hostess trolley and electric plate-warmer and the best sherry glasses, polished and permanently out on display. She knew she was a world away from her own mother's careful domesticity.

The meal progressed slowly, but Helen forced herself to swallow everything Daphne put on her plate, even though her stomach churned with nausea, until, unable to take any more, she had excused herself, claiming tiredness.

'Of course,' agreed Daphne. 'You must be exhausted. I've made up the blue room for you, my dear. I hope you'll be comfortable.' Richard had already told her they'd be in separate rooms. His parents were old-fashioned like that.

'I'm sure I will,' she said. 'Thank you, Mrs Tide.'

'Oh, please, call me Daphne. We're going to be family, after all.' The false note of cheer fell flat in the room.

'Yes, thank you, Daphne . . . Well, goodnight, everyone.'

'Goodnight,' they cried valiantly at her retreating back.

Helen felt immense relief as she carried herself up the creaking stairs to the guest bedroom. She lay down fully dressed on the generous brass bed and breathed deeply. The faded grandeur continued up here. The bedroom was beautiful, its walls lined with flocked wallpaper in the softest duck-egg blue; a pretty dressing table stood in one corner, a velvet covered stool pulled up in front of its speckled mirror. Dusty, leather-bound books lined a solid mahogany bookcase; a smattering of white lace cushions lay strewn across the window seat, perfectly positioned to look out across the gardens below. A tiny jug of snowdrops had been placed on the bedside table, and at the foot of the bed lay a cosy hand-embroidered quilt, its colours bleached with age and sunshine. Away from the candlelight and conversation downstairs, Helen suddenly felt the night chill close in around her. She shivered and pulled the quilt up over her legs, drinking in the heady smells of fresh laundry, beeswax and money.

It occurred to her then that entering Clifftops was like entering a whole new world, a world whose ground Helen wasn't quite sure of; it certainly felt as though it were shifting beneath her, as though she could trip or stumble at any given moment. She rested her hands on her belly, wondering for the millionth time if she'd made a mistake deciding to keep the baby, if she was truly ready to give up her dreams and ambitions for the tiny curled being nestled inside her, if she was crazy to tie her life to a man she sometimes felt as though she barely knew, and to a family whose assured sense of place in the world appeared to be so far removed from her own careful, suburban upbringing. And all the while she tried, in vain, to ignore the sounds of angry raised voices drifting up the staircase.

*

Things had seemed better in the morning. Everyone was more relaxed after a night's sleep and there was no further mention of weddings or babies as they took breakfast in the conservatory, but Helen was still grateful when Richard suggested a walk, just the two of them.

'Why is it called Golden Cap?' she'd asked, feeling clumsy in her borrowed boots and billowing raincoat as they strolled up the coastal path running beside the house.

'Well, that cliff you can see ahead of us is the highest point on the south coast of England. It gets its name from the exposed yellow sandstone you can see at the summit. I've always thought of it like its golden crown.'

Helen gazed at the bald patch crowning the top of the cliff. In the gloom of the overcast skies it didn't look golden, more of a dirty mustard colour.

Richard read her mind. 'It's probably more impressive on a sunny day, but the views are great, it will be worth it, I promise.'

'So how long has your family lived at Clifftops?'

'Oh, quite a while now,' Richard mused, reaching for her hand and tucking it into his warm one. 'It's rather romantic actually. Mum and Dad stumbled upon the house whilst on their honeymoon. It was incredibly rundown back then. The farmer who owned the estate had lost a lot of money and then been taken ill so it was little more than a ruin when my parents came upon it. Dad convinced the old chap to sell and then presented the house to Mum as a wedding present. It's been a labour of love for them both ever since, a complete money pit, of course, but they adore it. I think it was seeing their passion for Clifftops that convinced me to follow in my father's footsteps and study architecture at university.'

Helen nodded. 'It's certainly an unusual old place.'

'Isn't it just? You do like it, don't you?'

Helen sensed her answer was important to him. 'It's like nowhere else I've been before,' she replied, and she wasn't lying. Wandering around the house felt like being on a film set; it was like a box of delights to roam and explore on a rainy afternoon. But an afternoon – a weekend even – she knew would be enough for her. Secretly she couldn't help thinking she'd go mad rattling around such an isolated and draughty old house, perched as it was on top of the cliffs, with nothing but the tiny hamlet of Summertown within walking distance. Thank goodness their future was to be in London.

'Come on,' urged Richard suddenly, 'I'll race you to the top!'

'Wait!' protested Helen. 'That's not fair. I'm carrying two of us here . . .'

But Richard was already flying up the hillside, the wind inflating his Barbour coat and blowing his thick fair hair in such a comical fashion that Helen couldn't help but laugh at his retreating figure.

It was as she had packed her bag later that afternoon that she'd heard voices from the garden below. She'd peeked out of the open window and seen Daphne and Alfred, side by side in the flower bed running along the back of the house. They were clearing winter mulch from the plants.

'She seems so . . . quiet . . . aloof, perhaps. Do you think she really does love him?'

Alfred had muttered something she couldn't hear.

'She's lovely looking, beautiful, I suppose,' Daphne had continued, 'but I just can't understand how he could have been so stupid. By all means, he's a red-blooded young man; of course he'll want to sow his wild oats. I just thought we'd taught him better than that.'

'What's clear to me is that we've taught him a sense of responsibility. I'm proud of the way he's handling it.' Alfred tried to cheer his wife.

Daphne lowered her voice, but Helen could still make out the words that followed. 'I mean, how well does he *really* know her? He's a good catch. How does he know that the baby is even his? Do you think she's playing games . . . trying to trap him?'

Helen flushed an angry red but she couldn't pull herself away.

'He's no fool, love. And he says he loves her.'

'But Richard as much as admitted last night that they've only known each other for a matter of weeks. It's sheer madness if you ask me.'

'You're forgetting though, buttercup, I knew with you from day one,' Alfred replied, holding Daphne's gaze.

'You old softie, come here.' As Alfred leaned in to the tender embrace of his wife, Helen withdrew from the window, an ugly churning feeling settling in the pit of her stomach.

How dare they presume she was nothing more than a grubby gold digger? How dare they think she had deliberately trapped their son? There she was, trying to do the right thing by the baby – by *their* grandchild – and they stood there accusing her of *that*? She was enraged. After all, things for Richard would carry on as planned. He would finish his Architecture degree. He'd still be able to work at the family firm and carve out his illustrious career. No, it seemed obvious to Helen who was really trapped. It was *she* who would be giving up her dreams of travel and teaching, *she* who would be swapping smoky Parisian cafés and sultry Spanish sunshine for dirty nappies and sleepless nights. How dare they think her so pathetic and impoverished that she would stoop so low? Helen flung the rest of her belongings into her overnight bag. She couldn't wait to get away from Clifftops and bloody Daphne Tide.

Things had moved quickly after that; Helen had graduated in the summer and she and Richard were married soon after in a quiet register office ceremony in London. Cassie was born just a few months later – a tiny bundle of wrinkled pink skin, blue eyes and fuzzy golden hair. As soon as she clapped her eyes on her daughter, Helen knew she'd done the right thing.

There would be plenty of time for her career, later. Then, it was simply enough to just hold her baby close and breathe in the warm, sweet scent of her. Motherhood brought with it an intense love like no other, organic and pure, and Helen felt transformed by it.

Their daughter had an equally softening effect on Daphne Tide. To Helen's surprise, she appeared at Helen's bedside in London the day after the birth, carrying with her a small arrangement of late summer flowers.

'From the garden at Clifftops,' she'd explained to Helen as she handed them to a harried-looking nurse. 'Put these in some water, would you?' She turned back to Helen. 'May I?' she asked, holding out her arms for the baby and Helen, swallowing back the urge to clasp her daughter even closer to her breast, handed her over.

'She's beautiful,' Daphne cooed, offering the baby her little finger. 'She looks just like her father.'

Helen allowed herself a thin smile of triumph and watched as Daphne pulled an extraordinary range of clownish faces at the baby.

'Tell me, Helen, why did you choose the name Cassandra?'

Helen shrugged. 'I've always loved it. We'll call her Cassie.'

Daphne gave a sniff. 'I don't know my Classics as well as you, of course, but wasn't Cassandra rather a tragic figure?'

'Yes, in the end. But she was a princess, one of King Priam's daughters . . . and a prophet. Besides,' added Helen, seeing Daphne's scepticism, 'it's only a name, after all.'

The two women fell into silence, both gazing admiringly at the snuffling bundle in Daphne's arms.

'I've something else,' Daphne said suddenly. 'Something you should keep for Cassandra until she's a little older. It's in my handbag, there.' Daphne indicated that Helen should open the bag and Helen reached across and pulled out a tiny leather jewellery box. She carefully undid the clasp and there inside, nestled on black velvet, was an exquisite antique brooch in the shape of a butterfly. The body of the insect was made from the finest gold filigree and encrusted with tiny diamonds while the wings were formed from delicate sheets of shimmering mother-of-pearl. Helen held it up to the light, twisting and turning it so that the diamonds dazzled under the harsh hospital lights.

'It's beautiful.'

'Isn't it. It's the first piece of jewellery Alfred ever gave me. It belonged to his grandmother. Now I'd like Cassandra to have it – my first grandchild. Will you keep it for her?'

'Of course.' Helen looked up at Daphne and smiled. 'Thank you, it's very kind.'

'Yes, well . . .' Daphne looked around, suddenly embarrassed. 'Where on earth can those chaps have got to? It can't take that long to find a coffee machine in this place, can it?'

Helen had carefully secreted the tiny jewellery box into her own bag before reaching out to reclaim her baby.

Eighteen months later, Dora had been born, and with the second arrival of the new generation of Tides came a deeper confirmation of Helen's place within the family. Daphne and Alfred doted on their granddaughters and Helen only had to look at their faces to know she was, in part, forgiven for the 'entrapment' of their son. Yet twelve years on and Helen still never felt completely comfortable visiting the elegant old house. She still wandered through the rooms and hallways, unsure of her place within its walls, never truly feeling part of the Tide family, and, if she were being really honest with herself, never really feeling quite good enough for Daphne's perfect, blue-eyed boy.

'There it is!' exclaimed Richard, breaking through her memories. He pointed to a sparkling wash of ocean in the distance. 'There's the sea, girls; and look, the sun's coming out.'

Dora leaned forward, pushing against the back of Helen's seat. 'I see it!'

Helen saw it too, and even though she wasn't particularly looking forward to the holiday, she couldn't fail to feel her spirits lift at the sight of the spectacular emerald-green valley of fields and forest sprawling down the hillside to meet the sea. She rolled down her window and let the fresh spring air wash over her. London suddenly seemed a long, long way away.

'Nearly there,' said Richard, navigating the car through twisting lanes lined with hedgerows bursting with primroses and wild daffodils, his foot heavy on the accelerator. Just a few hundred yards later they were crunching their way up the long driveway towards Clifftops.

It stood there, as it had for well over a hundred years, gleaming white against the pale blue sky and wholly unchanged since Helen's first visit. As they approached, Helen could see the arched front door had been thrown open, and in its shadow stood Daphne and Alfred, side by side, waiting patiently to greet their guests. Helen wondered how they knew; did they stand there for hours, waiting for them to appear at the end of the driveway? The thought made her smile.

Richard saw the curve of her lips and patted her hand encouragingly. 'Your palace awaits,' he said, addressing Cassie and Dora over his shoulder.

As soon as they pulled up beside the front steps Dora leapt out of the car and raced towards her grandparents. 'Grandma! Granddad! We're here!' She hurled herself into Alfred's waiting arms and shrieked with delight as he swung her up into the air.

'Your father's going to put his back out one of these days,' muttered Helen to Richard, as she watched Alfred spin Dora about his waist. 'She's getting too big for that.'

'Oh let him have his fun,' said Richard gently.

It seemed Cassie wasn't going to wait around either. She grabbed her bag and stomped across the gravel to greet her grandparents while Helen and Richard still struggled with seat belts and an assortment of maps and sweet wrappers.

'Cassandra!' exclaimed Daphne, reaching out for her eldest granddaughter and pulling her into her embrace. 'Look at you, so tall . . . and all that lovely long blond hair, so pretty. Isn't she pretty, Alfred?' Daphne took a step back and peered at Cassie until she shifted and lowered her eyes, uncomfortable under such close scrutiny.

'She certainly is,' agreed Alfred, 'just like Rapunzel. Hello, Cassie, my girl. How are you?' He squeezed her tight while Dora bounced up and down beside him, giddy with excitement.

'Daphne, Alfred,' said Helen, greeting them each at the door, 'it's lovely to see you both. Happy Easter.'

'And to you, my dear. How was the journey? Not too much traffic on the roads, I hope?'

'Oh not too bad. We're here now.' Helen smiled politely.

'Well we're pleased to have you all, aren't we, Alfred?' Daphne pulled her cardigan a little closer around her shoulders and turned to look for her son. He was staggering towards them, laden under a collection of bags and buckets and spades. 'Goodness, Richard, dear,' exclaimed Daphne, 'leave all of that. There's plenty of time to unpack. Come in, come in, I've made hot cross buns. You must all be gasping for a nice cup of tea.'

'We are,' agreed Dora, 'we're all *gasping*. Mum and Dad had a huge row about whether to stop. Mum wanted to pull over but Dad said we should just push on!'

Helen felt her cheeks flush red.

Richard gave a little cough. 'It wasn't a big row, Dora, just a little . . . *discussion*.'

It was Daphne's turn to smile politely. 'Well, never mind all that, let's get you inside, shall we? Cassandra, Pandora, follow me.'

They trooped into the house, Helen hanging back to help

Richard with the bags. 'Why does she insist on calling them that? She knows the girls hate it,' she hissed under her breath.

Richard shrugged. 'It's what we called them, isn't it?'

Helen shrugged. She couldn't argue with that.

Helen didn't need to look around as she walked through the entrance hall towards the drawing room to know that everything would stand exactly as it had on her last visit, and the visit before that. There was the same smell of flowers and polish wafting on the air, the same worn Persian rugs spread across the flagstone floors. In the drawing room, amidst the golden dust particles shimmering in the sunshine, she spied the ancient carriage clock ticking noisily on the mantelpiece, the familiar faded wallpaper and the usual creaking wooden furniture. Clifftops was like that. Nothing ever changed.

'Sit down!' bustled Daphne. 'You must be exhausted. Make yourselves comfortable while I sort the tea. I'll just be a minute.'

Helen sat herself on one of the chintz sofas, sinking into an eclectic mix of scatter cushions, most of which Helen knew Daphne had made herself. Across the room Cassie slumped into the sunken leather chair, the one nearest the door. Richard ruffled her hair affectionately as he passed by, before seating himself on the sofa opposite Helen. Then Dora launched herself at Richard, who laughed and pulled her onto his lap. With that one simple action Helen instantly saw the growing gulf between her two daughters. Dora, at nine, was still so naive and childlike, while Cassie seemed to be growing sharper, more independent and self-aware by the day.

It was a creeping change that was stealing slowly over their girl. Cassie's bedroom door, once insistently open for the reassuring light from the landing, was now more often than not shut tight; and only last weekend a small but forceful handwritten sign had gone up, demanding that they all now knock before entering. Helen knew it was a natural part of growing up, but it still stung when she noticed Cassie hanging back from her in the shops, walking a couple of paces behind as they shopped for groceries or new school shoes, as if embarrassed to be seen with her. Dora, on the other hand, was still a little girl, happy to hold hands and cuddle at the drop of a hat.

She supposed, when she really thought about it, the two girls had always been opposites, right from the start, and not just physically, although that was perhaps where the most obvious differences lay. Cassie's fair hair, pale skin and ice-blue eyes resembled Richard's side of the family. Dora was all Helen; she had her mother's dark hair, olive skin and green seaweed eyes. Richard called her his little gypsy girl.

Cassie had burst into the world with a symphony of noise, opening her lungs with their full force and carrying on that way for quite some time. She had been a difficult baby, hard to read and always fighting sleep. Helen had worried herself silly over reflux and routines, until gradually Cassie had transformed into a bolshie little toddler and then into a tempestuous young girl. Now they were nearing puberty and Helen could see that they would soon face a whole new raft of challenges. Helen loved Cassie's fiery spirit, but it ran her ragged at times.

Dora's birth, though, was in stark contrast to Cassie's – she had slipped into the world quickly and quietly – so quietly Helen had been terrified there was something wrong, until the midwife gave the baby a firm slap on the bottom and Dora had opened her little mouth to let out a gentle mewl of protest. And unlike Cassie, from the very first moment they had brought her home Dora had just fitted in. She was happy to sit in a baby bouncer and suck on her fist, her green eyes following her mother peacefully around the room until Helen remembered to change her nappy or give her a feed.

Cassie was the one who had lain on the supermarket floor and kicked and screamed until she got the breakfast cereal she wanted; Dora was happy so long as she had the same as her sister. Cassie was the one who pulled all the clothes out of the dressing-up box and tried them on one after the other until the room was a bombsite; Dora was the one who would pick them all up and place them neatly back so her sister didn't get into trouble. Cassie was the one who snooped and peeked at Christmas presents; Dora would wait patiently for the Big Day, worried about spoiling the surprise. Cassie was the one who would dive straight into the deep end of the pool; while Dora would dip a tentative toe before sliding in carefully off the side. It puzzled Helen that she could have given birth to two such different and fascinating creatures, but if she knew one thing, it was that their differences were only getting more marked the older they got.

As Helen sat and studied her girls she noticed for the first time the brilliant colour of Cassie's painted fingernails – they were the exact same letterbox red as the expensive nail varnish Helen had treated herself to at the Chanel beauty counter last week. Cassie, noticing her mother's stare, glanced down at her fingers before looking up and smiling innocently back at her. Helen swallowed down her anger. She'd have a word later, in private. Yes, Cassie was certainly entering a difficult phase.

'How are you girls getting on at school?' Alfred asked, breaking the silence. 'Your father told me you did well in your Eleven Plus, Cassie?'

Cassie nodded. 'Yeah, I guess so.'

'She did really well,' said Helen. 'The teachers think Cassie's got a very bright future ahead of her, if she applies herself.'

Cassie dropped her head, seemingly embarrassed.

'And Panda Bear is doing well at school too, aren't you?' added Richard. 'She came third in a spelling test last week.'

'Yes,' said Dora. 'I had to spell P. H. I. L. O. S. O. P. H. Y. Philosophy.' She spelt the word out slowly. 'I got a red star.'

'Well done,' cheered Alfred.

'What clever granddaughters I have,' said Daphne, entering

the room with a tray of toasted hot cross buns wafting warm cinnamon and cloves, and a steaming teapot. 'Don't stand on ceremony – help yourselves.'

Cassie was the first up. She grabbed half a bun and then wandered towards the French doors. 'OK if I go outside for a bit?'

'No, darling,' Helen started, 'we've only just arr—'

But Daphne had already cut her off. 'Of course, Cassandra!' she said brightly. 'You go right ahead. I'm sure a good dose of country air would do you the world of good. You might find Bill down in the orchard. We've had some terrible storms down here recently; he was talking about building a bonfire.'

Helen bristled. They hadn't been in the house ten minutes and Daphne was already undermining her. She took a deep breath. Stay calm, she willed. It didn't matter. Cassie was better off out of the way anyway.

'Don't tell me old Bill Dryden's still managing the estate for you, Dad? He must be nearly seventy,' Richard marvelled.

'Not far off,' agreed Alfred, 'but he's as fit as a flea, that man.'

As father and son began to talk about the challenges of managing the land around Clifftops and Cassie drifted away through the French doors, Daphne turned pointedly to Helen.

'When did Cassandra start wearing nail varnish, Helen? Isn't she a little young for all that nonsense?'

Helen smiled sweetly, irritated by the disapproval written all over her mother-in-law's face. 'Oh, it's just a little bit of fun for the holidays. I don't let her wear it every day.' Why was she lying? Why didn't she just say that it was the first time she'd ever seen Cassie with painted nails and it certainly hadn't been her idea? Because it made her seem weak and incompetent as a mother, that's why.

Daphne tutted. 'Young girls these days are in such a rush to grow up. Boys, clothes, make-up . . . there's plenty of time for all of that.' Helen braced herself for a sermon but Daphne surprised her by suddenly changing tack. 'So how is London, Helen? You're all well? Keeping busy?'

'Yes,' nodded Helen. 'We are.'

'No plans to move out of the city just yet then?'

Here we go again, she thought. 'No, Daphne,' Helen said firmly, 'you know our lives are in London.'

Daphne sniffed. 'I just think you'd have a much better quality of life if you moved to the countryside.'

'We have a great quality of life. London is a wonderful, vibrant city. It has so much to offer the girls.'

'I'm sure it is an exciting place – *for a young couple*,' added Daphne pointedly. 'I just can't help thinking a family would be better off in a more rural setting. I do worry about the girls.'

'There's no need to worry about them. They're thriving. At their age they need stimulation, opportunities and adventure, don't you think?'

'Well . . .' murmured Daphne noncommittally.

'What?' asked Helen, rising to the bait. 'You don't think so?'

'I can't help noticing Cassie seems a little withdrawn. She's such a serious thing, so *inside* herself. I've heard about those inner-city schools. No fresh air, no green outdoor spaces. It can't be good for her.'

Helen's cheeks flushed red. 'Cassie's fine. She's happy and healthy.'

'I just think—'

'We can't uproot our lives, Daphne. I've got my work . . . my research at UCL. I won't give that up. It's an important part of my life.'

Daphne sniffed. 'I suppose I'm just a bit different to you *modern* women. I always chose to put my husband and family first.'

Helen bridled at the accusation. Daphne thought she was selfish for keeping the family in London but there was no way they were going to uproot everything to come and camp on

Daphne and Alfred's doorstep, just so Daphne could meddle in their lives. Helen couldn't think of anything worse.

'You're not talking about us moving again, are you, Mum?' Richard intervened, coming to Helen's rescue. 'We've only just arrived! At least give us a chance to have a cup of tea and a hot cross bun before you get started. Speaking of which,' he segued seamlessly, 'these are delicious. May I have another?'

'Of course, dear,' said Daphne, rewarding her son with her warmest smile. 'Help yourself. You're looking a little thin. I'll have to feed you up while you're here. We can't have you wasting away now, can we?'

Give me strength, thought Helen, and turned her face towards the garden to hide her flaming cheeks.

'She doesn't mean to upset you,' Richard said a little later as they unpacked their suitcase upstairs.

'She knows exactly what she's doing,' Helen huffed, slinging a handful of pants and socks into a drawer. 'She's been doing it for as long as I've known her.' It was hard to make Richard understand how Daphne's put-downs and comments made her feel so small and insignificant. It was true that taken individually they probably seemed little more than a touch insensitive, tactless at worst. But add them all up, and Helen felt as if she were facing a fearsome barrage of criticism and complaint.

'She's just a lonely old lady who misses her family and would like us to live a little closer.'

'She's not *that* old. And lonely? Give me strength! She's still got your dad, and, from what I hear, she's obviously the life and soul of the local community. If it's not WI cake stalls and fêtes it's amateur dramatics and charity garden parties. And it's not us she misses. It's *you*. You and the girls!' Helen opened the wardrobe and grabbed a hanger for her crumpled silk dress.

'Don't be like that.'

'Like *what*? I'm just sick of her criticism. I know she

doesn't understand it, but I need my work. It helps keep me sane. I can't do cosy country domesticity, you know that.'

'I do.' Richard moved across the room and reached for her hand. 'And that's why I love you. Helen, no one is saying you should give up your job.'

'Really?' She eyed her husband.

'Of course not. At least, *I'm* not. I know how important it is to you. I think it's great you've found something you love doing, and frankly, if it's good for you, then it's good for us, as a family. Right?'

Slightly mollified, Helen released her hand from his grasp and reached for her dress.

'I just sometimes wish you wouldn't act like it was some terrible penance being down here,' Richard tried softly. 'I mean, it's not so *completely* dreadful, is it?'

Helen didn't answer. Instead she smoothed at the wrinkles in her dress before hanging it in the closet.

Richard sighed and tried again. 'It would mean so much to me if you could both get along.'

'I've been trying for twelve years now, Richard. Perhaps it's your mother who you should be having this little conversation with.' Helen threw her make-up bag onto the dressing table. The sight of it suddenly reminded her of Cassie's painted nails and she scowled again in irritation. Things between her and Richard were usually pretty even-tempered, safe and stable – sometimes boringly so – but whenever it came to Daphne and Clifftops, it always got tense. It didn't seem to matter what Daphne did, Richard always defended his mother. Helen used to think it was an admirable trait, but it was starting to grate. What about her? She was his wife after all, and she was growing increasingly sick of always coming second. She grabbed her coat and stalked towards the bedroom door.

'Where are you going?'

'Just out. I need some fresh air.'

'Would you like company?'

'Not right now.' She knew it was wrong to take it out on Richard, but she couldn't help herself. There was something about being back in the old farmhouse that drove her a little crazy.

'Well, don't be late for dinner,' Richard called out at her departing back. 'Mum's cooking a roast – my favourite, apparently, and we both know how terribly malnourished I am, don't we.' He patted his ample waistline and Helen smiled in spite of herself.

Tensions between the two women simmered gently all week, but Helen was careful never to let them reach boiling point. And, if she were honest, Richard was right: it wasn't *so* dreadful being back in Dorset. The family slowly began to relax into their surroundings and a new pace of life gradually washed over them. The girls roamed the grounds, filling their lungs with fresh sea air and their bones with sunshine. They played poohsticks in the stream at the bottom of the orchard, tramped out across the cliffs on long scenic walks and were allowed to stay up later than usual, playing cards with Alfred or watching old movies in the den. Helen found time to curl up on a window seat with one of the dusty novels lining the bookshelves in the library, or even to just sit and watch the clouds drifting across the endless sky. Daphne cooked up a storm in the kitchen, the Aga churning out a seemingly endless parade of cakes and pies, delicious casseroles and roasts. On the Sunday, Alfred and Richard rose early and hid chocolate eggs all over the garden for the traditional Easter egg hunt. Helen wore her green silk dress and forced the girls into matching embroidered dresses too, just for Daphne. And with the weather on their side for once, they spent hours down on the beach, flying kites, combing for shells, paddling in the rock pools and sharing picnics on rugs strewn across the pebbles.

The sea was too cold for swimming but on their very last day, for a dare, Richard stripped down to his underpants and threw himself into the waves. Helen sat on a rug and watched him for a while as he splashed about in the water, the girls giggling at him from the shore. It was hard not to admire the strong muscles in his shoulders and his long, lean legs. He was a handsome man, and really not all that changed from the one she had met at university over a decade ago; a little less hair on the crown of his head perhaps, and a few crows' feet around his eyes, but that was all. He was aging well. Watching him, she imagined his wet arms around her, his cold salt-water skin pressing against her own, and was surprised to feel a sudden rush of desire. It had been a while since they had made love. Perhaps she would make an effort later, put on some decent underwear and persuade him to have an early night.

As Helen watched from the beach, Richard raced out of the waves, his skin pink from the cold. He held a long strand of seaweed above his head and chased first after Dora and then Cassie, making them scream with delight as he flapped the slimy green kelp at them. Helen smiled and reached for the camera lying beside her. It took her a moment to focus the lens and the three of them were almost upon her when the shutter finally snapped; a single image captured for ever. Cassie loomed in the foreground with her blond hair wind-whipped across her face and serious eyes staring straight down the lens, Dora a little behind, all rosy cheeks and wide laughing mouth, and Richard furthest away, grinning from ear to ear as he shook the water from his hair like a dog. It was an innocent moment captured and bottled for posterity like a fine wine and as Helen watched them she realised with a sudden start that this, after all, was happiness. It might not be quite the life she had imagined for herself, but it wasn't half bad.

As she sat on the pebbles, her arms wrapped around her knees, watching her husband and daughters dart about the beach with carefree laughter, Helen smiled to herself. The saying was true: when all was said and done, it *was* family that mattered most of all.

DORA

Present Day

The rain falls steadily on London all week, until Saturday dawns with a tentative new light. Dora draws the curtains to see the sun blooming like a pale yellow daffodil in the sky. It glints off the surrounding Hackney rooftops and transforms the steel grey landscape into something brighter and cleaner.

'It's a sign,' says Dan, giving her shoulder a little squeeze as he passes her at the kitchen table, coffee mug in hand.

Dora hopes he's right. She's been a mess all week, distracted at work during the day and disturbed by a head full of crazy dreams at night. She can't even remember what it's like to feel normal any more, and now that the day has arrived for her trip to Dorset, she's feeling physically sick. She's spent the week replaying the awkward telephone conversation she conducted with her mother and the unspoken question that had hung heavily between them: *why now?*

'I still wish you were coming with me.' She knows Dan has to work, but secretly she's been hoping that he will change his mind.

'Sorry, babe, you know I would if I could but I really need to crack on now. Besides, it's probably better that I'm not there, don't you think – a chance for a bit of mother–daughter bonding?'

Dora bites her lip.

'Anyway,' he continues, 'your news might be exactly what you both need to bring you closer again, you know, a time for celebration . . . hugs and tears of joy. I'm no expert but isn't that what mums and daughters are supposed to be good at?'

Dora doesn't say anything. The Tides have proved, over the years, to be very good at tears, although they aren't often the joyful kind. 'It's not *my* news, it's *our* news,' is all she says, eventually.

Dan reaches for her hand. He seizes her fingers and strokes each one in turn. The gesture makes her want to cry. 'I know it's scary going back after all this time, but it'll be OK, you'll see. Helen will be pleased to see you,' he says, pulling her closer still and kissing the tip of her nose. 'Nothing bad is going to happen. Trust me.'

'Yes,' says Dora, 'you're right,' but she holds him extra tight and breathes in his scent, committing it to memory, just in case.

She leaves after breakfast, hoping to avoid the weekend crush, but it's a good hour and a half before her little car squeezes its way through the city's clogged arteries and filters out onto the M3. Just as her foot is beginning to protest against the constant rise and fall on the clutch, space begins to open up between the cars and it's a relief when she is finally able to put her foot to the floor. She loses her favourite London station and retunes the radio, settling on a channel with an inane DJ chattering about how 'large' he had it the previous night. Thankfully he runs out of steam and begins to play a string of soundalike dance anthems, which distract Dora from the knot of tension building in her gut.

Eventually she leaves the motorway and follows a convoluted series of A-roads, which soon give way to more familiar lanes and landmarks, and although she hasn't yet seen the sea she rolls down her window and takes in great gulps of fresh air. The gear stick crunches audibly as she revs the engine up the steep incline of a hill and then finally, as she crests the top, she sees the little sleepy seaside town laid out before her like a patchwork blanket. After the monochrome tones of London the jewel-like colours are shocking in their intensity. She feels the beauty of the landscape like an ache in her soul.

As she drives the final roads Dora takes in the candy-coloured houses, the weather-beaten stiles leading off to cliff-top walking tracks, the hawthorn hedgerows and pretty cottage gardens. It is ten years on and yet it all feels so familiar, so unchanged. She indicates right, gives a little wave to a group of ramblers shuffling in front of the car, and then accelerates up through the wrought-iron gates and into the driveway. As she does she looks up and drinks in the view of Clifftops.

Ever since she was a little girl, the house has seemed magical to Dora, picturesque in its position and enchanting in its design. As she approaches now its white stone walls glow a dusky pink in the afternoon sunshine and she is surprised to feel a tiny thrill leap through her. It isn't the gloomy place she has been remembering in her dreams. It is beautiful. She heads up the drive and the house darts in and out of view behind sycamore trees and hedgerows. She can almost hear her father's delighted cry: '*Your palace awaits!*' She almost expects to see her grandparents standing on the doorstep with their warm smiles and arms thrown wide, welcoming her back. Those childhood days are long gone, however, and she shakes her head to clear the memories.

All too soon, the car comes to a crunching halt on the gravel outside the house. Dora sits for a moment, listening to the gentle tick of the engine as it settles in its resting place. She stays where she is. The knot in her gut has grown to the size of a bowling ball. Ignoring it she reaches across for her mobile phone and punches out a quick text to Dan. *Made it! x*. She presses send and turns the phone over and over in her hand, turning her gaze towards the arched stone entrance. All she has to do is get out of the car, walk across the gravel driveway and knock upon the worn oak door, but now that she's here, those few final feet seem insurmountable, like a sheer and slippery rock face she must somehow clamber over. She shudders at the thought.

It's not too late to turn back. She could turn the car around and drive away before Helen has even realised she's arrived. She could be home before it's dark, cradled in the familiar bustle of London and in the comfort of Dan's arms. Her life isn't so bad. On paper she is a success – a flourishing career, a dilapidated home, a loving boyfriend – her life in London is something to be proud of, to be envied, even. If she can just keep skating across the surface, if she can just avoid those jagged cracks that have started to appear, and the terrible feeling that she is about to fall into the abyss below, if she can just bury the nightmares and quell the panic attacks she knows she will be fine. Why dredge through the murky waters of the past? What does she really hope to achieve? She doesn't need to do this. She's been mad to come. The past is the past; it should remain buried.

As she plans her escape, Dora feels the beat of her heart slow. She reaches for the keys in the ignition, but as her fingers brush the cold metal her mobile lets off a shrill bleep. She glances down: it's a text from Dan. *Be brave! x*

She swallows.

Dan.

The baby.

Suddenly it is clear: there is no retreat. There is life growing inside her. She remembers Dan sitting opposite her, only a week ago, holding out the antenatal vitamins on the palm of his hand with hope and expectation burning in his eyes. It is enough to make thoughts of her hasty flight back down the motorway disappear. She can't run away now; she must confront whatever waits for her inside. She owes it to Dan, and to their future, whatever it might hold.

With a deep breath and trembling hands, Dora removes the keys from the ignition and opens the car door. 'Time to face the past,' she whispers, and steps up to the entrance to the house.

CASSIE

Fifteen Years Earlier

Cassie stood at the edge of the breakers and looked out towards the horizon. The sea stretched before her, peculiarly flat, like a sheet of metal pressed smooth by the heavy grey sky. Only a thin shard of winter sun pierced the cloud, illuminating a strip of water directly in front of her so that it shone like a mirror. It was this patch of silver water that Cassie focused on. She was skimming pebbles, flicking each one artfully beyond the messy surf and watching them skip and bounce across the shimmering surface until they lost momentum and sank from sight. Her best was six bounces. She bent down to pick up another stone, rubbed at its cold, wet surface with her fingers, before turning to skim it out across the water. She held her breath as it bounced – bounced – bounced and then fell below the waves.

'Not bad,' said her father, crunching his way across the beach towards her.

Cassie shrugged. It was a far cry from her grandfather's record of nine.

'It's getting cold.' Richard shivered and pulled his coat collar tighter around his neck. 'We should head back to the house. Your mum and sister will think we've fallen in.'

She couldn't muster a smile. Instead, Cassie flung her last stone out towards the horizon and turned towards the track leading up from the beach. She could just make out the winking lights of Clifftops high up above them.

'Are you OK, Cass?' Richard asked, putting one arm around her shoulders as they walked unevenly across the pebbles. 'It's been quite a day. You know, it's perfectly normal to feel sad . . . or angry . . . or both. Grief can be pretty bewildering.'

Cassie gave a little nod. She didn't really know how she felt. Her grandparents had only been dead a matter of days and their bodies lowered into their earthy tombs just a few hours ago. It still didn't feel quite real.

'I'm OK.' She paused, thinking for a moment. 'How about you, Dad? Are you OK?'

He seemed startled by the question. 'Yes, love, I'm OK,' he said a little sadly, and reached for her hand. 'It just seems like such a waste, doesn't it? One minute they're here, and then the next, they're gone. It's hard to take in.'

Cassie nodded and pretended she couldn't see the tears glistening in his eyes. The sight of them made the hard-to-swallow ache return to the back of her throat, like a cold marble sticking somewhere around her tonsils.

'They would have liked the service today though,' Richard added.

'Yes,' agreed Cassie. He was right. Daphne would have been thrilled with the standing-room-only turnout at the local church, and Alfred would have approved of the sombre hymns and the Tennyson poem Richard had read in a brave, unfaltering voice. The funeral had been long, slow and serious and Cassie personally would have preferred to remember her grandfather digging in the flower beds at Clifftops and her grandmother bustling around the kitchen than the image she now had stuck in her head of two dark wooden coffins being lowered side by side into the cold, damp earth. The sound of the first clods of earth striking the wooden boxes had made her feel sick. But at least she had been there. She had been part of the serious, adult world of loss and grief. Just for once they hadn't treated her like a little kid.

'Do you believe in Heaven?' she asked suddenly,

concentrating on the steady stomp of her feet across the beach rather than meeting her father's gaze.

It was a question she'd been preoccupied with ever since that midnight phone call had woken them a week ago with the news that her grandparents were dead, killed in a car accident on an icy country lane as they'd returned from a show in Bridport.

Cassie had tiptoed out onto the landing, curious. She'd peered between the banisters and seen her father, far below, standing in the hallway cradling the phone in the crook of his neck. Next to him, on the bottom step, sat her mother, her long silk nightdress pooling like water around her feet. Even though she couldn't hear what was being said at the other end of the telephone, everything about her father's appearance told her it was serious. He reminded her of one of Dora's puppets, when the strings got all tangled and the tension left its limbs. He looked broken.

He had hung up and Cassie watched as Helen had patted and shushed him until, eventually, Richard straightened his shoulders and wiped his eyes on a sleeve. Then he'd turned to look at his wife, for once seemingly unsure.

'What do you suppose happens now?'

Cassie hadn't waited to hear her mother's answer. The sight of her father's tears had been enough to tell her she shouldn't be spying. Instead she'd stood and tiptoed back to her room, knowing full well that whatever did come next, it wouldn't be good.

What had followed had been a week's worth of high emotion, tension and grief, her parents oscillating wildly between affectionate embraces and ferocious arguments. Things were particularly heated when it came to the funeral. Richard had worried it was inappropriate for Cassie and Dora to attend; he worried it would be too much for them, too distressing. It was Helen, however, who had insisted. 'We can't shield them from real life for ever, Richard,' she had argued. 'They're not babies any more.' And Cassie had been secretly pleased. She didn't want to be protected from anything and she certainly didn't want to be excluded from the most serious thing that had ever happened to their family. She wanted to be treated like the grown-up she nearly was. After all, she *was* almost thirteen.

'I . . . I'm not sure,' stammered Richard, his words pulling her back to the present and the windswept beach. 'That's a pretty big question, Cassie. There are lots of different theories about life and death, and what comes after.'

Cassie regarded him with surprise. Usually he could answer any question she threw at him. It was disconcerting to see him so uncertain.

They reached the stile at the far end of the beach. Richard clambered over and then held out a hand to Cassie before they both began to climb the walking track leading up towards the house. It was hard going and their breath fogged in the cold winter air.

'But what do you believe?' she asked, glancing up at her father.

'Do you know, I'm not really sure. I suppose I'd like to think that there is something after this life. I don't know if I like the idea of reincarnation, though. What if I came back as a pig?'

'Or a rat?' she offered.

'Or a slug?'

Cassie giggled.

'Heaven seems like a pretty sensible idea,' said Richard eventually. 'I'd like to think of Mum and Dad up there somewhere, watching over us. I think that's what I believe in.'

'So you believe in God?'

Richard paused. 'Yes, I suppose I do.' They walked for a moment more. 'What about you, Cassie, do you believe in God?'

Cassie shrugged and sucked on a strand of hair. She hadn't really thought about it before. She sang those boring hymns at school and joined in with the prayer at the end of each assembly, but that was only because the teachers made them; they got detention otherwise. It wasn't as if she went to church, or said prayers, other than the generic please-don't-let-me-get-caught sort of ones. And if she really thought about it, it seemed a little silly to think of some invisible, grey-haired man sitting up there in the sky watching over them all. Where was he, after all, when her grandparents drove off the road the other night? Why wasn't he watching out for them? They were good people; she didn't suppose either of her grandparents had done anything really bad in their lives, not like her, stealing sweets from the corner shop and teasing Charlotte Crumb on the school bus until the silly scarlet-faced girl had cried huge, snotty tears. It didn't make any sense. Maybe people just came and went. Maybe once you were dead you just disappeared, sinking without trace, like the pebbles she had flung into the sea only moments ago.

'I don't think I do believe in God,' she said finally. 'Too many bad things happen.' She bit her lip. 'And anyway, if there is a God, why does he stay invisible? Why doesn't he prove he's out there once and for all, instead of keeping us all guessing? He would solve a lot of problems if he just showed up one day and said, "Ta dah! Here I am!" '

Richard gave a small, sad smile. 'It's good to question things in life, Cassie. You're really growing up, aren't you?'

Cassie nodded. She certainly didn't feel like the same girl who had woken earlier that morning.

Dora and Helen were seated at the kitchen table as Cassie and Richard let themselves in through the back door.

'Here you are,' said Helen. 'I was just about to send out the search party. Did you have a nice walk?'

'It was all right.' Cassie wriggled out of her coat and boots, grateful for the warmth radiating from the Aga. She held her frozen hands out towards the stove, rubbing them briskly before shuffling off towards the hall.

'Not so fast, young lady,' called Helen. 'Your father and I would like to talk to you.' Helen indicated an empty chair at the table and Cassie reluctantly plonked herself into it. Richard came and sat beside her. He suddenly looked nervous.

'What's going on?' asked Dora. She looked from her mother to her father and then at Cassie. Cassie shrugged her shoulders; she had no idea.

It was their father who broke the silence. 'We wanted to ask how you would feel if we were to move down here . . . to Clifftops?'

Dora's mouth fell open. 'Us, live here?'

'Yes,' said Richard.

'For ever?' asked Dora.

Cassie rolled her eyes. 'Not for ever, dummy. Aren't you planning on leaving home one day?'

'I know what you meant, Panda,' Richard soothed. 'Yes, it would be a permanent move. We'd give up the London house and transfer our lives down here. It could be fun, don't you think? All of us together in my old family home.'

There was a resounding silence.

'And it's what your grandparents wanted,' he added. 'They've said as much in their wills.' He looked at each of them in turn. 'It was their dearest wish that Clifftops stayed in the family. It was so important to them . . . restoring this house, together . . . and that makes it . . . well, it makes it important to me.' They all heard the crack in Richard's voice.

'What about school?' Dora asked, still trying to grasp the enormity of her father's suggestion.

'You'd both go to the local school here,' Helen answered, giving Richard a moment to compose himself.

Dora looked thoughtful. 'Can we get a dog?'

'Hmmm . . . we'll have to see,' stalled Helen.

'Cassie, you're very quiet,' Richard said finally. 'What do you think?'

Cassie shrugged. She didn't know why her parents were bothering with the charade. 'You've already made up your minds, haven't you?'

'Well . . . what you think *is* important to us.'

'So if I said I didn't want to move here then we could stay in London . . . in our *own* home?' Cassie asked, eyeing him evenly.

'Well . . . not exactly,' stumbled Richard, 'but there are things we could do to help you with the transition.'

'What about you, Mum?' Cassie asked, turning to Helen. 'Do you want to move?' She couldn't stop herself; she could feel that tickle deep in her gut that made her want to stir things up.

'Your father . . . he . . . er . . .' It was their mother's turn to stumble. Richard shot her a look and Helen quickly corrected herself. 'What I mean is *we* think it's the best thing for the family. An exciting fresh start: a new school . . . and new friends. Your father can manage some of his projects from here, and some from London. He'll travel back and forth a bit, for a while.'

'What about *your* job?'

Helen gave a small defeated sigh. 'Well, I suppose *I* can find a new job when we get down here.' No one could miss the edge in her voice.

Cassie thought for a moment. It would be a big change. She'd miss her friends, the shops, the freedom of the city, just being able to jump on a tube or bus and find a new corner to explore. But there would be other freedoms living at Clifftops: the beach, the sprawling countryside, the rambling walks and most excitingly, the cavernous old house. There would be no more queuing to use the bathroom in the morning, no more tripping over Dora and her parents in the kitchen at breakfast time, or having to jam a chair against her bedroom door whenever she wanted a little privacy. They would rattle around in the huge old house like the lonely pennies in her money-box. It could be amazing.

'So *is* it decided then?' asked Dora.

Cassie watched her parents gaze at each other for a moment. The silence closed in around them.

Finally, Richard swallowed. 'Yes, Dora,' he said gently, 'it's decided. It will be a new start for *all of us*.' He reached across and gently took Helen's hand in his and Cassie watched as her mother flushed slightly and turned her face towards the window. She wondered if she was the only one who could see the pulse throbbing at her mother's temple, a fast drumbeat visible just below the surface of her skin.

In was late February when the Tide family eventually packed up their poky London terrace and moved down to the space and grandeur of Clifftops. The days preceding had been a tedious round of sorting and packing, clearing out books, clothes and old toys for the charity shops, watching as their life's possessions were bubble-wrapped, boxed, sealed and stored ready for the big move. There were endless arrangements, phone calls and goodbyes, most of which were punctuated by fierce and frequent arguments between her parents, until at last they stood on the doorstep of their terrace, locked the front door one final time and left London for good. Cassie found it a relief to be going, finally.

The afternoon light was fading fast as they arrived at Clifftops and tiptoed, intruder-like through the back door.

'Well,' said Richard, 'here we are.' He shivered and stomped his feet on the kitchen flagstones. 'Let's get the heating on. It's freezing.' He fiddled with a thermostat on the wall before leaning over the Aga.

'I'll make tea,' volunteered Helen. She opened a cupboard and was confronted by a towering stack of roasting trays and cake tins. She tried another, and then another. 'Where are the mugs?'

'Try that one over there,' offered Richard, pointing to a corner cupboard near the fridge.

Helen sighed and stomped across the room, and Cassie, sensing another argument building between her parents, sneaked silently out of the kitchen door.

It was strange wandering through the old house. She skulked down hallways and tiptoed through rooms, flicking on lights and testing how it felt now that it was to be officially their home. Everything stood as her grandparents had left it: each chair still perfectly in place, each cushion plumped, the table in the conservatory cluttered with gardening gloves and seed trays, the airing cupboard piled high with linen tablecloths and crisp white bedding, even the antique clocks in the sitting room still tick-ticking, marking the time as if nothing of any consequence had changed. Cassie came upon a half-finished crossword in her grandfather's study, and an embroidery frame of her grandmother's, the needle and thread tucked carefully into the last, uncompleted 'e' of the 'Home is Where the Heart Is' proverb. And there was that smell, that particular scent that Cassie would always associate with the house; a strange, dusty cedar-wood aroma that filled her nostrils and reminded her, by its very presence, how far they were from London and their old lives.

Cassie went from room to room, jumpy and uncomfortable, half expecting Daphne or Alfred to appear at any moment. It was eerie. The old house still seemed to echo with their presence and she was grateful when she came upon her sister outside the kitchen, perched at the bottom of the back staircase.

'It feels strange, doesn't it?' Dora said in a hushed voice.

'Yes,' Cassie admitted, 'it does.'

She pushed on the swing door and came upon her parents, embracing in the middle of the room. Cassie watched in silence as her father pulled back and studied her mother's face.

'We've done the right thing, haven't we?' he asked, and

Helen gave a small, serious smile and smoothed the furrowed lines of his brow with her fingers.

'Stop worrying,' she said. 'We'll make it work. We have to.'

They drank tea out of Daphne's cups and saucers and watched as the removal vans disappeared down the drive and it was only then, as the radiators clicked and groaned and the cardboard boxes towered over them that the enormity of the move began to sink in.

It surprised Cassie how quickly she adjusted to her new life. Once she'd unpacked the last of her possessions, got used to the scratchy new school uniform and attuned to the sound of the sea lulling her to sleep at night, she found that there was a lot to like about her new home. There was a simplicity and freedom that came with living in the countryside. In London her parents had always wanted to know exactly where she was and what she was doing, but somehow, by the coast, they didn't seem as tense or cautious. Cassie revelled in her new-found freedom and as winter gradually receded, she took to pounding the cliff-top tracks, often stopping to perch on a creaking stile or a fallen tree while she watched the waves and daydreamed.

Dora was still a pain, bounding around, snooping through her stuff and always wanting to follow her or know what she was doing, but whether it was the space of their new home, or the vast openness of the landscape around her, Cassie found she didn't mind her sister's stealthy pursuit quite so much any more. It was actually fun to wander down to the village shop together on Saturday mornings, spend their pocket money on penny sweets, and then sit on the sea wall, watching the crashing waves and the seagulls flap and spin above them on the breeze.

Their father seemed to love it too. He did his best to balance his weekly commute to London, and while there were plenty of evenings when he couldn't make it home, he always walked through the door on a Friday night with bear hugs for each of them and a beaming smile spread across his face.

It appeared that all of them had adapted easily to the change. All of them found the transition to their new home relatively straightforward. All of them, except Helen.

Helen, it seemed, was riddled with regret. Almost as soon as the boxes had been unpacked her mood changed. She stomped around the house like a stroppy teenager, grimacing as she opened yet another closet or wooden chest to be faced with teetering piles of fine bone china, crystal wine glasses, or bags of old clothes no one had the heart to throw out. She reminded Cassie of a caged tiger, frustration and bristling anger rolling off her in waves.

'What on earth are we going to do with all this *stuff*?' she would moan, despairing of all the dusty relics.

'Whatever we like, my darling,' said Richard, attempting to pacify her with a comforting arm around her shoulders. 'This is our home now.'

'So why do I feel like I'm living in some kind of museum?' Helen shrugged him off. 'I feel as though your mother is watching me.'

'It's bound to take us all time to settle in. The kids seem to love it though?' he offered, glancing hopefully at Cassie and Dora who nodded back obediently. 'I know it's daunting, Helen, I feel it too, but I owe it to my parents to look after this place. It's their legacy, after all.' Helen didn't reply, so he persevered. 'And I know it's a little cluttered and that not everything is to your taste, but you should consider it yours now. Treat it like a project, if you will, now you're not working. It could be exciting, don't you think? Do whatever you need to, to make it feel like *your* home.'

Helen looked at him sceptically. 'A project?'

'Yes, my darling. Whatever it takes for you to be happy here.'

And Cassie watched as her mother folded her arms across her chest and turned her gaze back towards the room, noting the dangerous glint in Helen's eyes.

While the Tides adjusted in their individual ways to the move, some things stayed the same. Bill Dryden remained a familiar face around the estate, his hunched figure often visible from the house, stooped over a flower bed or digging in the vegetable patch, just as he had when her grandparents were alive.

Cassie liked Bill, he was what her grandfather would have called *a good egg*, and sometimes, when she was bored with roaming round the big house, she would wander out, following the lazy drift of his tobacco smoke until she found him. She liked to sit and watch him work, sometimes in companionable silence, sometimes engaging in easy conversation. He didn't treat her like a little girl. He talked to her like a grown-up and always seemed interested in her opinions.

She was heading out to find him early one Saturday morning, when Dora caught her by the back door.

'Where are you going?'

'Just out.'

'*Where* out?'

'Nowhere special.'

'Can I come?'

Cassie sighed. 'I suppose so. You'll need your boots though, it's muddy.'

Dora was already rummaging in the pile by the back door for her red wellies. 'Got them!' she called. 'Let's go.'

Cassie held the door open for Dora and they began to clomp their way down the lawn towards the stream, their boots squelching in unison through the wet grass. It had finally stopped raining. There was a freshness to the air that made their cheeks sting but every so often the sun appeared from behind a fast-moving bank of grey clouds and showered them in a pale, golden warmth. Cassie could see clusters of bright yellow daffodils dancing in the flower beds.

'Where are we going?' asked Dora after a little while.

'I don't know. Just around.'

She took a running jump over the narrow stream and then continued along to the old rusting gate that led into the fruit orchard at the bottom of the garden. The first buds were just emerging on the tips of the branches, a faint green hue against the brown bark. For a while the two sisters wandered amongst the trees aimlessly, companionable in their silence, until the sound of metal against wood carried towards them on the breeze.

'Listen!' Cassie said. 'It's Bill . . . come on!' She set off at a run down the hillside, leaving Dora to chase after her, and arrived in the clearing at the bottom of the orchard just in time to see the stooped grey-haired man hefting a large axe at a gnarly branch of wood. 'Bill!' she called out. 'Bill, it's us!'

The elderly man turned and squinted before breaking into a broad smile. 'Well, if it isn't my two favourite girls. Hello there, how are you both?'

Dora rushed past Cassie at full pelt and launched herself into the man's arms.

'Whoa there, Nellie!' he cried, taking the full, buffeting embrace of the little girl. 'You nearly knocked me for six!'

Dora giggled. 'I'm not Nellie. I'm Dora!' It was their little joke.

Cassie caught Bill's eye and smiled.

'And Cassie too,' he said in his West Country lilt. 'Aren't I the lucky one. My Betty is still on at me to have you round to the house. She wants to make one of her chocolate cakes especially . . .'

'We'll come,' said Cassie readily. Betty Dryden's chocolate cake was legendary.

'Good-oh,' smiled Bill.

'What are you doing?' asked Dora, poking at a pile of logs with the toe of her wellington boot.

'Just clearing up after winter, chopping firewood for next.'

'Maybe we could help you?' said Dora hopefully.

'Well, you'd be welcome to. I've got plenty of branches to clear still. It's hard work, mind.'

Dora did a little jig of excitement. 'I'll start over here.'

She raced off and Cassie watched with amusement as her little sister began to fight with an oversized branch lying in the long grass.

Bill chuckled. 'She's nowt but determined, your sister. Reminds me of a young pup. More energy than she knows what to do with.' He reached for a handkerchief and mopped his brow.

Cassie grinned. She knew just what he meant. Dora did look like a puppy wrestling with a giant bone. She sat on a tree stump and watched her for a moment, swinging her dangling booted feet back and forth.

'So how are things going up at the big house, Cassie? Are you girls enjoying life by the sea?'

'Yeah, it's great.'

'School OK?'

'Uh-huh.' Cassie watched with fascination as Bill took a pipe from his pocket, filled it with tobacco and then placed it in the corner of his mouth.

'Making friends?' he asked, lighting the pipe with a match.

'Yep.' It was true. Cassie hadn't had any trouble making friends with the pupils in her class. Everyone had been very welcoming, if not a little in awe of the fact that she had arrived all the way from London.

'And how are your folks?'

Cassie paused. She wondered how much to tell him. She decided to be honest. 'Dad's good. He loves being back here, but I think Mum wishes we'd stayed in London.'

'Is that right?' He took several long puffs from the pipe and then exhaled smoke in a long, slow stream.

'Yes. Dad's away with work a lot, but now whenever he is here they just seem to fight all the time.' Cassie shot a glance towards her sister, checking she was out of earshot. 'Dora hates it. It makes her really upset.'

'Does it now?'

'Yes, I think she's scared they're going to get a divorce and then we'll have to move back to London and we'll never be allowed to get a dog.'

'And what about you, Cassie, are you worried?'

Cassie shrugged. 'Not really, I don't want a dog.'

Bill let out a small cough.

'I think Mum needs a job.'

Bill nodded sagely. 'You're probably right.'

'You know, sometimes I wonder if they even really love each other.' She'd blurted it out before she'd realised and blushed at her daring.

'Love's a funny thing, Cassie.'

Cassie looked up.

'It's like this here orchard. Look around you. Not much to see right now, is there? It looks a little sleepy, forlorn even. But it's all a cycle. Winter, spring, summer, autumn. Real love, I mean deep, true love is like that. It takes root, grows, and changes shape. Sometimes it seems to fade, other times it's in full bloom. Nothing stays the same for ever. Things change, life moves forwards. But if it's true love, like the love that entwines a family, then it's always there simmering beneath the surface, just waiting to burst forth again.'

Cassie looked up at the branches of the apple tree she sat beneath. They were brown and bare, but here and there she could see green shoots of life sprouting, buds that would soon bear beautiful blossom and before long heavy apples that would bend the boughs.

'So do you . . . do you love Mrs Dryden like that then?' Cassie held her breath, unsure if she was allowed to ask such a personal question.

But Bill nodded his head solemnly. 'Yes,' he said. 'We've been married fifty years this summer and I wouldn't have missed a single day, not even the ones when we fought like cat and dog. I'm sure your parents are like that too, Cassie. Deep down they love each other.'

Cassie nodded, feeling a little better.

'What are you two talking about?' asked Dora. She was dragging her giant branch triumphantly behind her.

'Just putting the world to rights,' said Bill smoothly.

'Oh.' Dora looked disappointed. 'Should I go and get some more trees then?'

'I'd be happy for your help, I surely would,' smiled Bill, 'but tell me, isn't that your father I can hear calling for you up at the house?'

Cassie turned her head and sure enough she heard their dad's bellows from the top of the garden.

'Beach time!' shouted Dora. She took off up the hill at a sprint, calling out her goodbyes over her shoulder.

Cassie gave Bill an apologetic look. 'Sorry about that, Dad's promised us a trip to the beach.'

Bill laughed. 'I understand; my bonfire is no competition for that. But we'll see you both at the house sometime? Drop by whenever you want. My Betty would love to see you.'

'We'll be there.'

'Good-oh.'

Cassie waved and then turned on her heel, heading off up the hill to her waiting father.

There were other familiar faces too; faces from their old life in London. In May, Violet Avery came to stay. Violet was Helen's oldest friend. The two women were like chalk and cheese, but they had been friends since their earliest school-days – Violet loved to tell the girls how their mother had stuck up for her against the school bully in the playground one day, kicking him in the shins after he'd called Violet a roly-poly-pudding – and Cassie and Dora adored her.

She was fascinating too, so different to their mother, with her bright red lipstick, throaty smoker's laugh and unmissable, jiggling cleavage. She drove up to Clifftops in her ancient yellow 2CV, sending a spray of gravel flying as she came to a jerking halt by the front door.

'Cooeee,' she cried, wobbling up the steps on vertiginous high heels clutching a large spray of yellow roses and a bottle of gin. 'What's a girl got to do to get a drink around these parts?'

Cassie and Dora had spied her from the living room window and rushed at her with delight.

'You came!' squealed Dora.

'Of course I came. You didn't think you'd get rid of me that easily, did you? Easy, girls,' she urged as they pulled at her excitedly, 'these shoes aren't really made for walking . . . or hugging.'

'Your hair's yellow!' exclaimed Dora.

'Yes, do you like it? I decided to see if blondes really *do* have more fun.' Violet fluffed at her hair and winked in Cassie's direction. 'The jury's still out. Here, Dora, you take the flowers. Cassie, you take this.' She pressed the large bottle of gin into Cassie's hands. 'It's for your parents, mind. Now,' she said, looking up at the house, 'I think you girls had better show me around your castle.'

Dora led her by the hand through the front door while Cassie followed, clutching the bottle to her chest as she scrutinised and then tried to mimic the alluring sway of Violet's hips.

They monopolised her for a good hour before Helen sent them packing, promising tea in front of the television if they went outside to play for a bit. Dora raced off immediately, but Cassie, reluctant to leave the beguiling inner sanctum of the adult world, backed out of the kitchen and lingered surreptitiously by the open door, listening to the clink of ice in glasses and the women's fascinating private conversation.

'So,' commenced Violet in hushed undertones, 'tell me *everything*.'

Helen gave a slight snort. 'What is there to tell? You can

see how things are here. Sleepy doesn't even begin to describe it.'

'It seems perfectly idyllic to me. This house is *too much*. There are women the world over who would kill for what you've got, Helen . . . a lovely husband, great kids, a country pile.' Cassie could hear Violet's silver bangles jangle as she gesticulated.

'I know,' sighed Helen. 'I feel like an ungrateful cow but it's just so deadly here. I feel trapped. Frankly, I'm terrified I'm turning into my mother-in-law.'

'Fat chance! When you start baking cakes and going for blue rinses, then you'll be in trouble. Until then I think you're pretty safe.'

Helen laughed. 'It's good to see you, V.'

'And you.' The two women clinked glasses and silence filled the room as they drank.

'I'm just so bored,' sighed Helen eventually. 'It's all right for Richard. He still has his job, and the move here is all about him really – him and his overblown sense of duty to this house and what he perceives as his parents' great, enduring legacy. God forbid we should disappoint Alfred and Daphne and sell this place!'

'He's still grieving, Helen,' Violet said softly.

'Oh I know I sound terribly selfish, I feel for him, I really do, but we're his family now. I always told him I couldn't do cutesy country domesticity. Yet here I am. I'm trying to be supportive but I just can't help wondering where *my* life has gone.'

'Ha!' snorted Violet. 'Old-life-old-schmife. Start a new one. Become a lady of leisure; God knows I'd envy you that. What I wouldn't give to leave behind those four a.m. starts at the flower markets each week.'

'But you love your job!' exclaimed Helen indignantly. 'If someone suddenly took your shop away you would miss it, trust me.'

'Well . . . maybe, but this isn't about me, is it? This is

about you, and what you need is to embrace the changes. I don't know, why don't you become a lady who shops and lunches? Join the PTA. Start a book group. Learn to cook.'

'Hey, I can cook!' Helen was indignant.

'And I'm Mother Teresa.'

Cassie smothered a giggle. Only Violet could get away with that. Privately they all agreed that Helen's enthusiasm for cooking far exceeded her skill in the kitchen. They had all waded through her roasts like old boots, catastrophic cakes and indefinable piles of gloop supposedly masquerading as puddings. It was just that none of them had the heart to burst Helen's bubble, none of them except Violet.

'Why not get another teaching job?' Violet continued. 'What is it they say: they always need good teachers?'

'Hmmm . . .' said Helen noncommittally. 'I'm not sure that holds true for Classics lecturers.'

'Oh stop feeling sorry for yourself!' Violet admonished.

Cassie heard the sound of more ice cubes clinking into glasses and the fizz of tonic being poured. 'The fact of the matter is you can do anything you like here. You're young, talented and not half bad looking. Get a job. Take up knitting. Have another baby. Just take control, OK? You'll feel much better if you do *something*!'

It was then that Cassie knew that Violet had had too much to drink. Her mum wasn't young, and she certainly wasn't going to start knitting or popping out more babies – just the thought of it made Cassie feel a little queasy.

'Richard's a good man,' said Violet, suddenly wistful. 'Don't take him for granted, Helen. Believe me, it's no fun out there on your own. Just last weekend I went out with this one guy, Roger, and you'll never guess what he did – on our first date, before we'd even finished our prawn cocktail . . .'

Cassie could tell Violet was gearing up for a long and emotional outpouring and decided that she'd probably heard enough. She backed silently away from the open door and headed off to practise walking around in Violet's outrageously high heels.

It was the painting that eventually brought about a change in Helen. She carried it home one Saturday afternoon, after a shopping trip into town, staggering into the house with two bags of groceries and a huge, rectangular parcel wrapped in brown paper.

'What's that, Mum?' Cassie asked, poking at it with her foot.

'That, my girl, is art – beautiful, soul-enlightening art.'

'Can I look?'

'Of course. You can *all* look. We'll have a grand unveiling this evening.' Helen handled the parcel carefully, caressing its string ties and brown paper reverently. It was the happiest Cassie had seen her since the move.

'Is it for the house?'

'Yes.' There was a fire burning in Helen's green eyes. 'It's just what this old place needs. Run along now, Cass, will you? I've got some things to take care of.'

Just before dinner Helen summoned them all to the living room.

'Ta dah!' she revealed, ushering them into the room with girlish excitement. They filed in one by one and took in their surroundings. The room was utterly transformed from how they had known it. Cassie, Richard and Dora stood in stunned silence while Helen waited behind them, shifting her weight from foot to foot in anticipation. 'Well, what do you think?' she asked.

Helen had been busy since she'd returned from town. A lot of the old furniture that had filled the room had been shifted to the edges or removed completely. Daphne's beautiful Persian rug had been rolled up and stored in one corner. Gone were the ornaments, the antique clocks and the dusty old barometer permanently stuck on 'stormy'. The faded chintz sofas remained, but had been repositioned in a horseshoe shape facing the fireplace, while side tables and their elegant lamps had been removed completely. The room was a stark, pared-down version of its former incarnation; the only real focal point, as Helen had clearly intended, was the enormous new painting that now hung on the wall opposite and held them all in its thrall.

'Isn't it breathtaking?' Helen asked again, this time turning to Richard.

Cassie eyed the picture with suspicion and felt Dora sidle up next to her as Richard cleared his throat.

'He's a genius, isn't he?' Helen gushed.

'Who, exactly?' Richard asked, confused.

'Tobias Grey. He's a local artist. I went to his gallery in Bridport and just fell in love with this painting. I had to have it. I knew it would transform this room.'

Cassie turned back to the painting and tried to take it all in. It was a Dorset seascape painted in thick oils. The ocean lay in a threatening splash across the canvas, viscous whorls of paint layered inky blue upon green to create an expanse of seething water, dark and forbidding. A pebbled shore, nothing more than a thin strip of land the colour of pale bone ran across the bottom of the painting while rocks and weather-beaten cliff tops towered off to one side. And above it all, from the depths of the storm-filled sky, fell a lone shard of light tracing silver upon a small patch of water. It was the only glimmer of light in the otherwise brooding landscape. Cassie shivered.

'It's part of a collection called *Dreams of Drowning*. Isn't it incredible?' Helen continued.

Richard cleared his throat again. 'It's . . . er . . . rather gloomy.'

'That's the point!' Helen cried, clearly exasperated. 'It makes you feel something. That single shaft of light dancing across the water, isn't it beautiful?' It seemed she didn't want an answer for she carried on breathlessly. 'He was telling me it represents the raw brutality of nature.'

'I don't like it,' Cassie heard herself say.

'Oh rubbish. Don't any of you appreciate great art?' Helen cried.

'It's big; *really* big. It looks expensive,' Richard added.

'Oh I see,' scowled Helen. 'That's what you're worried about, is it? The money?'

'Well, no, but . . . how much *did* it cost?'

'I thought you said "whatever it takes to make me happy"?'

'Yes.' Richard agreed. 'I did say that.' Cassie noted her father was speaking in his patient voice, the one he used when he was trying to help her with her maths homework. 'But we can't just go around spending money on lavish new paintings. What was wrong with the watercolour that was over the fireplace before?'

'Richard, do you really want me to answer that?' Helen asked, a distinct chill to her voice. 'You might be happy to live in your mother's house, but I'm not. It's time to change things.'

'And we will,' Richard tried again, 'with time, and together. I know I suggested you treat the house like a project, but I'd still like to be consulted. I'd like to pick out some things with you. But all this . . .' he flung his arms out to indicate the transformed room, 'it's so fast.'

'Richard, it's been weeks. We can't live in a mausoleum for the rest of our lives.'

'I don't expect us to live in a mausoleum.'

'But you would like me to check with you every time I shift a chair, every time I move a photo frame?'

'You're being ridiculous now.' Richard sighed, aware that he was fighting a losing battle. He looked up at the painting again and outwardly flinched. 'It's just so dark . . . and . . .' he struggled to find the right word, 'depressing.'

'Well I can't take it back. The artist gave me a special price. He knocked two hundred pounds off . . .'

Richard's eyes widened. 'Two hundred pounds *off*? How much did it cost in the first place?'

'Three.'

'Three hundred?' Richard asked, confused.

'No, three thousand.' There was a pause. 'What?' Helen asked. 'Why are you looking at me like that?'

'Helen, we just don't have that kind of money to throw around.'

'Rubbish! What about the money your parents left you?'

'It's not a bottomless pit, love. There's inheritance tax and the upkeep of this place to think about. The damp-proof course is going to need work, and the boiler is on its last legs.' Richard ran his hands through his hair and sighed. 'We're not rolling in money. It's all tied up in this old place and the estate. We have to be careful.' He looked round, suddenly aware of two sets of ears flapping madly, and then turned back to Helen with a meaningful look. 'Girls, why don't you run outside and play.'

'What about tea?' Dora asked. 'I'm hungry.'

'Have some toast,' Helen snapped. 'I'll come and make something in a bit.'

Cassie shrugged her shoulders and trooped across to the door. 'Come on, Dora. I'll make cheese on toast.'

The two girls shuffled out of the living room, trying to ignore the sound of raised voices as the door swung shut behind them. They both knew dark storm clouds had swept in off the horizon again.

DORA

Present Day

Feeling like an unannounced guest, Dora knocks tentatively at the front door. She is greeted by resounding silence. Realising her mother must be in the garden, she makes her way round to the side of the house, lets herself through a wooden gate and then makes for the terrace, all the way trying to shake the feeling that she is somehow trespassing.

From a distance Clifftops had exuded its usual picture-book appeal, but as Dora enters the garden she notices things are a little different. It's still lovely. The trees in the orchard are laden with late spring blossom and the garden rustles and stirs in the warmth; but there are little things that give the property an unkempt feel. There's a wheelbarrow that's been left to rust by the manure pile; the lawn is overgrown and littered with scruffy tufts of daisies and dandelions; piles of leaves, the remnants of last autumn, are clumped around the terrace and Dora notices a dripping gutter and paint peeling from the window frames. Individually they are all small over-sights, nothing that an efficient handyman couldn't put right in a few days, but collectively they make the house feel tired and a little shabby. It's not how she remembers the old place.

'Hello there, you're just in time for tea.'

Dora jumps at the sound of a voice. 'Hello, Mum, gosh, you startled me!'

Helen appears from behind a trellis of clematis and walks towards Dora, carefully removing her gardening gloves and straightening her shirt before embracing her. Their hug is stiff and awkward and Dora notices her mother's lips only just graze her cheek.

Helen pulls back and regards her through narrowed eyes. 'You look tired,' she says finally.

Dora realises she's fiddling with the hair that has blown loose from her ponytail and jams her hands back into her pockets. 'A bit, yeah.'

'How was the drive?'

'Fine, thanks. You're looking well, Mum. And the garden is . . . blooming.' Dora winces. She's more nervous than even she realised.

'Yes,' agrees Helen, surveying the garden with concern. 'It's certainly a handful for me on my own now.' The two women stand side by side for a moment, silently regarding the enormity of Helen's responsibilities. 'Well, come on inside. I'll put the kettle on.'

Dora follows her mother into the shade of the house, taking the chance to study Helen as she walks in front. She hasn't changed much. She is a stylish woman, not yet fifty and trim in cotton trousers and a sage-green shirt. Dora notices a fresh peppering of grey in her thick, dark bob, a few more lines around her jade-green eyes, but she is still beautiful.

Helen lays her gardening gloves on the counter and moves to fill the kettle. 'I'm out of tea leaves, I'm afraid. I didn't make it to the shops this morning. Do you mind a bag?' She holds up a box of expensive-looking Earl Grey tea bags.

Dora gives a little smile. She usually drinks what Dan refers to as 'builder's brew': one bag of own-brand left to stew for ten minutes. 'That's fine, thank you,' she says. 'So,' she adds, eager to keep the conversation flowing, 'how is village life treating you?'

'Oh, not too bad. We've been having a wonderful spring, lovely and warm. The locals have been in a tizzy about the village shop closing down – petitions and all sorts. And of course preparations have begun for the *event of the year*.'

Dora looks up at her mum questioningly.

'You know,' Helen continues, 'the annual village flower show? The local spinsters are elbow-deep in a flurry of cake baking and flower arranging. They say it's going to be very competitive this year, particularly in the jams and fruit cake categories.' Sarcasm drips from her mother's voice and Dora can't help but smile. Helen has never been one for the politics and gossip of village life. It's nothing short of ironic that her mother should be the one left living in the old house, like Daphne Tide reincarnated.

'Oh yes,' Helen continues, 'did you hear that dear Bill Dryden passed away a few months ago? Pancreatic cancer. You remember him, don't you? He used to manage the estate here. His wife Betty was distraught, poor thing.' Helen pours boiling water into a teapot and arranges mismatching china on a tray. Dora watches, filled with a sudden sadness. She recalls in a flash Bill's big, strong arms swinging her round and round until her giggles had turned to dizzy protests and he'd put her down. It has been years since she has seen him but the memories are still fresh. 'Such a good man,' Helen continues, rattling teacups and digging silver spoons out of the overflowing cutlery drawer. 'He was so dedicated to his job here and wonderful with you kids. They held a lovely service for him. The church was packed.'

'That's nice,' Dora murmurs, still shocked. 'I always liked Bill.'

'Anyway,' says Helen, suddenly brisk again, 'shall we take our tea in the conservatory? It's lovely in there at this time of day.' She's talking in her polite 'visitors' voice and Dora realises her mother must be as nervous as she is. It makes her feel slightly better.

Helen picks up the tray and Dora follows her out of the kitchen, wandering past the open door to the library, glimpsing her mother's old oak desk overflowing in its usual fashion with papers and books. She passes a table in the hallway clustered with a collection of family photos, their silver frames dusty and spotted with age. There is one of Daphne and Alfred's sepia-toned wedding photos, a shot of Cassie sitting sullen and straight-backed in her school uniform and one of Dora as a baby lying on a tartan blanket chewing on her fist. Behind them all is a smaller framed photo she has forgotten all about, until now. She peers at it more closely and sees it is of her, Cassie and their father, down on the beach. Cassie looks lovely; all of about eleven or twelve, with her blond hair blowing in the wind and her serious blue eyes staring straight into the camera. She sees herself running behind, a skinny, young girl lost in a fit of toothy giggles, and behind them both stands their father, his cheeks ruddy and his smile broad as he shakes saltwater from his damp, fair hair. He looks as though he's just been for a swim and while she can't really remember the day, she has a vague recollection of a chilly Easter picnic. Still, the image is startling to her. It is the sight of the three of them down by the shoreline – so young and happy and innocent – that makes her stomach twist. She wonders how her mother can stand to look at it. She gives a little shudder and turns away from the photo, racing to catch Helen who has already disappeared down the hallway with the tea tray.

They enter the brightness of the conservatory and settle themselves in creaking wicker chairs. Her announcement weighs heavily upon her but she daren't speak just yet. She needs to get it just right so instead she lets Helen continue with her monologue of Summertown life while Dora half listens, keeping one eye on a huge, luminous bluebottle scrabbling in vain at the only shut window. It hurls itself at the glass, desperate to escape the stifling atmosphere. I know the feeling, thinks Dora.

'And so what of you? How is life in London . . . and how's Daniel?' Helen's questions break through her daydream.

Dora decides to start with the safer topics. 'Dan's good. His last exhibition went well and he's got some new commissions. There's a lady in Highgate who wants three of his bronzes for her garden. That's why he couldn't make it this weekend.' Dora pauses, wondering if now is the moment, then chickens out. 'And I've been promoted at work.'

'Oh yes?' says Helen.

'Yes . . . I've just been made Senior Account Manager. We won a new client, breakfast cereals. We stole the business from our biggest rivals. I only found out yesterday but to be honest, it's a bit of a coup in the advertising world – my boss is over the moon,' she adds, aware that she's gabbling.

'That's wonderful,' Helen says again, taking another sip of tea and Dora pauses for a moment, watching the shadow of a bird flit across the far wall. She is unsure how to continue.

The bluebottle suddenly stops its agitated buzz at the window and the room falls deathly silent.

'And you, are you well?' Helen asks, glancing up. 'You look a little pale.'

First tired. Now pale. Dora marvels at how her mother's simple observations can sound more like criticism rather than concern. 'I'm . . . fine.' She thinks for a minute. 'Yes, fine,' she says again, and then, taking a deep breath, Dora finally says it out loud. 'Actually, I'm pregnant.'

There is a heavy silence.

'Only seven weeks or so, but definitely pregnant.'

Whether it is speaking the words out loud into the charged atmosphere of the room, or the relief of unburdening her news, or perhaps just the sheer terror she is consumed by, Dora doesn't know, but suddenly she is horrified to find that she is crying. Her body heaves and shakes as she releases noisy sobs into the stillness of the room.

She cries uncontrollably for a minute or so, a cascade of messy wet tears, before, in a vain attempt to compose herself, she runs her fingers under her eyes to catch the streaks of mascara, wipes her wet face on her sleeve and then reaches across for her cup of tea. She is mortified. This isn't what she'd intended. She takes a couple of slurps of her cold tea and then looks across at her mother. Helen is still seated, seemingly frozen in her chair, her face tight and suddenly pale. Dora gazes at her searchingly, waiting for the questions, a comment, the slightest registering of concern or joy but Helen remains utterly still, like a statue.

Dora waits a little longer. The room feels airless and Dora suddenly has the strangest feeling: maybe she isn't really there at all. Maybe this is just another one of her nightmares. Perhaps she is nothing more than a ghost. She feels light-headed. Insubstantial. Invisible.

Finally she can stand it no longer. 'Mum?' she asks. 'Aren't you going to say anything? *Anything at all?*' Her embarrassment is morphing quickly into fury.

Helen pauses, her teacup midway between her lap and her lips. Then she lets out a small sigh, a sound like a gust of wind passing through the branches of the trees outside.

Dora stares at her mother. 'Mum? I'm having a baby. Did you hear me?'

Finally Helen turns to look at her daughter. 'I heard you, Dora.'

'And?'

'What do you want me to say?'

'Well, I'm no expert in these matters, Mum, but "congratulations", I believe, is still the usual response.' Dora can no longer keep the anger from her voice. She isn't used to speaking so bluntly with her mother; in the past she has always been keen to avoid confrontation, to play the peacemaker. But this is too much.

'Congratulations then,' says Helen, but Dora notices she still cannot meet her eye.

She shakes her head in amazement. 'You just can't be happy for me, can you?'

Helen remains silent.

'I don't know why I bothered to come. I hoped things might be different. I hoped we might be able to put everything behind us. I thought my news . . .' she trails off. 'But I was wrong, wasn't I? Nothing's changed.'

Helen keeps her face turned to the garden. It feels like a dismissal and Dora wears it like a physical slap to her cheek. The blood rushes to her face. She slams her teacup onto the table between them and stands quickly. And then, unexpectedly, a rush of words comes.

'You know something, Mum,' she says as she moves towards the doorway, 'I had almost convinced myself that I was wrong; that I had imagined it all these years. I told myself that deep down you really *did* still love me but that you just couldn't show it any more, not after what happened.' She lets out a bitter laugh. 'I felt sorry for you. I figured you were . . . too . . . too damaged to show me how you feel. But I see now I was wrong.' She shakes her head and gives a bitter little laugh. 'God, was I wrong. The truth is that now that I carry the blame for what happened on *that one* day we can never go back. You'll never forgive me, will you? Years later and you can still barely bring yourself to look at me.'

The room falls silent and finally, Helen's head turns to meet Dora's. Even from her distance she can see the flecks of golden-amber glinting in the depths of her mother's green eyes.

'I . . . I . . . I want . . . I'm trying . . .' Helen stammers and then falls silent. She gives a defeated shrug of her shoulders and turns back to the garden once more.

'"*I . . . I*" what? What is it, Mum? What can't you say to me? Why are you still punishing me like this? What is wrong with you? Why can't you talk to me?' She is at the door. She waits, tearful and wild-eyed, hoping that her mother will tell her she is wrong, that she will stand and pull her into her arms and murmur comforting words in her ear; but her mother's shoulders remain twisted away from her and her gaze resolutely fixed on the swaying trees outside.

Dora stares a moment longer as another wave of anger floods through her body, then she turns and stalks out of the room. It takes all of her self control not to slam the door on her way out.

CASSIE

Fourteen Years Earlier

It was bad news. Cassie knew it the moment Dora sprinted into her bedroom, tripping in her baggy pink pyjamas and bursting with her first burning question of the morning.

'What's a happy accident, Cassie?' She threw herself shivering onto the end of the bed and shoved her feet under the duvet.

'Where did you hear that?' Cassie asked, pulled from a warm haze of sleep by Dora's words and the shock of ice-cube toes against her skin.

'Mum. On the phone last night to Violet,' Dora explained. 'Most accidents end in tears, right? That's what Dad always says, anyway.'

'Yeah,' Cassie agreed. Grazed knees, broken limbs, smashed crockery, and crashed cars – she couldn't think of one accident that didn't end in upset. Nothing good, as far as she could tell, ever came of an accident.

'Maybe we're getting a puppy?' Dora suggested hopefully.

'Mmm . . .' murmured Cassie doubtfully from beneath the covers. It was never going to happen.

'Do you think the boiler will freeze up again at school and we'll all be sent home?'

'I don't know, Dora,' Cassie sighed wearily. 'Why don't you go and bother Dad with your questions. It's too early.'

Dora stomped off with a little sniff, leaving Cassie to settle beneath her still-warm duvet; just enough time to try to block out the cloud of ugly thoughts suddenly filling her mind. No, nothing good ever came from an accident.

Richard and Helen sat the girls down that morning and told them the news.

'A baby?' Dora exclaimed.

'That's right,' said Richard proudly.

Cassie and Dora looked at one another.

'Is this the happy accident?' Dora asked, turning back to their mother.

Helen burst out laughing. 'Have you been eavesdropping on my phone calls?'

'No . . . Well, maybe,' Dora blushed.

'Yes, I suppose it is,' Helen agreed with a smile. 'We weren't planning on having any more children. It's a bolt from the blue. But it turns out we're rather pleased about it.' Helen reached over and squeezed Richard's hand. 'We hope you will be too.'

'Couldn't you have used contraception?' Cassie asked bluntly.

Richard coughed.

'What's contraception?' Dora asked.

'Well,' said Helen patiently, 'contraception is something two adults use when they make love, but don't want to have a baby.'

'It's what Sharon Tate in Year Ten should have used,' added Cassie knowingly to Dora.

'Yes, well, like your mother says, sex and contraception are for adults. Adults who love each other,' Richard stressed. 'And you're right, Cassie, we could have used contraception,' he agreed, trying to cover his embarrassment. 'But now that your mother is pregnant, we think it's wonderful. So . . .' he paused, expectation heavy in his voice, 'what do *you* both think?'

'I think it's wonderful too,' said Dora with a happy sigh. 'A baby sister.'

'Or a brother,' Richard reminded.

'It'll be a sister,' said Dora definitively.

There was silence. Cassie felt the weight of her parents' expectation pressing down on her.

'Well, Cassie, what do you think? Are you pleased?'

'Yeah,' Cassie said finally. 'It's great.'

There was a rush of air as Richard exhaled loudly. 'We knew you'd be pleased. Didn't I tell you, Helen? I *said* the girls would be pleased. A baby!' He smiled broadly at them all. 'Don't worry, we'll have you girls making up bottles and changing dirty nappies before you know it.'

'Ewwww . . . dirty nappies, no thank you!' Dora giggled.

'A baby,' Richard said again, shaking his head in wonder. 'Who'd have thought this old house would see another Tide arrive into the world? Mum and Dad would have been so pleased.'

There was something about the softness in her father's face that Cassie couldn't bear to see. She turned away, focusing her gaze on the scene outside the kitchen window. The ground was covered in frost and above it hung a thin strip of pale sky. Higher up a blanket of dark cumulus lay heavily upon the air, as though trying to press it into the frosted earth below, suffocating it slowly. Suddenly, she longed to escape. Never mind the cold, she wanted to launch into the void outside and run and run until her lungs were bursting and her legs collapsed. Then she would lie on the ground, let the frost from the grass soak into her clothes, crawl over her skin and wrap her in a cloak of ice.

'Earth to Cassie!' Richard was waving his hands in front of her face, trying to get her attention. 'Goodness, you were away with the fairies then! Did you hear me? I asked if you wanted another cup of tea?'

Cassie shook her head and turned back to the window. She couldn't even bring herself to smile. A baby; it was not good news.

*

Pregnancy transformed Helen. Over the coming months she seemed to swell and ripen, like the giant peach in Dora's favourite children's story. She had never been one for housekeeping, but she suddenly took to washing, cleaning and, most unfortunately, cooking with a newly found zeal, until Richard gently suggested she might want to conserve some of her energy for the baby's arrival; but the truth was none of them could stomach another of her elaborate and inedible family meals.

Her sister basked in Helen's glow, flitting moth-like around her mother with irrepressible excitement. Helen had told them that the baby could already hear their voices and Dora chattered away to the bump about anything and everything, but Cassie felt self-conscious the one time she had tried and couldn't think of anything to say, so she left it to Dora to babble idiotically at their mother's belly.

Their father too, could barely contain his excitement. He bounded round the house each weekend, preparing for the arrival. There was a new nursery to paint and an old crib to sand and varnish. He built wooden shelves which he stocked with new books and toys, and attacked his projects with vigour, as if by hurling himself into them he could somehow encourage the baby to arrive more quickly.

It didn't help that as Helen blossomed and grew, Cassie's own body was undergoing a strange and uncomfortable transformation. Overnight, it seemed, hair had begun to sprout in awkward places. Her skin broke out in greasy red pimples and she got hot and sweaty at difficult times, particularly whenever Miss Mackintosh, the prettiest teacher at school, addressed her in class. And worst of all, breasts had started to grow where once had only been flat, pink nipples. She studied and poked at them in the bedroom mirror, half annoyed, half fascinated. She wasn't sure she liked the new additions and felt self-conscious in her too-tight school blouses. Secretly she hoped that Helen might notice and suggest a shopping trip, like the other girls in her class; a mother–daughter rite of passage, it seemed: a new bra, a milkshake, and even her ears pierced if she were really lucky, like Tamara Hopkins. But Helen was preoccupied with her own life, and the new one growing inside her. As the days passed and Cassie's growth spurt went unnoticed, she grew increasingly annoyed, until eventually she raided Helen's purse, pocketed a twenty pound note and took herself off to the department store in Bridport.

All she wanted was a bra. How hard could it be? She drifted round the ground floor on her own for a while, trying to summon the courage to grab something from the bewildering array of lingerie on display. There were little lacy numbers, sporty T-shirt bras, pretty ones covered in flowers and bows, and giant hammock-like contraptions terrifying in their complex construction. Finally, a kindly grey-haired assistant with gold-rimmed spectacles perched high on her nose took pity on her. 'Can I help you there, love?' She smiled down at her.

Cassie would have run, but she really didn't want to return home without a bra; it was getting impossible at school. Her shirt was virtually see-through and she'd seen some of the boys staring.

'I need a bra, please,' she finally muttered.

'Well, you're in the right place. Let's get you into a changing room, shall we? I'll measure you up and then you can try on some different styles. We'll have you fixed up in no time, all right?'

Cassie nodded and followed the lady into the changing rooms. The assistant pulled out a tape measure and continued with her small talk as she took Cassie's measurements. 'You on your own today, love?'

'Yes.'

'First bra, is it?'

'Yes.'

'I remember when I got my first bra. My mum and I went

to a funny little shop in Exeter. Terribly uncomfortable it was. Not like these things nowadays. So soft and stretchy. It's the Lycra. It's revolutionised life for us women. Whoever invented Lycra should be given a bloomin' medal, if you ask me. Your mum off buying groceries, is she? Left you to get on with it alone, like a big girl?'

'My mum's dead.' Cassie wasn't sure why she said it, but the words were out of her mouth before she could stop them.

'Oh!' The woman's hands froze and the tape measure unfurled into a long tangled heap on the floor. 'Oh my gosh. I am sorry. There's me prattling on. Oh you poor dear.' There was an embarrassed silence. 'Well, don't you worry, my love. We'll get you fixed up and comfy as we can in no time. You're in expert hands here. Never met a pair of breasts I couldn't fit.'

Cassie gave the lady a weak smile and was mortified to see the assistant had tears in her eyes. She didn't really know why she'd lied, but it was out there now and she couldn't take it back.

The woman made a big fuss of her. She measured her and then brought four bras back into the cubicle. She had Cassie try them all on and sent her on her way just twenty minutes later in her first virgin-white 32A-cup; a simple cotton number with a tiny purple bow in the centre. 'She'd be very proud of you, she would,' the lady told her on her way out of the shop.

Cassie looked at her in confusion.

'Your mum, my love, she'd be so proud, you all grown-up . . . a proper woman!' and she'd winked down at Cassie and made her blush with shame.

Cassie thought about it on the way home. The shop assistant was wrong. Her mother wasn't proud of her. She hadn't even noticed Cassie was growing into a woman. Her mum may as well be dead, for all the attention she gave her these days. Cassie sat simmering quietly as she rode the bus home on her own, cursing her mother, her unborn sibling and the new bra straps digging uncomfortably into her shoulders.

She was still angry at the world that evening, and the sight of Dora seated at the kitchen table, her head bent intently over the misshapen blanket she was learning to knit for the baby was too much. She straddled the chair next to Dora and waited for her sister to look up obligingly from the tangle of yellow wool in her lap.

'You do realise,' she said, 'that things are going to be very different when this baby arrives, don't you, Dora?'

Dora looked startled. She had been mid-count, her tongue still caught between her lips in concentration. 'Dropped one! What was that, Cassie?'

'I said things are going to be different when the baby arrives.'

'Different how?'

'Babies need a lot of attention and Mum and Dad . . . they'll be tired and distracted.'

Dora nodded. 'Uh-huh.'

Cassie continued. 'It will be their favourite, you know, the *baby* of the family. It will get the most attention. You won't be the youngest any more, Dora. You and I, we can't compete with that, can we?'

Dora thought for a moment. 'I didn't think it was a competition. Surely Mum and Dad will just love us all the same? Anyway, they seem happy again, don't they? I like it.' Dora lifted the needles to regard her progress and Cassie noted several large holes in the long and strangely triangular-shaped fabric. The blanket was going to be a disaster but Dora just gave it a tug here and there and returned to clicking her needles together in a slow and steady rhythm.

Cassie shook her head. 'Oh, Dora, you're so naïve. Believe that if you want, if it makes you feel better, but deep down you know I'm right. Everything's about to change.' She just couldn't stop herself. She felt a hot spite raging within and she needed to release it, to share it. 'So you'd better brace yourself. It's you and me now, Dora,' she continued. 'It's you and me against the world. You know that, right?'

Dora seemed to consider her sister's words for a moment, before she nodded. 'I s'pose so.'

Cassie was chastened slightly by the sight of Dora's glum face, but she tried again in a softer voice. 'We've got to stick together, haven't we? It's what sisters do.'

Dora nodded again, but it seemed she didn't want to continue the conversation. She dropped her head and continued with her slow and steady knit-one-purl-one rhythm until Cassie got bored and retreated from the room.

A few nights later, Cassie woke from sleep to a hot, damp feeling between her legs. She flicked on her bedside lamp and looked down to see a bloody stain blossoming on the pale cotton of her nightie. She sighed.

Her period: it had finally started.

They'd talked about it in PSE lessons at school, Mrs Nelson battling on regardless, ignoring the girls' sniggers and embarrassed jokes, explaining to them that it would be worth keeping a small supply of towels or tampons handy for such a momentous occasion: 'their initiation into womanhood', she had called it. Since that class Cassie had been meaning to broach the issue with her mother but she had never found the right moment. She regretted it now.

Cassie hauled herself out of bed and padded silently down the landing to the bathroom. As she reached the doorway she heard a strange, strangled cry. She'd investigate just as soon as she'd sorted herself out.

First she pulled the nightdress over her head and washed herself with a damp flannel. In the bathroom cabinet she found an old packet of sanitary towels belonging to her mother. They looked enormous, far bigger than the ones the teacher had shown them in class. She pulled off the strip from the back of the pad and settled the giant wedge into an old pair of knickers from the airing cupboard. It felt stiff and fat between her legs, not at all comfortable. Still, it would do for now. Grabbing a pair of flannel pyjamas, Cassie pulled them on hurriedly and then set about furiously scrubbing the livid red stain from her nightdress. *Out damn spot!* She was suddenly reminded of the line from Macbeth. The mark had transformed from livid red to a tea-brown tinge, but it was still there. She stuffed the nightie, sodden and crumpled, to the back of the airing cupboard before switching off the light and heading back into the hallway.

It was still dark, but a sliver of light escaped from underneath her parent's bedroom door. Again, a cat-like wail broke the eerie silence. Cassie walked towards the door, uncertain if she really wanted to go any further, but unable to turn back. As she got closer, she noticed the door was slightly ajar. The mewling grew louder, and then stopped. She heard her parents talking in soft, low voices. She paused at the entrance to the room, took a breath, and then gently pushed the door open. Her eyes widened as she saw the scene before her.

Helen and Richard sat together on the bed, propped up on pillows. The sheets and duvet lay in a tangled heap at the bottom of the bed. Her father looked dishevelled, as though he hadn't yet been to sleep, his arm slung protectively around Helen's shoulders as they both gazed in rapture at a small bundle nestled in her arms. Another piercing cry broke the quiet and Helen shifted the bundle of blankets in her arms and unbuttoned the front of her nightdress with her free hand. Then a small, pink head appeared and seemed to settle peacefully at Helen's breast. 'He's hungry,' she heard her mother say.

Cassie bristled with discomfort. She felt as though she were intruding on a private moment, something sacred that she wasn't a part of. She started to back out of the room, willing her presence to go unnoticed but something had given her away because suddenly Richard's head swung up.

'Cassie!' he exclaimed, startled to see her standing at their bedroom door. 'Come in. Come and meet your brother.'

Cassie padded reluctantly across the carpet, leaning in to peer politely at the swaddled infant. He was pink and puffy with bow lips and eyes scrunched shut. His face looked swollen and his nose squashed, as if he'd gone ten rounds in a boxing ring. She could see a fretwork of blue veins pumping blood under his papery skin, and a smattering of blond down on the top of his head, the exact same colour as her father's. The baby was oblivious to anything but the breast he was latched to and Cassie was suddenly reminded of the newborn Labrador puppies they had gone to see in Farmer Plummer's barn last summer, disappointingly slimy and translucent, wriggling blindly at their mother's swollen teats.

'What do you think?' Richard asked. 'Isn't he adorable?'

'Mmm . . .' Cassie agreed. 'I thought you were going to have him at the hospital?' she addressed Helen, accusingly.

'Well, that was the plan, but it seems this little guy had other ideas. You should have seen your father, Cass, all in a tizzy, until the midwife at the end of the phone took him in hand and explained what he had to do. It was just as well because this baby was in a hurry.'

'To be honest I didn't really do that much. Your mother and brother did all the hard work.'

There was a loud creak of the door and they all looked up.

'What's going on?' yawned Dora. 'Why is everyone awake?'

'Come and meet your new baby brother,' Richard urged, beckoning Dora into the family circle.

'He's here? Already? Why didn't anyone wake me?'

'Come on, poppet, come and meet him,' Richard urged.

She didn't need any further encouragement. Dora launched herself at the double bed, landing on the mattress with a thud.

'Careful!' warned Helen, clutching the bundle protectively to her chest.

Cassie saw Dora bite her lip and glance across at her. Cassie rewarded her sister with a knowing look, one that said: *see, I told you so.*

Dora's cheeks flared red and she dropped her gaze hurriedly, before sidling apologetically up to her father's side of the bed. 'Sorry.'

'It's OK, Panda,' Richard soothed, putting an arm around her. 'Just go gently. He's only tiny.'

Dora nodded and poked at the baby in Helen's arms. 'What's he called?'

Cassie and Dora shared another quick look. First Cassandra. Then Pandora. They were both keen to know what trials from Greek mythology Helen would inflict on this new Tide child.

'He's Alfred, isn't he, Richard?'

Richard looked up at Helen with a start. 'I thought you had your heart set on Hector?'

'No.' Helen shook her head. 'Look at him. He's an Alfred if ever I saw one.'

'Alfie!' exclaimed Dora. 'Like Granddad?'

'Yes,' smiled Richard, his voice thick with emotion. 'Like Granddad.'

'Baby Alfie,' repeated Dora with satisfaction. 'It suits him.'

'Yes,' said Helen. 'Yes it does.'

Just then little Alfie gurgled and gave a small cry.

'He's so cute,' Dora exclaimed. 'Look at his tiny fingernails.'

As Helen, Richard and Dora all cooed over baby Alfie's ten perfect fingers and ten perfect toes, Cassie retreated quietly from the cosy family scene, slipping away unnoticed from the room. No, nothing good ever came from an accident; she could feel it deep in her bones.

DORA

Present Day

Dora runs down the oak-panelled hallway and bursts through the front door into the blinding afternoon sunshine. She doesn't know where she is going; all she knows is that she has to escape the house and, somehow, banish the image replaying over and over in her mind of her mother's face – tight and pale – turning away from her and the news of her pregnancy. At that moment Dora can't stand to be under the same roof as Helen.

She's oblivious to her surroundings as she half runs, half walks down through the garden and across the fruit orchard before joining up with the muddy walking track heading out towards the cliffs. The ground is boggy after weeks of spring rain and she concentrates on jumping the puddles littered along the way. Her impractical ballet flats squelch and splash as she goes and cold water is already seeping around her feet, edging up the hems of her jeans, but she doesn't care. She marches on, head down, stewing on the events that have just unfolded in the conservatory.

Helen's reaction has shocked Dora to the core. It was never going to be an easy conversation, but Dora realises now that she had, at least, dared to hope for a little more from her mother – an expression of joy or support, perhaps, amidst the obvious grief and distress. Instead it feels as though Helen has pulled yet another shutter down between them. There is an insurmountable divide that they just cannot seem to bridge.

What has happened to the mother she remembers from her childhood? The one who would gather her into her bed at night and hold her close as a midnight thunderstorm raged outside? Or cover her with pink calamine lotion when she itched with chicken pox? The woman who sewed name tags into her school uniform, packed her lunches, tucked her in at night, bathed her grazed knees, kissed her feverish brow and wiped away her tears? The mother she remembers from childhood seems wholly unrelated to the ice-cold woman sitting up at Clifftops. It makes Dora want to cry out with frustration and pain.

She reaches the trail's end; the hawthorn hedgerows on either side peter out and Dora finds herself standing on the cliffs overlooking Lyme Bay. She has, she realises, unconsciously returned to the well-trodden walking tracks of her childhood. To the left lies the beach. To the right stands an old weather-beaten church. Directly ahead lies the placid, shimmering sea. She watches the sunlight dance across its surface, a sheet of silver rippling in the breeze. Slowly her heart begins to calm in her ribcage. Fine gauze cloud is building high up in the sky but it is still warm and Dora knows it will be light out for a few more hours yet. In for a penny in for a pound, she thinks, and with a grim smile, she turns right and heads for the church.

It is exactly as she remembers it, a humble, whitewashed building with arched stained-glass windows and a roughly hewn wooden cross hanging over the doorway. It is surrounded by a crumbling stone wall, and dotted all around are the markers of a hundred or more graves, the headstones seeming to push up through the ground like the wild spring flowers dancing on the breeze. Dora hesitates for just a moment before entering through the wooden gate.

For a minute or two she wanders among the graves, trailing her hands across the warm stone, reading the names and the dates of the deceased. Some of the graves are overgrown, their headstones nothing more than ruins, the words once so carefully engraved onto the stone now weathered and worn until illegible; but others are well maintained, with carefully placed bunches of flowers indicating the human grief and loss that still lives on. Many are sailors, she realises, souls lost over the years to the raging sea. As Dora slowly makes her way towards her grandparents' resting place, she wishes she had thought to bring flowers.

She stands in almost the same spot as she had fifteen years ago, when she had watched Alfred and Daphne's wooden coffins being lowered into the earth. The memory of that day is strangely hazy, but standing there, she is reminded of the feeling of her father's cold hand clutching at her own mittened one. His grip had been bone-crushing, like that of a drowning man. Afterwards they had all returned to Clifftops and Dora had sat shivering on the front doorstep watching a steady stream of creaking, elderly people arrive from the village. Her cheeks were soon bruised from their sympathetic pinches and the fridge fit to bursting with the casseroles and cakes they'd brought with them. After a while she'd realised Cassie had the right idea. She'd left the serious business of adult grief behind, and wandered upstairs to find her sister.

'Cassie?' She'd rattled the door handle to her sister's room.

'What?' had come the muffled reply.

'Can I come in?'

She'd heard a sigh, followed by the sound of chair legs scraping across the floor. When Dora had tried the handle again the door had flown open. Cassie was resettling herself on the bed, a bottle of nail varnish in her hand.

'What are you doing?'

'What does it look like?'

Dora knew it was best not to say anything. When Cassie got into one of her strops it didn't take much to tip the balance; sometimes even the most innocuous of comments could see her ejected from the inner sanctum of her sister's room. So she'd sat quietly, watching from a careful distance as Cassie artfully applied a thick layer of black nail varnish to each of her toenails. Their mum was going to go spare.

'Cass?' she'd tried, eventually.

'Uh-huh?' She didn't bother to look up.

'What do you think it feels like when you're dead?'

Cassie turned to regard Dora with her cool blue-eyed gaze, her hand paused halfway between the bottle and her toes. She seemed to consider the question for a moment. 'I think dead probably feels OK. You know, peaceful . . . calm . . .' She paused. 'Like when you're in a warm bath, just floating, floating and you've got nothing in your head.'

'So it doesn't hurt?'

'No, you don't feel anything when you're dead. Everything just stops.'

Dora remembered she'd felt a little better. She'd watched as Cassie had leaned over and removed the twists of toilet paper from between her toes, before testing her nails with a finger. Seemingly satisfied she'd turned to Dora. 'I'm bored, are you coming?'

'Where?'

'Outside. I can't stand all these old people everywhere. It's so depressing.'

Dora hadn't needed to be asked twice. She'd followed her sister down the stairs, grabbed their winter coats and shoes, and run out into the back garden. They'd tripped across the lawn and down to the stream below the orchard, silently watching as their poohsticks slipped away towards the ocean.

Dora winces at the sudden onslaught of memories and although the sun still holds a glimmer of warmth, she shivers and wraps her arms tightly around her body. Was that when it had all begun to unravel – for it had only been a matter of weeks before the family had left London and moved down to Clifftops – was that when things had started to come undone? Like a tiny hole in a tightly woven cloth, was it the move to

Dorset that had tugged loose the first thread and begun to unravel the fabric of their family?

Dora looks down again at her grandparents' graves. She is unable to offer flowers but there is something she can do. She kneels on the ground and begins to clear the weeds that have sprung up around their headstones, ignoring the damp earth seeping through the knees of her jeans. As she works, her ear tunes in to the ebb and flow of the waves washing against the cliffs below. The sound is strangely soothing, like the rise and fall of her breathing – in and out, forwards and backwards, the perpetual motion of the waves is ceaseless in its rhythm.

She works until she has pulled every weed from the mounds of earth covering her grandparents' coffins, then stands and looks out towards the horizon. The sun is paling in the sky, sinking slowly towards the earth. Dora knows she must return to the house. It is too late to drive back to London now. She'll have to stay the night.

She picks herself up, still unable to even glance at the newer, cleaner headstone standing next to her grandparents', and turning her back on the church she makes her way through the gate and out towards the muddy path that will take her home.

HELEN

Eleven Years Earlier

It was the usual morning of chaos. No matter that it was the last day of term, there they were, racing around the house like lunatics, trying to get out the door on time. Helen felt like pulling her hair out.

'Have you seen my trainers, Mum?'

'By the front door, where you left them, Dora.' She turned and threw milk and cereal bowls onto the table. 'Alfie, get down! You'll fall and hurt yourself.' Alfie grinned at her from his precarious position hanging over the back of one of the kitchen chairs. 'Alfie, I mean it. Get down now.'

Slowly he clambered down.

'Where's Cassie?'

Dora shrugged. 'Still in bed.'

Helen let out a groan. 'That girl!' She raced out of the kitchen and stood at the bottom of the stairs. 'Cassie! Get down here now. You're going to be late for school.'

Richard appeared at the top of the stairs, struggling with a tie. His hair was still wet from the shower and his face bore a livid shaving rash, an angry red against his pale skin. 'Morning, love.'

'Will you tell Cassie to get herself down here, now. She's going to miss the bus again.'

Richard turned and huffed back up the stairs.

Honestly, thought Helen, sometimes it was like having four kids to look after. She headed back to the kitchen.

'I can't find them, Mum, they're not there.'

'What's not there, Dora?'

'My trainers.'

'Well maybe if you put them away each night, like I asked you to, we wouldn't have to go through this every morning. Have you thought of that?'

Dora rolled her eyes and stomped off in the direction of the conservatory.

Helen hurried into the kitchen, turning her attention back to breakfast. 'Did you tell her?' she asked as Richard reappeared. She danced around him, simultaneously removing toast from the toaster and filling glasses with orange juice.

'I told her.'

'Is she coming down?'

'She was still in bed when I went in, but she got the message.' Richard sat himself at the kitchen table and reached across for a slice of toast. 'Did you buy more marmalade?'

'You know I've been flat out this week. Just when would I have had time to get to the shops?' She sounded more defensive than she'd intended, but Richard, thankfully, didn't rise to the bait.

'Would you like *me* to stop at the supermarket on my way home from work?' he asked carefully.

'No.' She shook her head. 'Thanks,' she added after another moment.

Richard shrugged. 'You know,' he continued, spreading butter across the slice of wholemeal in front of him, 'if Cass went to bed at a sensible time we wouldn't have this problem every morning.'

Helen sighed. She'd tried, but Cassie was going through yet another phase. No one, it seemed, could tell their daughter what to do. 'Did you find them?' she asked, glancing up as Dora entered the room, grateful to change the subject.

'Yes.'

'Where were they?'

'In Alfie's toy box. He must have put them in there.'

Richard smiled indulgently. 'Funny boy. Hello, Panda, did you sleep well?'

'Yes thanks.'

Helen couldn't miss the meaningful glance Richard threw her way. He was always drawing comparisons between the two girls, but it wasn't fair. They were so different. Chalk and cheese. Dora was just like her father in temperament, solid and dependable. Cassie was more spirited. It was a good thing.

'Talking of Alfie,' said Helen, 'where is he?'

All three of them went still, listening for traces of a little boy making mischief. It was ominously quiet.

'Great,' sighed Helen. 'I'll go.'

She found him, moments later, on the sofa in the den. He was perched in front of the television set, still in his dinosaur pyjamas, his straw hair even more electric than usual. Piled beside him was a mountain of corn flakes. The empty packet lay on the floor and Helen could just see the rim of a bowl poking out from beneath the landslide. 'Did you help yourself to breakfast, Alfie?' she asked, surveying the wreckage.

He nodded and reached a chubby hand into the pile for a flake, angling it into his mouth, his gaze never leaving the cartoon on the screen.

'Were you hungry?'

He nodded again. 'Alfie spill it.' He looked up at her then with his cornflower-blue eyes. 'Sorry, Mummy.'

Any frustration she felt about the mess instantly faded. 'That's OK. Just ask me next time, or one of your sisters. We will help you.'

'I can do it myself,' he asserted, ever the independent, shovelling more dry cereal into his mouth.

'All right, Alfie, but we don't just help ourselves, OK?'

'Why?'

'Because if we all helped ourselves to the food in the cupboards we'd run out very quickly.'

He looked up at her with interest. 'Why?'

'Because Mummy only goes shopping once a week.'

'Why?'

'Because Mummy is very busy, working and looking after all of you.'

'Why?'

'Because that's what mums do.'

'Why?'

Helen sighed. It seemed he had entered *that* phase. She opted for the fail-safe conversation closer. 'Just because.'

It seemed to work. He turned back to the television, silenced for a moment, until he twisted back to her with a smile. 'Mummy's nice.'

She grinned back at him idiotically, his words swelling her heart.

Eventually, after several more attempts to prise Cassie from her room, a battle with the dishwasher, a curt goodbye to her husband and a fight with Alfie about a plastic dinosaur he refused to leave behind, Helen bundled the girls down the driveway, fastened Alfie into his child seat and then leapt into the car. It was going to be one of those days.

She got as far as the end of the lane when a tractor came into view. 'God damn it!' she cursed, thumping the steering wheel with frustration. She was going to be late for work, again.

'Damit, damit, damit,' Alfie babbled at her from the back.

She looked at his chubby little face in the rear-view mirror with a guilty start. Richard was always warning her about minding her language in front of the kids, but she always forgot.

'Rabbit, rabbit, rabbit, Alfie. That's what Mummy said,' she tried cheerfully.

'God damit!' Alfie giggled back at her. He was nearly three and no fool.

Helen sighed. No doubt that would be another black mark

against her. She was already in Mrs Kendall's bad books at Alfie's nursery. She had been taken aside just yesterday and told with stern disapproval that she really did need to collect her son *on time* each evening. They wouldn't mind if it had just been the once, but unfortunately it was becoming something of a habit. Still, she consoled herself, just one more day and then she and Alfie and the girls would all be home for the summer holidays. No more late nights sitting up preparing lectures for uninterested, yawning students; no more mad dashes across the Dorset countryside; no more guilt as she realised yet again that she would be late to collect Alfie; at least, not for the next six weeks anyway.

Guilt: it was an emotion she felt consumed by these days. Helen loved her job but it was proving harder and harder to juggle all the pieces of her life, and she felt constantly as though she were falling short in every single area. Wife, mother, employee – she tried hard to make it all work; to fit the pieces together like a complicated jigsaw puzzle, but she felt that as soon as she got one piece slotted into place, the table was jostled and another piece came springing free. She had complained to Richard about it at the weekend but he had only infuriated her by gently suggesting that if she couldn't cope perhaps she should consider giving up her job at the university. It wasn't as if they really needed her wages, he'd reminded her, and it might be nice for her to spend a little more time around the house. He'd helpfully pointed out the moth-eaten curtains in the drawing room that needed replacing, and the thick layer of dust caking the library bookshelves.

'What?' he'd asked, confused at the fury spreading across her face. 'Why are you looking at me like *that*? I'm only trying to help . . . I know you enjoy your job, but we shouldn't let the house just fall down around our ears. You don't have to put yourself under this pressure, not for us. Why not relax a bit, enjoy the peace and quiet here, instead of haring off to Exeter day after day?'

She had nearly thrown the saucepan she'd been holding at his head. Did he really think she would give up her job to stay at home and dust bookshelves? Did he really know her so little? She had no intention of giving up her job, not now. It was one of the few things that gave her a thrill. It was one of the few times that she actually felt like herself again, and not just a frumpy housewife or exhausted mother.

Helen followed the tractor round yet another hairpin bend and was about to release another string of profanities unsuitable for the tender, young ears in the back seat of the car when the vehicle finally pulled up onto the grass verge, allowing her past. The road was pleasingly clear in front and just twenty minutes later she was running back across the nursery car park to her car. Thankfully she'd managed to avoid grumpy Mrs Kendall, plonking Alfie into the arms of a pretty young minder she didn't know the name of, and waving cheerfully to him as she said goodbye. 'Have fun, little man, see you this afternoon.' Alfie's bottom lip had wobbled slightly but the young woman holding him had artfully distracted him with a big red train that lay at their feet.

She still hated leaving him, but she couldn't deny she'd grown to love the sensation that descended upon her just minutes later as she clambered back into her car, turned up the radio and put her foot down on the accelerator. She knew what it was she felt: sheer, unadulterated freedom. Was it normal to long for these solitary moments so much, she wondered? Or did that make her a bad mother? A bad wife? Well, she thought with a sad smile, pulling onto the dual carriageway and putting her foot to the floor, she already knew she was a bad wife, and she didn't need Richard to remind her of it, as he did so frequently these days. Last night's row had been no exception. She couldn't even remember how it had started now. But it had been awful. She could still hear Richard's bitter words echoing in her ears.

'Do we really have to live in this perpetual chaos?' he'd

asked, hurling the remains of his uneaten dinner into the bin. 'I can't bear it. I'm not asking much, am I?'

'No, of course *you're* not asking much!' she'd spat back. 'And Cassie's not asking much! And Dora's not asking much! And Alfie's not asking much. None of you *think* you're asking for much; but add it all up and you'll soon see that I'm being torn in four different directions. I don't have time for *me* any more. I can't even remember who *I* am.'

'Oh don't be so melodramatic. Other women seem to balance work and family just fine – and I already told you just this weekend—'

'Well perhaps you should have married one of those superwomen then!'

And round and round they had gone, all the recent family niggles and annoyances rolled into one angry mess. She'd looked at Richard as he'd stood across the kitchen from her, his mouth opening and closing in a 'Charlie Brown' *wuuh-waah-waah*, and all she could focus on was a small, irritating tuft of hair that had made a break from one of his nostrils and flapped helplessly in time to his words. It was then that she knew her feelings for him had faded beyond recognition. She didn't know what she felt for him any more, but it was a long way from the early romance of their youth. She had stood there in a sort of daze, wondering how they had come to this.

She'd thought about it plenty over the years, wondering why she had accepted his proposal of marriage when they barely even knew each other. The only conclusion she had been able to draw was that he had seduced her with a false promise. Not a malicious one, but something sly and subtle. Because when Richard had sat across from her on the night he'd proposed, his eyes full of adoration and hope, it had seemed so romantic, so spontaneous that she'd convinced herself Richard might just be the man for her. He wasn't merely attractive and intelligent and what her mother would have deemed to be a *good catch*, he'd seemed passionate and adventurous too.

But as the years passed, Helen's simmering disappointment grew and grew as slowly she realised that Richard's sense of spontaneity and adventure was a short-lived thing; a tiny, hot flame that had burned brightly for just a moment and then extinguished itself for ever. He'd acted in a way that had promised her something that she knew now he simply couldn't deliver. He seemed aware of her disappointment – how could he not be when she was so frustrated, so spiky and volatile – but his cautious tiptoeing around her, his gentle, soft-spoken attempts to pacify and smooth the waters only served to irritate her more. Frankly, she would have preferred it if he'd shouted and raged and shown her a fiery, passionate spirit; but every day that she endured his cautious, wary glances, his dry, conservative views, the careful way he kissed her, his perfectly lined-up shoes in the wardrobe or his habit of folding the newspaper just so, she felt more and more angry, like a tightly coiled spring about to explode.

The truth was that they had reached a critical point in their relationship, a sort of stalemate that they just couldn't move beyond; for now, whenever one of them tried to draw close, whenever one of them reached out to reconnect, they always seemed to put a foot wrong. His well-meaning attempts to lighten her load only made her feel defensive and guilty, while her attempts to swallow back her frustration and disappointment only seemed to make it spew forth more furiously when she did, inevitably, lose her temper with him. Their few clumsy efforts to reconcile only sent them spinning further away from each other, like two magnets repelling each other.

In essence, she mourned the life she thought she should have, the life she'd believed they would share. She wanted bright lights, culture, a bustling city landscape, travel and adventure. To have ended up cloistered away in a sleepy seaside hamlet of all places, rattling around the rambling old farmhouse of his childhood, seemed unfathomable. She'd told him from the start that she wanted a career . . . that she wanted to be in London . . . that the life his mother had lived wasn't for her, and yet here they were, Daphne and Alfred Tide reincarnated. Thanks to his overblown sense of familial duty she'd foregone her dreams and traded her ambitions, all to service the legacy of his dead parents.

It always came back to that damn house! It seemed to stand between them, casting a huge, dark shadow over their faltering relationship. She was no fool; she knew now they were there for good. She knew that the only way he would leave Clifftops would be to be carried out in his bloody coffin; she just couldn't bear to go the same way. She wasn't yet forty, far too young to resign herself to a sedate life of quiet country pursuits. The thought made her shiver.

Helen sped onwards, solitary in her little car, winding down the window so that the breeze blew her hair loose from its clip. A warm weekend had been forecast and she was grateful that the holidays were nearly upon them, but for now it was just enough to be on her own, on her way to work, enjoying the sunshine. It was far too nice a morning to spend it dwelling on her unhappy marriage. Pushing all thoughts of her family from her mind, Helen began instead to think about the day that lay ahead. She had one lecture to give, a few papers to mark and then she would be free. She turned up the radio and put her foot to the floor. For once, she could feel her blood pumping and her skin tingle in the summer breeze. For once, she felt alive. It was going to be a good day.

A little over twenty minutes later Helen pulled into the faculty car park. Miraculously she was on time. She tried to resist glancing at the space opposite hers but failed. The little green MG was there already, its battered bonnet winking cheerily in the sunshine. She felt a sudden heat flood through her body and tried to ignore the sensation, instead grabbing at the books and papers that had spread themselves across the back seat and making her way into the Classics department. Just a silly housewife's fantasy, there was no harm in that.

'Last day with the buggers for a while eh?' Dean Childs called out as she walked by his open door. 'Are you joining us at the pub later to celebrate?'

'Yes,' she agreed, caught off guard. She had forgotten about the faculty end of year lunch.

'Good, good,' the grey-haired professor nodded. 'Nice to have a respectable turnout and I'd be interested to hear how your module has gone this semester. I've heard good things from the students.'

'Great!' Helen exclaimed with false enthusiasm. 'See you then.'

Eager to avoid any more chitchat she sped to the end of the corridor and unlocked the door to her office. She entered and closed it behind her with a sigh. That ruled out lunch in the staff canteen then, and any possible chance of bumping into *him*.

Just thinking of a possible encounter again made her stomach twist with lust. She glanced at herself in the little mirror she'd hung on the back of her door. Her shoulder-length hair was wild and curly after the car journey, and there was a pink flush to her cheeks where the wind had whipped at her face. She'd dressed carefully, eager to look youthful, but careful not to overdo it. She thought she'd struck just the right note in a brightly patterned calf-length skirt, a fitted white shirt and wide brown leather belt and boots. She didn't look half bad for a mother of three, although she supposed it didn't really matter now. She sighed. It was probably just as well.

The lecture theatre was half empty when Helen entered, just a smattering of unusually prompt students already in their place. She moved to the lectern, arranged her papers and ran through the slides one final time. By nine thirty she was ready and as the last stragglers slipped into their seats Helen dimmed the theatre lights, cleared her throat and began.

'*The Iliad.* Of all Homer's orations, this one is perhaps the most celebrated, the most popular. And at its centre, at the very heart of the tragedy lies one woman: Helen of Troy. Daughter. Sister. Wife. Adulteress. Victim . . . or perhaps . . . villain?' She paused for dramatic effect. 'She has been called many things over the centuries . . .'

Helen looked out across the room. In the dim half-light a number of students had begun to scribble furiously in notepads. She could see one or two others leaning back in their chairs, arms folded, their eyes on the screen overhead. To the far right she saw another student with his head resting upon the desk, clearly settled in for an hour's sleep. She pressed her clicker and flashed up a series of images, details of Helen taken from frescoes and vases, pausing on a slide showing Evelyn de Morgan's famous nineteenth-century portrait.

'Undoubtedly she is one of the most alluring women of ancient mythology. She was the face that infamously launched a thousand ships, and yet even before we meet her in *The Iliad,* she has experienced a life of tragedy and controversy.'

Out of the corner of her eye Helen saw the door to the lecture theatre open. For just a moment the figure of a man stood backlit in the doorway. He slid quietly towards the nearest empty chair and the door swung shut again, returning the room to darkness once more. The surprise entrance only took a second or two, but it was long enough for Helen to recognise the unmistakable silhouette of her uninvited guest.

'We . . . we know . . . er, we know, of course, that Helen was a great beauty.'

Helen struggled to maintain her composure. *Focus on the lecture. Focus on the lecture.* She glanced back to the slide on the screen, swallowed back her discomfort and then continued. 'But you have to delve deep into the text to really understand the essence of Helen and what it was she stood for. If we look at Euripides' play *Helen*, which he wrote in the fifth century BC, we find a very different portrayal of the woman. In the opening scene Helen stands . . .'

She had soon forgotten the presence of her unexpected guest as she lost herself in the lecture and before long Helen found herself opening up the floor to questions. As usual the undergraduates were reluctant to step into the spotlight, but then, miraculously, one student stuck up her hand. Helen nearly keeled over with surprise. 'Yes, Jenny, you have a question?'

'Um, yes, I wanted to ask if there is any chance of an extension for our final essays?'

Helen's heart sank. She'd been hoping for something a little more pertinent to the lecture. 'Essays are due in the first day back next term. You'll need to come and speak to me in person if you have a problem meeting the deadline. Does anyone else have a question?' She was just about to wish them all a happy holiday when a deep baritone broke the silence.

'I do.'

Helen's heart sank. 'Er, yes, Mr . . .' She feigned ignorance.

'Grey. Tobias Grey, Artist in Residence here at the university. I hope you don't mind me sitting in on your lecture today. I found it fascinating.'

'Thank you, Mr Grey,' Helen replied formally. 'You have a question?'

'Yes. I was interested to hear you talking about the tension between duty and desire that Helen faces,' he continued. 'What do you think Homer was saying about her dilemma? Was it a warning to women of the follies of adultery? Or is he saying Helen was right to abscond with Paris to Troy? To follow her heart?'

Helen took a deep breath. She felt the beady eyes of her students gazing up at her. 'Well, you raise a good point, Mr Grey. That very tension is one of the themes I've asked the students to explore in their papers.' She forced herself to turn away from the heat of his gaze and look around the room. 'I believe it's more complicated than a simple "right or wrong". There are other factors at play in Helen's life, and other forces at work in the tragedy as a whole. Helen is a complex woman in a precarious situation and so, without giving too much away right now, let me just say I'm really looking forward to reading my students' interpretations of her dilemma in more detail next term.' There was an audible groan as the few still listening realised they weren't going to be privy to Helen's own theories. No easy pickings for their essays. 'Now, does anyone else have a question?'

Nothing. Just the shuffle of papers and bags as students began to pack up their belongings.

'Well, then. I hope you all have a wonderful break and I look forward to seeing some of you in my module next year on Sexuality and Gender in the Ancient World.'

There was a rush for the door and the room suddenly swelled with the babble of students, energised and excited by their impending freedom. Helen shook her head and gathered her belongings. She'd never understand undergraduates. She was certain they had been more responsive and interested in her day.

'Wow.' Tobias was bounding up the aisle towards her. 'That was great, Helen.'

'Hello.' She was mortified to find herself blushing. 'What are you doing here? I thought you'd be busy finishing up your own classes today.'

'I finished yesterday. I just came in to tidy up my office and decided, on a whim, to come and check out what was happening in the Classics department. You didn't mind did you?'

'No. I just hope you didn't find it too boring?' She knew she was fishing for compliments, but his approval was important to her.

'It was fascinating. You're a natural up there, you know. Those kids were riveted.'

'Ha ha! I don't think so. Didn't you see Kim Winslow fast asleep in the back row?'

Tobias shook his head with a smile. 'You're too hard on yourself. From what I know of Kim it's a miracle she even turned up.'

Helen grinned and they fell into an awkward silence.

He cleared his throat. 'Listen, do you fancy lunch today – a last hurrah before the holiday? I'm buying.' She felt his eyes boring into hers and she turned back to the lectern, distracting herself with a stack of papers. 'After all,' he continued, 'I don't have to write your essay; you can tell me more about Helen's conflict between duty and desire.'

She knew he was flirting with her. It wasn't the first time either; but this *was* the first time he had invited her out. She felt the hairs on her arms prickle with excitement. 'The faculty has an end of term lunch,' she said, ruffling her papers.

'Oh. That's a shame.' Tobias looked crestfallen. 'I know the perfect little place . . . Another time then.'

Helen felt a terrible panic wash over her. 'I suppose I could try to get out of it . . .' She'd blurted the words before she could stop herself.

'Really?'

'Yes. It's only the old fogies from the department. There will be plenty more lunches.'

'That's great, Helen. If you're sure?'

Helen thought for a moment. 'I'll have to feign a headache, and then we can slip away once they've all gone. They might take it a bit personally, you see.'

'Very sensible.' He grinned at her, his eyes crinkling attractively, and she felt a flush of heat radiate from her very core.

'Why don't I call you when they've all left? We can head off then, if that suits you?'

'Absolutely. You won't regret it, Helen. This place is great; they do the best crab linguine.'

She smiled. 'Sounds delicious.'

For the rest of the morning the minute hand on Helen's watch seemed to be stuck in slow motion. She tried to busy herself with filing notes and reshelving reference books, but nothing could distract her from thoughts of Tobias.

It was a long time ago – over three years – that she had first stumbled into his gallery to take refuge from the driving rain outside. She'd fled the house that day in a terrible rage after yet another furious argument with Richard, driving into Bridport just to escape the confines of the house. She'd wandered the streets aimlessly until a sudden downpour had forced her to seek shelter and she'd entered the little artist's studio with no intention other than drying off for a few minutes.

The gallery had been empty as she entered so she'd leaned her dripping umbrella against the wall by the door and then turned to view the paintings hanging from the walls. She'd been spellbound from the start.

They were dark oil paintings of the Dorset coast, real and graphic in their depiction of nature unleashing its full force on the landscape. She'd wandered through the exhibition space, eyeing each one carefully, feeling a surge of excitement at the sight of them. They perfectly captured the storm of emotion she felt raging within her, ever since they had moved to the coast. She knew she had stumbled upon something, or perhaps *someone* wonderful.

'Can I help you?' A young man had appeared from out the back. He was tall and muscular with broad shoulders and a head of close-cropped dark hair. His face was strong and tanned, with startling brown eyes and attractive laughter lines etched either side of his mouth. He was dressed simply in jeans and a paint-splattered pale blue shirt, the sleeves of which were rolled up to reveal a Celtic-style band tattooed around the smooth skin of his biceps. 'Did you want some help?' he'd asked again, wiping his hands on a rag.

'I'm just browsing. Is that OK?' she'd asked. As he moved closer Helen felt something odd happen. Her stomach did a funny flip-flop and she had turned to look at the nearest painting, unable to meet his eye.

'Do you like it?' he asked.

She could feel him moving even closer but she kept her eyes fixed on the canvas. 'Yes I do, very much.'

'Nature; we're at her mercy, right?' He turned and nodded to the foul weather lashing at the window of his gallery. 'That's why you're in here, I take it? Driven in by the rain?'

Helen was embarrassed but he just grinned back at her. 'Don't worry, I always get more visitors on rainy days. You don't have to be polite. You're my first today so I'm glad to see you.'

Helen nodded and gave a shy smile, suddenly self-conscious of her bedraggled appearance. He spoke with a Gaelic lilt, Irish perhaps, although she couldn't quite place it. She was terrible with accents.

'This is what I'm interested in.' He turned to survey the painting again, a depiction of a tiny sailing boat dwarfed by a huge, roiling ocean. 'The brutality of nature.' He paused. 'It's awe inspiring, isn't it?'

She realised she was still staring at him so she turned back to the painting and nodded. She wasn't sure if he was talking about the weather, or about his work, but either way he was right. He moved closer and she felt the warm air shift around them.

'Let me show you around,' he offered with a sudden smile. 'My name's Tobias. Tobias Grey.'

'I'm Helen,' she said, shaking his outstretched hand and jumping back in alarm at the sudden bolt of electricity that seemed to shoot up her fingers as their skin touched.

His smile widened. 'Come on, I've got loads more paintings upstairs.'

She'd spent an hour following him around the two levels of his studio as he explained his techniques and influences at great length, and was surprised to find herself standing out on the pavement at the end of the tour with a large canvas wrapped up in brown paper and string and a little card with his telephone number secreted into her pocket.

'Just call me if it's not right for the room,' he'd urged as he'd shown her back out onto the street. 'You can exchange it for something else. It's important to me that you're happy with it.' He'd paused for a moment. 'Or . . . you could just call me anyway?' The mischievous look in his eyes had said it all.

She hadn't been able to speak. She'd just blushed and turned on her heel, running away up the little side street without so much as a backwards glance.

Helen looked at her watch again. There were still twenty minutes or so to go before her department would begin to gather for their lunch. She closed her eyes, unable to even keep up the pretence of working now, and surrendered herself to her memories of Tobias.

She'd only realised exactly how good the painting was when she had got it home and taken off the wrapping. It was wonderful, and had looked perfect installed above the fireplace. She felt energised just looking at it; and it didn't hurt that the canvas also reminded her of those deep brown eyes boring into hers. She'd sat there, turning the little card with his phone number on over and over through her fingers, convincing herself that she must never see him again.

She hadn't. Instead, feeling the spark of something hot and insistent reignite in her belly, she had thrown herself at Richard and, surprised and delighted, he had responded in kind. Six weeks later she was staring at the thin blue line on the pregnancy test, scared and excited in equal measure.

Alfie. She only had to think of him to smile. He was her last pregnancy and an unexpected gift. Whenever she thought about that fuzz of straw-blond hair, his toothy lop-sided grin and the sound of his cheeky, infectious giggle she felt a little part of herself melt. He was utterly adorable. Everyone said so.

Of course there were moments. What family didn't have them? Occasionally Alfie would tire of Dora's dressing-up games, or resist his bedtime and a fierce tantrum would erupt. And there were Cassie's histrionics whenever he invaded her bedroom or went through her stuff. More often than not Alfie would get into some kind of scrape or other, his curiosity pushing him through life like a little kamikaze missile, but then that's what little boys were like; you couldn't wrap them in cotton wool.

Yes, it had been Alfie who had pushed all early thoughts of Tobias into nothing but a pleasant, distant memory. Occasionally she had found herself staring at the painting above the fireplace and imagining what might have been, but it was a secret guilty pleasure; nothing more than a fantasy. It simply wasn't meant to be.

Until nearly four years later when she arrived for a new term of lecturing at Exeter University, only to find the celebrated local artist, Tobias Grey, installed as Artist in Residence. It was then that she knew Fate had intervened, and that life was about to get complicated.

After a few interminable minutes spent clicking refresh on her email inbox and gazing out the window at the steady flow of students making their way towards the campus bar, there was a knock on her office door.

'Come in!' Helen called out in relief.

'I just wanted to check if you were feeling any better?' Joan White, the motherly department secretary asked, sticking her nose around the door.

Helen rubbed her temples. 'Sorry, Joan, my head is still thumping. I think I'll have to go home.'

'Oh you poor thing. You do look a little flushed.' The woman winced at her in sympathy. 'Terrible timing for you, especially with the school holidays.'

'Yes, typical, isn't it?' Helen said, trying to conjure up some semblance of regret. 'I'm sorry to miss out. Have fun, won't you? And have a wonderful summer . . .'

'Yes, thank you, Helen, you too.' Joan closed the door gently behind her and just a few moments later Helen heard the rest of the faculty leave the department. She waited until it was completely silent outside and then picked up the phone. He answered almost immediately.

'They've gone. I'm a free woman.'

Tobias let out a low laugh. 'You know, Helen, I really wish you were.'

It was the first time he had voiced his desire and she felt her breath catch in her throat. What was she doing? Was she mad? She was a married woman with three lovely children at home. Was she really prepared to risk it all for some wild flirtation with a man she barely knew? Besides, she'd heard on the university grapevine that Tobias was married too. What about *his* wife? Maybe she was reading this all wrong. Maybe he really did just want to be friends. God, she was acting like a teenager. It was ridiculous.

She closed her eyes. It wasn't too late. She could call it off now, before anyone got hurt. She could jump in her car and drive home and be back at Clifftops within the hour. Back to the stifling walls of the draughty old house; back staring at piles of dirty washing that had mounted up in the laundry; back wondering yet again what to cook Alfie for tea; back lying motionless next to the soft, snoring body of her husband as she watched her life spiral slowly away.

'I'll meet you in the car park in two minutes,' she said, hanging up on him before she could change her mind.

*

They drove out of the city along the A30, Helen following Tobias in her own car, careful not to lose sight of the battered bumper of his old MG. She turned the radio up in an attempt to stop her brain churning over the mad recklessness of her actions. At each junction she willed herself to turn around, to go home, to put a stop to what she had started; but she couldn't. Her whole body tingled with anticipation.

After a few more miles they turned off and drove through a pretty village, past picturesque cob houses and an old cider press, before pulling into the gravelled car park of the King's Arms. They parked their cars next to each other and then stepped out into the sunshine, Tobias smiling a devilish grin at her. 'I'm pleased you're here. I had this funny feeling you might change your mind. I kept checking my rear-view mirror to see if you'd turned around.'

'I wanted to,' she admitted.

'Well, I'm glad you didn't. You can run away anytime you want, but we've come this far, so let's at least have a drink before you flee?'

Helen nodded and they crunched their way across the gravel drive, Tobias putting a warm, steadying hand on her back as they entered the smoky interior of the pub.

They found a quiet booth in one corner and Tobias went to order drinks. As she settled herself into the velvet seat she looked around nervously. They were miles away from home, but she couldn't help but feel conspicuous. One of the men propping up the bar appeared to be staring at her and for a horrible moment she wondered if he knew her, or Richard.

'You look lovely. I like your hair like that.' Tobias had returned with their drinks, placing them on the table between them. Amusement danced in his brown eyes. 'Why are you blushing?'

'I'm not. It's just a little warm in here, that's all.'

Tobias smiled. They both knew it was a lie.

She grabbed at her wine glass. 'Cheers,' she offered.

'Cheers.' He drank long and deep, his eyes never leaving hers. 'So, are you hungry?' he asked when he'd placed his pint glass back on the little cardboard coaster.

She shrugged. 'Not really.' Her stomach was cartwheeling with such outrageous excitement that she knew she wouldn't be able to eat a morsel.

'Me neither,' he agreed.

They sat looking at each other for a moment before they both burst out into nervous laughter.

'This is a bit strange, isn't it?'

'Yes, it is.'

'You know, I've wondered about you . . . ever since you came into my gallery. I couldn't believe it when I saw you on campus. It was like a sign.'

'You remembered me?' Helen was astonished and flattered.

Tobias nodded and hung his head, a little shamefaced. 'Here we are now and I can't actually think of a thing to say. Isn't that terrible?'

Helen was surprised. Tobias was nervous too. 'I'm the same,' she confessed.

'Words aren't my forte. I'm better with a paintbrush.' He paused. 'You know, I'd love to paint you sometime. You've got such wonderful bone structure. And your skin . . . it's luminous.'

Helen looked down at her wine glass.

'Sorry.'

'It's OK.'

'I don't mean to scare you.'

'I know.'

Gradually, as they grew used to the setting and started on a second round of drinks, they began to relax and the conversation started to flow. Tobias was good company. He amused her with stories of his students and eccentric customers at his gallery and soon they were laughing and joking more easily.

'Tell me something,' he asked suddenly, 'what *is* a woman like you doing closeted away in a sleepy seaside town?'

'What do you mean?' Helen asked. Her eyes ran over the dark tattoo encircling his biceps. She had to stop herself reaching out to touch it.

'You just seem rather different to the usual sort round here.'

Helen was flattered. 'Different? I don't think so. I used to believe I was. I had dreams of making a difference, you know, of really making something of my life. But it's like I've woken up seventeen years later and I'm just a middle-aged housewife living the middle-England dream. It's depressing!'

'You seem anything but to me, Helen.'

'I never really wanted to move to Dorset,' she confessed. 'I felt sure I'd go mad trapped out here.'

'So why did you come?'

'Because it was important to the rest of my family.'

'You put them first.'

Helen nodded.

'Duty won over desire,' he grinned, then fell serious again. 'You're a good woman.'

Helen shrugged. At that very moment, sitting there opposite Tobias she felt like a very, very bad woman. She glanced at his watch. It was three thirty in the afternoon. How had that happened?

'Do you have to go?' he asked.

'No. I've drunk too much. I don't think I can drive anywhere. Not yet.' Helen did feel drunk, on a heady combination of alcohol and lust.

Tobias nodded. 'Me too.'

'So what should we do?'

Her question hung between them, suggestive on the air.

He looked at her for a moment and then reached into his pocket and slowly pulled out a large brass chain with one solitary key dangling off it, his eyes never leaving hers. 'It's for a room upstairs. You can walk away now and I won't think any the less of you, Helen. I'm not pressuring you.'

She swallowed.

'But,' he continued, 'if you would like to . . . If you feel at all how I feel right now . . .' He reached across with one hand and caressed her cheek and it felt like the most natural thing in the world to lean her face into the curve of his hand. As she did he rubbed his thumb across her lips, a strange, sensuous gesture that made her head spin.

'I'm older than you.'

'So?'

'I'm married.'

'Me too.'

'I have three children.'

'I know.'

'And you still want me?' she asked.

He nodded. 'I've wanted you ever since you walked into my studio on that wild, wet day.'

Helen swallowed and closed her eyes. It was now. It was now that she should get into her car and drive away and never see this man again. It was now that she should get up from the table, thank him for the drink, and leave the pub, putting as much distance between them as possible.

She opened her eyes. The key chain winked between them on the table. She reached out one hand and took it in her palm, testing the weight of it carefully. 'No one can ever find out.'

Tobias smiled.

'I mean it.'

He nodded. 'No one ever will. It's our secret, Helen. I promise.'

She nodded once, satisfied, gulped back her last mouthful of wine and then turned to him.

'Well, are you coming?' she asked.

*

They took the narrow staircase that led upstairs, giggling and grabbing at each other until they fell through the doorway and into their room. Tobias shut the door behind him and leaned against it, suddenly serious, his eyes holding hers.

'Are you OK?'

Helen nodded. 'You?'

Tobias nodded. 'And you're sure about this?'

Helen nodded again.

He walked towards her and pulled her into his arms, kissing her deeply until she pressed herself against him, dizzy with desire. Then he pushed her away, holding her at arm's length.

'God you're beautiful. Unbutton your shirt. Let me see you.'

'I . . . Um . . .' She was flustered.

'Shhhh.' He put a finger over her lips. 'No words.'

Helen slowly unbuttoned her blouse, holding Tobias's gaze and fighting the urge to cover her breasts with her hands. She hadn't been naked in front of anyone except Richard for such a long time and she was conscious her body was no longer the figure of her youth. Childbirth and the steady march of time had taken its toll. Tobias seemed to sense her anxiety. He smiled and pulled her into his embrace once more, kissing her lips with such passion she forgot her nerves and concentrated instead on the warm, velvet feeling melting her insides.

'You are lovely,' he whispered. 'I would like to paint you, standing there in that shaft of sunlight, your eyes closed like that.'

He reached out and slowly traced the contour of her collarbone, running a fingertip trail all the way down to her wrist. For a moment they linked hands, their eyes still locked in a steady gaze. Then he reached across and undid the belt at her waist. Helen felt herself shiver as he lowered her skirt to the floor and knelt to kiss her. As his lips touched her skin she let out a small sigh of surrender and closed her eyes.

*

She woke with a guilty start. Tobias was still lying there next to her, sprawled naked across the ugly floral bed cover they hadn't even found time to pull back. She gazed for a moment at the curve of his broad shoulders, the dark hair that spread across his chest and ran down towards his groin, to the long muscles in his legs, the flush of colour that had spread across his cheeks as he slept and the long sweep of his eyelashes. He was very much a man, and yet strangely vulnerable in his sleep, almost boy-like. She felt another twinge of lust and checked herself. The sun had moved lower in the sky and the room was now bathed in a warm amber light. She reached across and held Tobias's wrist so that she could see the face of his watch.

'Shit. Shit. Shit, oh shit.' She leapt off the bed.

Tobias opened one eye lazily. 'What's wrong?'

'I'm late. That's what's wrong.' She ran around the room collecting her clothes, pushing her arms through her blouse and tripping over her skirt all at the same time. There was a stickiness between her legs. She tried to ignore it; there wasn't time for a shower.

'Tell me you're not going, not yet?' groaned Tobias from the bed.

'I have to. It's Alfie. He'll be waiting at the centre for me. Mrs Kendall has already told me off once this week for being late.'

'Correct me if I'm wrong,' yawned Tobias, 'but don't *you* pay *them* to look after your son?'

'Yes,' cried an exasperated Helen as she searched frantically for her underwear. 'But they close at five thirty and at this rate I won't be there until after six.'

'Just tell them you got stuck in traffic.'

Helen retrieved her knickers from underneath the antique writing desk across the room and jammed them into her handbag. 'You don't understand. It's not just them. Poor Alfie. He'll be waiting for me.' A rush of guilt suddenly overwhelmed her. She pictured him alone at the centre, the last one left as Mrs Kendall paced impatiently around him. What on earth was she doing here, in this room, with this man? She had a family – a husband – children that needed her, for God's sake.

Tobias read the emotion in her face and leapt up from the bed. 'No, no, no. Don't do this, Helen.' He seized her by the shoulders and forced her to look at him. 'Don't feel guilty for what we've just done. We're not bad people. We're not hurting anyone. We're just two adults, having a bit of fun.'

'But we're both married, Tobias.'

'Yes, we're married, but they don't *own* us, do they? You're not an object for Richard to keep under lock and key . . .'

Helen tried to interrupt. In fairness Richard had never made her feel that way, but Tobias just shushed her, putting his fingers up to her lips. She smelled herself on him and swallowed hard, overwhelmed by a heady combination of guilt and lust.

'Helen, you deserve a little happiness. Trust me, we've done nothing wrong here, OK?'

Helen was silent. She didn't *feel* as though she'd done nothing wrong.

'OK?' Tobias asked again.

'OK,' Helen sighed.

'Now, when am I going to see you again? And don't tell me in the autumn when we go back to college because there is no way I can wait that long.'

'I just don't think . . . it's the holidays . . . the kids . . .' Helen gabbled nervously.

'I'll call you.' He raised a hand as Helen opened her mouth to protest. 'It's OK. If you can't talk just tell me I've got the wrong number and I'll hang up.'

Helen nodded. She grabbed her handbag and slipped on her shoes. 'I'm sorry. I really do have to go.'

'I know.' He kissed her hard on the lips, as if claiming her one last time. 'No regrets?'

She smiled up at him, his brown eyes boring into hers as his body pressed against her. She could feel he was hard again and a little groan escaped from her lips. He smiled back at her in triumph.

'No,' she said finally. 'No regrets.'

It was a sultry summer full of sex and dangerous excitement. Several times, overwhelmed by guilt, she tried to end the affair. But in the end it proved too hard to give Tobias up. Each time she left him with the sting of sex and guilt burning inside her, she told herself it was the last time. But he was like a drug and she couldn't bear to let go. He was so different to Richard. He was so youthful, so soulful and so persuasive. He made her feel beautiful. He made her feel cherished. She rationalised that he was her one guilty pleasure, her one adventure. She put everyone else first the rest of the time – Richard, the kids – and all she wanted was a little fun. She wasn't hurting anyone. It was just a harmless little dalliance between two consenting adults. No one need ever know.

To compensate, they grew increasingly careful about where and when they met. He never came to the house. Instead she visited him at his studio, or in small, out-of-the-way village pubs, often stopping off like displaced teenagers to lie amongst the golden wheat fields. And it was magical. Summer had finally arrived and began to roam across the country, spreading warmth and beauty in her wake. On days when the birds were in full song and the trees offered up their dappled shade, it felt like the most natural thing in the world to lie in Tobias's arms looking up between branches at the blue sky. It was here she let her real life simply fade away, like the fleeting lace clouds drifting high above them.

Even in the last week of the holidays, knowing that they would soon be back on campus, she couldn't resist him.

'I know we're due back at college soon, but I have to see you,' he murmured down the telephone. 'I miss your body. I miss your skin. I miss your smell.'

Helen swallowed. Dora was right there in the kitchen, shovelling cereal into her mouth, seemingly in a dream world. Alfie was skidding matchbox cars around the kitchen floor, performing an impressive range of screeches and crash effects. Cassie was upstairs, still in bed, enjoying one of the last lie-ins of the holiday. She should spend the day with them. The girls would be back at school next week and then the merry-go-round of real life would start up once more.

'I promise, if you come, I will kiss you from the nape of your neck where your hair grows in that little curl, all the way down to the tips of your toes.'

Helen let out a small involuntary sigh. 'I'll be there.'

'You will?'

'Yes. Give me an hour.'

'Great. See you at the usual place.'

'Yes.' Helen put the phone down and turned to Dora with a smile. 'That was work, I'm afraid, darling.'

Dora looked up at her. She didn't say anything; she just kept spooning cereal into her mouth.

'I have to go onto campus; it's a last minute thing. Will you and Cassie be OK babysitting your brother today?'

Dora paused with her spoon halfway between the bowl and her mouth and regarded her mother for a moment. 'Today?'

'Yes,' said Helen patiently. 'It's just for a few hours.'

Dora sighed. 'Do we have to?'

Helen felt her blood start to rise. 'Yes, you do.'

There was a pause. 'It's not fair,' Dora whined. 'Why today?'

'Because I have important things to do.' Helen sighed. 'I need to tidy my office, sort through some papers, go through timetables with the Dean.' The lies tripped easily off her tongue.

'Can't Alfie go with you?' said Dora.

'No.'

Dora stood, flung her cereal bowl into the sink and kicked at the side of the fridge angrily.

'Dora!' exclaimed Helen. 'That's enough. Now, I haven't asked much of you all summer. You girls have been living the life of Riley these last few weeks. I haven't even asked you to tidy your bedroom! The least you and Cass can do is look after Alfie for a few hours.' She expected tantrums from Cassie, but Dora was usually so placid. Helen hoped she wasn't about to start her own brand of teenage rebellion. She didn't think she could take it from both girls.

Dora scowled. 'Can we at least take him to the beach?' she asked.

So that was what was bothering her – Dora wanted to go to the beach. Helen studied her daughter for a moment. They both knew the rule: the beach was off limits to Alfie unless a parent was present. Helen looked at her watch and then back at Dora, exasperated. She supposed they were old enough now. 'You can take him with you, but you girls must stick together and keep an eye on him. And *no* swimming, OK?'

'Not even if we take his armbands?'

'Don't push it, Dora.'

'Beach!' Alfie exclaimed excitedly from the kitchen floor. 'Ice cream?' he asked hopefully.

'Yes, darling. You can have an ice cream.' Helen reached into her purse and pulled out a ten pound note. 'This is for you all. Now I'm trusting you, Dora, OK? Don't let me down.'

Dora took the ten pound note from her outstretched hand. 'OK.'

Helen let out a sigh of relief. If she left soon she would still be on time.

It took her ten minutes to get ready. She changed out of her jeans and into a pale blue skirt covered in tiny daisies that she knew Tobias liked. Then she dragged a brush through her hair, splashed perfume onto her neck and wrists and dusted a trace of blush onto her cheeks. She looked in the mirror. Not bad; and there was no time for anything else. Grabbing her handbag, she ran down the stairs, calling out to Dora at the bottom.

'Bye, love, I'll be back later.'

'Bye, Mum.' It was a muffled cry from deep within the kitchen.

'Be good,' she added, feeling like a prize hypocrite as the front door slammed behind her. She sprinted down the steps and into her car and as she reversed down the driveway she saw Dora standing with Alfie at the kitchen window. They were grinning and waving, Alfie's corn-coloured hair tickling Dora's face and making her laugh. Helen gave a smile and a little wave of her own, and then spun out of the drive in a spray of gravel. If she put her foot down she would be on time, assuming there were no bloody tractors, of course.

Helen was in luck.

She made it to the dual carriageway in record time, and it was only as she pulled across into the outside lane and put her foot to the floor that she realised in her rush to get to Tobias she had forgotten to kiss her children goodbye.

DORA

Eleven Years Earlier

The air was thick like honey as Dora stomped across the beach. In one hand she held Alfie's backpack, in the other she clutched her brother's hot little fist. Ahead she could see Cassie giggling with Sam. They skulked along the shoreline; their heads bent together, one blond, one dark. She glowered at them and tried to concentrate instead on her steady stomp across the uneven pebbles, cursing her mother for the hundredth time that day. Dora had hatched a thousand plans for her last day of freedom and *this* had not been one of them.

'Hurry up, will you,' she urged Alfie. 'We're going to lose sight of them if you can't keep up.'

'Too fast,' panted Alfie, stumbling on the shifting stones.

'Well maybe if you weren't wearing those wellies and that stupid cape you'd be able to walk a bit faster.' Dora was cross. Alfie had insisted on wearing his Superman outfit for their beach trip and no amount of wheedling or cajoling could persuade him otherwise.

'You'll be hot,' Cassie had tried.

'You'll look like a wally,' Dora had added.

But Alfie was adamant. 'I need it.'

'Why can't you go as Clark Kent, before he turns into Superman? You could just wear your ordinary clothes and no one would know who you are? You'd be in disguise!' Dora had said.

'Or even better, come as the Invisible Man?' Cassie said drily.

'No. Superman. Superman is the bestest superhero of them all.'

The girls rolled their eyes at each other. Alfie had recently entered an action-figure phase and they'd heard a lot about the 'bestest superheroes'. They left him to his costume, deciding to turn their attention to the more annoying matter of the toys.

'You can't take Lego to the beach,' Cassie had said, scanning through the growing heap of goodies Alfie was lining up by the door. 'You'll lose it. And look,' she said, kicking at a lump of brightly coloured plastic. 'Why do you want to take this car? The batteries don't even work!'

'It's not a car,' he replied. 'It's a digger.' Alfie whizzed the toy along the floor, expertly wielding its bucket and performing the appropriate digging noises.

Cassie sighed. Both of them knew it was impossible rationalising with him, but Dora tried again with a little more patience. 'How about we take a rucksack? You can wear it on your back, like a special rocket pack.'

'Superman doesn't have a rocket pack,' Alfie corrected.

'OK,' Dora tried again. 'But if Superman was going to the beach and he wanted to take his special gadgets, where would he put them?'

'Down his underpants?' offered Cassie.

Alfie giggled.

'Thanks, Cassie. That's *really* helpful. No,' she said, turning back to Alfie, 'he'd put them in a rocket blaster backpack. Right?'

Alfie looked at her uncertainly.

'Right, Cassie?' Dora urged, appealing to her sister for help.

'Sure,' replied Cassie with another laboured sigh. 'Look, I really don't care what toys you kids bring, but if you don't hurry up I'm going to the beach on my own, and that's final.'

Dora was stung; not just by the indignity of being lumped

into the 'kids' category with Alfie, but more by the total injustice of it all. 'You can't. Mum said we *both* had to look after Alfie today,' she argued.

'Well get a move on, otherwise I'm off and you can look after him here by yourself instead.'

Dora fumed. Bloody Cassie, with her new friends and her superior attitude; and their mum wasn't much better, always off behind closed doors having her private conversations, or racing off to campus for important meetings. Weren't they all supposed to be on summer holiday? The last thing she wanted was to spend the day tromping round after Cassie and Alfie. It was going to be a scorcher and she had planned to spend it down at the beach, splashing in the waves, sipping cold Cokes straight from the bottle and watching sunburnt campers squabble and pack up their pitches ready for the long drive home. It should have been perfect; the perfect last day before she woke on Monday, jammed her feet back into shoes and socks, picked up her school bag, and took herself off to start what both her parents kept calling *One of the most important years of her life*. GCSEs. They hung over her like a curse; them, and Sam Skinner.

Cassie had met Sam a week earlier. She'd arrived at the local campsite with her parents in a flashy new caravan. She wore the standard teen uniform: torn jeans, scuffed trainers, T-shirt from some gig or other, an army shirt and her long black hair falling over her pale face like a curtain. Dora wasn't sure how the two girls had met, but she'd seen them skulking around at the beach together, smoking cigarettes behind the skips in the car park or perched on the sea wall, sharing chips and talking to boys. Frankly it didn't take a genius to realise that Dora was now redundant, replaced by Sam, a new and improved model.

'I'm thirsty,' Alfie piped up from beside Dora. 'Can we stop?' His little legs were working hard but it wasn't easy for him to keep up with Cassie and Sam's long stride across the uneven pebbles. Heat rose off them like roasted chestnuts beneath their feet.

'Soon,' replied Dora, cursing her sister and that annoying girl. 'Hey!' she shouted at them. 'Slow down, will you? We can't keep up.'

Cassie's snigger travelled back to them on the wind. 'Told you not to bring all those toys, Dora.'

She could have killed her.

Even though Cassie hadn't bothered to say, it was obvious where they were headed. She'd seen Cassie and Sam sneak off to the Crag earlier in the week with a couple of boys. She hadn't been spying so much as keeping a lookout. Everyone knew teenagers only went to the Crag for two things: partying and making out. It was the perfect place for both. Dora had been there once before, as part of a silly schoolgirls' dare, and she didn't relish the thought of returning there now. But she didn't have a choice; they'd been told to stick together.

It wasn't yet midday but the sun was beating down and making the air around them waver and shift in a surreal dream-like haze. The beach shimmered, as though she were looking at it though a funfair mirror. Dora wiped a trickle of sweat from her brow and then looked up for her sister. Cassie and Sam had finally come to a halt. They stood, dark silhouettes against the skyline at the far westerly corner of the beach where the sheer cliff face slashed the horizon at a perpendicular to meet the shore. They gazed intently out to sea. Dora squinted, following their line of sight. She could see a stain as dark as blood across the pebbles closest to water. The tide was going out. They'd timed it perfectly.

Sam reached out and secured a footing on a piece of rock jutting out from the base of the cliff. She pulled herself up, her long hair catching in the breeze, and then reached out for Cassie's hand. As Cassie crested the top, she half turned to look back at Dora and Alfie.

'Are you coming or what?' she yelled.

Dora sighed. 'Come on then, Alfie. Time for an adventure.'

Her brother squeezed her hand tightly. 'Don't worry,' he said, looking up at her with big, round eyes. 'I've got my cape. I can protect you.'

He looked so sweet and earnest as he flapped his cloak about him importantly. Dora smiled down at him, and then turned to face the cliff. Helen would kill them if she knew what they were doing.

The Crag was a sacred place in Summertown; a spot known only to local teens, and a secret location so closely guarded that only a few young holidaymakers from out of town had been initiated into its existence. At the far end of the beach, where the Lyme Bay cliffs descended into a jagged outcrop of rock pools and boulders stood a secret cave, tucked away deep within a stone gully. Its magic lay in the fact that it could only be reached at low tide and it took a certain determination, or recklessness, to seek it out. Once found, its limited accessibility added to the sense of danger and excitement. Inside the Crag's depths you were safe from both the incoming tide and prying eyes, but if you missed the shift of the tide you could be stuck there for hours waiting for your exit route to be cleared at the whim of the ocean. The story at the local high school was that someone's elder brother had stumbled upon it while looking for a new potholing challenge. The brother had told a few friends, who had told a few more. The news had spread and before long teenagers were heading there in droves for illicit parties and secret meetings. As the legend grew, so did the stories surrounding it. First it was an old smuggler's den; then it became the home of a local crazy-eyed hermit; and most recently, myth had transformed the cave into a tomb for the victims of a notorious serial killer. Dora knew the stories were all made up, but she still hated going there.

Dora and Alfie drew in close to the jut of rock Cassie and Sam had disappeared over. Sam's head popped up suddenly on the other side.

'You'd better send Alfie over first,' she suggested. 'I'll pull him up. His little legs won't manage the rock face.' It was the most she'd heard Sam utter in the week she'd known her.

'This is crazy,' Dora replied. 'Why can't we all just hang out on the beach? It would be much easier.' She averted her gaze from the warning signs nailed to the cliff face that screamed of eroding cliffs and falling rocks and looked back helplessly towards the car park. It was nothing but a distant dot on the horizon.

Sam ignored her plea and turned instead to Alfie. 'You want to see the special bat cave, right, Alfie?'

'Yeah!' Alfie cried. 'Bats!'

Great, thought Dora. Now there was no getting out of it. She seized her brother by the waist and pushed him roughly up the stone face, his red cloak flapping wildly in her face.

'Hold out your hands,' Sam urged. 'Attaboy. I've got you.'

Suddenly Alfie was weightless in her arms. She let go and Sam pulled him up and over the rock face. She saw two kicking red wellies before they vanished completely from view.

'I can fly!' she heard Alfie shout from the other side of the stone buttress. His voice echoed wildly around, a hundred Alfies suddenly filling the cavernous space. She looked up at the dizzyingly high walls looming overhead and shivered, in spite of the heat.

'Are you coming?' Sam asked.

It was her turn. Dora scrambled up the side of the wall, finding natural footholds in the rough stone. Sam towered above, holding out a hand to her, but she ignored it, too proud and too annoyed to accept her help. She was almost up and over the ledge when her left foot shot away from beneath her in a skid of loose rocks and gravel. Scrabbling to steady herself Dora lunged at the rock face, seizing at the ledge in panic and wincing as her hands fell heavily on a sharp shard of stone.

'Are you OK?'

Dora nodded, fighting to control the sting of tears in her eyes. It was a stupid slip, that's all. She held her hands out and saw blood welling red and fierce amongst the gravel and small stones embedded in the skin of her palm.

'That looks nasty.'

'It's nothing. Just a graze.' She didn't want to admit it hurt so she stood for a moment, just looking at the vivid crimson fluid as it welled up at the gash on her hand. It oozed up into a little pool and then trickled slowly down her wrist until it fell with a lazy splash onto the slate-coloured rock below her. There it lay, a vivid jewel-like stain upon the warm stone.

'Are you sure you're OK?' Sam asked again.

Dora nodded. She looked up. The cliffs towered above her, dark and forbidding. She put her palm to her lips and sucked the wound, swallowing the metallic taste of blood until the throb dulled slightly. Then, with a sigh, she hauled herself over the rocky ledge and dropped down into the darkness below.

Sinister stone walls rose up steeply from the rocky floor. They leaned inwards, meeting about twenty metres or so above their heads. Only a small gap in the stone canopy allowed a finger of daylight into the cavernous room. Dora looked up and saw a chink of blue a long way above her, but then had to look away; she was still dizzy from the heat outside the cave. She turned instead to look at the dripping walls around her covered with clumps of lurid green lichen and glistening with slime. Dotted across the rock face were a thousand different graffiti tags; names and dates scrawled all over the walls, some scratched, some painted, and some carved, by possibly the most dedicated young lovers, into the stone itself. The gritty floor was littered with the detritus of past parties: cans, bottles, cigarette butts and worse were strewn around. Old fishing net, a rotten wooden pallet and a forgotten oil drum had been positioned at one end of the cavern, makeshift party decorations now surplus to requirements. There was a low stone shelf rising up from the centre of the floor at the rear of the cavern, and next to it a circle of ash indicated where a bonfire had last burnt; it shone in the dark interior as white as cleanly picked bones. Dora shivered. She couldn't think why anyone would want to hang out here. Sure it was private, tucked away safely from prying eyes, but it also stank. The air was cold and heavy with the smell of rotting vegetation and damp, salty kelp. It was plain creepy.

Alfie, however, appeared to disagree. He ran around the cavernous space shouting and whooping, his delighted cries echoing off the walls and bouncing around them wildly. A seagull shrieked out of the shadows, beating its wings and making Dora jump.

'A bat!' cried Alfie ecstatically. She didn't have the heart to correct him.

Sam and Cassie were at the far end of the cave. Dora saw Sam kick the oil drum with a toe and then shrug off her faded green army shirt. She laid it on the ground and Cassie sat down on one half. Sam then used the hem of her T-shirt to wipe down the low stone shelf in front of them. It was strangely sacrificial in design; like an altar she had seen in an Indiana Jones movie that had scared her more than she had cared to let on. As she rubbed at the rock, Sam gave a long, low whistle. 'Look at this, Cass,' she murmured. 'The perfect skinning-up table. Nice one.'

Dora didn't know whether to go and join them. She felt self-conscious and uncomfortable. She hadn't asked to come here, after all. She'd thought they were all going to hang out on the beach. Oh sod it, she thought. She huffed over to her sister and perched on the edge of the oil drum. 'Well, this is brilliant,' she said sarcastically.

Cassie shrugged. 'We didn't force you to come with us, Dora.'

'I didn't exactly have a choice, did I? Mum said we had to stick together.'

'Who says we have to do what Mum says all the time?

You're a big girl, Dora,' Cassie taunted. 'Can't you make up your own mind?'

'But there's Alfie too . . . It's not fair . . .' She saw Cassie turn to Sam with a roll of her eyes. 'Oh, forget it,' she tailed off.

Sam retrieved a packet of Marlboro Lights from her shirt pocket and pulled out a fat, misshapen roll-up from within. She lit it with a shiny Zippo, took a couple of quick puffs and then passed it to Cassie. Dora watched her sister take a long drag, before exhaling smoke upwards in a slow, steady stream. She looked like she'd done it a million times before. The smoke hung in the dank air like a shimmer of fine cobweb between them.

'Don't look so shocked, Dora,' Cassie said.

'I'm not,' she lied.

'You are. You're doing that thing you do with your eyebrows.'

'But . . . what if Alfie tells?' She looked around to where her brother was scampering happily across the sandy floor. He had found a long stick and was energetically whacking the rocky sides of the cave with loud thuds.

'Take that. And that,' he shouted at his invisible enemies.

Cassie shrugged. 'So? What are they going to do?'

Dora could think of lots of things her parents could do to punish Cassie, but she didn't bother to list them. Her sister obviously didn't care.

'Want a drag?' Sam asked, offering her the spliff.

'No!' Dora said, a little too quickly. 'Er, no thank you,' she repeated. 'I don't smoke.' It came out sounding very prim. Dora blushed.

Sam just shrugged and pocketed the lighter. She lay back on the sandy floor of the cave and Cassie sank back too, resting her head in her hands and closing her eyes. Now they were all here, Dora was uncertain what to do. She looked around for Alfie. He was standing on a stony ledge peering down into a rock pool, poking at something with the end of his stick.

'Careful, Alfie! Those rocks are slippery.' He ignored her. Great. Neither Cassie nor Alfie seemed to want her around. She looked back at her sister. She was whispering something to Sam that made the other girl let out a deep, throaty laugh.

She turned back to Alfie, the lesser of two evils. 'What have you got there, Alfie?' she called out.

'A crab.'

'Let me see.' She wandered over, grateful for distraction, and crouched down at the edge of the pool to get a better look. It was a tiny grey thing, almost translucent and disappointing in size. Alfie was tormenting it, using both hands to wield his stick.

'Snap, snap, snap, snap, snap,' he repeated, over and over. 'Snap, snap, snap.'

'Your cloak is trailing in the water, Alfie,' she warned. There was a dark red stain creeping up from the base of the material, leaving it soggy and caked in sand. Alfie didn't seem to care. He surveyed the damage with a nonchalant shrug and turned back to the pool.

'Snap, snap, snap.'

They stayed together like that for a while, Alfie digging and poking in the rock pool and Dora looking on, pointing out whelks and periwinkles and a crusty old anemone glued to the rock like concrete. When Alfie got bored with the pool they explored the inner recesses of the stone walls. Without discussion, they began to collect snarls of driftwood, dragging them into a huge pile at the far end of the cavern. Neither of them questioned what they were doing or why they were doing it. They were united in their work and set about it with a quiet dedication, building their wooden pyre until it stood almost a metre high. It seemed that once away from the beach, in the cool, quiet interior of the Crag, it was easy to forget there was a beach just a few hundred metres away littered with blankets and bodies, all sweltering in the sunshine; it was easy to forget about the thirty degree heat baking off the pebbles; it was easy to forget about a new school term just around the corner, and easy to forget all about the time and tides outside their private, enclosed world.

Dora lifted her head with a start.

'What's the time, Cass?' she called out.

Her sister's blond head raised an inch off the ground to look at her watch.

'Twelve fifty,' she replied, sinking her head down again. Another puff of smoke rose up languidly above her head.

'How long have we got before the tide turns?'

'Oh ages yet. Calm down, will you?' Cassie scolded.

Dora remembered the ten pound note in her pocket that Helen had handed her that morning. As if in unison with her brain, her tummy rumbled loudly. Alfie giggled.

'I'm hungry. Are you hungry, Alfie?' she asked.

'Yeah!' he cried enthusiastically. 'Ice cream!'

She sighed. It would take ages to walk back to the car park with Alfie toddling along beside her.

'Cass?' she called out.

'What?'

'We're hungry. I'm going to get ice cream. Do you want one?'

There was a muttering from the far corner as Sam and Cassie discussed the offer.

'Nah.'

'Get us a couple of cans of Coke though, would you?' Sam asked.

'OK. Won't be long. You've got Alfie, OK?'

Cassie mumbled something at the far end of the cavern.

'OK?' Dora repeated.

'OK,' Cassie shouted huffily.

Dora turned to Alfie. 'You stay here with Cassie and Sam. I'll be quicker on my own. I'll bring you back a ninety-nine.'

'Ohhh . . .' began Alfie in a whine.

'I'll be twenty minutes, tops. I promise.' She saw Alfie look up at her uncertainly. 'Anyway,' she tried, 'who's going to build the driftwood tower if we both go? See how big you can get it before I get back, OK?' She glanced at her sister. It was so unfair of her to just ignore them both. 'Or maybe you could go and play with Cassie and Sam,' she added spitefully.

'OK,' agreed Alfie. 'Two flakes?' he asked hopefully.

'Sure,' agreed Dora. 'I'll get you two flakes. See you in a bit.'

'Bye, Cassie,' Dora yelled out again, making sure her sister knew she was going.

There was a giggle from the far end of the cavern.

'Bye-bye-ye-ye,' echoed back at her off the walls.

Dora shook her head with frustration. She was such a mug. How come she was the one that ended up babysitting Alfie all morning? And the one that now had to trudge back across the beach to get ice cream? It was so unfair. She looked back one final time. Alfie was plodding slowly towards Cassie and Sam, dragging a twisted branch of driftwood behind him. His boots scuffed noisily through the silt and his little shoulders were hunched with resignation. Dora felt guilty, but she was pleased to be leaving the stinking cave. She craved the sunlight and the fresh air.

Getting out of the Crag proved to be much easier than getting in. The rocky walls were less steep on the inside and someone had chipped helpful footholds into the stone, so that Dora was able to pull herself up without trouble and hop down onto the hot pebbles on the other side. She was out within seconds and her feet landed with a crunch. She dusted off her hands and allowed her eyes a few seconds to adjust to the brightness. The white-hot shimmer of beach was a shock after the cool interior of the Crag.

As her eyes refocused she realised there were two adults, only thirty or so metres from the entrance to the cave; two women, laying out towels in the thin shadows close to the face of the cliff. They were the only other people for a long way, everyone else choosing to stay up the other end, preferring the proximity of the car park, the ice cream van and each other. Sensible, thought Dora. She glanced again at the women as she walked past. One was now lying face down on her towel, but the other was standing and seemed to be watching her with interest. Dora could see long dark hair and snake-like hips. Too thin for a woman. As she passed she saw the skinny man's mouth open and a flash of white, a grimace or a smile, she wasn't sure. As he bared his teeth he raised his hand in a jaunty salute. She dropped her head, guilty at having been caught scrambling about on the eroding cliffs, and started to crunch her way back along the beach, ignoring the trickle of sweat that had already begun to inch its way down her back.

She chose a path along the shoreline. It was easier to walk on the densely packed shingle than the larger pebbles further up the beach, and the sea offered up a cooling blast of spray every now and then. Besides, it was the clearest path back to the car park; the further she got, the denser the bodies became, strewn across the beach in their positions of sun worship. Bare-bottomed children ran up and down between parents and the shoreline, shrieking and laughing; ladies with huge jiggling bosoms and magenta-coloured skin sat slumped in deckchairs; she passed a pack of teenagers, all long bronzed limbs and brimming confidence in skimpy bikinis, and tried not to imagine the worst as their hoots of laughter rang out as she passed. An old man baiting his fishing rod gave her a friendly nod. She nodded back and then returned her gaze to the horizon and her eventual destination: the ice cream van. It occurred to her for the first time that transporting ninety-nines back to the Crag without them disappearing into puddles of melted mush was going to be a mission in itself. Bloody Cassandra.

Finally, she turned away from the shoreline and waded up the beach, past the lifeguard slumped in his chair until at last the ice cream van came into view. It was parked in all its pink and turquoise glory in the turning circle at the edge of the sea wall. Nirvana. She could see a queue, orderly and polite, but only six or so people in front of her. Her hand went into her shorts pocket and fingered the grimy note Helen had given her. She had enough for ice creams and Cokes, but it would be a job carrying them all back to the Crag. Cassie and Sam would have to share. It would serve them right.

'What'll it be, missy?' the rotund man asked when it came to her turn.

'Two ninety-nines, please. Double flakes. And three cans of Coke.'

'Right you are.' The man turned and delved his arms into a deep fridge behind him.

'Here you go,' he said, handing her the cans. 'Icy cold.'

'Thanks.' She pulled them towards her and then lifted one to her forehead. The cold metal stung her skin but she held it firm, enjoying the shock as the chill worked its way through her skin to her brain. Then she popped the lid and drank deep. Bubbles rushed out, too fast, and she choked, cold fizz finding an escape route through her nostrils and down the front of her T-shirt.

'Bit thirsty, are we?' asked an amused voice from behind.

Dora turned, embarrassed, and saw Steven Page, the coolest boy from her year standing behind her in the queue. She was mortified and flushed deep red. 'I . . . er . . . yeah.' She couldn't think of anything to say. She busied herself by rubbing at the sticky mess on her white T-shirt. It seemed to spread beneath her fingers.

'Good summer?' he asked.

'Not bad, thanks. You?' She was glad she sounded calmer than she felt.

'You know, same old,' Steven replied.

'Yeah,' agreed Dora. She knew.

'What are you up to?'

'Now?' Dora asked.

'Yeah,' he grinned.

'Just getting ice cream.' God, talk about stating the obvious.

Steven didn't seem to mind. He shuffled closer, digging his hands into his jeans pockets and looking up at her with clear blue eyes from beneath his floppy brown hair. 'Cool. Me too.'

'Then I'm walking up to the Crag. My sister's up there.'

Steven raised an eyebrow. 'The Crag, eh?'

Dora blushed. Everyone knew about the Crag. 'Er . . . yeah. My little brother too . . .' She didn't want him to get the wrong impression.

The ice cream man cleared his throat loudly above their heads. '. . . And two ninety-nines, doubles. That'll be seven pounds fifty, love.'

Dora handed over the ten pound note. As she pocketed the change Steven spoke up.

'What happened to your hand?' he asked, indicating the angry red graze on her palm.

'Just a silly fall. I tripped. It's nothing.' She rubbed at her sore hand self-consciously.

'Well, it looks like you're going to need some help with those,' he said, indicating her drinks with a nod of his head. 'Want me to walk with you?'

'Sure.' Dora blushed deeply again. 'That'd be great. If you don't mind?'

'Cool, hang on a sec. I'll just tell James.' Dora looked across to where Steven had nodded with his head. James Buchan, another boy from her year sat on the sea wall observing them both with interest.

Dora felt her heart thumping wildly in her chest and she felt a little sick suddenly. Ice cream dripped onto her hand and she licked at it quickly, eager not to make any more mess. Why had she asked for a ninety-nine? It was so childish. And in this heat she'd have to wolf it down before it collapsed into a sticky mess. She saw Steven and James exchange a few words. The boy on the wall gave Steven a big grin, punched him on the arm and then dropped down off the wall, heading back onto the beach alone. Steven sauntered back to her.

'Ready?'

'Yep.'

'Cool. Here, you'd better let me carry those.'

She handed him the two unopened cans of Coke and they set off down the beach, Steven ambling casually along, with Dora next to him, frantically licking at the edges of both ice creams in vain.

'So, what've you been up to over the summer?'

Dora's mind went blank. 'Oh, you know, this and that.'

Steven nodded. 'Me too.'

Silence. Dora concentrated on the steady crunch of her flip-flops on the shingle, willing the ice cream to defy its chemical properties and stay frozen.

'I went to see that Austin Powers movie in Bridport,' he offered finally.

'Cool,' Dora replied, watching a trickle of white goo make its way down the cone to the crease of her hand.

'Yeah, it's pretty funny.'

Silence again.

'Have you been swimming?' Dora tried, nodding her head at the sea.

'No way! Too cold for me,' Steven replied.

'It's lovely once you're in.'

Steven looked at Dora, impressed. 'Serious?'

'Yeah. It's the warmest it'll get now. You know, after the summer . . .' She trailed off.

'Nice one. Maybe I'll give it a go then.'

'You should.'

'OK, I will.' He grinned at her and Dora felt her stomach flip.

'Watch out!' he yelled, his eyes flicking towards the ice cream she held in her left hand. She turned just in time to see the whole vanilla head tumble off its cone and fall splat onto the pebbles. An incoming wave caught it and within seconds it had disappeared without trace into the salty foam. Dora looked at the empty cone in her hand and sighed.

'Oh shit!' Steven cursed. 'Sorry, I should have said something . . .'

'No, don't worry,' said Dora suddenly. 'I didn't really want it anyway.'

'Well, you've still got that one,' he said, indicating the ice cream in her right hand.

'It's for my brother.'

'OK. We can do this,' said Steven, suddenly getting into the spirit of the challenge. 'We can get this ice cream to your brother in one piece. It'll be like *Mission Impossible*.'

Dora giggled.

'Don't laugh,' he urged. 'This is a serious undertaking . . .'

'Sorry.' Dora copied Steven's serious expression, trying not to let her lips curve back up into a smile.

'Come on then, full steam ahead.'

They picked up the pace across the shingle, dodging kids and inflatables and the remains of sweaty picnics strewn across blankets. Most people, Dora noticed, lay prone upon towels, or slumped in chairs, dozing and dreaming in the heat of the sun. It seared down on them now, razor sharp, baking the beach in its glare. Dora pushed stray strands of hair, now slick with sweat off her forehead and marched onwards next to Steven. It was a relief when they finally arrived at the far end of the beach.

'I've not actually been to the Crag before,' Steven confessed as they pulled up to the base of the cliffs.

Dora was surprised. She thought all the cool kids from school hung out there. 'Well I've only been here once, before today,' Dora confirmed. 'It's nothing special.'

'How do you get in?'

'Just up here. You wouldn't know, unless you knew what to look for. You see that shadow on the rock face, just to the left of that dead tree?' Dora pointed with her free hand to a gnarled tree stump, bent over like a broken old man.

'Yeah.'

'Well, just underneath there, there's a gap in the rock. It's hidden from the beach, sort of a trick of the light. You can only see it when you get really close.'

Dora and Steven moved up towards the rock face. 'Look, do you see now?' she asked.

'Oh yeah,' whistled Steven. 'Very clever.'

'Just follow me.'

Dora hopped up onto the stone cliff face. It was harder with one hand holding an ice cream and the graze on her palm an aching reminder of her earlier stumble, but she was desperate not to look like an idiot, not in front of Steven. She misjudged one handhold and nearly lost her balance, but her fingers met with a clump of golden samphire and the roots held firm as she regained her grip. It was a major relief when she dropped down the other side and into the cool interior of the cavern.

'OK?' she called out.

A moment later Steven's head appeared. 'Blimey, you made that look easy.'

Dora smiled. 'You get the hang of it . . . Here, throw the drinks down to me and then work your way down these gaps in the stone.'

Two cans of Coke landed on the sandy floor next to her, and then Steven dropped down beside her.

'Well, well, well,' he said, surveying his surroundings. 'So this is the famous Crag.'

'Yep. See, I told you, nothing special.'

'Where are your brother and sister then?'

Dora looked around. She could see Cassie and Sam huddled where she had left them, strands of Cassie's blond hair fanning out on the ground, mingling with Sam's own raven-black hair.

'Hey,' she yelled out. 'We're back.' She didn't know how

Cassie would react to her bringing Steven. She hoped she wouldn't embarrass her. It would be just like Cassie to say something awful.

'You took your time.' Cassie sat up. She rubbed her eyes, as if she'd been asleep. 'Did you get us our drinks?'

'Yeah, only one, sorry.'

Cassie sighed and grabbed the can from Dora's outstretched hand.

'You're welcome,' Dora replied, her words dripping with sarcasm. 'This is Steven,' she added.

Cassie looked him up and down. 'Hey, Steven,' she said finally. 'I'm Cassie. This is Sam.'

Sam gave a little wave and then returned to picking at her split ends.

Dora breathed a sigh of relief. It looked as though Cassie was going to behave herself. 'So where's Alfie?' she asked, looking around the cavern. The ice cream she held had virtually disappeared, just a tiny white blob remained on top of the cone, with two wilting flakes for company.

'Ha ha,' laughed Cassie sarcastically.

Dora looked at her sister, confused. 'What do you mean "ha ha"?' Where is he? I've got his ice cream here and it's not going to last much longer.'

Cassie glanced around the cave before returning her gaze to Dora. She gave her a strange look. 'He left with you, didn't he?'

'No. I told him to stay with you guys.'

'But . . . you said you were taking him with you.'

'No I didn't. I told you to look after him. When I was leaving I said, "You've got Alfie." I told him to go play with you.'

'No, Dora, you said *you'd* got Alfie. I distinctly heard you. Didn't you hear her, Sam?'

Sam just shrugged.

'Well, whatever, Cassie, he didn't come with me, OK?'

Dora said, looking around the cave with irritation. 'So he must still be in here.'

Cassie stood up, brushing sand from her denim skirt, before peering into the gloomy interior of the cavern.

'Alfie?' she called out. 'Alfie, Dora's got your ice cream.'

Silence.

'If this is a joke, Cassie, it's not bloody funny. I've just walked for twenty minutes in the heat for this ice cream. Just tell him to come out, all right?'

'This isn't a joke.' Cassie looked Dora straight in the eye. 'I don't know where he is.'

The two girls looked at one another for a moment, each trying to read the expression in the other's face. Dora willed her sister to break into a smile, to throw her hands up and to admit to the bad gag, to have Alfie run giggling out of some dark corner, the joke on her. But Cassie just stared back at her blankly, and in the end Dora had to turn away. She couldn't bear to see the fear welling up in her sister's face.

'Come on, he'll be here somewhere. He's just hiding . . . making a game of it,' Steven said, trying to break the suddenly serious atmosphere.

Dora wandered towards the pile of driftwood she and her brother had busied themselves with only half an hour or so earlier. 'Alfie!' she yelled, hearing his name echo off the walls. 'I'm going to eat your ice cream if you don't come out now. Mmmm . . . yum yum . . . Two more flakes for me!'

The silence was deep and still.

'Alfie! Alfie. Come out now!' Her sister's voice joined in, a little higher in pitch, a little more panicked.

They walked around the edges of the cavern, looking for a glimpse of their brother's cheeky face grinning out at them from his hiding place. Any moment now, Dora thought, he's going to jump out at me. She reached the old oil drum, back near the stone table where her sister and Sam had been lying. She knew it was silly but she turned it over anyway.

'Come on, Alfie. It's not funny now. Come out, will you? We need to go home soon.'

Nothing. She turned back to her sister.

'Where is he, Cass?'

'I don't know,' she replied, almost a whisper.

'Well, when did you last see him?'

Cassie thought for a moment. 'Not for ages. Not since you left.'

Dora ran her hands through her hair in exasperation. 'But what were you doing all that time I was gone? Didn't you see him, or even hear him, here in the cave with you?'

'No.' Her eyes were downcast.

There was a male clearing of the throat. Dora turned around to see Steven. She'd forgotten he was there.

'Look, he's either in here, right? Or he's found a way out of the Crag? Is that possible? How old is he?'

'He's only three . . .' Cassie wailed.

'Could he have made it up these footholds and out onto the beach, d'you think?' Steven's voice was calm. Dora suddenly realised she was glad he was here.

'I . . . I don't know.'

The two sisters looked at each other. It was true that Dora had found it easier getting out than she had getting in but . . . could Alfie have really clambered out, all on his own?

'I guess . . . if he followed me . . . *maybe* he could have managed it. But surely I would have seen him on the beach on my way back? Unless he headed the other way . . . you know, over to the rock pools . . .' Dora's voice trailed off. None of them wanted to think about that possibility.

Cassie let out a sudden sob. 'Oh God, we've got to find him.' She turned to Sam imploringly. 'We've got to find him, OK?'

Sam shifted uncomfortably. 'OK, OK. Let's think for a moment.'

'He's probably just headed up to the ice cream van,' said

Steven, 'thought he'd find Dora. Let's do one final check in here and if we're sure he's not still in here, head out and start looking for him on the beach. Right?'

'Right,' Sam and Dora agreed simultaneously. Dora patted her sister on the arm. 'Come on, Cass, it's OK. We'll find him, all right?'

Cassie didn't say anything, just turned and ran to the end of the cave, calling Alfie's name loudly.

For the next few minutes the four teenagers scoured the cavern from top to bottom for signs of Alfie. They looked in vain for hiding places they might have missed, called his name, coaxingly at first, then with increasing panic, and even tried to find little footprints in the silty earth that would reveal where he had gone. He had, it seemed, vanished into thin air. When they met back in the centre, moments later, it was clear to them all that the hunt would need to continue outside the Crag. They were silent as they took it in turns to climb up the rocky side of the cave and drop back down onto the beach.

It was only half an hour or so since she had first left the Crag to buy ice cream and yet as her feet landed back on the hot pebbles on the other side of the cave, it seemed to Dora as if the landscape outside had tilted slightly. On the surface it was still a picture-perfect postcard setting; the sun still shone down on a thousand happy holidaymakers; there were squeals and giggles floating in the air; pink bodies shone under greasy slicks of sunscreen like grilled saveloys under a hot plate; the grassy green slopes of the campsite rose up out of the distance, dotted with colourful tents and caravans winking at them in the brightness of the day. And yet the sun was even more shocking in its intensity. Dora could feel the skin across her shoulders prickle and tighten under its blaze. The seaside chorus of gull cries, the tinny call sign of the ice cream van and the shrieks of children all mingled in the air into one frenzied crescendo. And from somewhere far out across the ocean a breeze had picked up. Dora held a hand up to her eyes and squinted out to sea. She saw white caps topping the waves out towards the horizon and closer to shore her ear tuned in to the unmistakable *whoomph* of water dumping onto limestone. She looked nervously towards the rock pools. Sea spray flew up, glinted like diamante caught in the sun, and then fell, vanishing into the path of another incoming wave.

The tide had turned.

She swallowed back sticky-sweet bile and turned to Cassie with a renewed sense of urgency. 'We should split up.'

Cassie nodded but she seemed lost in her distress.

'We'll check over by the rock pools,' offered Sam.

'Yes, and Steven and I will go back up the beach and see if anyone has seen him. Let's meet back at the car park in twenty minutes. OK?' Then louder. 'OK?'

Sam and Cassie nodded again and then turned, walking quickly towards the rocky outcrop.

Dora wrung her hands.

'It'll be OK,' Steven tried to reassure her. 'You'll see. He's probably making mischief up at the beach shop. Or queuing up for more ice cream as we speak.'

'I hope so,' Dora agreed. 'I really do.' She felt Steven take her hand and give it a reassuring squeeze. Under other circumstances, she realised, she'd be delirious with happiness to be holding hands with Steven Page. Under other circumstances . . .

They looked at the beach spread before them. It suddenly seemed huge.

'Should we split up?' Dora asked, uncertain where to begin.

'Let's walk in parallel with each other, one down by the shoreline, one further up the beach. That way we can sweep the width of it together and one of us should spot him.'

Dora nodded, grateful for his calm logic.

'I guess I should ask what's he wearing? Can you remember?'

Dora gave a little sob, half laugh, half cry. 'Oh, I can remember. He's wearing a Superman costume.'

Steven smiled. 'Well, that's certainly original. Shouldn't be too many Supermen on the beach today. I reckon he'll be pretty easy to spot.'

'Yeah,' agreed Dora, suddenly more optimistic. 'You're right.'

They started off towards the car park. Steven opted for the harder route, taking the higher path along the shore across the baking pebbles while Dora retraced her steps for the second time that day along the shingle near the water's edge. Her eyes scanned the water's edge for signs of a little boy, and every so often she would turn in vain to the ground, looking for some sort of imprint of her brother's footsteps on the ever-shifting stones. As she got closer to the car park she scanned the camps of families set up on the beach for a flash of red and blue, asking every so often if anyone had seen a little boy in a Superman costume. Every time she was met with an indulgent smile and the shake of a head. And once in a while she'd turn her gaze to the water. The waves were slapping onto the shore with increasing violence. She saw a little girl on a lilo, her father beside her in the water, suddenly flip with the force of a wave and disappear under the wash of foam. She appeared, seconds later, all tangled hair and limbs, her shock turning to hilarity when she saw her father reach for her and she realised she was safe. They chased the inflatable out of the water onto the beach in front of her. Dora couldn't look any more. She turned her glance back to the bodies strewn across the seashore and tried desperately to banish the thoughts that had suddenly flooded into her head. Alfie couldn't swim without his armbands.

Steven met her at the sea wall. He shook his head as he walked towards her and Dora felt another nugget of hope disintegrate.

'Sorry, no one's seen him.'

Dora bit at her nails. 'What should we do?'

They decided to split up again, Steven heading into the shop while Dora walked back to the ice cream van and wandered around by the sea wall. There was a smiley old couple sitting on a bench gazing out in silence towards the horizon; a sunburnt family squabbling over who would carry what back up to the campsite; and a harassed-looking father laden with fish and chips. None of them had seen her brother.

Minutes later Cassie and Sam appeared, red-faced and sweating from their walk back up the beach. Dora peered at them, willing the figure of a small blond-haired boy to appear mirage-like beside them. But they were on their own. As they drew closer Dora saw that Cassie's knee was grazed and bleeding and she held something in her arms. Cassie spotted them and ran over.

'Is he here?' she asked with a gasp.

Dora shook her head.

'Oh, Dora,' she gasped, holding out a wet tangle of material. 'It's his Superman cape. Sam found it on the rocks by one of the pools. It's soaking wet.'

Dora swallowed. 'Are you sure? I mean, is it definitely his?'

Cassie didn't answer. She just gave her a look that made her stomach churn and her eyes sting with tears.

'Well what now?' Dora asked. She realised she could hardly breathe.

Blessedly, Sam took charge.

'Dora, you should go home. Go see if Alfie has somehow made his way back there. If he's not there you should call your parents. Tell them what's happened. The three of us will carry on searching here. I think we need to talk to the lifeguard and maybe even get some more people looking with us.'

Cassie moaned. 'Oh, Alfie. Oh God, where is he? We are going to be in so much trouble.'

Dora's mind was whirring. Images of Alfie flooded her

brain. Alfie standing on the edge of a rock pool as a giant wave washed in. Alfie being led away from the beach by shadowy strangers. Alfie wandering the lethal laneways of Summertown as a huge caravan bore down on him. Alfie wading into the breakers, his little boots filling quickly with water. Alfie standing precariously on a cliff edge, his cloak flapping wildly in the breeze. The images crowded her mind and kept her frozen to the spot. She didn't want to leave the beach. Not without Alfie.

'Dora!' Steven shook her by the shoulder. 'Dora, go now. Hurry.'

She took one last look at the three of them standing there in the car park, and then she ran.

HELEN

Present Day

Helen is sitting in the conservatory lost in thought when Dora returns. The slam of the back door signals her arrival. She doesn't know how long it has been since her daughter broke the news of her pregnancy, but the early evening sun is just starting to brush the tops of the trees and its warmth slants down onto the conservatory, making the old wooden joists click and creak like arthritic joints. Helen knows she has handled things badly, even for her. It's time to make amends. She stands stiffly and tidies their plates and cups, placing the china back onto the tray and carrying it into the kitchen. Then, wearily, she climbs the staircase.

She finds Dora in Alfie's room. She's sitting in the old rocking chair by the window, her face turned to the garden, her legs – now mud-spattered – are tucked beneath her. Unobserved, Helen stands in the doorway and takes in her daughter's profile; her elegant neck taut with tension; her pale skin and seaweed eyes; her nose, thin and straight; a smear of early freckles on her skin; her unruly dark hair scraped back carelessly into a ponytail. Although now a young woman, Dora doesn't look all that different from the girl Helen remembers racing around the house just a few years ago, twirling a giggling Alfie in her arms, or curled up in Richard's lap as they pored over some book or puzzle. How have they arrived at this? Two damaged women unable to communicate with each other in anything but brutal jabs and sharp thrusts of confrontation and pain.

It's obvious Dora doesn't know how attractive she is and it comes to her now that perhaps it's her fault. She tries to remember the last time she complimented either of her daughters and can't, and allows herself a fleeting moment of regret. She knows she hasn't been a very good mother. She has neglected each of her children at crucial moments in their lives and now she is paying the price. Is it too late to change? Dora sighs and shifts in the chair. Yes, she is beautiful, beautiful but troubled.

As Helen watches her daughter, it occurs to her that she sits in the very same chair she herself occupied thirteen or so years ago, nursing Alfie day and night and rocking him gently to sleep. She remembers the sweet, talcum powder smell of him, the impossibly soft skin and the rhythmic suck and pull of his mouth at her breast; mother and baby connected in the nocturnal hours to a universal force that is as natural and insistent as the ebb and flow of the waves down on the shoreline. And now, in some strange twist of fate, here is Dora, seated before her, pregnant and distraught.

She's known this day would come. She's imagined it in her head a million times, one of her daughters sharing the news that she is to become a mother. She and Richard even talked about it in the early days when the girls were little more than babies, imagining the glorious days of wedding celebrations and the births of their grandchildren. They'd lived with such innocence then, made so many naive assumptions, for she'd only ever imagined those moments to be filled with joy. And she *is* happy for Dora. Of course she is. But what she hasn't expected, what Helen hasn't banked on is the indescribable feeling of jealousy that surged through her body at Dora's announcement. It had been physical; a violent force that stole the breath from her lungs and left her speechless and shaking with the sheer ugliness of its existence. How *could* she?

Surely she is a monster; to feel such burning jealousy for

her daughter who has been given a fresh start, a new life, while all Helen has left are her mistakes, her regrets and her overwhelming grief? There are no second chances for her. She has had her time and she has squandered it.

But she has, at least, swallowed down her seething jealousy. It is under control and buried now, smothered beneath the more pressing need to make amends with Dora. She wants to go to her, to draw her into her arms and reassure her daughter that everything will be all right; but she can't. It is as if she is anchored to the spot, pinned down by fear and regret and the aching desire not to make things even worse, and so she just stands there, right where she is, barely breathing until Dora turns suddenly, startled to see her mother watching her from the doorway.

'I didn't hear you come up.' Her daughter's voice is flat and she turns her tear-stained face back towards the window. She is still angry.

'No,' says Helen. She is unsure what to say. She doesn't know how to start the conversation that hangs unspoken between them but she forces herself to enter the room and sits down on the bed in the corner, smoothing the blue comforter beneath her.

'I'm sorry.' Helen pauses but Dora doesn't interrupt. She knows this is her stage now. 'I didn't expect . . . I didn't know what you wanted me to say earlier . . . downstairs.' She draws a breath and carries on. 'How are you feeling? With the pregnancy?'

Dora's gaze remains fixed on the blossom outside. 'Sick most mornings, and so tired by the evening. I'm tired like I've never been before, as if it's burrowed deep in my bones.'

'I was the same with Cassie,' Helen remembers with a small smile. 'It should pass in a few weeks.' Another pause, then, 'Was it an accident?'

She sees her daughter flinch. It is the wrong question. She tries again. 'What I mean is, you seemed so upset earlier. It threw me. I thought, perhaps this was something you weren't pleased about.' Helen wonders privately if Dan is giving Dora a hard time. He seems like a nice chap but you can never be too sure.

Dora sighs and finally turns to her mother. 'I'm scared.'

Helen takes a moment to form her response. 'Well, that's completely natural, most first time mums are. Your body is going through an enormous transformation. All those hormones rushing around—'

'No. It's more than that,' Dora interrupts. 'I'm scared of the past. Of what happened. I'm scared it could happen again. I already feel like I've lost one family. Starting another is too much responsibility . . . it's too much to lose all over again. I can't do it. It would break me.'

There. It has been said. Helen closes her eyes momentarily, trying to find words of comfort. 'What happened was terrible . . . tragic. But it's done now. It's in the past.'

'How can you know that, Mum? I mean, honestly, none of us would have thought, you know . . . none of us would have imagined what happened . . . the impact it had.' Dora's words trail off again. She seems unable to continue, but then she finds the words in a rush. 'I don't think I can handle the responsibility of becoming a mother. You know, I still wonder whether things might be different if I had acted differently that day, if I had *been* different. I mean, how can I possibly be ready to be a parent when I still feel like a child inside, the same child that I was on the beach that day?'

'But that's exactly it, Dora. You *were* just a child, a girl.' Helen puts her fingers to the crease between her brows and tries to smooth away the headache she can feel building. 'I think we'd all do things differently a second time round,' she finally admits. God knows she would if she could. She has so many regrets of her own to bear. She wonders if now is the time to admit her own guilt, to air her own dirty little secret. But Dora is speaking again.

'I can't let it go. I think about it every day.'

'We all do, darling. But at some point, you have to. You have to say to yourself, "This was not *my* fault."'

'Wasn't it?' Dora looks at her mother searchingly. 'Do you really believe that?'

Helen swallows. She knows what Dora needs to hear. She knows Dora needs to be absolved of her guilt. And she could say it out loud now. Helen could say the words she has rehearsed in her head over and over since that day. *Say it. Say it*, she wills herself. But again, a stifling fear prevents her and seconds later she sees the hope that flared in Dora's eyes die as quickly as it arose. She burns with shame for her cowardice and tries another approach. 'Some days, I wake up and just being here, in this house, well, it brings me great comfort. Other days it's different. I know before I even open my eyes that I can barely muster the strength to get out of bed, because to do so means facing another dark day; another day when we all face our future, and our lives, stuck in this horrid black hole.' Helen pauses, looks at her daughter pointedly and adds, 'Without him . . . without each other.'

Dora nods. She understands. They've been ripped apart and scattered on the wind, each locked away in their own private purgatory. 'Do you ever wonder if the police got it wrong?'

Helen gazes out at the garden. 'No,' she lies.

'I do, all the time.'

Helen thinks of all the possible scenarios she has churned over night after night and winces in pain.

'Sorry, is this too hard for you?' Dora asks.

'No, it's good to talk about him. We've never . . .' She breaks off.

Dora nods. 'Dan says this is our opportunity. He thinks that we should grab it with both hands. He thinks this baby is a chance for me to start over, but he doesn't understand. There's no such thing as a "fresh start" is there? There's no full stop. No clean page. Our lives just carry on. And yet, I had to come here. I can't let go of this feeling . . . it's the not knowing.' She stops and rubs her belly unconsciously. 'I have dreams.'

'What sort of dreams?'

'Dreams of falling. Dreams of drowning. I have this one dream where I lose something really important. It can be anything, but I am haunted by it. It's such a terrible feeling that overwhelms me when I realise that it's gone . . . for ever. I keep dreaming it, over and over. Then the other week, on the Tube, there was this crush. It was rush hour and I got caught up in it. It was terrifying, like being caught in a rip . . . I panicked. That feeling . . . of floundering, suffocating . . . it tore me apart.'

Helen closes her eyes again.

'Sorry, Mum, I know this must be painful. But don't you ever wonder if one day we will find out what happened?'

'Would it really make such a difference now, after all this time? Dan's right. You should grab this opportunity with both hands.'

'And I want to,' insists Dora. 'I really do. I don't want to push Dan away. I just don't know if I can move forwards when I feel as though I'm standing on such a precarious ledge. How can you just accept that this is it? Don't you want answers?'

'There are no answers, Dora. Don't you think we searched for them? We searched and searched but there weren't any. I've had to accept that. It's the hardest thing I've ever had to do, but I did it.'

'But there are still so many unanswered questions . . .' Helen sees her daughter close her eyes and rub at her temples, a gesture so reminiscent of Richard it almost takes her breath away. 'I just don't believe . . . I can't believe it until—'

'Dora,' urges Helen, desperate to stop the words tumbling from her daughter's mouth, 'you have to let go. It's time.'

Dora shakes her head. 'No,' she states flatly. 'I can't. Not yet.' She turns back to the window. 'Not yet.'

It seems their conversation is over.

Helen sighs. The opportunity has passed her by, again. She is ashamed of herself for not speaking out, for not at least trying to ease her daughter's burden. But then whatever she says, whatever her own private guilt, she knows she can't change what has happened. There is nothing she can say, after all, that will fix what has been broken.

Dora stays the night. Helen makes up the bed in her old room and once Dora has showered and changed the two women sit in the kitchen and eat supper together. It is an uncomfortable meal. Both are awkward, embarrassed by the half conversations they have shared, but no mention is made of *the day* again, or of Dora's pregnancy and by nine thirty Dora cries tiredness and takes herself off to bed.

Helen sits up a while longer in front of the television set as it fuzzes and drones in the living room. She pays it no attention. Instead she pictures Dora lying upstairs, in the same brass bed that she slept in on her first visit to Clifftops. She was pregnant then too, with Cassie. It is like some bad joke; history is repeating itself and despite the reassurances she has tried to offer Dora that afternoon, there is no escaping the fact that it plain terrifies her. She can't comfort Dora or promise that her fears are unfounded because deep down she doesn't know that they are. Helen has learnt the hard way that life can throw its absolute worst at you; and if she could say anything to her daughter at all, if they were having the conversation all over again, with the raw, brutal honesty she hadn't felt able to speak with earlier that afternoon, she would tell her daughter to run; to run as fast as she can away from the tears and the grief and the terrible pain life is about to bestow on her.

As Helen sits in the living room and contemplates Dora's dilemma, her head begins to fill with a carousel of images from the past. They crowd into her mind's eye like faded Polaroids: the girls shell-seeking on the beach, skinny and sunburnt in swimsuits; Richard cloistered away in his study at Christmas, his fair head bent in concentration over a drawing board; Alfie giggling, his chubby limbs flailing wildly as Dora pulls him along the polished wooden floorboards in the laundry basket; Cassie stomping moodily up the stairs after yet another telling-off about a broken curfew; her husband running ahead of her up to Golden Cap, his coat flapping in the wind; Alfie drawing a smile on the kitchen table with uneaten peas; her three children, two fair heads and one dark, bent together as they thread summer daisies into long looping chains; and finally, Dora's stricken face as she bursts into the kitchen that summer's afternoon with the unbearable news that pulled their world apart.

Scenes from her life wash over her until, overcome by emotion, Helen's carefully preserved countenance dissolves. As the television strobes colour across the living room walls Helen cries an endless river of fat, silent tears. She weeps for a decade of regret and she mourns, all over again, for a little life lost to them for ever.

HELEN

Eleven Years Earlier

The house was deathly quiet when Helen returned. She let herself in through the front door and closed it behind her with a gentle click, leaning her forehead against the coolness of the wall for just a moment. There was the familiar hum of the ancient fridge in the kitchen, and the soft reverberations of the house breathing on its foundations, but all sounds of human life were absent. The children were still out, probably down at the beach making themselves sick on ice cream and fizzy drinks. She smiled: it was the last day of the holidays; a little indulgence wouldn't do them any harm. She'd make them something healthy for tea, extras for Richard. He'd be grateful for a home-cooked meal when he got in off the train from London.

She felt flushed and giddy. Tobias had been rough with her and she could still feel the weight of his body pressing down on hers in the long grass of the field they had found that morning. There had been nothing romantic about their encounter; it was sordid and hasty. But Helen had submitted to his desires, excited by his need to possess her. And afterwards, she had lain in his arms and abandoned herself to his daydreams of a life without husbands and wives and children and responsibilities. It was a game Tobias was fond of playing, a re-imagining of what life might be like for them in another world, and she was happy to indulge him. They'd lain together on the warm earth, planning their alternative life as long blades of grass and the seed heads of hemlock danced against the blue sky overhead.

Gathering herself, Helen floated through the hallway humming quietly, an inane pop song that had stuck in her head on the drive home. She always felt so alive after time with Tobias. It was like having a jolt of electricity flow through her body, recharging her tired limbs and refreshing her mind, clearing away the banal cobwebs of her life for just a few short hours. Tobias was right; he did do her good.

As she wandered down the hallway she checked her watch. It was nearly three. If she were lucky she would have time to shower and change before the kids returned. Reaching the bottom step of the staircase she turned to regard herself in the long mirror. Yes, the difference was noticeable; she looked lighter, happier. Would it be obvious to anyone else? As she surveyed her reflection carefully in the mirror her eye was suddenly caught by a dark green smudge ground into the daisy-patterned fabric of her skirt; a grass stain. It must have happened when she was with Tobias. Damn. She rubbed at it but she knew she'd never get it out of the pale cotton; it was ruined. With a sigh she turned to head upstairs but as her foot touched the bottom step she heard the slam of the back door.

'Mum? Mum are you home?'

Damn. It was Dora. They were back already.

'In here,' she called out airily, running her fingers through her hair and patting at her face self-consciously. She could have done with five minutes to herself, at least.

Dora emerged from the kitchen. Her cheeks were flushed red and she seemed to be struggling to breathe, drawing air into her lungs with great, ragged gasps.

'Is he here?' she panted, her eyes flicking nervously around the hallway.

'Is *who* here?' Helen forced an innocent smile but she couldn't help the slow blush that crept over her face. There was no way Dora could know about Tobias. It was impossible.

But her daughter's face burned an even deeper red and there were tears welling visibly in her eyes. Helen swallowed nervously.

'Oh, Mum,' she cried, 'something awful's happened.'

'What is it? What's happened?' Please God, she willed. There was no way she could know about the affair – anything but that.

'It's Alfie,' Dora sobbed. 'He's missing.'

The innocent smile that had been playing on Helen's lips froze as her daughter's words slowly sank in. She shook her head. 'What do you mean *missing*?'

'We can't find him anywhere.'

Helen moved closer. She seized her daughter's arm and looked searchingly into her wide eyes. 'Where is he, Dora? Where's your brother?'

Dora couldn't hold her mother's gaze and Helen, feeling the first coil of fear twist in her gut, dug her fingers deeper into the flesh of her arm. Dora flinched and tried to squirm out of her tight grasp but Helen wouldn't let go.

'Where is he?' she demanded again.

Dora let out a hysterical sob. 'I don't know! We've looked and looked but he's vanished.'

'Vanished? Where's Cassie?' Helen stopped for a moment. 'Is this some silly prank you kids have cooked up to scare me? If it is, it's not funny.'

'No,' Dora whispered. 'I swear. We were at the beach. I went to get ice creams. I thought he was with Cassie. But he must have followed me, and now we can't find him. Oh, Mum . . .' She couldn't finish her sentence. The tears were flowing fast and heavy now.

'Where's Cassie?' Helen asked again.

'She's still at the beach.'

Helen moved quickly. Her car keys were sitting on the hall table where she had thrown them only moments ago. 'You stupid girl! I *told* you to all stay together. Wait here. I'm going to find him. I'll deal with you when we get back.'

'Mum, I'm so sorry, I really didn't—'

Helen held up her hand to silence her daughter. 'We'll talk about your punishment later. When Alfie's home.'

She didn't stop to listen to Dora's pitiful sobs. Instead she ran from the house, leapt into her car and raced down the driveway as fast as she could.

It was only a short drive to the beach, but by the time Helen pulled into the car park, she had convinced herself she would find Cassie and Alfie sitting astride the sea wall waiting for her. She could see them now, their two fair heads shining in the afternoon sunshine as they waved and swung their legs carelessly in front of them. It was all just some silly mix-up. Dora had overreacted.

She parked in a disabled spot and leapt from the car, running through the throng of holidaymakers all laden with deckchairs and picnic hampers, rugs and inflatables as they started to leave the beach. A few gave her curious glances as she pushed past, but she ignored them. She had to get to the foreshore. She had to get to Cassie.

And then she saw her, exactly where she had pictured her only moments before, standing by the sea wall. But as she drew closer, she could see that the second fair head she had imagined next to her daughter's was missing. Cassie was standing next to a girl Helen didn't recognise, a girl with long, black hair and the whitest skin. There was no sign of Alfie.

Helen moaned and ran towards them blindly.

'Where is he?' she gasped as she drew closer. Then when Cassie didn't reply, she screamed it again, 'Where's Alfie?' She seized Cassie's arms and shook her violently until she went limp like a rag doll in her arms and she felt someone restraining her from behind and murmuring soft, reassuring words.

'Calm down . . . we're searching for him . . . Coastguard on its way . . . we will find him.'

'You don't understand,' she said, turning to the woman who held her, 'he's only a baby.'

'I understand this is very distressing for you,' the young woman soothed. 'If you'll just come with me for a moment, Mrs Tide . . .' Helen noticed for the first time that the woman was wearing a police uniform. She let herself be led away into the shade of the awning of the little beach shop. There seemed to be a crowd gathering around them, but Helen ignored the stares and whispers, scanning the crowds frantically, willing the face of her son to appear in front of her. Why were they all just standing there? Why weren't they looking for Alfie?

Helen gazed out across the beach in desperation. The sun had begun its slow descent towards the horizon and a light scattering of amber-coloured clouds was forming out at sea. She could see fishing boats making their way in to shore, spent from a day on the ocean. There was a sudden flurry of activity down by the breakers as a series of gulls flapped and squawked territorially over the remains of a picnic. Further up the beach a plastic bag blew towards them across the pebbles. Helen's heart leapt as she saw a little boy chase it across the stones, but hope turned to dismay as she realised it wasn't her son. It wasn't Alfie. She looked around again and realised Cassie had disappeared from view.

'Where's my daughter?' she asked, rounding on the police-woman next to her.

The woman put a reassuring hand on her arm. 'They're just asking her a few questions.'

'I want to see her. I want to hear what she has to say. Where have they taken her?'

'She's in the shop, but it might be best if . . .'

Helen didn't wait to hear the rest. She lunged through the doorway into the shop, and then, finding it empty, barged through into the back room where she could hear the murmur of voices.

The stockroom was dark and cramped. Cassie was perched on a pile of boxes in front of a policeman who scribbled hasty notes into a pad. Cassie's gaze seemed to be fixed on a spot of tatty linoleum on the floor in front of her and she was picking agitatedly at the torn corner of a box, shredding the corrugated cardboard into a million little pieces which fluttered slowly to the floor. She looked up nervously as Helen entered the room, and then returned her gaze to the floor.

'Do you mind,' Helen addressed the policeman. 'I'm her mother. I'd like to hear this too.' It wasn't a question.

The young policeman nodded and turned back to Cassie. 'So you all walked down together from the campsite.'

Cassie nodded.

'What time did you arrive at the beach?'

'It was about eleven o'clock this morning. We met Sam first and then headed to the Crag.'

'Who's Sam?' Helen asked sharply.

The policeman shot her a look. He wasn't angry but it was clear that he thought it best if he were the one asking the questions.

'Is Sam the girl outside?' he asked.

Cassie nodded. 'She's my friend.'

'And where is the Crag, Cassandra?' the policeman asked.

Helen's head swam. Helen had never heard Cassie talk about 'Sam' before.

'It's at the far end of the beach,' Cassie continued, 'near the rock pools. It's just a cave, where teenagers hang out sometimes . . . you know . . . to just . . . just hang out.'

The policeman nodded. 'Could you show us where this cave is?'

'Yes, but we already looked there. He's not there.'

'OK, but we'd like to take another look. So you headed to the cave at around eleven o'clock this morning with Alfie and Sam?'

'Yes. And Dora, my sister. She was there too.'

The policeman scribbled in his book again. 'Were you all together in the cave for long?'

'Yes. We were there for an hour or so. Then Dora said she

was going to get ice creams.' Cassie thought for a moment. 'No, it was more than an hour. I remember she asked me the time before she left. It was just before one p.m.'

The policeman nodded his head again and scribbled in his pad.

'When she returned Dora asked me where Alfie was. I thought she was joking. Sam and I hadn't seen Alfie since she'd left. We thought she'd taken him with her.'

Helen felt her stomach plunge and let out an audible whimper. 'So neither of you were looking after him? What did I tell you girls?'

The policeman held up his hand. 'If you wouldn't mind, Mrs Tide, I know it's hard but time is of the essence here.'

Helen nodded and bit her tongue.

'So the last time you saw Alfie was just before one p.m. today?'

Cassie nodded her head. Helen looked at her watch. It was nearly four.

'Do you think he left the cave? Followed Dora down the beach? Do you remember him saying anything about what he'd like to do? Where he might want to go?'

Cassie shook her head. 'He was happy in the cave.' She suddenly remembered something and let out a small sob. 'He thought it was a bat cave. He thought the seagulls were bats.'

Helen felt tears sting her eyes. Her little boy was out there, alone.

'And what were you and Sam doing while Dora was off buying ice cream?'

Cassie blushed. 'Just . . . chatting . . . and, you know . . . smoking.'

Helen felt her blood rise. Cassie smoked?

'I see.' The policeman scribbled something else into his pad.

'What was Alfie wearing the last time you saw him?'

'A Superman costume.'

The policeman gave a small smile as he scribbled in his pad.

'Can you describe it for me?'

'Blue pyjama bottoms, red wellington boots, a blue T-shirt with the Superman logo on it, and a red cloak.' Cassie glanced up at Helen for a moment and then looked away again. 'Mum had sewn a big yellow "S" onto it. But we found the cloak, up by the rock pools. Sam did.'

Helen's stomach took another sickening plunge. She wanted to scream, but she forced herself to remain quiet, jamming her fist into her mouth and biting down hard on her fingers. It hurt; but she didn't care.

The policeman nodded again. It seemed he'd already seen the item of clothing.

'Do you remember seeing Alfie take his cloak off in the cave?'

Helen held her breath but Cassie shook her head.

'So he might have left the cave and then removed it, near the rocks?'

Cassie gave a slow nod. Helen wanted to reach out and shake her, but she just bit down harder on her hand, feeling the ache of her flesh beneath her teeth.

'OK. That's very helpful, Cassandra. We'll need to ask you and Sam some more questions but I think we've got enough to start with. Is your sister here?'

Cassie looked at her mother and Helen shook her head. 'Sorry, officer, I asked her to stay up at the house in case Alfie found his way back there. I thought it was best. I came here as soon as she told me what had happened.'

The policeman scribbled a final detail in his notebook and then snapped it shut. 'OK. We'll speak to Dora up at the house.' The policeman mumbled something quickly into his crackling walkie-talkie, and then stood. 'Cassandra, you've been very helpful,' he repeated before turning to Helen. 'Don't worry, we'll find him, Mrs Tide. We've got two officers down on the beach looking for your son right now and I'm about to radio the coastguard. It's just a precaution, of course. No doubt he's off playing with some other kids, or building sandcastles somewhere on the beach. You know what kids are like.'

Helen nodded and tried hard not to think about why they might need to call the coastguard.

Alfie couldn't swim.

Helen felt her knees start to buckle but the policeman moved quickly and his strong arms were underneath her before she hit the ground.

'Do you want to sit down, madam?'

'No, no, I'll be OK.' She pushed him away. 'My husband,' she said. 'He's in London. I should call him.' She couldn't bear the thought of breaking the news to Richard, but he needed to be told. He would know what to do. Suddenly, Helen was overwhelmed by the need to feel her husband's strong arms around her. He would find their boy.

'Where does he work?'

'Tide Associates. Fitzhardinge Street.'

The policeman nodded. 'We'll contact him now.'

Helen gave a small, grateful nod and then left the little shop, stepping out into the noise and confusion outside.

It was like being underwater. She knew it was important to listen to what the police were telling her, but she found it hard to focus on anything but the crowds of people leaving the beach. She wanted to scream at them all to stay where they were. She wanted to freeze them in time and run from cluster to cluster, searching for Alfie's face amongst them. And so, when the police had finally finished with their questions she and Cassie began to scour the crowds, stopping everyone they met to check if they had seen a little boy in a home-made Superman costume. But it didn't matter who they asked, each time their question was met with a wary but sympathetic shake of the head and soon the beach became emptier and emptier as sunburnt holidaymakers extricated themselves from their carefully chosen plots and made the long trudge back to their cars and their campsites. Eventually they were left with nothing but the deserted beach and the inevitable detritus from a thousand careless tourists. Helen kicked her way wearily through cans and plastic bottles, ice cream wrappers and empty chip cartons as she made her way back to the car park.

At seven o'clock Helen broke off from the search to call Dora up at the house. She knew it was wishful thinking, she knew the police would have notified her if he had arrived at Clifftops but she couldn't help but hope Alfie might have found his way home, somehow.

Dora picked up on the first ring.

'Is he there?' Helen asked.

'No,' said Dora.

Helen was about to hang up but Dora continued.

'Should I come down there and help look? I'm going crazy up here on my own. Perhaps I could—'

Helen hung up and turned back to the police officer next to her.

'I need to see the cave. Take me there, before it gets dark.'

The policeman opened his mouth to say something, but the look in Helen's eyes stopped him. Instead he gave a curt nod. 'Follow me.'

Helen struggled to get into the Crag. Her cotton skirt was desperately impractical for climbing the cliff face and her espadrilles slipped dangerously on the rocks. The policeman who accompanied her, however, ably assisted her over the ledge with strong hands. As he lowered her down her feet touched the gritty floor of the cavern and she sucked in a deep breath.

It was a desolate place; dank and gloomy and stinking with the smell of slimy vegetation, rotting fish and worse. What on earth had possessed the girls to go there? Helen couldn't understand. She wandered around for a minute or two, her jaw clenched tightly as she ran her hands across the towering stone walls. It was as if she hoped the touch of her fingers might open up a secret doorway in the rock and allow her son to be released back into her arms, returned from the underworld into which he had been stolen.

'You've searched every inch of this place?' she asked.

'Yes,' the policeman confirmed. 'We'll get the sniffer dogs in tomorrow, if we don't find him before then.'

Helen shook her head. 'Why did they come here?'

'Your daughter tells me it's a secret haunt for local teenagers.' He pointed up at the walls. 'You can see from the graffiti they weren't the first ones.'

Helen looked at the spray paint scrawls and shuddered. She couldn't bear to think of little Alfie playing in there. It was no place for a child. She swallowed. 'I think I'm ready to leave now.'

The officer nodded and they both moved to the narrow gap in the stone. As Helen hauled herself up and out onto the other side she noticed the sun was beginning to set. Alfie would be hungry. He'd missed his tea.

They stayed at the beach until it got dark and a young WPC gently suggested they return home. Helen didn't want to leave, she couldn't bear to return home without her son, but it was obvious there was nothing more they could do in the faltering light. The coastguard's helicopter had already been called in for the night and although they could see the lights of the search boats out in the bay, they'd been told even they too would be returning to shore soon. It was too late and too dark. They would have to wait until daybreak to start the search up again.

Helen thought her heart might split wide open with the sheer ache of it all as she climbed into her car and drove Cassie the short distance back to the house. They both saw, but neither of them commented on the empty child seat glaring at them accusingly from the back seat and it took every ounce of her willpower for Helen to keep her foot on the accelerator and not turn the car around and hurl herself back onto the beach, screaming out her son's name.

'Is Dad coming home?' Cassie asked finally, breaking the silence.

'Yes. He's on his way back from London. He'll be here soon.'

It was obvious they were both hoping Richard would know what to do.

Helen thumped the steering wheel. 'Where is he, Cass? Where did he go?'

Cassie fiddled anxiously with the frayed hem of her denim skirt. 'I don't know,' she whispered. 'I honestly don't. I thought he was with Dora. She told me she was taking him to get ice cream. Then she came back with some boy from school . . .'

Dora was seated at the kitchen table when they got back. There was an untouched mug of tea in front of her and she sat nervously biting her fingernails. She leapt up as soon as they entered. 'Is he with you?'

Cassie shook her head and Dora slumped back into her seat, wilting like a sunflower as night approaches.

Helen walked over to the kitchen sink and leaned against the draining board. She dropped her head and let out a loud sigh, releasing a tiny drop of her pent-up anger and tension. She couldn't think; she couldn't breathe. It was as if she had entered some strange twilight zone, a parallel universe where everything seemed to be imploding on itself. As she stood there, with her head bent over the sink, her eyes slowly focused on a brightly coloured object in front of her. It was Alfie's plastic breakfast bowl. It sat in the sink where she had dumped it only hours earlier; it still had a half-eaten Weetabix glued to its sides. With a surge of emotion, she rounded on the girls.

'What the hell do you think you were doing today?' Her

voice was icy cold but there was fire in her eyes as she looked searchingly first at Dora, then Cassie, and then back to Dora.

The girls glanced nervously at each other. She could see fear in their eyes.

'Look at me,' Helen shouted. 'Tell me what happened.'

'It was my fault,' Cassie started. 'It was my idea to go to the Crag. Dora didn't really want to, but I told her I was going and she said we should stick together.'

Helen shook her head. 'I told you girls to keep an eye on him. I thought I could trust you. You're not kids any more.' She shook her head in disbelief. 'I don't understand how a little boy can just disappear on a crowded beach.'

Cassie hung her head in shame.

'He's three years old, for God's sake!' Helen's voice trembled. 'He's just a baby.'

'Mum,' Dora pleaded, 'We're really—'

Helen shook her head. 'I don't want to hear it, Dora. I told you girls to stick together. You left your brother and sister and wandered off on your own to get ice cream! And Alfie followed you, and now he's lost.' Helen shook her head again. 'I *told* you to stick together.'

'Mum,' Dora pleaded in a small voice, 'I'm sorry.'

'Sorry!' Helen turned on Dora. 'You're *sorry*? Do you think "sorry" will help Alfie, who's out there now, all on his own, in the dark . . .'

Dora began to sob.

'Do you think "sorry" will make this all right?'

Dora shook her head.

Cassie opened her mouth to speak but Helen held a hand up to stop her.

'Sorry doesn't bring Alfie home and tuck him in upstairs, warm and safe in his bed. Sorry doesn't keep him out of harm's way with a tummy full of food and our loving arms around him. There are lots of things I want to hear from you right now. But I certainly don't want to hear that you are *sorry*, young lady!' Helen could feel her body trembling, but she couldn't stop herself. 'I just don't know what you were thinking,' she continued, shaking her head in bewilderment. 'He's just a little boy . . . a baby.' She paused, and then suddenly all the anger left her and she felt herself collapse slowly to the floor, like a puppet whose strings had lost all tension. 'Oh my baby,' she cried. 'My poor, poor baby . . .'

For a moment the room was filled with her noisy sobs. She felt a hand on her shoulder but she shrugged it off angrily.

'Mum . . .' she heard Dora plead. 'Mum . . .' But she couldn't listen.

'Just go away. Get out of my sight. I can't stand to look at you right now, Dora.'

'Mum?' It was Cassie this time.

'Get out!' screamed Helen. 'Get out, the both of you! Get out of my sight!'

They didn't need to be told again. She heard the girls run from the room, Dora's noisy cries reverberating all the way upstairs to her bedroom.

Helen remained curled in a foetal position on the kitchen floor until her back ached and the chill from the kitchen tiles had numbed her flesh through the flimsy summer skirt. It was uncomfortable but it was nothing compared to the fear that gripped at her insides when she thought of her little boy out there in the dark, lost and alone. She'd thought she could trust the girls; she'd thought they were old enough to act responsibly. But she had been proved wrong. She had asked them to stick together but Dora had disobeyed. If only they had all stayed together, Alfie would never have gone wandering off.

There was a jangle of keys in the front door. Helen unfolded herself stiffly and went to meet her husband. He walked through the door, ashen-faced and crumpled in his business suit, and pulled her into his arms. They stood together for a long while, just holding each other and letting the enormity of the situation sink in.

'Our baby,' she whispered, 'our poor baby. He's out there,' she cried.

Richard stroked her hair and shushed her like a distressed infant. 'We'll find him.'

There was a creak on the staircase. Helen didn't look up but she felt Richard turn his head and then slowly, he opened his arms and she felt the warm body of their daughter join their embrace. She breathed in the sweet smell of Cassie's golden hair and closed her eyes. Richard was right; they would find him.

For a few moments the three of them stood together in the hall, clinging desperately to each other, and the hope that Alfie would be back in their arms at first light. When Helen did eventually open her eyes she looked up and saw Dora standing alone at the top of the stairs. She was watching them anxiously through tear-stained eyes. Helen gazed at her coldly for a moment. How could she have broken her promise? How could she have left Alfie and Cassie and gone off with that boy? She stared at Dora a moment longer, unable to hide her disgust, before turning her back and heading into the kitchen to fix Richard some tea.

'I've been speaking with the police,' Richard said a few minutes later. He'd joined her in the kitchen and sat fidgeting at the kitchen table. 'They're going to start up the search again at first light. They're bringing dogs with them. We'll find him, Helen, I promise.'

Helen didn't say anything. Instead she concentrated on the steady cloud of steam rising out of the mouth of the kettle. She wondered how long she would be able to stand the scalding heat of it if she were to hold her hand out over the vapour.

'Apparently they've had lots of locals volunteering to help too,' he continued. 'Bill Dryden's coming to the house first thing. We'll get search parties organised and head out across the cliffs to the beach. Alfie's probably just got himself lost and is tucked up asleep in a warm little nook somewhere on the cliffs; or in a ditch in Farmer Plummer's fields. We'll be laughing about this in a few days, you'll see. It will be one of those stories we'll tell at his twenty-first to embarrass him.' His smile was forced.

Helen nodded, wanting to believe him. 'At least it's a warm night,' she relented. 'Thank goodness he's got long sleeves and trousers on. I never thought I'd be so grateful for his Superman obsession.'

Richard gave a small smile.

'Are you hungry?'

He shook his head.

'Shall I make you a cup of tea?'

'I'm fine.'

The kettle released its piercing whistle into the silence and Helen turned it off, uncertain what to do next. In the end she turned and pulled a chair out opposite Richard at the kitchen table. The wooden legs scraped against the floor tiles with a slow, painful scream.

'The police offered to send a GP up to us, but I said it wasn't necessary.'

Helen nodded.

'I doubt we'll sleep tonight, but I couldn't bear the thought of taking painkillers and being out of it when they find him. Did I do the right thing?'

Helen nodded. She knew exactly what he meant. She didn't want anything to numb her pain; she needed to feel every shard of it deep in her heart.

'Do you think the girls are OK?'

Helen shrugged.

'It's very quiet upstairs.'

'They've probably gone to bed. Best place for them. I'm not sure I can face them right now. I'm so disappointed in Dora.'

Richard raised his head and looked at her.

'I *told* her they had to stick together. I told her they could only go to the beach if they *all* stuck together.'

Richard looked down at his hands. 'I thought we'd always said the beach was off limits for Alfie unless you or I were present.'

Helen looked up at him guiltily. 'They're nearly adults, Richard. I thought I could trust them. But it seems Dora decided to head off on her own. She went to buy ice cream and met up with some boy from school.'

Richard sighed and they sat in silence a while longer, before he cleared his throat. 'I didn't realise you had to work today, Helen. I thought you weren't due back for a week or so.'

Helen felt a flush of shame spread across her face. It seemed like a lifetime ago now that she had lain in that field with Tobias and made love to him while the birds rustled and the crickets chirruped in her ears. 'I had to go in . . .' she blustered. 'I had to go through my timetables with the Dean.'

Richard nodded. 'Sorry, I'm not . . . it's not . . .' He held up his hands. 'Nothing matters but us finding him, first thing tomorrow.'

As Helen looked into the tired, troubled eyes of her husband she wondered, for just a split second, whether she should tell him. It was only ever supposed to be a bit of fun. Nobody was ever supposed to find out. What would she achieve now if she were to lay this secret upon Richard and expose her infidelity to him? Would it really help the desperate situation they found themselves in?

No.

She couldn't do it. They had enough to deal with right now; and really, what difference did it make where she was? What if she had actually been called onto campus? They would still be living the same nightmare now. No, there was no need to confess about the affair to Richard. It wasn't her fault. Helen swallowed back the cold, hollow feeling nagging insistently at her belly and reached across for Richard's hand.

The warmth of his skin surprised her and she gripped it tightly in her own icy hand.

'I keep wondering if he could make his own way back to the house,' Richard murmured. 'Do you think he knows the way?'

Helen shook her head. 'I don't know. I've wondered the same myself. He's a bright kid.' She looked out at the blackness of the night pressing against the windowpane and shuddered. 'I just keep thinking if he could come home, he would.'

Richard looked up sharply. 'What do you mean, "if he *could* come home"?'

Helen swallowed. 'I want to believe, I really do.' She faltered and swallowed again. 'It's just his cape,' she said finally, in a quiet voice. 'Why was it on the rocks, by the pools? Why did he take it off there?'

Richard shook his head quickly. 'It doesn't mean anything. Don't think like that. We have to stay positive. We won't get anywhere if we give up now.'

'I'm not giving up. It's just—'

Richard held up his hand. 'Stop, Helen. Just stop.' He stood up with another loud scrape of wood against tiles. 'I'm going to take a shower. It's going to be a long night.'

Helen slept in Alfie's room; at least, she lay on his bed underneath his duvet and inhaled the sweet little boy smells of Johnson's shampoo and vanilla Play-doh and baby breath as soft and sweet as a delicate summer breeze. And as she lay there she submitted herself to the strange, twilight world between waking and sleep where dreams become most surreal and vivid. Her head whirled with a crazy mix of images: Tobias moving over her with his eyes closed and perspiration forming on his brow, Alfie gleefully crayoning vivid scrawls onto the dark walls of the Crag, Dora bursting into the house with that fearful look on her face and Richard, strong, dependable Richard, squeezing her cold hand in his warm one and reassuring over and over, 'We'll get him back. I promise, we'll get him back.'

She didn't think she slept, but she must have done, because Richard was suddenly shaking her from her strange slumber and whispering in her ear, 'It's nearly daybreak; time to find our boy.'

After he had left the room Helen lay for a moment on the little bed and let the enormity of Alfie's absence engulf her all over again. She felt it tickle the back of her throat and then slowly pour down through her insides like cold, liquid mercury, moving faster and faster before it settled in a painful, heavy pool in her gut. She sighed and pulled herself up from the mattress, feeling her fear slosh and settle as she moved. It was still dark outside but she could hear Richard clattering downstairs in the kitchen, preparing for his departure. Before she left the room she made Alfie's bed carefully; he would be tired when they brought him home.

In the bathroom she splashed cold water on her face and stared at her reflection in the mirror. It was like looking at a stranger. Her green eyes were red and lifeless and there were dark rings of make-up smudged around them. She needed to change too. She was still in the same clothes she'd been wearing the day before. She pulled her T-shirt over her head, unclasped her bra and slipped her crumpled cotton skirt down over her calves. As it landed on the floor she saw, once again, the dark grass stain from the day before. It stared up at her accusingly. Helen looked at it for a moment and then swept the skirt up into her arms and flung it with a sob into the rubbish bin under the sink.

Then she sat on the edge of the bath and gave in to deep, painful sobs that made her body shudder and shake. She sat naked and alone with her hands wrapped around her belly, keening for her baby, feeling the ache of his absence deep in her core.

*

Richard was letting Betty and Bill Dryden into the house when she came down the stairs. Bill shuffled awkwardly by the front door, holding his cap before him in his weathered hands, but Betty walked straight over to Helen and pulled her into her motherly embrace.

'You poor dears, you must be going out of your minds with worry. I'll get the kettle on, shall I? Make us a nice cup of tea?'

Helen nodded into the top of Betty's grey, curled hair, grateful that somebody seemed to be taking charge.

'We'll be off, Helen,' said Richard. 'We're meeting the police down at the car park. I'll call you as soon as we find him.'

Helen nodded again and watched as Richard and Bill let themselves out of the front door.

'Come on.' Betty ushered Helen into the kitchen. 'Let's get this kettle on. The girls will be up soon and you'll all need breakfast. Got to keep your strength up – for Alfie.'

Helen followed Betty into the kitchen and watched as the elderly woman fussed and bustled around the kitchen, finding tea bags and putting mugs on a tray.

'I'll put a little sugar in your tea, Helen,' she said. 'You look like you could do with it.'

Helen nodded again. It seemed she had lost her voice. Instead she turned to look at the colourful paint scrawls she'd tacked to the wall earlier that year, all abstract masterpieces by Alfie. She'd looked at them many times in the past, but she observed them now as if through fresh eyes, drinking in every brush stroke and every splotch of colour as if it were the first time she'd seen them. One was called 'Pirate Ship and the Moon'. Another, 'Dinosaur on a Slide'. It hurt to look at them, but Helen couldn't drag her eyes away. He was out there, somewhere. They would find him.

If anything, the second day was worse than the first. The house quickly filled with police officers and well-meaning friends who descended upon them, everyone desperate to help, but no one really knowing what to do. They flapped and flitted from room to room, conducting intense, hushed conversations while Helen remained seated at the kitchen table, in a state of disbelief, watching the machinations of the search revolve around her, while her head remained fixed in one position, turned towards the telephone, waiting for Richard to ring with the triumphant news that they had found Alfie.

At lunchtime she glanced out of the window and saw several cars and a large white van parked at the end of the driveway.

'What do they want?' she murmured to a passing police officer, carrying a tray of tea out of the kitchen. She noticed absent-mindedly that he had used Daphne's best china cups.

The man followed her gaze up the drive. 'The vultures are circling,' he said apologetically. 'The media have got the sniff of a story.'

Helen shrugged. 'Perhaps they can help? Perhaps if they cover the story someone will remember something important from yesterday?'

The policeman gave a polite nod and left her alone in the kitchen.

Betty bustled in moments later. 'Do you want me to fix you some lunch, Helen? You haven't eaten a thing all morning. You really should try to eat something . . .'

Helen shook her head. 'I couldn't, really.'

Betty looked worried. 'Well, what about the girls then? Can I do something for them?'

Helen shrugged. She hadn't seen either of the girls since breakfast. Cassie had shuffled into the kitchen, made herself a cup of tea and taken herself off somewhere. Dora had gone out at first light, following Bill and Richard at a distance down the driveway. Helen had been glad to see her go.

'You're very kind but really, we're fine. I'm not sure anyone is terribly hungry.'

'Well at least let me fix some sandwiches for those nice policemen? They'll need something in their tummies to keep them going.'

Helen nodded and then excused herself from the kitchen. She didn't think she could stomach the sight or smell of food. She felt like a gulping grey fish, washed up on a sandbank, drawing in her last gasps as the tide sank further and further away from her. Each breath she took physically hurt, a terrible searing pain that gripped at her insides, each breath signifying another moment without Alfie.

She was in the conservatory when Dora found her a little later. Helen didn't hear her approach until she stood just metres behind her and gave a loud cough, making her jump and spin with surprise.

'Oh, it's you.' Helen turned back to the garden with disappointment.

'Mum, there's something I need to tell you. Something important.'

Helen swung around again, eyeing Dora carefully. 'Go on.'

'Yesterday, when I left the Crag, there were two people near the cave. They were lying in the shade of the rocks. Grown-ups. A man and a woman. I remember he smiled at me and waved. It was a bit strange.'

Helen felt her breath catch in her throat.

'The man had long dark hair,' Dora continued, pulling at her T-shirt sleeves nervously. 'I thought he was a woman, at first. He was wearing jeans. And a T-shirt, red, I think. Yes, definitely red.'

'Did you see the woman?'

'No. I didn't get a good look at her. She was lying down.'

Helen felt her heart begin to pound wildly in her chest. Witnesses. They must have seen something. Why hadn't they come forward yesterday? They might be able to tell them which direction Alfie had gone in. They might be able to help. It was something to cling on to.

'Why didn't you say anything yesterday?' she snapped, rising quickly from her chair.

Dora backed away slightly. 'I forgot. There was so much going on.'

Helen looked at her in disbelief. 'You *forgot*?'

'It was confusing. I was so worried about Alfie—'

Helen could feel her body trembling. She stalked to the doorway, grabbing Dora's wrist as she went.

'Come with me.'

They half ran, half walked all the way down the oak-panelled hallway until they reached the door to Helen's study. She pushed it open without knocking – it was her house God dammit – and blurted her words before the officers inside could speak.

'My daughter has just remembered something. Something important.' She looked down at Dora. 'Go on; tell them what you told me.'

Dora looked up at her with alarm and fear.

'Go on,' Helen urged. 'Quickly!'

Richard was out all that day and late into the evening. He eventually returned home exhausted and grey. Helen knew from the look on his face not to ask how the search had gone.

'The police want to talk to us in a moment, in the lounge. Are you feeling up to it?'

Helen nodded. She was desperate for some news, something to hold on to. She'd heard nothing since she had dragged Dora in to face the police. Of course she felt up to it.

She joined him in the lounge moments later and they sat next to each other, holding hands as a senior-looking police officer took the seat in front of them. Helen watched the careful way the man pulled his trousers up over his knees as he sat and noted the starched collar of his white shirt. He had strong brown hands and a kind face. No doubt he had a loving wife and a happy family waiting for him at home right now and she felt a sudden stab of jealousy for his simple, uncomplicated life.

'Your son has been missing for over twenty-four hours now,' he began.

Helen bit her lip and nodded.

'We've covered a significant area today with the help of our own search teams and the assistance of local volunteers. I don't need to tell you that we have very grave concerns for Alfie's safety.'

Richard squeezed Helen's hand tightly but they both remained quiet.

'The land search has failed to offer any clues about what might have happened to your son. We've found no traces of a possible route away from the cave and no evidence that he might have decided to strike out on his own, perhaps heading to the car park in pursuit of Dora, or even trying to find his way home. Despite the crowds on the beach we've had no witnesses come forward. The only real evidence we have is the clothing found by the rock pools.' He looked them both in the eye. 'I don't need to tell you that this is very worrying indeed.'

Richard coughed. 'It doesn't mean . . . he's young, but he's not stupid, officer.'

The policeman gave a slight nod. 'I know, Mr Tide. But the rocks would have been slippery and at that time of day the tide was turning. Little kids are fascinated by water. It would only take one wave to knock him off his feet and the shelf drops away steeply off that side of the beach. We know there is a dangerous rip . . .'

Helen pressed her head into Richard's shoulder, trying to block out the mental picture that suddenly swam before her eyes.

'This is a very real scenario we are looking at. We need you to be prepared; do you understand?'

Helen couldn't move. She kept her face pressed into her

husband's shoulder, concentrating on her slow, steady breathing as she drank in the warm, reassuring scent of him.

'What about the couple Dora saw by the cliffs?' she asked finally, turning to address the policeman, fumbling desperately for something else to cling to.

Helen felt Richard shift his weight slightly.

'We interviewed your daughter this afternoon,' he continued. 'Dora does remember seeing a man and a woman near the Crag when she left to buy ice cream. She didn't get a close look at them but we have a basic description and it's enough for us to go on for now. We're going to try to track down the couple. We'd like to ask them some questions.'

'Yes!' agreed Helen. 'You have to find them. They might have seen which direction Alfie went in.'

It was only slight, but Helen saw the policeman hesitate. 'Possibly, yes.'

'You have to find them,' she urged again, hope suddenly surging through her body. 'They're sure to have seen him.' She turned to Richard. 'Aren't they?'

Richard gave a tiny nod of his head but he didn't meet her eye. Helen couldn't understand it. Why weren't they all over this? It was a real lead. 'You know,' she continued, 'I can't think why Dora didn't mention this before.'

The policeman intervened. 'I believe, Mrs Tide, in all the panic and confusion she just forgot. It's quite normal. And you see,' he continued, 'she doesn't remember seeing them when she returned to the Crag with the ice creams. Only as she left the cave that first time.'

Richard gave a little cough. 'So you have another scenario in mind, officer?'

The policeman looked down at his lap and an ugly thought suddenly buzzed in Helen's imagination, nagging at her like a dirty, pestilent fly. She tried to shoo it away but it buzzed straight back again, loud and insistent.

'You think they might have taken him?' she said. It was barely a whisper.

It was the policeman's turn to look away, averting his gaze ever so slightly to the empty space above their heads. 'We want to talk to all possible persons of interest. As soon as we have any leads, any at all, we will let you know.'

'You can't just snatch a little boy off a crowded beach. Someone would have seen something. It doesn't make any sense. He's out there, lost. He just can't find his own way home. You have to find him.' Her voice was rising hysterically in pitch and Richard put a hand on her arm, trying to restrain her.

'Shhhh, darling,' he soothed. 'Getting upset now isn't going to help anyone, is it? It isn't going to help Alfie.'

Helen clenched her teeth and fell silent. Damn Dora. How could she forget this vital piece of information? First her blatant disobedience in leaving her brother and sister to go off with some boy from her class, and now this; she had wasted precious police time by forgetting important details. She was angry with Cassie too, of course she was, but Dora's mistakes made her blood boil.

'As I said,' repeated the policeman, beginning to rise from his armchair, 'as soon as we have any leads you will be the first to know. We're doing all we can. Now you both should try and get some rest. Don't get up, I'll see myself out.'

Richard thanked the man and then pulled Helen into his arms. 'Stay strong,' he urged. 'We have to stay strong.'

Helen nodded, but inside she felt her heart crumble slowly, like an old fire-eaten log collapsing into a pile of cold ashes.

That night the rain came. Helen heard it pattering softly on the creeping foliage outside her bedroom window. She looked across for Richard but saw only an empty hollow on his side of the bed and feeling a rising panic, she pulled herself up and ran to the window. The weather was turning.

The night was dark as ink. Thick clouds shrouded the moon. Helen couldn't even see as far as the orchard. Alfie was out there, somewhere, and wherever he was, it was raining down on him.

She shrugged her dressing gown on and padded quickly down the stairs to the kitchen. It was dark and empty, quiet except for the low whirr of the dishwasher. Betty must have put it on earlier. Letting herself out of the back door, she stepped onto the drenched patio tiles, hardly noticing the wetness of the stone under her bare feet or the cold drops of rain as they began to fall on her hair and skin and night-clothes. *Cats and dogs*. That's what Alfie would have said. He still hadn't grasped that the expression wasn't to be taken literally, rushing to the window to look for animals falling from the sky whenever a heavy rain came. The thought made her wince.

She moved through the garden, wandering down the sodden lawn towards the dripping trees in the fruit orchard. She didn't know where she was going. She didn't know why. All she knew was that she couldn't lie there in the house, while her son was out there, somewhere, afraid and alone.

Rain streamed down her face, mingling with warm, salty tears. She felt her body begin to shiver under the wet chill of her clothes, but she carried on, regardless. Alfie was out there, she knew it.

'Alfie!' she cried, her voice desperate and high. 'Alfie! Where are you?'

Her cries were met with nothing but the thick splatter of rain drops falling onto the leaves of the pear trees and the distant sound of the surf breaking below.

'Alfie, it's Mummy. Where are you?' she called. 'Alfie!'

She listened again, but there was nothing.

Helen fell heavily to her knees. She felt the dampness of the grass rise up through her nightdress but she didn't care. It was nothing, nothing to what he would be feeling out there. She needed to feel the fullness of his pain, just to feel close to him again.

Helen lay on the wet grass, curling up into a tiny ball and

clutching her knees to her chest, letting the hard rain wash down over her. And as she lay there she sobbed and sobbed, calling his name out over and over and screaming at the sky, 'Take me, take me instead. I'll do anything, just give me my baby back', until her voice was hoarse and her body was overtaken with uncontrollable shivering. But still she couldn't move; she *wouldn't* move from that spot until Alfie was returned to her. Because she knew she couldn't go on without him.

She lay there for a long time, in the cold and the wet, until she felt strong, warm arms lift her gently and carry her back into the house. She felt herself stripped of her wet clothes, and wrapped in a blanket. She felt the sting of a hot water bottle as it was placed in her lap, and the chatter of her teeth as a cup of sugary tea was held to her lips, and the soft sound of Richard's anxious voice as he phoned for the doctor. And all the while she wanted to cry out in agony, 'Leave me be. Leave me to suffer. Let me feel this pain.' Because deep in her heart, she knew it was nothing compared to what Alfie was feeling, wherever he was.

Even with the little pink pills the doctor had given her, the long hours that followed were awful. It was like living on a rollercoaster. One minute she would feel a fresh surge of confidence, a conviction that her baby was out there, alive and well, just waiting to be found. But then the smallest thing – the sight of his ketchup-stained clothes in the laundry basket, his toothbrush in the mug in the bathroom, or his little shoes lined up by the back door – would be enough to send her plummeting into another spiral of despair and guilt. She slept in small snatches, falling into a fitful sleep until she would wake, with a start, and experience the horror of Alfie's absence all over again. And all the while, the search continued fruitlessly around them.

Everyone wanted to help; everyone wanted to offer their support and assist with the hunt for Alfie. But no one searched as hard as Richard. As if trying to make up for his absence on the day Alfie disappeared, he barely stopped to rest. He left the house at daybreak and didn't return for hours. When he did, it would be merely to shower and change his shirt, before heading straight back out again, often stopping to exchange a few words with the band of journalists who remained camped out at the end of the driveway. A little boy lost made tragic headlines and sold newspapers. Helen's initial acceptance of them had worn thin. She thought them increasingly ghoulish and found it hard not to be rude to their faces, but Richard was more tolerant. He thought their interest in the story might help to throw up a few leads, or keep the police search active, and so he would stop every so often for a few brief minutes to update them on their progress as he came and went.

And as he searched, Dora followed. She pursued him like a shadow. Helen saw her come and go from the house, pale faced and anxious. And once or twice she stood at the kitchen door and watched as Dora sat at the table across from Betty, who held her hand or wiped the tears as they trickled down her daughter's face. But Helen couldn't stand to watch for long. She had no words of comfort to offer, so she always left the room quietly, before Dora saw her.

Cassie was equally quiet and elusive. She spent hours cloistered in her bedroom, only really coming out for any length of time at night, when the others had retreated to their beds. Helen could hear the floorboards creaking as she passed back and forth outside their bedroom door. And occasionally, during daylight hours, Helen saw her out in the garden, drifting through the long grass, brushing the tips of the hot pink Japanese anemones Daphne had planted or caressing the trunks of the sycamore trees, with their leaves turning a slow, burnished yellow. She was a long way away, but Helen could still see her daughter's lips moving frantically, as though she were talking to herself, or offering up desperate prayers.

Helen knew she should draw them close. She knew that

her daughters needed comfort and compassion, but she just couldn't do it. She had to be alone, with her grief and distress. She had nothing to give, and so they revolved around each other like distant planets, remote and elusive. It was as if each of them were locked in their own private sphere of pain; none of them could confront the others, none of them could meet the others' eyes, none of them could bring themselves to speak of the torment they endured. They had been torn apart, like the yellowing leaves that had started to tumble and drift on the cooling autumn breeze.

As forty-eight hours became seventy-two, and seventy-two hours became four horrific days without Alfie, Helen, even in her catatonic state, began to notice that the faces around her grew a little more grim; mouths began to set into thin, hard lines and eyes remained downcast whenever she rustled by. She overheard a great deal of discussion about tides and currents in the bay, and felt a terrible chill run up her spine the morning she came downstairs and heard one senior policeman discussing the odds of finding a *body*.

A body.

They were talking about Alfie's body, his chubby little legs, his cheeky smile and that fuzz of straw-blond hair that refused to stay flat on his head no matter how many times she brushed it straight. Until then she'd still entertained a small ember of hope that he might be brought home eventually, tired and smiling, wrapped in a blanket and demanding fish fingers and beans before a bath and bed. She'd allowed herself to imagine the indulgent smiles and cheers of the locals as Richard carried him back into the house, hoisted triumphantly on his shoulders. But as she heard the serious talk of the operations around her, she realised, suddenly, that the images were nothing more than an indulgent fantasy.

And then, midway through the first week, there was a sudden flurry of excitement. Police examinations of the registrations at the local campsite had discovered a convicted paedophile had been staying at the time of Alfie's disappearance. He had not come forward, but left the very same day that Alfie disappeared. To Helen, it seemed perverse to suddenly wish Alfie abducted by a paedophile. But at least that way there was hope of him being found alive. There was a series of lengthy conversations between Richard and the police that Helen simply couldn't bear to be a part of. But in the end it turned out there was nothing to suggest the man's involvement. He had a watertight alibi playing bingo in Lyme Regis on the day Alfie had disappeared. It seemed it was nothing more than an eerie coincidence. And with the two adults Dora had witnessed on the beach near the Crag still frustratingly elusive, it seemed all other leads were drawing to a dead end. They were back on the downward slope of the rollercoaster, and it seemed the carriage was speeding faster and faster into a deep, dark tunnel.

Time passed in a fog, each new day melting into the last until on the twelfth, the nice policeman with the strong brown hands and the kind face came back to the house. He sat in his usual position in the living room and broke the news to Helen and Richard that the search would be called off the following day and the enquiry taken back to the station. There were no leads, no evidence of foul play and no proof of any suspicious circumstances. It seemed Alfie's disappearance was nothing more than a beach outing gone wrong.

'Nothing more? Nothing more?' Helen had whispered. 'How can you say that? Our son is missing. Until I know what's happened to him how can I give up hope that he is still out there, that he might still be alive? Tell me that. You haven't even found that couple Dora saw. Where are they? What kind of an investigation are you running? They could have our son,' she sobbed. 'They could have our son!'

'Mrs Tide,' the officer had said gently, 'it has been nearly two weeks. We've explored all the possibilities, but I'm afraid we believe it to be most likely that Alfie was playing on the rocks. If he were swept into the ocean he would have stood very little chance. The water is very deep off the promontory there and the currents are strong.' He paused for a moment before continuing. 'I'm afraid, Mr and Mrs Tide, that we may never find his body.'

Helen closed her eyes and put her head in her hands.

'Just a few more days, please, officer,' Richard pleaded. 'If it's a case of money I'm sure . . .'

'It's not about money,' the policeman assured him. 'We'll keep the file open, of course, in case of any developments but we need to scale back the operation, move resources. There will be an inquest at a later date.'

'You can't!' It was Dora. She was standing at the door, her eyes wide with horror, her face drawn and pale. She looked awful. 'You can't do this! You have to keep looking,' she shrieked. 'You have to. He's out there. I know he is.'

Helen turned to look at her daughter. 'Get out,' she hissed.

'But Mum, they can't do this. He's out there.'

'I said get out. You've done enough already.'

'I . . . I . . . I only want . . .' Dora clutched at the door handle, the blood draining from her face. Helen didn't let her continue.

'If it wasn't for you Alfie would still be—'

'Helen!' It was Richard. 'Dora, your mother is distraught. She doesn't mean what she says. Why don't you go into the kitchen? Put the kettle on for us. I'll come and explain what's happening in just a moment.'

Dora stood transfixed in the doorway like a statue, frozen under Helen's icy stare.

'You think it's my fault?' Dora whispered, still staring at Helen.

'Dora, go into the kitchen. Now!' Richard commanded.

Dora turned on her heel and fled from the room and Helen, seeing her go began to rock back and forth in her seat. She bit down on her cheek and tasted blood as a strange keening sound left her body.

'It's my fault. It's *all* my fault. I'm his mother,' she cried, 'I'm his mother. I'm supposed to protect him. He's innocent, just a baby. It's *my* fault, isn't it? I'm the one who was supposed to protect him. Punish me. Punish me. But not my baby.'

It hit her then, like a sledgehammer. It *was* her fault he was missing. It was her fault her baby was gone. A mother was supposed to protect her children. A mother was supposed to fight like a tigress when it came to the safety of her babies. Yet here she was, an abomination, a monster, more concerned with her own selfish pleasures than the care of her children. She had brought this upon Alfie; she had brought this upon all of them and she didn't think she could bear the guilt or the shame of it any longer. If only she hadn't answered his phone call. If only she had said no to meeting him. If only she had stayed home with her children instead of sauntering off to play her sordid games with Tobias. If only . . .

As Helen silently ran through the weight of her unbearable guilt Richard pulled her into his chest and gripped her tightly.

'Ssshhh,' he urged. 'Sssshhh, none of that, you hear me?'

She could make out the thud of his heart through his sweater. It sounded too fast.

The policeman looked down at his shoes. 'I'm so sorry, I really am.' He couldn't meet their eyes. 'On behalf of the whole force I'd like to offer our sincere condolences for your loss.'

Helen let out another sob.

'I'm so sorry, but we really have done all we can; you understand.'

They didn't understand. They couldn't.

But there was nothing more they could say. The search was drawing to a close.

The following day the police packed away their files, drank their last cups of tea in the kitchen, rinsed out their mugs and bade the family a solemn farewell. Even the one remaining journalist, who had stayed doggedly at the end of the drive for the last two days, had packed up her belongings and driven away. The scent of a big story had gone. There were new tragedies to chase. The world, it seemed, had given up on Alfie. And there they were, just the four of them, left to pick up the pieces of their lives, a family in tatters, never to be the same again.

DORA

Present Day

It is obvious from the stillness of the air around her that the flat is empty but Dora still feels compelled to yell out as the heavy metal door slams shut behind her. 'Dan, I'm home!'

Silence.

She throws her weekend bag down by the door and makes her way through to the living room. She is pleased to be back and has been looking forward to seeing Dan, so she is disappointed to find the place empty. Dora walks through the echoing white room until she stands by the closed door to Dan's studio. She knows what lies behind it. It is an austere, concrete-floored room with a soaring skylight and wide glass windows, the perfect sculptor's studio. Dan had fallen in love with the space at first sight and it was at the initial viewing, as he had stalked around the room, stroking the brick walls with his hands, that she had known the flat was meant to be theirs. It is where he designs his sculptures, casts his wax moulds, and pours his bronzes.

Cire perdue. The lost wax method. Memories suddenly come flooding back of their second, or perhaps third date, when Dan had shown her around his modest rented studio in Camden and the handful of completed bronze sculptures awaiting shipment to a gallery in Bristol. They were large, ever so slightly distorted figures of people, in poses that suggested the flash of a camera capturing a random moment in time. An old man stood in one corner, painfully hunched as he reached for something on the floor. A little boy with socks sagging round his ankles was caught in an energetic kick at a football. A tall, elongated figure – a businessman, she assumed, from the briefcase in his hand – strode out confidently, mobile phone to his ear and his mouth open in a brash shout. A tired-looking young woman with a shopping basket slung over one arm stood on tiptoes with her other arm outstretched to an unseen aisle of food. The figures crowded the small workspace with their solid metal presence.

She had walked around them slowly, marvelling at the intricate, lifelike detail on each one – fingernails, hair, a scabby knee. Each was strangely realistic and yet, at the same time, oddly impressionistic in its surreal, slightly stretched dimensions. The harder she had looked at each one, the more they had seemed to blur into indefinable pieces of molten lava.

Dan had explained the painstaking process he undertook to produce each one and she had sat spellbound. She had never really thought about it before. She had supposed he would just take a big lump of metal and chip away at it until the image he had been striving for emerged. But the reality was, of course, very different. She found it fascinating that he should have to produce an initial clay cast, absolutely perfect in every single detail that would then form the basis for his bronze sculpture. When he was happy with the detail in this first sculpture, he would slather it in a layer of wax, and then another layer of clay. And finally, when this wondrous layer cake of clay and wax had been created, the mould would be heated, the wax melted and drained, and a hollow cavern created between the layers of clay into which he would pour his molten bronze.

'It's very expensive. Not a process you want to get wrong,' he admitted.

'No, I can see that,' she marvelled, stroking the bronze sleeve of the businessman. He wore tiny cufflinks in the shape of chess pawns. 'But all that work in clay and wax, just to create a void into which to pour the metal, isn't it frustrating? Doesn't it feel like a waste, just to see it melting away, or being chipped off afterwards? Why not just work in clay?'

'But that's the beauty of it, you see,' exclaimed Dan passionately. 'That moment, when you remove the clay and there it is, like a butterfly emerging from its cocoon, standing before you. It's a moment of truth, in pure bronze. And there's something about bronze that's just so solid; so permanent. It's so *real*.'

'But what about those first sculptures, you know, the ones in clay and wax? You spend so much time on them, only to then discard them. I feel a bit melancholy just thinking of it. *Cire perdue*. It even sounds sad!'

Dan had laughed. 'You are so sentimental. Look at it this way: those earlier sculptures are necessary. They are what give life to this final bronze sculpture that stands before you. If they hadn't existed, this now couldn't exist. It's all part of a process, a life cycle.'

Dora had nodded, still a little unconvinced. 'I just don't know if I'd have the patience,' she admitted.

Dan shook his head. 'It's not patience. It's passion. Or perhaps,' he admitted truthfully, 'more like obsession. I'm obsessed with capturing that moment, that single moment of movement in a human being's life when everything can change. I try to find that moment, and then capture it in a split second; I freeze it in time.' He paused and then shook his head, 'Actually, it's more than that. It's not just about freezing it. The challenge for me is to cast fluid movement permanently, in one of the most fundamentally enduring and fixed materials available. It doesn't get much more permanent than bronze, after all. Transient movement versus enduring solidity, do you see?'

Dora was a little lost; but she knew she loved his sculptures. They were alive and exciting and breathed vitality into the dingy workroom they wandered around. Looking back now, she knows that was the moment she fell in love with him. Seeing him standing there amidst his work, his flushed face illuminated by a shaft of light as dust particles danced all around; she had felt his passion and something warm and fluttering and terrifyingly real had stirred deep within her.

That had been nearly three years ago, and here she is, in the home they share, standing on the other side of a shut door, listening for sounds of him. There is nothing but silence and she knows he is out. She is tempted for a moment to sneak inside the studio and take a peek at his latest work, but then thinks better of it. It doesn't seem quite right without him there. Like spying. There'll be plenty of time to catch up properly. First she needs a cup of tea.

In the kitchen there is evidence of Dan everywhere. Half-drunk mugs of coffee and dirty plates are stacked precariously by the draining board. A pad of scribbles and sketches lies discarded by the telephone. Dora flicks through the pages and glimpses Dan's distinctive hand in the rough sketches of women's necks, arms, legs and shoulders. The images are eerie in their dislocation, an array of dismembered limbs stark in dark charcoal against the whiteness of the page. Next to the pad is a stack of invoices from his suppliers. It is obvious it's been a productive weekend. She is glad. It makes his absence in Dorset more bearable, knowing that he's knuckled down to his new piece. As she turns back towards the sink to rinse out a mug she sees his note on the table. It is held in place by a dirty cereal bowl.

Welcome home babe. We missed you.
Hanging with the Grizzlies.
Come join us xxxx

Dora smiles. 'The Grizzlies' is their private name for the grumpy old men that prop up the bar at their local. She picks up Gormley's water bowl, rinses it out and refills it with fresh water from the tap. It sloshes onto the lino as she places it back on the floor. Maybe she doesn't want tea after all. It is the kind of night that calls for soft jazz and a chilled bottle of white wine, a chance to enjoy the last gasp of the weekend before the realities of Monday morning descend. She switches the kettle off and grabs her keys.

She had made good time on the drive home from Summertown and it is still light as she wanders along the Dalston backstreets towards the pub. All around her the urban sprawl seems to buzz and hum. Returning to London is like being wrapped in a comforting blanket; the reassuring blare of traffic and humanity converging on her until she barely notices individual sounds. It washes over her, a backdrop of noise, like the friendly hum of an old refrigerator. Dora rolls her shoulders to release their tension and suddenly realises how immensely relieved she is to have left behind the static order of Helen's life at Clifftops and the picture-perfect Dorset vistas. It was a confronting visit, and yet she has come away ultimately dissatisfied. She hasn't found what she was looking for.

The whole city seems to be celebrating the first truly warm weekend of the year. A car speeds by with its windows rolled down and hip hop blaring. She passes a couple strolling arm in arm and sees them stop to steal a kiss. As she crosses the road a gaggle of hoodied kids on skateboards sweeps past her, laughing and cursing loudly, full of confidence and the daredevil bravado of youth. The city is pulsating in the glow of early evening sunshine. Dora realises she can't wait to see Dan and quickens her pace.

The Fox is conveniently located a mere stone's throw away from their home. 'Scarily close', Dan had joked. 'We'll be alcoholics before the month is out,' he'd toasted over a bottle of red wine on their first night as homeowners, seated at one of the pub's rickety wooden tables.

Dan and Dora love it there. It is their adopted second home. They'd stumbled in that first time, on a dark winter's afternoon, after the oily estate agent had shown them around the old button factory. It was there, sitting on tatty red velvet banquettes beside the smoky coal fire, that they had gone through the pros and cons of the flat purchase. They'd tried to be rational, tried to maintain a sense of gravity as they'd discussed the leaking roof and worn out floorboards, the dilapidated kitchen and stained wall tiles, but inside they both knew the space was meant to be theirs and as they'd talked their mounting excitement had been impossible to conceal. It was there that they had exchanged Cheshire cat grins and clinked their handled pint glasses together, sealing the deal on their first home. And it was there they had returned just a few months later after the contracts had been signed and the keys collected, to celebrate and drink and giggle nervously at the enormity of the project they had taken on.

Dora pushes open the heavy wooden door to the pub and enters its dark interior. There is the customary collection of men slumped at the bar, all beer bellies and jowls. She can see Dan on the other side, sitting at his usual table with his head bent over one of the Sunday supplements and a half-drunk pint of bitter in front of him. She takes a moment to watch him, enjoying the rare perspective it gives her, a moment to regard him with unobserved detachment, as others might.

He is sitting on a favourite wheel-backed chair. It is clearly too small for his long, lean frame, but Dora knows by now that he will never change. No matter how many times she tells him he looks uncomfortable he always gravitates back to that one spot. He seems to like the hard, bone-jarring seat and the cramped confines of its austere wooden frame. He sits there now, his long legs wrapped underneath him and his shoulders hunched over the table, like a modern-day Gulliver among the Lilliputians. He is dressed in his work overalls and she can see a smear of red clay across his cheek. He has obviously come straight from the studio, not really surprising judging by the state she has found the flat in. His lovely face is still, his brown eyes fixed on the papers before him; and he must be tired, she realises, for he is wearing his gold-rimmed glasses; he doesn't usually bother. His black hair skims the tops of his ears and is beginning to curl at the nape of his neck. He'll need a haircut soon. He turns a page of the supplement and then moves his hand unconsciously onto Gormley's head who is lying faithfully at his feet. The Labrador opens one eye and nuzzles his nose into his master's palm in gratitude.

Dora understands how Gormley feels. It was Dan's hands that she had first noticed the night they'd met. She'd been drinking warm Chardonnay at a friend of a friend's book launch when someone had introduced them. 'Dora. You should meet Dan. He's Alice's cousin, and a genius artist.'

Dora didn't know who Alice was . . . someone attached to the book, she assumed, but she didn't mind. It was as he'd reached out to greet her that she'd noticed his hands. They were huge and rough with heavily lined palms that felt raspy to the touch. His knuckles were marked and gnarly and a livid red scar ran across the back of his left hand. Dora stared, entranced. They were a workman's hands; the hands of someone who knew accidents and pain, hurt and healing; the hands of someone who knew who they were, and where they were going; the hands of a real man; the hands of someone who had already lived a life. She had stood there, wordlessly, as he had greeted her, trying to control the slow flush spreading across her face; she couldn't help it; she couldn't stop thinking about how those hands would feel on her skin. She'd been lucky enough to find out later that night.

Dora hadn't planned on falling in love and, at first, she had comforted herself with the fact it was nothing but pure lust; just a hot, hungry sexual attraction she couldn't resist. She liked the way he made her feel in bed, the way he made her forget who and where she was. When she was with Dan she found she could just live in the moment, and with him, the moment felt good. She didn't plan on opening herself up to him. She didn't plan on laying bare any of her secrets. They simply met up, had dinner, fell into bed and then let themselves out of each other's flats the next morning, skulking away to complete their respective walks of shame until the next time.

But then something had changed. It had crept up on her when she wasn't looking, a feeling that had sneaked into her heart and made leaving him each morning harder and harder. She found herself thinking of him when he wasn't there, longing for his arms around her and his lips on her skin. But more than that, she wanted to spend time with him out of the bedroom. She wanted long, snowy walks on Primrose Hill and hand-holding in the cinema. She wanted newspapers and freshly squeezed orange juice on Saturday mornings, and lazy Sunday afternoon pints with friends in the sunshine. Most of all, she realised, she wanted to share her life with him.

The thought terrified her. And yet losing him wasn't an option either – he made her feel the most sane she had felt in a long time, and so, fighting the voice inside her head that screamed 'Don't do it! Don't let him get too close!', she had let him into her life – and her heart.

As if sensing her gaze Dan looks up from his seat across the bar. He frowns in her direction, his eyes refocusing for an instant, and then breaks into a broad grin. He is standing by the time she reaches the other side of the room.

'Hey, you're back already. Fantastic.' He pulls her into his arms, planting a generous kiss on her lips. 'How are you?'

'OK. I made good time, didn't I?' she agrees, checking her watch. 'The traffic wasn't too bad. I guess everyone decided to stay put and enjoy the sunshine. What are you doing in here on such a beautiful evening? I thought you'd have your head down in the studio, or at least be out the back here, soaking up the last rays of sun.'

'Nah, you know me. I fancied a bit of good old-fashioned pub grunge. But how are you?' He asks again, his eyes full of concern. 'Are you tired? Do you want some fresh air? Shall we move outside? Would you like a drink?'

'Dan, chill out, will you. I'm pregnant. Not infirm. I'm fine just here. And what I would really love to drink is a double gin and tonic, ice and a slice of lime . . .'

Dan gives her a worried look.

'Joking!' She holds up her hands in supplication. 'I'll have an orange juice. Straight up.'

Dan lets out a palpable sigh of relief and nods his head. 'Coming right up.'

Gormley is thumping his tail in languid acknowledgment of Dora's arrival and so she bends down to pat him. 'Hey, Gormley. Did you miss me?'

Gormley thumps his tail again and yawns, showing off a fleshy pink tongue and blasting her with warm, meaty breath.

'I'll take that as a yes.'

Dora settles herself at the table and reaches across for the newspaper Dan has been reading. It is some article about environmentally friendly house renovations; all grey-water tanks, compost buckets and solar panels. Nice if you can afford it, she thinks, pushing the pages back towards Dan's empty seat. When Dan returns he places a glass of orange juice in front of her before folding himself back into his seat.

'So how was the trip?' he asks.

'Oh, fine. I missed you and Gormley though. How was your weekend? Did you get much done?' It is a clumsy deflection but Dan lets it pass for now. She knows he is a patient man. He will bide his time.

'All good here. I spent the entire weekend in the studio.'

'I can tell.'

Dan looks at her quizzically.

'The flat . . . it's a tip!'

'Ah, yes. Sorry about that. I was going to tidy up, but Gormley here, he bullied me into coming to the pub to celebrate. He wouldn't take no for an answer.'

'And what are you both celebrating?' Dora asks with a smile.

'Oh you know,' Dan throws his arms out expansively, 'the

sunshine, a free bone from the butcher, the start of a new sculpture, you coming home . . .' he pauses and looks her in the eye, 'the baby.'

Dora reaches across for her drink and takes a big gulp. It is thick and treacly – the sort of orange juice that has spent too long collecting dust in a bottle at the back of a shelf and not enough time soaking up the sunshine on a tree somewhere glorious in Spain. It leaves a furry pulp on her tongue. 'So how's the sculpture coming along?' she asks. 'Are you going to tell me *anything* about it?'

Dan looks at her evenly. 'Not this one, sorry, but it's a surprise. I'm really pleased with it though. I started the clay model this weekend. It's different, for me. A real "departure" as they say.'

'Sounds interesting.'

'Yeah, I'm excited. The Grimshaw commissions are all well and good. They'll pay the bills, but they're not exactly ground-breaking, are they?'

Dora nods.

'Oh, before I forget, your dad called.'

'Did he?' Dora pauses. 'Everything OK?'

'Yes, all fine. He invited us for lunch. Do you fancy it? I can make up an excuse if you don't want to go . . .'

Dora thinks for a minute. 'I suppose we ought to. It's been ages since we went to their place. Besides, we should tell him our news, I guess?'

'*You guess?* Does that mean . . . ?' Dan trails off.

Dora shrugs her shoulders. 'Well, I've told Mum now, haven't I?'

'OK,' says Dan slowly, clearly confused. 'So tell me, how did it all go down there? How was your mum?'

'Oh, Mum was Mum. Nothing ever changes.'

'So no breakthrough?'

Dora pauses for a moment. 'I guess not.'

'Really?' Dan asks, taking a sip from his pint. 'She must have been pleased about the baby though?'

Dora can hear the hope in Dan's voice. She feels his expectation weigh heavily on her and she chooses her words carefully in response. 'Mmm . . . more startled, I think. Pleased? I'm not so sure. She so rarely gives anything away.'

'But she must have said something?' Dan pushes. 'It's not every day you're told you're going to be a grandmother.'

Dora doesn't know how to explain the conversation she had with Helen. She doesn't like to tell him of her tears, of how she'd screamed out in frustration and stormed out of the conservatory, and their subsequent awkwardness with each other before she had climbed back into her car the next day and driven home. Dan knows a little about Alfie, but he can't know, can never understand just how much it has affected them all. She doesn't want to disappoint him, she really doesn't. But she also knows she can't lie. 'We talked. We talked about the pregnancy . . . and about Alfie. I finally found the courage to ask her if she blamed me for what had happened.'

'What did she say?'

Dora thinks for a moment. 'She told me it was time to *let it go*.'

'There you go then, and she's right, you know.'

Dora shakes her head. 'But she couldn't say it, you see. She couldn't say, "Dora, it's not your fault." '

Dan rubs at a smear of clay on his hand. 'I'm sure what she meant was—'

'No.' Dora shakes her head. 'I'm sick of making excuses for her. I've made so many in the past. But I'm tired of it now. She told me I was only a child back then. She told me to let it go. But she couldn't answer me when I asked her if she still thought it was my fault. So you see, I've been right all along. She's always blamed me for losing Alfie.' She feels tears welling up in her eyes as she speaks the words out loud and Dan reaches across and gives her hand a gentle squeeze.

'Well, perhaps you have your answer then. As painful as it is, perhaps you needed to go down to Dorset to discover that you won't ever be able to rebuild the bridge between you and your mother. But you can certainly tell yourself that you've tried, right? Perhaps, if your relationship with her is as dysfunctional as it sounds, well . . . maybe you shouldn't see her for a while. If that's what will make you feel better?'

Dora nods and bites her lip. 'I just hoped . . . you know . . . I just wanted . . . *she's my mother*.' The tears are running silently down her cheeks.

'I know.' Dan gives her hand another squeeze.

'There was this time,' Dora said, 'ages ago. Before Alfie, before he was even born. We hadn't been at Clifftops that long and Dad was away. A huge storm blew in off the sea.' She gives a little laugh. 'I thought the house was going to blow away.'

Dan smiles at her indulgently.

'Cassie and I climbed into bed with Mum and the three of us lay there listening to the wild weather as it battered the house. We just huddled up together, warm under the duvet, sharing the moment. And do you know what Mum said to me then?'

Dan shook his head.

'I'll never forget it. She looked down at me with the softest look in her eyes and she said, "Don't be scared. We've got each other. Nothing else matters."' Dora gives a little sob. 'I believed then that she loved me, that she'd do anything for me. But here I am.' She shrugs. 'I went to her for help. I went to her for answers. And she as good as turned me away.'

Dan strokes her hand with his warm fingers.

'But I suppose it actually doesn't matter now. It still doesn't change anything, does it? It still happened. We all still live with it every day.'

'Yes, but you have to accept it, Dora. Accept it and move on. Live *your* life. Live it to the best of your ability with the people who *do* love you surrounding you. Don't dwell on the past.'

Dora bristles. 'I'm not dwelling on the past, Dan. I *am*

living my life, right now, the one that was given to me, the only life I have . . . with all the good, and all the messed-up *shit* that comes with it. But I just can't ignore this . . . this *thing* that happened to me. To all of us. I can't forget him.' She stops, trying to control the tears, and looks up at Dan imploringly. 'Can't you understand? *Alfie* happened to me. To us. And I just can't forget him. I can't let go. And if I can't forget him, can't live with my part in what happened, then how can I expect to move forwards and be a good parent, a good mother to an innocent child? It's a whole new life, for Christ's sake. And it will be my responsibility. It's too much. I don't think I can do it.'

'It's *our* responsibility, Dora. I'm with you in this too, remember? I'll be right here.'

Dora looks up at Dan again. His eyes are filled with so much love and concern that it makes her want to weep. 'Oh God, these hormones. They're doing my head in. Sorry,' she apologises and reaches for the hanky he holds out to her.

'Dora, I don't know how to help you any more. But one thing is for sure; you need to make a decision. Time is not on our side.'

'I know that.'

'And you know how I feel, don't you?' He looks at her earnestly. 'Dora, I want to keep this baby, desperately. But if you don't think you're ready . . . if you need to make a different choice . . . well . . .' His voice trails off.

'I thought Dorset would help. You know, going back, remembering . . . talking to Mum. But it feels like I still only have one tiny piece of the puzzle. Does that make sense?'

Dan shakes his head. He doesn't understand.

'I just need a little more time.'

Dan sighs. He grabs his glass and swallows back the last of his pint. 'I think I'm ready to go home. You?'

She leaves her glass of orange juice on the table, half drunk. A ring of condensation has formed underneath it, creating an ugly white stain on the dark wood. She rubs at it half-heartedly and then stands to follow Dan out of the pub.

They walk back through the half darkness in silence. Dora wills Dan to stop and take her hand, but he strides on the whole way, just a pace ahead of her with Gormley trotting along loyally at his heels. This isn't how she'd imagined their reunion. The comforting sensations of the city have left her now. She hears the shriek of a siren in the distance and sees the ugly smears of litter, broken glass and dog shit strewn around the street. Even the familiar silhouette of the button factory seems cloaked in ominous shadows. They plod silently up the stairwell and it is a relief when Dan puts his key in the front door and lets them into the flat.

'Do you want a drink?' she asks, keen to defuse the tension between them.

'No. I'm going to put in a bit more work before bed.'

Dora feels the rebuff, but lets him go without another word.

She stands at the sofa and watches him walk towards the studio, push on the door, turn on the lights and then shut the door definitively behind him, closing himself off from the rest of the world, and more importantly she knows, from her. She sighs. She knows what he wants to hear. She knows he needs to hear her say that she wants this baby; that it is the best thing that has happened to them; that she can't wait to become a mother. But she just can't. She is terrified. She is terrified of the change it will bring to their relationship and terrified by the responsibilities of parenthood and, most of all, terrified of losing not just this tiny being growing inside her, but of everything that she and Dan have built together. Families are fragile. She knows this better than anyone and Dan, for all his talk, doesn't understand. He can't, because he has not lived her life. For so long she has protected herself. She lived like one of Dan's sculptures, hollowed out, her warm clay interior and pliable wax coating removed until there was nothing inside of her but a vast, empty space. Alone, she coped, hidden from the pain and the hurt that could come from giving too much of yourself. But she isn't alone any more. There is Dan, and now there is their baby. How has she got herself into this mess?

With a sigh she turns to survey the living room. The few surfaces they own are cluttered with the detritus of their lives. She ushers Gormley into the kitchen before grabbing a black bin bag and working methodically, dumping old papers and bills, dead flowers, empty wine bottles, half-eaten crusts of toast and the stumps of misshapen candles into the rubbish sack. She stacks Dan's art books back onto the bookshelves and carries dirty mugs and dishes into the kitchen. It takes her twenty minutes to do the washing up, and another ten to wipe down the dusty surfaces and whiz the vacuum round, but by the time she has finished the flat looks pristine again.

She looks back at the closed door to the studio and can just make out movement beneath the gap in the door. He is lost in his work, or angry at her still. Either way she knows she'll be going to bed alone.

That night she dreams she is diving for coins. The water is green and murky but she can see them glinting silver on the bottom, drawing her down. She dives again and again, her hands scrabbling through the silt, her lungs burning as she seizes upon the cold metal and returns to the surface each time with a triumphant rush of air.

There is one more down there. She has seen it winking at her. She can't leave it behind. With a final gasp she forces her body down below the surface. She can feel her lungs ache but the coin is within reach, she knows it; just a few more metres.

Her hands stretch before her in the gloom and she feels grit sift through her fingers. Nothing.

She has to return to the surface; her body needs the air, but her mind is insistent: it is there, just one more second, keep going.

Her hands pat blindly at the ground and suddenly she touches something; not cold metal but something warm, something strangely flesh-like. Something human. Her eyes open wide with panic in the darkness. She can't breathe. Her body is on fire, her mind dizzy. She tries to rise to the surface but the thing she has touched has hold of her now. Fingers, insistent and strong, grip her, refusing to let go.

She pulls one more time, her body thrashing under the water as her final survival instincts kick in.

But the hand's grip is firm and tight. *It will not let her go.*

With a final desperate wrench, she pulls away from its death-like hold and opens her mouth to scream.

She wakes to the shriek of her alarm clock. It is seven a.m. She turns it off and lies in bed for a moment, listening to the sound of rain drumming on the roof and water dripping rhythmically into the buckets and pans scattered around the bed, as the remnants of her nightmare fade away. Another wet Monday morning: she doesn't know how she is going to muster the energy to shower, dress and get herself on the Tube to work, particularly with the revolting queasy feeling already welling up inside her. She hasn't even opened her eyes yet, for God's sake. The last few mornings she's felt like this Dan has been so sweet. He's made her tea and toast and brought it to her in bed. She reaches out a hand for him now but finds nothing but empty space. His pillow lies chastely next to hers, perfectly plumped. He hasn't come to bed so he must have crashed out on the couch in the studio. She hates it when they go to sleep separately, still upset with each other.

She staggers into the bathroom and loses herself under a jet of steaming water for a few minutes, then dresses and heads into the kitchen, swallowing back bile as she goes. She makes tea and throws down a bowl of dog biscuits for Gormley before noticing the furry bulge sticking out of the black bin bag she filled the night before. Reaching in she pulls out the mystery object by one fuzzy leg. It is a teddy bear, the old-fashioned kind with soft tawny fur and moveable joints. He still wears his price tag: £65; not cheap. Dan must have bought him for the baby. As teddy bears go he is really rather sweet: a round podgy tummy set off by oversized paws and ears. The sight of him in her hands, his fixed black eyes looking up at her with a sad, doleful expression is almost too much to take. She puts him to one side on the kitchen table, ties off the bin bag, and sits gazing at the bear for a few more minutes. Then, before she can change her mind she reaches for the telephone.

'Hello?' The voice at the other end answers midway through the first ring, as though the person has been standing by the phone all this time, just waiting for her call.

She takes a deep breath. 'Dad, it's me . . . it's Dora.'

CASSIE

Ten Years Earlier

Cassie sat on her bed surrounded by revision notes. She was supposed to be studying for her history A level, but her brain felt like mush and all she could think about was the little butterfly brooch tucked away at the back of her bedside table. There was an itch spreading across her skin and she couldn't ignore it.

Kicking her notes to one side, she reached across and pulled the diamond and mother-of-pearl ornament out of the drawer, turning it over and over in her hand. It was so pretty, shimmering its muted pastel colours back at her, even in the gloom of a rain-soaked afternoon. She gazed at it a moment longer before unhooking the clasp and testing its pin for sharpness against her fingertips. It was good enough.

She pushed her sweater sleeve up past her elbow and pressed the point against the pale skin in the crook of her arm, the spot where the skin was most sensitive and the results of her work could be hidden. Then, sucking in her breath, she pressed harder and winced as the metal punctured her flesh. Ruby red blood sprang up around the pin and as she watched the beads bubble and form she dragged the spike down in one long, painful stroke, exhaling deeply as the metal did its work. She repeated the action several more times, watching with satisfaction as a crazy criss-cross pattern sprang up on her skin and the warm blood began to seep down her arms. Then, feeling a little dizzy, she lay back on the bed and let the pain wash over her. It felt good to feel something.

As the knife-sharp sting gradually subsided to a dull ache, Cassie returned to the present. The world flooded in around her once more and she lay there for a while just thinking about how much her life sucked. It sucked more than Jessica Goldstein getting off with Charlie Simpson right in front of her at the rugby club dance last weekend. It sucked more than her mum telling her in no uncertain terms that she could not get her belly button pierced before she passed her A levels. It sucked more than being stuck in her bedroom listening to the dull thump of Dora's pop music while she tried to concentrate on her history revision. And it sucked even more than the incessant rain belting down outside keeping her trapped in the house like a prisoner, again. Yes. Life sucked, more than all of those things put together, and then some.

She pressed a tissue to her bloody arm and then reached out and banged on the wall. 'Turn it down, will you?'

Dora's latest girl-band fixation shrank a decibel or two until it was just a dull, unfathomable noise from the other side of the wall; it was slightly better, but she still couldn't concentrate. The Reformation really was *so* boring and with Dora safely secreted in her bedroom, the house lay quiet and inviting below. Her mother had left over an hour ago – Violet was staying for a few days and they'd gone off in her battered little car to trawl some local farmers' market. Richard was safely ensconced at work and the only other sound she could hear was the faraway buzz of a saw on wood; probably Bill tending to the garden somewhere. The house was all hers.

She pulled her sleeve down over the wound, tucked the brooch back into its hiding place and then left her bedroom, tiptoeing silently down the landing past Dora's door before heading on to the guest room where Violet had set up camp. She tapped very lightly on the door, just in case, and then pushed it open, ducking inside and shutting it behind her in one smooth movement. She stood, listening for a moment, but Dora's music continued its muffled thump and she knew she was alone.

Violet's suitcase lay open at one end of the bed, a colourful array of clothes spilling out across the floor. Cassie plucked at a few of the garments. Violet's taste was tight and bright and Cassie winced at each in turn as she held them up to her body in the mirror – not her style. She replaced each item carefully where she had found it and then moved across to the dressing table. Violet was not a tidy woman. The surface was strewn with bottles and jars, compacts of pressed powder, lipsticks and eye shadow, jewellery and scarves. She reached for a bottle of perfume and sniffed at the nozzle; a pungent floral scent raced up her nostrils. She put the bottle back and reached instead for an expensive-looking moisturiser. She gave it a suspicious sniff before smothering a dollop onto her face, then seized a ruby red lipstick and smeared it over her lips. She finished the look with a heavy ring of black kohl around each eye and stood back to assess her reflection in the mirror. She looked like one of Dora's old Sindy dolls after a particularly frenzied attack with the felt-tip pens. Beneath the make-up Cassie saw violet bags the colour of four-day-old bruises; she hadn't been sleeping well recently. She wiped the lipstick off with a tissue and scrubbed at her ringed eyes.

Bored with the oddments on the dressing table Cassie turned to survey the rest of the room. There was a splayed paperback lying on the bedside table that, according to the quote splashed across the front, promised a 'raunchy and irresistible' read. Violet's scarlet lace nightdress peeked out from underneath one pillow, and several pairs of impossibly high heels stood lined up on the floor underneath the window ledge, but other than that the room held little of interest. Cassie slipped out into the hallway and wandered downstairs in search of other forbidden treasures.

Her mother's office was the next obvious place to try. Since Alfie, Helen had taken to spending even more time cloistered behind its door, her head bent over some book or other. Cassie sometimes wondered if she even remembered she had two daughters who were still very much alive, the amount of attention she paid them some days. Still, there were certainly benefits to being ignored. She got away with things most of her friends would have been grounded for weeks for.

The room was dark as she entered and she could smell a heady mix of paper, leather and Helen's familiar lemony scent hanging on the air. Cassie flicked on the overhead light and moved to the desk. She sat herself in the leather writer's chair and swivelled round and round for a few moments, until she felt dizzy and had to stop. The surface of the desk was covered in papers. She plucked at a few and scanned the text, before placing them back on the surface. More boring work stuff. She rummaged through the desk drawers, discarding a packet of extra strong mints, some of her mother's personalised stationery, elastic bands and paper clips, old biros and post-it notes. She was about to give up when her fingers grazed the edges of something stuffed right at the back of the drawer. Curiously, she grabbed at the object and pulled it out.

Cassie's heart skipped a beat when she saw what she held: a bundle of Alfie's baby photos. They were worn and tatty, as if aged by a thousand caresses and stained by a flood of tears. Cassie stared at them for a moment, taking in her brother's wide toothy smile and brilliant blue eyes. In one he sported a large scab across his forehead: Cassie could still remember the awful sound of his head connecting with the coffee table and the piercing wail that had followed. In another he sat on a swing, his chubby little legs flailing wildly as he went higher and higher into the blue sky. And in another he peered up at the camera from beneath a voluminous, floppy straw hat with flowers decorating its brim; one of their grandmother's, she supposed. As she sifted through the images an uncomfortable lump formed at the back of her throat. She shoved them back into the drawer and slid it shut with a bang. That would teach her for snooping.

She was just double-checking for telltale signs of her spying and planning her exit when the telephone rang. Without thinking, Cassie reached for the handset.

'Hello?'

'Helen, is that you? Don't hang up.'

Cassie swallowed. She didn't recognise the man's voice, but there was a desperation in his words that made her pause.

'Helen?'

'Yes,' she whispered.

'Helen, just listen to me. Please. I'm going out of my mind here. I need to see you. I know you've said you can't have anything to do with me, but I can't let you go. I can't eat. I can't sleep. I certainly can't paint. God knows, I've tried, but nothing feels right without you. I love you. It's as simple as that. Don't you feel the same way? Don't you think of me at all?'

Cassie was frozen to the spot, paralysed by the words spilling from the telephone.

'Helen, say something, please!' the man urged. 'I beg you.'

At a loss for what else to do, Cassie placed the receiver gently back on the hook and ran quickly from her mother's study, her face burning with shock and anger.

She was shivering on the patio, puffing on an illicit Marlboro Light when Violet came upon her.

'It's OK,' Violet said as she leapt in alarm, 'I won't tell. Got a spare one?'

Cassie breathed a sigh of relief and handed over the packet. She watched as Violet, clutching a cocktail glass in one hand, struggled to free a cigarette from the packet, her bracelets jangling wildly with her endeavours. She eventually managed, stuck one between her red lips and leaned in to accept Cassie's offer of a light. For just a second the flare of the match lit up Violet's round face, before they were both plunged into darkness again. They stood side by side, clutching themselves for warmth, and puffed on the cigarettes companionably.

'You wouldn't believe it was almost summer, would you?' laughed Violet. 'It's bloomin' freezing out!'

'No,' agreed Cassie. She thought she'd try a little small talk. 'So, how was the market?'

'Oh, muddier than Glastonbury and full of hippies selling over-priced organic honey and hemp clothes. Not really my scene, to be honest.'

Cassie smiled in the darkness.

'There was a beautiful flower stall, though, with some gorgeous hand-tied bouquets. I enjoyed that.'

Cassie knew Violet ran her own florist's and nodded politely. 'You enjoy your work, don't you?'

'Yes,' said Violet. 'I do. I'm lucky. I couldn't stand to spend my days doing something I hated, like so many poor people end up doing. I love flowers. Oh, I know lots of people think they're frivolous and unnecessary, but imagine the birth of a baby without a celebratory bouquet, or a bride walking down the aisle without an arrangement of beautiful flowers in her hands; a sick person in hospital with nothing pretty to look at to cheer their spirits, or a grave without a floral tribute?'

Cassie winced at the last example but Violet was lost in her monologue and didn't seem to notice.

'My work marks the passing of time, just like the very seasons the plants themselves grow from. It celebrates all those important moments in life, and follows us from beginning to end.' Violet shook her head in wonder. 'A florist's work is actually quite wonderful when you think about it.'

Cassie nodded. She'd never thought of it like that before.

'And how are you, Cassie dear? How is life treating you?'

'Oh, you know.' Cassie scuffed at the moss on a paving slab with the toe of her trainer. 'It's OK.'

'I remember my A-level year. Pure torture. All I wanted to do was hang out with my friends and party.'

Cassie nodded in agreement.

'So, any nice boys on the scene I should know about? Don't worry,' she added hastily, 'I won't tell your mother.'

Cassie shook her head. 'Not really.'

'You surprise me, a pretty girl like you. I'd have thought you'd have boys beating down the door.'

Cassie eyed Violet evenly in the darkness. For a split second she wondered about telling her, but then she changed her mind. Violet was cool, but she didn't really know if she could trust her.

'What about Dora?' Violet continued. 'Has she got a boyfriend?'

Cassie shrugged her shoulders. 'I don't know. We don't talk about stuff like that. We sort of keep to ourselves these days.'

Violet took another drag on her cigarette and exhaled smoke upwards into the night sky. 'It's been tough for you girls, hasn't it? How do you think your folks are holding up?'

Cassie shrugged again. 'They're miserable. We all are.'

Violet gave a little nod. 'Yes, it's going to take time. You must be looking forward to university though? A fresh start?'

Cassie swallowed and gave a little nod. 'Did you go to university?'

'Me?' Violet let out a little laugh. 'Oh no. I wasn't clever enough for that. Left that to your mother, didn't I? I was very easily distracted back then.' She let out a little giggle. 'Yes, far too easily distracted . . . and between you and me, the thought of three more years of study horrified me. I couldn't wait to get into the real world . . . get a job, earn some money, start being really independent.'

Cassie looked up at her with interest. 'So you don't regret not going?'

'Oh, I don't know about that. Looking back now I don't know why I was in such a rush to join the real world. Another three years of larking about wouldn't have hurt – and it might have helped with the old love life too. Apparently almost twenty per cent of people meet their future spouse at university. Did you know that, Cass?' Violet took another long drag on her cigarette. 'Twenty per cent! Just think, your Mr Right is probably out there, waiting for you right now.'

'Hmmm . . . perhaps,' said Cassie with a small smile. 'I'm sure *your* Mr Right is still out there too, somewhere.'

'Do you think?' asked Violet. 'Well, that would be nice. One can but hope.'

They stood side by side in silence, smoking and shivering until Cassie steeled her nerves enough to direct the conversation to where her thoughts had been all afternoon.

'Do you think Dad is Mum's Mr Right?'

Violet's head swung up in surprise. 'Yes, of course; why, don't you?'

Cassie shrugged her shoulders. 'I'm not sure.'

'Your parents are made for each other, Cassie.'

'Mmmm . . .' Cassie thought again about the insistent voice at the end of the telephone: *I love you . . . don't you think of me at all?* Who was he?

'Trust me, Cassie,' continued Violet, swigging at her cocktail, 'what those two have been through is enough to damage the strongest of relationships. But they'll be fine. It's just going to take a little time to heal.'

Cassie looked up into the darkness. The heavy cloud had cleared finally and she could see a smattering of silver stars dancing in the night sky. *A little time to heal.* Was that really all they needed?

'Yes,' said Violet quietly, 'it's just going to take you all a bit of time.' She cleared her throat suddenly. 'And in the meantime, roll on September . . . heading off to carve out your own future . . . it will do you good, Cassie. I bet you can't wait, can you?'

Cassie nodded again, but stayed silent, hoping the effects of the alcohol would encourage Violet to keep talking, but she suddenly seemed to have clammed up.

'Gosh, it's really cold out here,' she said finally. 'We should go inside, Cass, before they all start to wonder where we've got to.'

Cassie nodded, disappointed not to have uncovered even the slightest hint at whom the strange man at the end of the telephone might have been.

'Oh, and not a word about the ciggies, OK?'

'Sure,' agreed Cassie, following a tottering Violet through the back door and into the warmth of the kitchen.

It surprised no one more than Cassie that she passed her exams; she opened the envelope and stared down at the white slip of paper, feeling disbelief and a cold, creeping dread as she read through her results.

'Well?' asked Helen nervously from the other side of the breakfast table.

She nodded. 'I passed.'

'All of them?'

'Yes.'

The relief seemed to temporarily jolt her parents out of their grief-stricken stupor. Richard even opened a bottle of champagne over one of Helen's less disastrous dinners that night and they toasted her with Daphne and Alfred's best crystal glasses.

'Well done, Cassie, you've made us very proud.'

Cassie knew she didn't deserve their pride but she threw back the champagne anyway. It was sour and fizzy in her mouth.

'So I guess that means Edinburgh this September,' added Helen, a little sadly.

Cassie noticed Dora's head sink a little lower over her plate. She didn't envy her sister, stuck in Dorset, rattling around their ghost house for another two years.

'We'll have to go shopping,' said Richard. 'Go and buy you a few things for your new room. It will be fun taking you up there. I haven't been to Edinburgh in years.'

Cassie decided it was as good a time as any to broach the

subject. 'Actually, Dad,' she started, 'I was wondering if I could take the train up to Edinburgh – by myself? I think I'd like to do the first bit on my own, you know, get settled into halls, meet a few people.' She saw her mother and father exchange a glance but she carried on anyway. 'You could all come and visit me after a few weeks, see how I'm getting on. I'll be able to show you around properly by then, and I'll be ready to see a few friendly faces from home. You could come too, Dora.' Her well-rehearsed spiel petered out and she waited with bated breath for their response.

Helen reached for her glass of water. Richard placed his cutlery down on his plate and folded his fingers together carefully, a sure sign that a 'discussion' was about to take place.

'You want to go up there on your own?' he asked. 'Take the train?'

Cassie nodded and cut into the last piece of chicken on her plate, refusing to meet his eye.

'But how will you manage all of your things?'

'I won't be taking that much, not at first. Just a few clothes, some books, a bit of bedding. I can buy most things up there anyway, right?' She looked around at them all again and smiled encouragingly. 'I just like the idea of striking off on my own, carving out my own future.' She deliberately chose the same words Violet had used. They sounded good, like something her parents would approve of. 'You understand, don't you . . . after everything that's happened?' She held her breath. This was the closest she had come to mentioning Alfie since the funeral last year. She didn't know if she'd overstepped the mark or not.

Richard gave a slow nod and cleared his throat. 'I suppose I do. Helen, what do you think?'

Helen sighed. 'I can understand you wanting some space. Are you sure it will be safe? Won't it be a little lonely? Most of the other students will have their parents with them and we'll certainly *try* not to embarrass you. We really don't mind the drive. We could make a weekend of it?'

'You can still come, Mum, just in a few weeks, once I'm settled in.'

'Well it would be fun for us to come and visit you there, wouldn't it, Helen?' Richard tried again, summoning up an enthusiastic tone at last. 'Maybe we could make the trip just before Christmas, combine it with some shopping and a nice hotel?'

'Yes,' agreed Cassie, seizing upon the idea. 'It's supposed to be lovely up there at that time of year.' Finally, they were getting somewhere.

'And you'll be OK travelling all that way on your own? You'll have to change trains in London. You won't get lost?' Helen worried again.

'Mum, I'm about to leave home. If I can't navigate my way from Dorset to Edinburgh on the train then I'm really going to be in trouble, aren't I?'

'Mmmm . . .' murmured Helen. The worried frown had returned to her face.

'So your heart is set on it?' asked Richard one final time.

'Yes,' said Cassie.

'Well, I suppose it will be OK.' Richard paused. 'But if you change your mind, it's no problem. I'd be happy to drive you.'

'I know, Dad, thanks.' She knew she wouldn't change her mind.

'Could you pass the water, dear?'

Cassie breathed a small sigh of relief. It seemed to be the end of the matter.

Richard leaned over and passed the jug across the table to Helen. Cassie noticed Helen's little jump of surprise as Richard's fingers accidentally grazed hers, as if his touch had burnt her. Yes, it would be good to leave.

*

The night before Cassie left, Dora tapped quietly at her bedroom door. Cassie let her in and watched as her sister eyed the oversized rucksack propped by her bed.

'All packed then?' she asked.

'Yep.' Too late, Cassie saw Dora's eyes flick to the vivid red hatch marks streaking up her arm. Hurriedly she pulled down her sleeves and threw herself onto her bed. She blocked out her sister's horrified look and, willing her not to say anything, returned to frantically scribbling in her diary as a heavy silence settled around the room.

Dora took the hint and grabbed an old *Cosmopolitan* from a stack next to Cassie's bed and began flicking through the pages carelessly. 'So, what time are you off?'

'Mum's dropping me at the station at nine.'

There was another pause.

'You're *so* lucky.'

'Am I?'

'Yes! You get to escape, start afresh, somewhere completely new.'

Cassie eyed her sister. 'University isn't exactly the be-all and end-all you know, Dora. It's just glorified school. You still have people telling you what to do and when to do it, what assignments to write and when to hand them in . . . which books to read and exams to sit. It's not *real* freedom. It's not real escape, is it?'

'It's better than nothing!' Dora wailed plaintively. 'I'm going to be stuck here on my own. Just me and Mum . . . and Dad, when he's around.' Dora paused for a moment to stare at a 'position of the month' feature, her eyes boggling, before flicking the page. 'Can you imagine anything more awful?'

'Mmm . . .' Cassie was chewing on her pen lid. She wouldn't want to be in Dora's shoes either. 'It'll be all right,' she lied. 'You'll be out of here too before you know it.'

'Can I come and visit you sometime?'

Cassie went quiet for a very long time. 'Yes of course. If Mum and Dad let you, that is.'

Dora nodded. They both knew how erratic and strange their parents' moods could be now; how one minute they would be cloyingly protective, demanding to know the ins and outs of every single social interaction or engagement, only then to be weirdly absent and distracted the next, as if they barely remembered the girls existed at all.

'Sometimes I'd give anything just to get away from here,' Dora announced suddenly. 'I can't understand why Mum and Dad stay. I think it's making things worse. You know, if we had all just left, had a fresh start somewhere . . . or gone back to London. Maybe it would be a bit easier. Maybe we would feel like a family again.'

'Maybe,' said Cassie.

'But then if Alfie is out there, somewhere, he wouldn't know how to find us, would he?'

Cassie shook her head. Dora still didn't get it. 'I don't actually think Mum and Dad want to go back to how it used to be. That's the problem,' she said. 'They enjoy the misery. They love wallowing in it.'

'I don't know . . .' Dora was sceptical. 'They don't look like they *love* anything at the moment.' She chewed on her lip. 'Cass . . . ?'

'Yes?'

'Do you think about him much?'

'No,' Cassie replied bluntly. It was another lie.

'I do.'

Cassie didn't want to talk about Alfie. She sat up, slammed her diary shut and threw it down onto the bed, hoping to bring a swift end to the conversation. As her diary thumped on the duvet a collection of sealed blue envelopes slid out from between the covers. They were all addressed to Cassie and whoever had sent them had taken the trouble to draw a tiny heart above the 'i' in her name, where the dot should have been. Cassie snatched them up quickly and stuffed them back between the pages of her diary, but it was too late: Dora had spotted them.

'Aren't you going to open those?' she asked, eyeing the letters.

Cassie shrugged. 'Nope.'

'Who are they from?'

Cassie sighed. 'Sam.'

'What? Sam from last summer?'

'Yep.'

'What does *she* want?'

Cassie shrugged. 'I don't know, I haven't opened them, have I?'

'Why not?'

Cassie scowled in frustration. How was she going to explain to Dora that the very last thing she wanted to do was confront whatever Sam had written inside those innocuous blue envelopes? She just wanted to forget all about Sam and that unbearable day on the beach.

But it was as if Dora could read her mind. 'Don't you ever wonder if it *was* our fault?' she asked in a small voice.

Cassie didn't say anything; she just pushed the diary under her pillow and sank back onto her bed, closing her eyes.

'You know, I can't help but think . . . if we hadn't gone to the Crag . . . and if I hadn't left you all to go and get those stupid ice creams . . .'

'Dora, shut up will you?' Cassie snapped.

Dora looked stung. There were tears in her eyes. 'We never talk about him, none of us. It's like he never existed. It's driving me crazy. All I want to do is talk to someone about him. About what happened . . . Just a few minutes. It's all I'm asking for.'

'Dora, I won't tell you again.' Cassie's cheeks flamed red with anger. 'Just shut up! Shut up, or get out of my room.'

'Why won't you talk to me? We used to hang out all the time. Now you just shut yourself away. It's like you can't bear to spend time with me.'

'Dora, I'm warning you.'

Dora sighed, and then got to her feet. She threw her magazine down on the floor in front of Cassie. 'What's wrong with everyone in this family? You all ignore me. All I want to do is remember him. I'm forgetting Alfie, and it makes me sad.' Dora looked close to tears.

Cassie felt like a bitch, but she couldn't help herself. 'Haven't you ever thought that it might make us all *more* sad to remember? That's why we are all trying so hard to forget. And there you are bringing Alfie up every five minutes. It's not helpful, Dora. No wonder Mum and Dad are barely speaking. That's probably *your* fault as well. And it's no bloody wonder I can't wait to escape this hellhole. I just want to find some peace away from this crappy place. Away from you! Let it *lie*, will you. For God's sake, you're not a kid any more! Stop acting like one.'

Dora didn't say another word. She marched out of Cassie's room and slammed the door.

Cassie lay back on her bed and tried to block out the sound of her sister's sobs as she fled down the hallway. She waited until she heard the slam of Dora's bedroom door and then she reached back under her pillow for her journal. Before she could change her mind Cassie seized the four pale blue envelopes and ripped the contents of each one into tiny illegible pieces, watching as the torn remnants floated to the ground like fragments of ash settling after a fire. Whatever had been written couldn't hurt her any more. The words were gone.

She lay back on her bed and closed her eyes. She could feel the start of the itch, crawling up the inside of her arms, tingling and hot. She tried to ignore it but it grew more and more insistent, until, unable to resist it any longer, she snapped open her eyes and reached across for the little butterfly brooch in her drawer. It was too hard to resist. Cassie reached for it and began to pick at her skin with the bloodied pin.

*

Her nightmare returned that night. She woke from it with a start, her pillow drenched with sweat and tears. She knew it was only a dream but she turned on her bedside lamp anyway, eager to chase away the dark shadows still lurking in her mind. She'd been in the Crag, clawing desperately at its walls, screaming and hammering on the unforgiving rock face for Alfie. Although she was wide awake now she could still feel the sensation of stone ripping at her hands, torn fingernails and bleeding skin. She shuddered and pulled her duvet up tight under her chin.

She'd thought it was getting better. She hadn't dreamt of him at all the last few weeks. But then, just like that, Alfie was back. Damn Dora and their argument. Why couldn't she try to forget like the rest of them? God knows none of them wanted to relive last year, night after night, like a never-ending horror movie stuck on repeat.

It had been horrendous.

Her stomach churned.

She looked around her bedroom desperately, trying to find something normal to fix upon, something mundane that would keep the nightmare at bay, keep it from being real. She tried counting the rows of CDs in the rack across from her. One, two, three, four . . . Unwanted images came crashing in on her from all directions.

Oh God. There she was, at the far end of the beach, sunburnt and foggy from too much spliff, stumbling around the rock pools at the far end of the beach with Sam. They were both calling Alfie's name in raspy, panicked cries. Her tongue was heavy with the taste of marijuana and she was thirsty – so thirsty, she could barely find her voice. She remembered a sudden rush of seawater breaking over the rocks and filling her sandals. The water had been cold enough to make her shriek. Then, Sam's shout. She had turned to see her holding something above her head. *Don't be ridiculous.*

she'd thought, we're looking for my brother, not beachcombing for washed-up junk, but then her eyes had readjusted and she'd realised with a horrified gasp that the dark, shapeless object Sam held aloft was, in fact, Alfie's Superman cloak.

She'd stumbled towards her, falling once and grazing her knees on the rocks, but moving forwards all the time until she reached Sam.

'No!' she'd shouted. 'No, no, no, no, no.' She'd started to cry.

Sam had looked on, shocked and silent.

She remembered running her hands through her hair and pulling it hard, and again harder still, trying to get a grip of the situation as it spiralled wildly out of control around her. She had turned and looked out at the surf crashing onto the rocks closest to the beach, scanning the water for a sign of Alfie.

'It doesn't mean . . . you know,' tried Sam, nodding her head in the direction of the waves. 'Maybe he was hot. Maybe he took it off and then headed back up the beach, to get ice cream? Perhaps,' she tried again, 'perhaps he went to look for your sister?'

Cassie looked at her hopefully. 'You're right.' She ignored the damp bundle of cloth in her arms. 'He's probably up at the car park now, with Dora and her friend. This doesn't mean anything.' She dried her eyes, suddenly hopeful. 'We should go find Dora and Steven, see if they've found him.'

'Yes,' agreed Sam.

Suddenly they were both keen to leave the remote outcrop behind. They wanted to return to the main strip, to surround themselves with the buzz and chatter of families going about the normal business of holidaying.

Cassie closed her eyes and swallowed hard. When she opened them again she could see light from her bedside lamp pooling onto the duvet cover, highlighting a small circle of pink roses on the material. She pleated the fabric frantically between her fingers, willing away the scenes flashing before her eyes. But it was no good.

Now there was Helen racing towards her across the car park. Even in her state of distress Cassie remembered thinking her mother looked strange. Usually so poised, there she was stumbling and tripping in espadrilles across the tarmac with her face twisted into a terrifying grimace like a theatrical Greek mask, half rage half fear.

'Where is he?' Helen had gasped as she got closer. Then when Cassie didn't reply, she screamed it again, 'Where is he, Cassie?' Her mother had seized her arms and shaken her violently. She remembered going limp like a rag doll, allowing her mother to buffet and bruise her in the painful embrace. There was nothing she could say.

'Er, miss. Are you Cassandra Tide?' A large man in police uniform was looking at her with concern.

'Yes, yes I am.'

'I need to ask you some questions. To help us find your brother. Will you come with me?'

Cassie nodded and let him lead her into the shade of the beach shop. It was hot and stuffy in there, but it was a relief to be away from all the staring faces. And she'd answered all of their questions. Even when Helen had burst into the claustrophobic storeroom and stood by the doorway glowering at her with barely disguised disgust, she'd kept her eyes fixed on a strange elephant-shaped stain on the floor and answered each question as best she could. And the only details she omitted were the ones she knew shouldn't be spoken out loud; like the smoky tang of the spliffs she'd shared with Sam that had burnt her throat and coated her tongue; like the slow creep of Sam's fingers as they travelled up her thigh and under the hem of her denim skirt; like the velvet-soft brush of Sam's lips on hers and the taste of her tongue, soft and sweet. Yes, there were some details she had left out, but she knew they wouldn't have helped with the search and so she hadn't spoken them out loud. They wouldn't change anything.

The horror had been never-ending. She still got chills thinking about the desperate hours she had spent pounding up and down the beach with her mother. Back and forth, back and forth they went until Cassie had thought the clank and crash of the pebbles under their feet would drive her crazy. She remembered, with guilt, that she had actually been relieved when the police had suggested gently that they return home. But the hardest moments were still to come; like when their mother rounded on her and Dora in the kitchen. Cassie had never seen her so angry. It was terrifying. She'd tried to speak up. She'd wanted to say something then. It was obvious Helen lay the most blame on Dora for leaving the Crag, for meeting up with Steven, but Helen had held up her hand and the words Cassie had wanted to speak, to defend her sister, stuck in her throat and she'd swallowed them back with a burning shame.

Richard had arrived home an hour later. Cassie heard the wheels of his car crunch on the gravel, his quick footsteps and then the slam of the front door behind him. She'd rubbed her red, puffy eyes and left her bedroom.

As she'd descended the staircase she'd seen her parents in an embrace in the hallway. Her mother had her back to her but she could see Richard's face. He was pale and anxious and his face lay half hidden in the shadow cast by the lampshade hanging in the hall. He held Helen to him with one arm, and stroked her hair with the other while she sobbed and clung to him tightly. He was talking to her in low murmurs, the exact same way she'd seen a horse whisperer speak to a wild foal in a documentary she had watched. Yet he must have heard her footsteps because he looked up as she approached and as their eyes locked Cassie remembered pausing, suddenly unsure whether to join them. For a moment it was as if they were all suspended in time; Cassie frozen on the stairs, one foot just hanging in mid-air and Richard looking up at her, his hand pale against Helen's brown hair while he just stared and stared. She couldn't read his expression. It was as if he wasn't really seeing her at all and she was afraid, but then, suddenly, the moment was gone. With a nod of his head, he beckoned her to them and she flew down the stairs, Richard opening his arms and the three of them clinging to each other, crying and hugging.

She remembered they stood there like that for a long time, holding on for dear life, each of them lost in their own world of pain.

It was as if they were drowning.

Drowning slowly in the tight embrace.

She was wide awake now. She knew it wouldn't matter if she reached across now or in an hour or so to turn her bedside lamp off; she wouldn't sleep again that night. It was all upon her at once, raw and unbearable. Twelve months on and it still felt as fresh as it had that first night. She glanced across at her bedside table. The alarm clock showed 03:14 a.m. There were still hours of darkness to get through. She pulled her duvet up to her chin and closed her eyes but it was no use.

Sam had phoned around the same time the police had packed up and cleared out. Cassie's heart had sunk as Richard handed her the phone. She'd known it was too much to hope she might just disappear with her parents and never be heard from again, but she'd clung to the thought anyway. She didn't want to talk to her. It was best they just stuck to their story and tried to forget all about it. She took the phone from her father and turned her back on him.

'Hello?'

'It's me. It's Sam.'

'Hi.'

'Are you OK?'

Cassie didn't know what to say so she stayed quiet.

'Is there any news?'

'No.'

It was Sam's turn to remain silent and there was nothing but the distant hum of the telephone exchange and the quietness of the two girls breathing for a moment.

'Have the police talked to you again?'

Cassie looked around for her father. He was gazing out the window, washing up mugs in the sink and looked to be a million miles away. She cleared her throat, 'They took statements from all of us . . . but they don't think they'll find anything now. They think he was swept off the rocks.' Her voice was barely a whisper. She could hardly say the words.

Sam made a funny strangled sound. 'God, Cassie, it's so awful. I can't bear it.'

'You don't have to, do you? He wasn't your brother.' As the words left her lips Cassie registered it was the first time she had used the past tense to describe Alfie. She felt sick with the realisation.

'I know, I mean . . .' Sam struggled to find the words. 'I'm sorry. It's just so awful. I'm so, so sorry. I don't know what to say.' She paused again. 'Cassie, do you think you should have told the police about—'

Cassie didn't want to hear any more. 'I have to go now. Someone needs the phone. Thanks for calling.'

'Wait, Cassie, don't go—'

But Cassie had hung up before Sam could say another word.

'Who was that?' her father asked, his face still turned to the window.

'Oh, just a friend from school – they wanted to say sorry about Alfie.'

Richard gave a nod. 'Good of them.'

'I guess.' She left the room before he could ask anything else.

*

Cassie had waited and waited for the sledgehammer of blame to come crashing at her door. She knew it was only a matter of time, and as the house emptied of well-meaning strangers and police officials, there was nowhere left to hide. She braced herself for her parents' questions and recriminations. It would be nothing that she hadn't already blamed herself for a million times already, but she knew it would be worse coming from them. To look into her parents' eyes and admit *yes, it was all my fault* would be more than she thought she could take. But it was what she deserved and it would be a relief in the long run, she decided. She spent hours in her bedroom, braced for the knock at the door.

But it never came.

Instead, the fights began.

They started over the funeral.

Richard wanted one. Helen did not.

'There's no body,' Helen had said as she stacked the dishwasher in the kitchen one morning, carelessly crashing plates and cutlery into random spaces. She spoke in the flat monotone her voice had taken on ever since the police had left. 'Why would we have a funeral if we don't have a body? That inquest was a joke, nothing but pure conjecture and speculation. I don't know how you sat through it like you did.'

Cassie froze. She was in the laundry folding clothes and didn't want to draw attention to herself.

'Because it was the right thing to do,' Richard replied, 'just as a funeral is now the right thing to do. We need to say goodbye.'

'I will say goodbye,' Helen said, 'when I see his body.'

'Darling, you know that might never happen. The police explained this to us. All their evidence points towards his drowning.' Richard was trying to be patient but an edge had entered his voice. It was clearly a wearing conversation for them both. 'Look, will you just stop that for a moment? This is important. The dishes can wait.'

There was a crash as bowls hit the kitchen counter. 'I just don't understand why you are so keen to move on, Richard. I would have thought that you, of all people, would want to get *all* the answers. You're usually such a stickler for the details.' Cassie heard the fury in her mother's voice. 'Shouldn't we try to find out what really happened to our son before we just give up hope and move on with our lives?' Helen paused. 'You know, I wish I could forget him sometimes. I'd like to blank this whole nightmare out too. But it's just too soon for me.'

'I haven't forgotten him!' Richard blasted. 'How could you even suggest such a hateful thing?' He was quiet for a moment. Cassie had to strain to catch his next words. 'I am consumed by Alfie. I am living this nightmare each and every day, just like you, since he disappeared. I ask myself every moment of every day what I could have done . . . if I might have done things differently . . . how I might have protected him, been a better father to him . . .' His voice wavered. 'How I could have saved him.'

'And you think I don't?' Helen had cried out, her voice suddenly hysterical with pain and rage.

'I don't know, Helen. Do you? I still don't really understand where you were that day or why the kids took him to the beach. We had rules – strict rules about that. Alfie was not to go there without one of us.'

'Oh, get off your bloody high horse, Richard. The *kids*, as you call them, aren't *kids* any more. They're teenagers . . . almost adults. I had to go onto campus. What was I supposed to do, take Alfie with me?'

Richard ignored the question. 'Dora told me you asked them to look after Alfie. She said you gave them permission to go to the beach. She said you gave her the money for the ice creams.'

There was a pause. When Helen next spoke her voice was

low and cold. 'Richard, have you been talking to Dora about this behind my back? Are you blaming me for what happened that day? Are you saying this is my fault?'

He didn't respond, instead choosing to change tack. 'I'd just like to know what was so important at the university that it couldn't wait until term started.'

'For God's sake, Richard, you've got a nerve. Have I ever asked you what's so important that you have to spend days up in London, working all hours?'

'That's different.'

'Is it? Why?'

'Because I wasn't supposed to be looking after the kids during the school holidays,' Richard blasted back at her.

Helen started to say something but Richard shouted over the top of her. 'If you'd told me you had work commitments maybe I could have shifted things around at the office. I could have worked from home that day. But you never mentioned that you had to be on campus. So how could I have known?'

'It was a last minute arrangement,' Helen screamed. 'The Dean needed us to come in and discuss timetables and—' She stopped herself suddenly. 'Seriously, Richard, what are we achieving here? Do you really want me to justify myself? Are you honestly looking for someone to blame? What about the girls? What about Cassie, spending the day doing God knows what with her new friends? Or Dora, playing on the beach, frolicking around with boys up in the car park when she should have been with Alfie?'

Cassie held her breath.

'Don't be ridiculous, Helen. Dora isn't to blame for this.' Richard's voice quietened again. Cassie couldn't hear what he said next. She put her ear right up to the door but it was no use. It was Helen's voice she heard next.

'Please, please just stop,' she sobbed. 'None of this is helping. None of this is going to bring Alfie back.'

'I know,' Richard replied coldly. 'And that's exactly why I think we should hold the funeral.'

And round they went, a merry-go-round of grief and anger, insults and tears.

Cassie tiptoed out of the laundry room, her clothes bundled under her arm. She didn't want to hear any more.

In the end Richard had got his way. The funeral had been held a few weeks later on a cold autumnal afternoon. Cassie dressed carefully in an old black skirt and dark polo neck and escorted her sobbing sister to the front of the chapel. The church was packed; its pews were full of familiar faces. She saw Sam standing at the back of the church with her parents as she walked by. For a split second their eyes locked. Sam seemed to be gazing at her urgently, as if she had something she wanted to say, but Cassie couldn't bring herself to stop and speak to her so she just gave her a little nod and continued to the front of the church, trying to ignore the sensation of the girl's eyes boring into the back of her neck for the rest of the service.

She remembered mouthing along silently to the hymns, and the sickening, dentist-drill feeling in the pit of her stomach. Someone, she didn't know who, had thought to put some of Alfie's favourite toys up near the coffin. It was heartbreaking to see his favourite little wooden trains lined up at the front, and his blue and yellow tricycle, a stark reminder of all the frenzied trips he had taken around the house on it, scuffing the skirting boards and driving Helen to distraction with the noise. Never again would she see that anarchic grin as he skidded around the house. Never again would she discover him in her bedroom, guilt written all over his face with his hands caked in make-up and loops of her necklaces draped around his little body. Never again would he joyfully catch snowflakes on his tongue and declare them 'yummy', or pester her relentlessly to play spaceships and dinosaurs, or to read him his favourite stories. Never again would he lean his little head against her leg and ask her where the moon had gone in the morning.

She remembered her father standing up at the lectern and with shaking hands and trembling voice, talking about his 'beautiful boy' until his voice faltered and the pastor stepped in to pat him awkwardly on the shoulder and offer a comforting word. She remembered her mother's hysterical sobs as the heartbreakingly tiny coffin, holding nothing but air, was lifted from its stand at the front of the church and carried out into the grey afternoon light. And she remembered standing outside in the graveyard, holding herself so completely still, her lips so tightly shut, her body so rigid with tension, terrified that if she were to let go for just a moment, even for just a second, she might open her mouth and scream at the very top of her lungs: 'It's all my fault! I killed him.'

After the funeral, when it had finally sunk in that Alfie wasn't coming home, the four of them had found themselves faced with the sorry task of picking up their lives. It struck Cassie now, looking back, that this had actually been the hardest time of all. No matter how painful and turbulent those first few days immediately after his disappearance had been, there had been something about the knife-edge anxiety and tension that had kept them all going; a strange adrenalin born out of the extreme situation that gave them the strength to dress each morning, head downstairs, and face the brutal days head on. But after the funeral, 'normal' life came knocking.

They reacted to it in different ways.

Her father disappeared, retreating to his darkened bedroom to lie amongst the shadows with his face turned to the wall. When he eventually stirred he was like a shadow himself – ghostly pale, creeping around the house with all evidence of his easy smile and jolly disposition gone.

Their mother, on the other hand, was volatile in her grief. It seemed to come upon her in waves. She set about the business of running the house, tight-lipped and stiff with tension, but then suddenly the pressure of maintaining her composure would prove too much and she'd take herself off in private to disintegrate into a pool of maternal grief. Cassie would hear her wailing and sobbing behind the bathroom door, or in Alfie's room, weeping into his pillow night after night.

Really, she had wanted to avoid them all. She didn't want to look at her father's grief-stricken face, or hear her mother's raw midnight wailing. But most of all, she didn't want to have to look into Dora's eyes and see the bewilderment, grief and the unanswered questions running endlessly through her sister's mind. Dora's face was like a mirror and all it did was shine a spotlight back at Cassie. So she avoided her, as far as she could, taking refuge in her school work, or busying herself with friends and parties, or when she *was* at home, closeting herself away in her own room, a 'do not disturb' sign pasted firmly on her door.

The irony was that she had never been so popular at school. Everyone seemed to want to get close to the girl who had actually *experienced* something. She heard them whispering around her, nudging each other and staring with barely disguised awe as she passed them in the corridors, even on her first day back. Suddenly she was invited to hang out with the most popular girls and to attend the wildest parties. When sleep failed to come, or the nightmares threatened to keep her up all night or she was simply too afraid to lay her head on her pillow, she would sneak out of the house, desperate to escape its confines and the cloying atmosphere of grief.

With the new friends came new experiences. Alcohol, pills, clubs, sex. She did it all, anything to dull the pain. She loved the warm tingle that filled her belly when she threw back the shots she was handed; and the beautiful golden-honey glow the world took on when she swallowed the little white pills pressed discreetly into her palm. Suddenly everything was OK again; everyone was smiling; everyone was happy. There was dancing, and clapping and laughing and she twirled under strobe lights with a manic intensity, never wanting the moment to end.

When the clubs closed she dragged them all down to the beach. 'Let's watch the sunrise,' she cried. 'It will be fun,' and swept up in the hilarity of it all they'd careen through the lethal laneways and park down in the turning circle by the sea wall, Cassie leading the way across the pebbles to the water's edge.

'Who's coming in then?' she dared, stripping off at the water's edge.

'You're kidding, right?'

'No chance! The water's freezing.'

'Pussies,' she taunted, shrugging off her bra and slipping her skirt down over her legs until, naked and giggling, she'd thrown herself into the ice cold waves, submerging herself until she could barely breathe.

'She's crazy,' she heard them whisper.

'You heard about her brother, right?'

'She's got serious problems, that girl.'

And slowly, one by one, her new-found friends would slip away into the darkness, leaving her alone on the pebbles to shiver and smoke and curse the fact she wasn't brave enough to stay under the waves for long enough.

She took to hanging out alone at the chippy, sitting in the window watching the condensation run down the side of her Coke can and her chips cool in the winter air. It was where she met the man with the thin gold wedding band and the peeling bumper sticker on his Ford Escort that said *Scream if you want to go faster*. He drove them to out-of-the-way lay-bys and did things to her body that made her sit in the bath for hours afterwards, weeping hot salty tears into the cooling water, wondering why she still couldn't feel anything.

It was why she'd started cutting herself. It was the only time she felt real. It was the only time she truly felt anything. The sting of metal on her skin, the rush of warm blood dripping down her arms, pooling in her hands or falling scarlet into the white porcelain of the bath, it made her feel alive. It made her feel present and in control. And most importantly, it made her feel punished, for what she had done, and what she would never be able to tell another living soul.

It was these nights that she wanted the world to end. If she could have stopped it on its axis and prevented it from turning one more millimetre towards another day, she would have. But the morning always came. And it was always bad. God, was it bad. When the grey light of dawn broke through the night and the hangover came knocking with a loud crash of cymbals at her temples, *then* it hurt. She'd crawl shivering and shaking under her bedclothes, her body cut and bruised, and squeeze her eyes shut against the reality of her life. She would will some kind of end to it all, and shudder in disbelief that her parents could be so oblivious, not just to her secret night antics but, more importantly, to the unbearable truth behind her pain.

Cassie could see a triangle of grey light forming where her bedroom curtains didn't quite meet. It would be daylight soon. She thought back to her argument with Dora the night before and felt bad. She didn't want to talk about Alfie, but she also knew she didn't have to be quite such a bitch about it. After all, she was the one who was leaving; Dora would have to endure another two years at home with Mum and Dad and the memories of that terrible day. There was no escape for her sister, not yet.

She tried to close her eyes again, one last time. She felt tired now. She had spent half the night reliving the tragedy in her mind's eye. It was wearing, enduring such intense grief, and such private guilt. She couldn't wait to leave Dorset, to leave it all behind. As her body relaxed once again into the mattress, and her mind began to submit to sweet oblivion, she was pulled back to the surface of consciousness by a strange sound; like a soft, sad sigh. She thought she was dreaming, but then she heard it again.

Cassie squeezed her eyes shut. No, no, no she implored silently. Not again. It can't be.

There was a shuffling sound, and another sigh.

Go away, she willed. *You're not real. I know you're not*.

But it was there again, a soft sigh carried on the air. It was coming from the corner of the bedroom.

Her heart pounded in her rib cage and her blood seemed to pump in her ears. She really didn't want to open her eyes, but in the end, morbid curiosity won. Tentatively she opened one eye and glanced quickly at the shadows in the far corner of her bedroom. Her eyes widened in fear when she saw the small figure crouched there.

He was cast in shadow, and hard to make out, but two unmistakable, piercing blue eyes stared up at her mournfully out of the darkness. She could just make out the familiar silhouette of his sticking-up hair and the grimy old blanket he had dragged around everywhere, clutched in his little hand. It was terrifying to see him so vivid, so lifelike, there before her. And yet it was the expression in his eyes that scared her the most: for they were filled with such terrible sadness and reproach.

'Cassie,' he whispered. 'Cassie, play with me.'

It was her baby brother. It was Alfie.

Cassie stifled a choking cry and scrunched herself beneath the bedclothes, sobbing wildly.

'Go away,' she willed again. 'Just go away. I didn't mean it. I didn't mean to hurt you.'

There was another sigh, a breath so close now that she swore she could feel it on her skin.

'Cassie . . . Cassie . . . Casssieeee.'

'Leave me alone. Please, just leave me alone.'

She stayed there, trembling under her duvet until the morning sunshine had breached her bedroom curtains and she could hear her parents moving around below.

*

In the end it was a mad rush. Helen drove like a maniac to get her to the station on time and they arrived with just minutes to spare. The train to Waterloo pulled in just as she was paying for her ticket. Cassie submitted herself to a last hug from her mother, scooped up her rucksack and then climbed up the steps of the last carriage. She gave a small wave as they began to pull away from the platform and then watched as her mother grew smaller and smaller, until she was nothing more than a tiny, indistinguishable grey dot on the horizon. As she disappeared from view, Cassie let a small sigh of relief escape from between her lips.

At last, she thought, and plunged her hand into her coat pocket to grasp the cold butterfly brooch secreted deep within.

DORA

Ten Years Earlier

Three days passed without word from Cassie. Dora watched as her parents went about their lives with a strange, quiet bravado. Outwardly they appeared calm about their eldest child's first foray into the big wide world and while they certainly put on a good show, Dora wasn't fooled. She could see the tremors of worry stirring below the surface. It was obvious from the swing of her father's head whenever the telephone rang, and from the soft sighs her mother emitted every time Cassie's name was mentioned that they were desperate for news of life up in Edinburgh.

'She'll call tonight,' Richard mused over dinner on the third night, the furrows in his brow deepening. 'She's having too much fun to worry about us – off meeting people and finding her way around, sorting out her classes. Quite right too.'

'Yes,' agreed Helen. 'It must be hard to find a phone. Everyone will be queuing up to call home, don't you think? I wish she'd taken that mobile we offered her.'

'Yes, she was funny about that, wasn't she? Very independent. You know, I admire that in her. Don't worry, love, I'm sure she'll call, just as soon as her hangover has eased off a bit.' Richard was trying to lighten the mood but it wasn't working.

Dora sat in silence. Personally, she thought Cassie terribly selfish not to ring. Surely she would know better than most how much their parents would worry? Just because she got to escape Clifftops and start again somewhere new, well, it didn't mean the rest of them were so lucky. It was bad enough to feel so jealous, but to then have to listen to her parents make excuses for her sister . . . it was enough to drive Dora more than a little crazy.

She was still silently railing at Cassie as she made her way into school on the bus the next morning. Rain poured down, fat drops splattering onto the window and streaming diagonal rivers across the glass. The bus was already steaming up – the driver reaching every few minutes to wipe the windscreen with a grimy cloth – and worse, everything smelt – of wet sports shoes and the revolting sulphuric stench emanating from Billy Cohen's lunchbox as he ploughed through his egg sandwiches. She leaned her head against the window, gazing out unseeing at the passing landscape as she channelled her anger towards an imagined image of her sister swanning around Scotland.

If the last few nights were anything to go by, the next two years of sixth form were going to drag. She simply couldn't stand being the only one left at home with their mum and dad. Sure, her parents were there in body, but in spirit? Not so much. It was a bit like living with those zombies you saw in the movies: two pale, silent bodies drifting around the house, seemingly devoid of life until suddenly they turned on each other, lashing out in a rampage of vitriolic anger and gnashing teeth. In truth, Cassie hadn't been much better to live with, but at least she'd offered some form of distraction with her music and her make-up and a different wardrobe of clothes to borrow from. Now that she had left, there was yet another gaping void in the house, another echoing space that couldn't be filled. There was no one to talk to; no one to hang out with. It was the loneliness that ate her up.

'Hey, how's it going?'

The greeting pulled Dora from her thoughts. She looked up

and found herself staring into Steven Page's calm blue eyes. He gazed down at her from the aisle, his floppy brown hair streaked with rain and falling messily across his face and Dora felt her heart skip a beat.

'Is this one taken?' he asked, indicating the empty seat next to her.

She was a rabbit in the headlights. She blushed and shook her head, watching in disbelief as he slid in next to her and rubbed roughly at his hair, sending droplets of water cascading over them both.

'Sorry,' he said, drying the drops on her arm with his sleeve. 'I got drenched waiting for the bus.'

Dora's skin tingled where he had touched her and she was conscious of the sudden warmth of his thigh pressing against hers. She swallowed. Say something, she willed. Anything. 'Yes,' she said finally, 'it's really raining out there.'

It's really raining out there! Was that the best she could do? She turned to look out the window again, desperate to hide her hot cheeks.

'Are you OK? I haven't seen you around much lately.' She could feel him studying her and Dora felt the flush across her cheeks deepen.

'Yes,' said Dora, 'I'm fine.' She felt anything but.

'It's strange, we've hardly spoken since that summer . . . since your brother . . .' His words petered out and they were left awkwardly staring at each other. 'I came to his funeral, you know?'

Dora nodded. She hadn't seen him at the time, but Cassie had told her afterwards that he'd been there. She swallowed. 'I know. Thanks, you didn't have to do that.'

Steven shrugged. 'Sure I did.' They sat in silence a little while longer before he spoke again. 'It's been a year now. Does it get any easier?'

Dora hesitated.

'Sorry,' he held up his hands, 'none of my business. I'm an idiot for asking.'

'No,' said Dora, 'it's OK. No one really talks about Alfie. Everyone tiptoes around what happened. It's actually nice to be asked. And no,' she added, 'it doesn't get any easier, at least, not yet.'

'I can't imagine.'

Dora closed her eyes. 'It's like living with a wound. You think it's starting to heal, you feel like it's getting a little better, that a scab is forming but then something happens, you hear something, or see something . . . anything . . . the sound of an ice cream van . . . the sight of a little boy learning to ride his bike . . . and it hurts like the first time, all over again. It's horrible. I don't honestly know if it will ever be any different.' She looked up at Steven, wondering if she'd said too much. A simple 'no' would have done. But he was staring back at her with sympathy.

'It must be awful.'

She shrugged.

'How are your folks?'

She gave a dry little laugh. 'Put it this way, our house isn't exactly a great place to be right now.'

Steven nodded and seemed to think for a moment. 'I was wondering . . . you know . . . perhaps you might like to go out sometime, you know, with me? We could get a pizza . . . or go to the movies? Some mates and I are going down to the Dog and Duck on Friday night. I passed my driving test last week. I could pick you up . . . you know, just in case you ever needed to get out sometime?'

Dora's breath caught in her throat. Was Steven Page, *the* Steven Page, really asking her out? *Yes, yes, yes* she wanted to scream, *of course I want to go out with you, what girl in her right mind wouldn't?* Her heart stirred and she felt a fluttering of . . . what was it – excitement? – happiness? – way down in her belly.

She was just trying to formulate her response, to assemble the right words into a coherent sentence, when a violent gust hurled yet more rain up against the window. It splattered loudly onto the glass, making them both jump.

'Jeez,' said Steven, 'it's really raining cats and dogs out there.'

Cats and dogs.

Dora felt the smile playing on her lips fade. Instantly, she was reminded of little Alfie, peering out of the rain-streaked windows at Clifftops, watching a summer storm lashing down onto the sea. 'Where are the cats and dogs, Dora?' he had asked, all childish innocence. 'I can't see them.'

And just like that, the ache was back in her belly. For a few blissful seconds she'd forgotten. She'd felt like a normal sixteen year old, being asked out on her first date by a boy she liked. But the euphoria was over as soon as it had begun. The wound had reopened and she felt it throbbing deep within her, pulling her down once more into the depths of her sadness. She couldn't go out with Steven. Who was she kidding? Hanging out with him would only serve to act as a reminder of that day on the beach, and of how she had failed them all. She didn't deserve to forget. She needed to feel it all, achingly raw and real, for Alfie, always.

'So, how about it?' Steven asked. 'Friday night?'

'Thanks,' she said, 'but I'm actually a bit busy at the moment.'

'Oh.' Steven looked crestfallen. 'And I can't tempt you, not even in a week or two?'

She shook her head. 'I don't think so.'

It seemed it was Steven's turn to blush. 'OK then.' They sat for a moment in uncomfortable silence until he shifted in his seat and opened up his rucksack. 'I've just remembered I've got some homework I didn't finish last night. You don't mind, do you?'

Dora shook her head, a little stung, and as Steven busied himself with a hefty biology textbook, she turned to look out of the window once more. The rain looked like teardrops on the glass. She put her finger against one and traced its slow trail down the pane. She'd done the right thing, she told herself. There was no way she could go out with Steven. It just wouldn't be right.

By the weekend, her parents' creeping worry had taken root.

'I'm going to call,' said Richard. 'It's Saturday morning. Even if she was out last night with new friends she should be in her room now, don't you think?'

Helen nodded. 'It's been a week and we've been more than patient. I think we should call.'

'You don't think it's too soon?' Richard asked.

'No. Call.'

Dora held her breath as Richard rifled around on the kitchen pinboard for a scrap of paper containing details of Cassie's halls of residence. He punched the number into the phone and then waited in silence for an answer.

'Hello, yes, er, hello. I'd like to speak to Cassandra Tide. She's staying in room 132. It's her father calling.'

Dora blushed. He sounded so old and stuffy. She could almost imagine the languid student at the other end of the phone rolling their eyes and stomping off to get Cassie.

'Yes, of course I'll wait. Thank you.'

Dora sat at the table running through the questions she would ask Cassie. She wanted to know what her room was like, if she'd made any friends yet, and most importantly, when she could come and stay. She'd sleep on the floor, she didn't mind, just as long as she could get away from Dorset for a little while.

Several minutes passed. She started to wonder if they'd been forgotten about, if there was a phone receiver lying off the hook somewhere in Edinburgh, while students flitted all around, heading off to lectures and parties, pubs and sports fixtures while the three of them sat there, frozen to the spot.

Finally Richard spoke. 'Yes, I'm still here.' He listened a moment longer and then frowned. 'I'm sorry, I don't understand. What do you mean she never showed up? She left home nearly a week ago. Perhaps you just haven't come across her yet. You know what students are like.'

There was silence again as Richard listened once more. 'But that doesn't make any sense! She must have registered! Where else would she be? What else could she be doing?'

Dora crept closer, trying to decipher the indeterminable burble at the end of the line.

'No, I'm sorry,' he said firmly, 'there must be some mistake with your registration records. Cassie left home last Saturday—' Richard listened again. 'No, by herself. She took the train up on her own. She insisted.'

It was then that Dora knew.

University isn't exactly the be-all and end-all, you know, Dora . . . It's not real freedom. It's not real escape, is it?

The truth sucker-punched her in the guts: Cassie hadn't gone to Edinburgh. She hadn't even intended to go. That was why she'd been so adamant about travelling on her own. It wasn't because she wanted to be independent and arrive at university on her own. It wasn't because she was embarrassed of being seen with them and was worried about navigating those excruciating first hours with her cumbersome family in tow. It was because she had never intended to travel up there in the first place.

As Richard wound up the telephone conversation and turned to them in shocked disbelief, a more pressing question flew at Dora: if Cassie wasn't in Edinburgh, then where on *earth* was she?

'What do you mean "there's nothing you can do"?' Richard sat opposite a police officer – distressingly for them all, the same one that had handled Alfie's disappearance the previous year – and wrung his hands in frustration. 'Our daughter is missing.'

'I understand your concern, sir, but Cassie is eighteen years old. She's an adult now, in the eyes of the law. She can leave home any time she chooses, and while I understand it is upsetting for you to not know where she is, it is, unfortunately, her prerogative. Do you have any reason to suspect criminal activity or foul play?'

Helen looked to Richard who shrugged his shoulders. 'It's very out of character.'

Dora thought of all her sister's long solitary walks, her late nights and the broken curfews. Then she thought of the violent scratches she'd seen on her sister's arms, when Cassie's careful cover-ups had lapsed for a moment and her bare arms had flashed their painful secrets. Cassie didn't know she'd seen the marks, but the sight of them had haunted Dora. She wondered now whether to mention it, but decided against it and bit her tongue.

'But you don't have any reason to believe a crime has been committed?'

'How would we know, we have no idea where she is! That's why we need your help.'

Dora flushed with shame at her mother's rudeness; the policeman was only doing his job, even she could see that.

'Did she give you any indication or clues as to where she might have gone? Does she have any friends or family she could be staying with? Any boyfriends she might be with?'

Richard shook his head.

'Do you remember what sort of state she was in when she left? Did she seem upset? Might she be capable of hurting herself?'

Dora swallowed hard.

'Of course not!' exclaimed Helen indignantly. 'She was looking forward to starting university.'

Richard shook his head. 'All we know for sure is that she left on a train to Waterloo. She was supposed to arrive in London around midday and then take the Underground to King's Cross, for a connection to Edinburgh.'

The policeman cleared his throat. 'London's a big city.'

Dora realised it was time to pipe up. 'She said something to me.' She could feel her parents' eyes boring into her but she continued, regardless. 'The night before she left she said something a little strange. She said university wasn't "real freedom . . . a real escape". I didn't think much of it at the time but now it sort of makes sense. I think maybe she wasn't planning on going to university after all.' She paused. 'I think perhaps she was having second thoughts about it all.' Dora looked up at her mother and felt daggers.

The policeman nodded encouragingly. 'That's good information, Dora. Did she say anything else? Does she have any friends you can think of, friends in London, or elsewhere who she might want to stay with?'

Dora shook her head. 'Only the friends we used to have way back when, before we moved here. But we lost touch with all of them years ago. There's no one.'

The policeman sighed. 'Well, I could ask the London Transport police to review their security camera footage for Waterloo station, around the time Cassie's train was scheduled to arrive last weekend. We might get lucky. Perhaps we'll be able to see if she met up with someone. Or which direction she went in. It's a long shot, but I can certainly ask the question.' He paused momentarily. 'You might want to phone round the hospitals too.' He didn't meet their eyes.

'Is that it?' Helen was aghast. 'Once again a child goes missing and you lot do nothing?'

'Helen!' snapped Richard. 'I hardly think that's fair.'

Dora noticed the policeman flush slightly. 'I understand your distress, Mrs Tide. I'll do what I can, but in the meantime, you could consider a private investigator – someone who can trace your daughter's movements independently. You might have some luck that way.' He was standing now, preparing to leave. 'I'm sorry, there's not a lot else I can do for you. I'm sure she'll turn up. From what I remember of Cassie she seemed pretty streetwise. Try to keep your phone line free and your spirits up. I'll be in touch as soon as I hear anything.'

And with that he was gone.

*

The hours that followed carried with them the painful echoes of Alfie's disappearance. Richard was frantic. He tore around the house, making urgent telephone calls and conducting intense, emotional conversations with Helen behind closed doors, all the while berating himself at every available opportunity for missing the signs that something was amiss with Cassie. Had she run away? Was she being held against her will? Perhaps she'd been taken ill? Or worse, was lying in a ditch somewhere, undiscovered. He shoved furniture, slammed doors and lashed out at inanimate objects. He was wild and terrifying and virtually unrecognisable in his panic.

By comparison, Helen was quiet, seemingly in shock. She sat on the sofa, her hands clasped around her knees as she rocked over and over to some inaudible internal rhythm. Her lips moved, but Dora never heard the words she whispered; frankly, she wasn't sure she wanted to. Instead she stayed at arm's length, circulating carefully around both her parents, bewildered and scared and riddled with disbelief: could it really be happening all over again?

As if on some strange autopilot, the three of them gathered together in the kitchen at dinnertime. Richard told them about the investigator as they pushed uneaten food around their plates.

'He seems very competent – the agency has a ninety-eight per cent success rate when it comes to missing persons and he's promised to handle Cassie's case himself.'

Helen nodded, cleared her throat as if to say something, but then fell silent, twisting her water glass around and around on the table. It made an annoying grating sound on the wooden surface and Dora saw her father throw Helen an irritated glance.

Richard pushed his plate away. 'I just feel so utterly helpless. I don't know what to do.' His voice cracked painfully. 'Tell me, what am I supposed to do?'

Helen looked up then and stared at Richard, as if really

seeing him properly for the first time. Slowly, she reached a hand across the table towards him. Dora could see a strange softness in her face, a vulnerability in her eyes that told her how scared she was too; but at the exact same moment Helen reached out to him, Richard, unseeing, pushed back his chair and stood from the table.

'Sorry, but I can't just sit here, eating dinner, playing happy families, pretending nothing's wrong.'

Dora saw her mother flinch and retract her hand.

He turned to them both at the door. 'I'll be in my study if you need me.'

They sat in painful silence as the door swung shut behind Richard's retreating back.

True to his word, the police officer phoned twenty-four hours later. Dora held her breath as he relayed his findings to a grim-faced Richard.

'What is it?' Helen whispered. 'We've lost her too, haven't we?' Her knuckles were pressed against her mouth.

Richard quietly replaced the handset and turned to them both.

'I don't know, love. I honestly don't know. They think they've found her on their CCTV footage.'

'Where? What was she doing?'

Richard carefully explained how the Metropolitan police had found a grainy image of a girl matching Cassie's description getting off the train at Waterloo around midday. Instead of making her way into the Underground, as intended, she had exited the station by foot. The cameras lost sight of her at the turning for Westminster Bridge, but the evidence was damningly clear: Cassie had left the station of her own free will and the police were no longer invested in the problem: there was nothing more they could do.

'At least we know she's OK, right?' Dora asked, nervously biting at her fingernails. 'I mean, she's clearly run away, not been . . . not . . .' Her words petered out.

Richard sighed. 'I just don't know, Dora.' He shook his head. 'I don't know anything any more.'

'But we'll find her, right? It's just a matter of time.'

For once Richard couldn't answer. Instead, he reached for the telephone. He had only one purpose: finding Cassie.

It was the anger that surprised Dora. It welled up inside her like white-hot lava. How dare Cassie run away like that? Wasn't it enough to be able to leave for university in a blaze of glory? She'd had the perfect excuse to escape and still it hadn't been enough. She'd had to go one better and disappear without a trace, leaving them all worried and distraught. How dare she be so selfish? It was so pointed, so cruel. Surely her sister would know better than most people how that would bring the anxiety and pain of Alfie's vanishing flooding back to them all? Didn't she care how they suffered? Were they not worth one phone call, one email, just to put them out of their misery?

And more to the point, why hadn't she told Dora about her secret plans? Why hadn't she treated her as a confidante? For Cassie to have planned her escape and not breathed one word of it to Dora, after all they had experienced together, well, it felt like the ultimate abandonment.

What about all that rubbish Cassie had spouted a few years ago? What had happened to the sister who solemnly told her, 'it's you and me against the world . . . we've got to stick together, haven't we . . . it's what sisters do.' What a load of crap! Her sister was full of it; the memory of those words made Dora's blood boil even hotter, for it only served to remind her, once again, how alone she truly was. Dora wasn't sure she would ever truly be able to forgive her sister for that.

An eerie atmosphere descended on Clifftops, like a thick winter fog rolling in off the sea. Things were painfully tense; Helen closeted herself away in her study while Richard seemed to come and go from the house at odd hours. Neither of them, it seemed, were much concerned with Dora's whereabouts and with both of them so distracted, she found herself wandering the corridors of Clifftops like some ghostly orphan. She made her own meals, dug around in the washing basket for clothes and went up to bed each night watching her mother's shadow moving in the gap beneath the closed study door.

As the hours ticked slowly by Dora struggled with the monumental loneliness. She considered calling Steven, wondering if it was too late to take him up on his offer of escape, but she could never quite bring herself to pick up the telephone; a creeping self-doubt paralysed her from contacting him. In the end, it was her mother she reached out to, daring to knock on her study door one morning before school.

'Is everything OK?' Helen asked, eyeing her wearily from the door. 'Did your father ring?'

Dora shook her head. 'I thought you might want this.'

Helen looked down at the cup of tea Dora held in her outstretched hands as if it were a strange, unidentifiable object. 'Oh, thanks.' She took it and placed it carefully behind her, on the edge of her desk.

'I think the milk's on the turn, sorry,' Dora added. Neither of them had thought to go shopping.

Helen nodded. 'You off to school?'

'Yes.'

Helen was clearly distracted. 'Did you find something for your packed lunch?'

Dora nodded. She'd rifled through the cupboards until she'd found some sultanas and an old packet of cereal bars.

'Good.'

They stared at each other for a moment and Dora could see the pain and worry etched in the violet shadows under her mother's eyes. It was like looking in the mirror. She wanted to reach out and touch her, to be pulled into her mother's embrace and feel the warmth of her arms around her, to breathe in the fresh, clean scent of her. At that moment, she realised, she would have given anything to be held by the woman who had comforted and soothed her as a little girl – the woman who had always chased away the nightmares and reassured her that everything would be all right. She felt the tears welling up in her eyes and forced them back.

Helen looked back at her desk. 'Well, thanks for the tea . . .'

'Mum . . .' Dora tried, desperate to keep the chink of communication open for a moment longer. 'Cassie'll be OK, won't she? I mean, she's eighteen, and tough. She can look out for herself, don't you think?'

Helen studied Dora for a moment. 'Yes,' she agreed finally, 'I suppose so. She's not exactly a *baby*, is she?'

Dora didn't know if Helen had intended to reference Alfie but she recoiled at her mother's words. Alfie. It was always going to be there, between them. Would they never get past it? Would she never let her in?

Dora turned silently and headed towards the front door, hearing the gentlest of clicks as Helen closed the study door behind her.

It was four o'clock the following afternoon when Richard burst through the back door.

'Helen! Helen, are you here?' Then, seeing Dora emerge from the living room, 'Dora, quick, where's your mother?'

'In her study, I think. What is it?'

'Go and get her. Go!'

Dora was turning on her heel as ordered when Helen appeared in the hall. 'What is it? Have they found her?'

Richard went straight to his wife and took her hands carefully in his. 'You need to stay calm, OK?'

'What is it, Richard? For God's sake, just tell me.'

'They've found her.'

Dora felt her stomach plunge. It was obvious it wasn't good news.

'Tell me, Richard, you're scaring me.'

'She . . . she . . .' Richard seemed to struggle with the words.

Dora noticed his hands were trembling. She swallowed.

'She . . . she threw herself off a bridge,' he managed finally, 'into the Thames.'

'What?' Helen looked at him, aghast.

Dora suddenly felt as though she had slipped into some other world; the day had taken on a surreal, shimmering quality.

'Is she . . . ?'

He shook his head. 'No, she's alive. She's in hospital.'

Helen gave a small sigh of relief. Dora thought she looked as though she might collapse.

'Oh thank God.'

Silence filled the room as they all processed the enormity of Richard's words.

'What do you mean "threw herself off"?' Helen asked finally. 'You mean . . .'

Richard nodded. 'Yes . . . she tried to kill herself.' His face was white and Dora could see how hard it had been for him to even say the words out loud.

Helen shook her head. 'No, it's not possible. Cassie would never do that.' She bit her lip. 'No. It must have been an accident. Perhaps she fell?'

As the three of them stood in silence once more, an image of Cassie's ravaged arms swam before Dora's eyes.

'No, it's true,' Richard continued. 'Someone saw her jump – thank God – and they were able to fish her out, just in time. They took her to St Thomas's. She was resuscitated and treated for pneumonia. She picked up a nasty water-borne infection too. They've kept her in all this time. Seems she gave a false name. That's why it's taken us so long to track her down.' He ran his hands through his hair. 'The investigator I hired just called me with the news. I'm going to head up there right away and meet him.'

'I'll come too,' said Helen immediately.

'No, love,' Richard urged gently. 'I think you should stay here.' Dora saw the meaningful nod in her direction. 'Anyway, this chap has suggested we take things slow with Cassie, and for what it's worth, I think he's right. We don't want to overwhelm her. He seems to know what he's talking about. I'll try and see her tomorrow, have a gentle chat with her then and convince her to come back with me.'

Helen shook her head. 'This just doesn't make any sense.'

'I know, love.'

'You'll bring her home?'

'Yes,' said Richard.

'Good, she should be here with us, at least until she's feeling well again.' Helen seemed to think for a moment. 'I'll call the university. I'm sure they'll keep her place on hold. We can bring her home, get her strong again and then take her up there ourselves in a few days. She shouldn't miss too much of the first term.'

Dora stared in disbelief at her mother. She couldn't quite believe what she was hearing. It seemed her father couldn't either.

'Helen, do you understand what I just told you?' He seemed visibly shaken. 'Cassie has tried to commit suicide. I hardly think a place at university is the priority right now, do you?'

'Well she can't just throw away her future.' Dora winced, but Helen was oblivious to the sad irony of her words and carried on. 'We need to get her back on her feet. This is no time for self-pity or silly stunts. She's got a future and a career to think of.'

'Silly stunts?' The colour was flooding back into Richard's face. 'I hardly think throwing yourself off a bridge into the Thames can be classified as a "stunt", do you?'

'What else is it?'

'I'd say it's a cry for help . . . or worse . . . a sign that she doesn't think life is worth living any more.' Richard ran his hands through his hair again. 'I just don't understand how we could have missed this. Certainly she's been quiet . . . more withdrawn since Alfie . . . but I really thought she was doing OK. I just didn't see what was going on . . .' He shook his head in anger. 'How could I have been so blind?'

'This isn't about you, Richard,' Helen spat. 'This is about Cassie. And I just want her home. I think I should come up to London too. If we caught the evening train—'

But Richard cut her off. 'No, stay here with Dora. I can handle it.'

Helen shook her head again. 'What on earth was she thinking? I've been going out of my mind with worry . . .'

'I know,' said Richard, 'me too. At least we've found her now. I'll bring her home, I promise. This will all be over by the weekend.'

Dora listened to their conversation with a creeping doubt. Surely they knew by now that nothing that involved Cassie was ever that easy.

Dora was in the living room flicking through the dismal Saturday night television schedules, bouncing haphazardly between an old Bond movie and a wildlife documentary, when her father's car headlights swung up the driveway. She'd been determined to act offhand about Cassie's return – she wasn't going to give her sister the satisfaction of knowing how much upset she'd caused, or how much she'd been missed – but when the moment came, she found herself standing on the top step of the porch, next to Helen, peering anxiously into the darkness for a sign of her sister's fair head. She had so much she wanted to say to her.

The driver's door opened, a car light came on and Richard appeared in the darkness. He slunk out of the seat, slammed the car door and stomped wearily up to the front door. Dora craned her head but there was no sign of her sister behind him.

'Where is she?' Helen asked, a high note of panic in her voice.

Richard reached the floodlit porch and looked up at them both. Dora could see the dark shadows under his eyes and was surprised to note how old he looked.

'She wouldn't come.'

Helen gave a start. 'What do you mean, "she wouldn't come"?'

'Just that. I tried my best, Helen, but she insisted on staying in London. I couldn't exactly force her.'

'But I thought she'd been discharged? I thought she was well enough to leave hospital?'

Richard nodded. 'She is; but it seems she wants to stay in London. It's not as if I could drag her back to us kicking and screaming, is it?' he added quietly.

'Why not? She should be here, with us. Not dossing in London, doing God knows what. Where is she staying? What is she doing for money? You said you'd bring her home. She's not well, for God's sake!' The panic in Helen's voice had shifted to accusation. Dora slid backwards into the shadows slightly. 'I knew I should have gone myself.'

'Helen, I honestly don't think it would have made any difference if you had been there. In fact, it might have made things worse. Cassie was adamant. She wants to stay in London. She doesn't want to come home. She wouldn't say very much, but she did say she couldn't face . . . well . . . any of us right now. She just wants some time and space.'

'Space from *what*?'

Richard stared at Helen for a moment; he seemed to be about to say something and then changed his mind. 'She says she needs to figure out who she is and what she wants from life.' He ran his hands through his hair.

'Who she is? What she wants?' Helen shook her head. 'So she's just going to chuck away a perfectly good place at university?'

Richard shrugged.

'I hope you told her what a mistake she's making?'

'Helen, she's eighteen. I couldn't force her. I did my best.'

'Your best? You did your best?' Helen spat the words. 'You promised you'd bring her home with you. Cassie's going to wreck her life, chuck it all away . . . just like I did!' Helen let out a sob.

Richard eyed his wife carefully. 'Just what do you mean by *that*?'

'Oh forget it. You wouldn't understand.'

Richard gave an irritated shake of his head. 'You could at least *try* me.' He paused for a moment. When he next spoke it was with more control. 'I did what I thought was best. She's our daughter. I thought I was doing the right thing.'

'The right thing? You just left her there to fend for herself!' She shook her head. 'It's pathetic, really. You're weak. Did you even try to change her mind, or did you just roll over and let her do whatever she wants? And how do we know she won't be jumping off the very next bridge she finds?' She shook her head again. 'I *knew* I should have gone with you.'

Dora swallowed and watched as her father pushed wordlessly past them both, disappearing into the hallway. Helen spun on her heel and followed after him, leaving Dora alone on the doorstep. She looked into the house and then up at the dark sky. There was a crisp, autumnal smell on the night air that carried with it the promise of falling leaves and bonfires. She could see a sliver of moon shining its pale light from behind a high veil of cloud but for the most part the garden was cast in darkness. She couldn't even see as far as the gates at the end of the driveway.

More angry shouts reverberated behind her. Dora knew she couldn't take much more. Choosing the lesser of two evils, she tripped down the stone steps onto the driveway and headed out into the darkness.

Halfway down the lane it struck Dora that it was much colder out than she'd first thought. She squashed a pang for the warm coat hanging by the back door and pressed on, ignoring the goose pimples prickling on her skin. She didn't care what her parents thought; she doubted they'd even notice she'd gone, but if they did so be it. First Alfie, then Cassie; they had both disappeared and yet it was she who felt invisible. Let her parents worry about her for a change.

A thicker bank of cloud moved across the moon and Dora struggled to adjust her night vision. Something rustled in the bushes next to her and far off she heard the plaintive shriek of a fox. Dora steeled her nerves. It was terrifying being out in the pitch black all on her own, but she wouldn't turn back. She didn't know where she was going, and she didn't much care. All she knew was that she couldn't bear to be in the house a moment longer. She didn't want to hear any more arguments or recriminations. She had been holding out for Cassie's return and now even that had been denied her.

Bloody Cassie. It was always all about her. Her moods. Her tantrums. Her needs. And now this; she had trumped them all. No matter which way she looked at it, Dora struggled to get her head round it all. Surely Cassie hadn't really wanted to end her life? She knew she was upset. She knew she was still grieving for Alfie . . . they all were. But she'd had a place at university. She'd had somewhere legitimate to run to. Why would *she* want to end it all? What could have possibly driven her to hurl herself off a bridge? It just didn't make sense.

As Dora stomped on through the darkness, tripping and stumbling down the laneways, she turned it all over and over in her mind.

It was the lights that eventually drew her. They flashed orange between the dark waving branches of the trees until she got closer and saw Betty Dryden at the window of the cottage, her grey head bent over a sink of washing up. Bill was in the background, sitting at a table reading the paper. It was such a cosy, contented scene that Dora stood in the darkness of the lane for a moment watching the elderly couple as they performed their nightly ritual. They looked so peaceful. So normal.

Betty turned to say something to her husband and Dora saw Bill look up from the table and give a gentle chuckle. She could almost hear the low, musical hum of it from where she stood on the grass verge. Why couldn't her family's life be simple, like that? When was the last time she had heard her parents speak to each other with kind, warm words? Why were they all so totally screwed up?

Betty had just rinsed the last of the plates and shuffled across to the kettle when Dora took a few steps further down the lane and set off a security light. It flooded her in a sudden and dazzling white beam. She froze awkwardly as Betty's head swung up with a start, embarrassed to see the recognition pass over the old woman's face as her eyes adjusted to the darkness and focused on Dora's static form. Damn.

Betty disappeared from view and, unsure what to do next, Dora jammed her hands into her jeans pockets and began to beat a hasty retreat up the lane.

'Dora? Is that you?' It was Betty, calling out to her from the front door.

Dora spun around, mortified. 'Yes, sorry, Betty.' The old lady stood on the doorstep, peering out at her. 'I didn't mean to frighten you both. I was just out walking.'

Betty nodded and Dora was grateful she didn't seem to need any further explanation.

'Would you like to come in? It's cold out there and I've just put the kettle on.' The old lady shivered and pulled her woollen cardigan tighter around her shoulders.

Dora hesitated. She didn't want to intrude, but she also knew she really didn't want to return home either.

'Come on,' Betty urged. 'Have a cup of tea with me. I could do with the company. Bill's got his head buried in the newspaper. I made flapjacks earlier . . .'

That swung it. Dora turned and skulked back towards the cottage, following Betty through the low wooden doorway and into the warm interior of the cosy flint cottage. She had to bend slightly as she entered the kitchen.

'Hullo there, Dora.' Bill greeted her with a warm smile. 'What brings you to our doorstep on such a cold autumnal night?'

'I . . . er . . . was just passing. I fancied getting out for a bit. You know, some fresh air . . .'

Dora saw Betty throw her husband a warning glance. 'Yes,' he agreed with an easy smile, 'it's as good a night as any for a walk, eh?'

Dora nodded, grateful she didn't have to explain further and Bill, sensing a shift in mood in the room, folded his paper and stood up from the table. 'If you'll excuse me, there's a gardening show on the telly I wouldn't mind catching. I think I'll leave you ladies to your tea and chatter.'

'Yes, be gone with you,' teased Betty. 'Never let it be said I kept you from your composting worms and hardy perennials.'

Bill left the room and while Betty busied herself for a moment with teacups and a biscuit tin, Dora took the opportunity to look around the kitchen. It was small but perfectly formed, with exposed stone walls, a large hearth and a hanging pot rack dangling shiny copper pans. A pretty arrangement of dried flowers stood in a vase on the windowsill and in one corner Bill's muddy boots stood drying on an old sheet of newspaper by the radiator. On the table a folder of Betty's prized recipes lay open, ready for her next culinary foray.

'You should write a cook book,' mused Dora, staring down at the spidery handwritten notes for a gooseberry and elderflower ice cream.

'Oh I'm a bit old for that now,' laughed Betty. 'Besides, I'd never live it down at the WI. I can hear them all now: "That Betty Dryden . . . always did have ideas above her station!" '

'Not true!' cried Dora. 'From what I've heard you'd give Delia Smith a run for her money!'

'What rot,' laughed Betty, but an attractive flush had risen in her cheeks and Dora could tell from the way she fussed with the knitted tea cosy that she was flattered by the compliment. 'Now then,' she said, carrying the tray to the table and pouring milk into the cups, 'what about you, Dora? How are you, dear girl?'

Dora took one of the flapjacks from the plate Betty had pushed towards her and nibbled at a sticky corner as she wondered how to reply. In the end she decided on the truth. 'Not so good, I'm afraid.' She paused, took a deep breath and then continued. 'It feels as though everything's falling apart, Betty . . .' she took another breath, 'and I'm afraid it's all my fault.'

'What's your fault, dear girl?'

'Everything. Alfie going missing; Cassie . . . leaving; Mum and Dad fighting all the time. It's all my fault.'

'And what makes you think that?' The concern in the old lady's eyes was enough to keep her talking.

'Because it all traces back to that day last year; the day when I went off by myself when I should have been looking after Alfie. The day I decided to hang out with a boy from school and took too long getting back to the Crag.' She dropped her head to her hands. 'Now Cassie's run off and it's set Mum and Dad off again. They're at each other's throats. I just feel like the whole horrid mess is all down to me.' She gave a hollow laugh. 'Mum named me well. That day, on the beach, it's as if I opened up Pandora's box and released a world of pain into our lives. It's like I've gathered up everyone's hearts and smashed them into a million pieces and now I don't know how to put them back together.'

Dora's final words came in a rush and although she couldn't meet Betty's gaze, she felt the old woman's papery hand reach for hers and was grateful for the warmth of her touch.

'Too much pain for one family,' said Betty, shaking her head, 'far too much pain. It's not your fault, Dora. It's not anyone's fault. A terrible thing happened to Alfie, but there's nothing to be gained by blaming yourself.'

Dora sighed. Betty didn't get it. No one did. They didn't have to live at Clifftops, surrounded by the pain and grief, dodging the haunted faces of her shattered parents, dislocated from her tortured sister and taunted by memories of a happier past and of what could have been.

'Terrible things happen to good people. It's a sad fact of life. But no matter what's happened in the past I do know one thing: you're still a family,' said Betty, squeezing her hand. 'You can find your way back from this.'

Dora shook her head. 'You're wrong, Betty. Our family disappeared that day on the beach . . . with Alfie. It's like we all drowned with him.' She dropped her gaze. 'You know, I can't remember the last time any of us said we loved each other.'

'But your parents love you, Dora, of course they do. They may not be able to show it very clearly at the moment . . . they have a lot on their plates right now . . . but your mother and father *do* love you, Dora.'

'No! They don't, and they shouldn't, you see, because it's my fault! I don't deserve their love any more. I don't deserve anyone's love. I ruined everything. I destroyed it all.' Blinded by the tears streaming down her face, Dora felt herself pulled into a warm, flapjack-scented embrace and clung to the old lady for what seemed like an eternity, letting her shush her over and over until Dora felt as though she had no more tears to cry.

'There there,' said Betty, handing her an embroidered handkerchief. 'It will all work out, you'll see. Nothing stays the same for ever. You'll all move forwards from this. It will be hard, but you will.'

Dora shook her head. She knew things couldn't stay as they were. None of them could carry on that way but she just couldn't see a way for things to get any better, as Betty clearly believed they could.

'One day, Dora, you'll have your own family. Then you'll understand.'

'No,' said Dora vehemently. 'I won't. I don't want a family if it means I could ever feel like this again.'

Betty eyed her. She could see the woman didn't believe her, but deep down Dora knew. She knew she couldn't ignore the feeling in the pit of her stomach that told her they were all still falling down the blackest of precipices, and that they still had a long, long way to go before they hit the bottom.

DORA

Present Day

Dora is hiding. She knows it's unprofessional. She knows she should be out there with the rest of the team, going through the concepts for the Sunrise Cereals presentation, but she just can't summon the energy – or the stomach. Some genius has thought it would be a good idea to open the sample boxes of Wheat Fizzies the client has sent to them and the smell of sugary, sweet-and-sour cereal hangs on the air, making her stomach flip dangerously. Bloody morning sickness. She swallows hard and eyes the waste-paper bin under her desk. It's her only option. She can't face running through the packed office floor to the ladies' loos. She takes deep breaths through her mouth and closes her eyes, trying to think of something that will make her feel less nauseous. She settles on snow. There is nothing offensive about snow, with its cool, white, wonderful nothingness; and it is a damn sight better than the thought of Wheat Fizzies.

Urgh. There she goes again – straight back to food. It is like some form of sadistic torture her mind puts her body through. Wheat Fizzies. They are the bane of her life right now. She opens an eye and glances quickly at the mood boards on her desk. She is greeted by images of clean-cut children's faces grinning back at her, all perfect toothpaste-white smiles and neatly combed hair as they sit around breakfast tables with their parents. They don't look like any kids she's seen recently, but it is too late to change things now.

The brief had been for an irreverent breakfast cereal launch; something the kids would love, and would eventually win around the parents. That was the challenge: to generate formidable pester-power. But what she sees staring back at her is no different to a thousand other breakfast cereal launches she's seen before. It is bland in the extreme, and while Wheat Fizzies can be accused of being many things, bland certainly isn't one of them. Her first taste of the puffed cereal had nearly sent her skidding to the bathroom at full pelt. The kids will go crazy for it, that much is a given. A cereal that can turn your milk fizzy is too cool for words, but it is definitely an acquired taste.

She holds up a storyboard and eyes it critically. Their hook, a superhero called Captain Fizz, is mocked up in a cartoon strip. He is battling the giants of the breakfast table, propelling himself off a spoon at a slice of dry toast, bursting through a bowl of unappetising-looking muesli, and fighting off the perils of a gloopy-looking porridge. It ends with the tagline: *You Can't Fight the Fizz*. It isn't the most original creative she has seen, but the directors at Sunrise Cereals are due at their offices within the hour. There is no time to change anything now.

She sighs. This is the part of the job she likes least: pitching ideas she doesn't believe in to clients, selling to them in such a way that they will walk out of their offices delighted with the agency and happy with the exorbitant fees they will be charged. Sometimes she hates advertising.

She has just about pulled herself together when their Creative Director Leela appears at her desk.

'Are you ready, my lovely?' Leela asks, adjusting a laptop and folder of papers in her arms. 'I'm going to head up to the boardroom and set up . . .' Her words trail off as she looks at Dora. 'Oh, you look like shit. Are you OK?'

Dora smiles in spite of herself. Diminutive Leela with her perfect coffee-coloured skin, lustrous black hair and tongue as sharp as steel. She has never been one to beat around the bush. 'Yeah, I'm OK; just a dodgy takeaway last night. I'll be all right.'

'Are you sure? I mean, I don't want to be rude but you really don't look too good.'

'Seriously, Lee, I'll be fine. It's just the smell of that bloody cereal.'

Leela laughs. 'Yeah, that's why I'm heading upstairs. It's making my stomach churn too. The things we do, eh? Dominic had better give us a bloody big bonus for this one.'

Dora nods. 'I'll be up in a moment, you go on ahead.'

'OK.' Leela looks at her with concern, turns to go and then swings back. 'Look, don't take this the wrong way, but you might want to try some blusher.'

'A bit pale?'

'Well, you know Cate Blanchett at the end of that movie *Elizabeth* . . .'

Dora laughs weakly. 'Say no more. I'll get the bronzer.'

The Sunrise executives arrive on time and the meeting begins well. The clients smile and nod encouragingly as Dora talks through the launch strategy and the rationale behind their Captain Fizz character. The Creatives pull up the graphics and storyboards and by the time they have lined up the showreel Dora is feeling confident. The Sunrise executives are buying into it.

Before they dim the lights for their finale reel, Dominic stands to address the group. 'Tina, Rick . . .' he addresses each of the executives in turn with his winning smile. 'I hope you're as excited by what you've seen here today as we are. We consider your account to be the jewel in the Fielding and Fey crown. It's a privilege to be working on your business; and even more exciting that we will be launching Wheat Fizzies as our first project together. I think the team here have come up with some sensational ideas and we're excited about moving these forward over the coming weeks.'

The Sunrise Executives smile benevolently up at Dominic. He has a way of putting people at ease, a way of making his clients feel like the most important people to walk the earth.

'To conclude, we'd just like to run you through a short promo reel we've put together with rough cuts of the Captain Fizz television spots. It's an indication of where we feel we can take this campaign. We really do believe we're on to something big here. As Dora has already said, if we can capture the attention of the three- to eight-year-old demographic, the sky really will be the limit.'

With well-timed efficiency the lights in the boardroom are dimmed and everyone turns their attention to the giant plasma screen running across one wall of the room. Dora swivels round in her chair for a better view. She hasn't seen the tape – it has been running late – and she is interested to see what Leela and her team have come up with to deliver the final, knockout punch. She sees Leela grin at her from across the room. She is obviously happy; it's a good sign.

The tape starts innocuously enough. There are roughs of the television ads and images of Captain Fizz battling against some of Sunrise's biggest competing brands. The Executives chuckle in their seats and Dominic turns to give her a little wink. Then the tape shifts. It shows images of young children, around three or four years old, she guesses, running around a playground. They are laughing and playing innocently enough, but as Dora watches the scene unfold, she feels something dreadful grip at her stomach. She sits there in the dark, mesmerised by the screen. The children are dressed as their new marketing icon, Captain Fizz. They wear red trousers, blue T-shirts and long, home-made capes. As they run and play they throw Wheat Fizzies around laughing. 'Take that! And that! You Can't Fight the Fizz!' they cry with cheerful glee and then, as the tape draws to its conclusion, one adorable blond-haired boy turns straight to camera and proclaims with an innocent, gap-toothed smile: 'I love Captain Fizz: he's the bestest superhero of them all.'

Dora feels something lurch sickeningly within and, without further warning, she leans over and vomits all over the Sunrise Sales Director's impossibly shiny shoes.

She is sitting at her desk with her head in her hands when Dominic finds her. He knocks lightly on her door before entering and seating himself in the chair opposite.

'What the hell happened to you back there?'

'It's . . . er . . . nothing, just a touch of food poisoning. I'm so sorry. I thought I was over it. I really hope I didn't ruin things for the team.'

Dominic waves his hand dismissively. 'Forget the team for a moment. A new pair of shoes and a spot of Febreze is all it took. Sunrise have gone away happy and we're committed to stage two. It's a great result. I can hardly believe it myself; I never thought they'd buy that Captain Fizz crap.'

Dora smiles weakly.

'No,' he continues. 'It's you I'm worried about. You haven't been yourself these last few weeks. And don't tell me it's food poisoning. I know you better than that, Dora. If something's bothering you then I want to know about it.'

Dora looks up at him in surprise. Dominic does not normally go in for touchy-feely management techniques. He is a renowned pit bull. She doesn't know what to say. She can tell him the truth; but then what is that, actually? That she is pregnant and falling apart with guilt from a tragedy that happened ten years ago? It would be hard for a pit bull to swallow.

'Look, Dominic, I will tell you, but not yet, OK? You have to trust me. This is personal. I know I need to sort it out.' She sighs. 'Can you leave it with me for now and if things haven't improved in a few days, well, then you're welcome to come back in here and sack my sorry arse.'

Dominic looks at her with concern. 'I'd like to help, if I can?'

'Honestly, Dom, trust me, you're not the one who can help me right now.'

He stares back at her for a moment and then throws up his hands in defeat. 'OK, I won't ask again. You've got two weeks. I don't want to see you back in the office until then, OK?'

Dora nods, grateful that he doesn't require any further explanation at this stage.

He stands and walks towards the door. 'You did good in there today, you know?' he says as he reaches the hallway. 'And I would never sack your "sorry arse", as you so sweetly put it – certainly not because of a small bout of food poisoning. Besides,' he says with a knowing wink, 'they *were* terrible shoes.'

Dora breathes a sigh of relief.

'Now, get yourself home to bed, young lady, before I see any more of your breakfast on my carpet!'

She still feels queasy so, rather than take the bus, Dora decides to walk for a while. It's warm out and by the looks of the puddles splashed across the pavement she's just missed a shower. The air is still damp and probably as fresh as it will ever get in London so as she walks she breathes in great lungfuls of the stuff, trying not to think about the exhaust fumes she's inhaling too.

She makes her way along Old Street, under the railway bridge plastered in fly-posters and past a celebrated Banksy mural, before cutting up through Hoxton Square, weaving past council estates, corner shops and old Victorian terraces made good by the affluent media set. The council have been busy; summer flowers burst from beds and tubs, their bright colours in stark contrast to the grey cityscape. She sees a fluorescent yellow police sign appealing for information about an assault, and further on, a wall of beer kegs stacked outside a pub. Sunlight peers cautiously through the cloud, as if checking it is safe to come out; its rays bounce down onto the silver kegs, blinding her momentarily with their glare.

She carries on through the maze of estates until she sees the canal. The sun is still out and the sight of it glimmering on the pond-green water entices her down onto the towpath. There is no one visible in either direction and she pauses for a moment, peering into the water, watching as it creeps slowly past. There is a sheen of rainbow-coloured oil at the surface and an empty plastic bottle floating near the bridge; it bobs up and down like a fisherman's float. Away from the hum of traffic and people it is suddenly and strangely quiet. Dora likes it; there is something about the unexpected stillness of the canal, the imperfect, dirty beauty of the waterway that appeals to her; she stays there for a few minutes, gazing into the dark, shifting mass of water, until a cyclist speeds towards her, dinging his bell. She waits for him to pass before heading down the towpath.

Halfway down the track she shrugs off her jacket. The sun has gained in confidence. Two ducks splash in the reed beds on the far side of the canal; Dora wishes she had some bread to throw. Every so often she passes a barge, moored to the side. Most are dilapidated old things: all crackled paint, rotting wood and grimy tarpaulin shrouds, but one or two are well cared for. She has just stopped to admire a beautiful red and blue boat with cheery checked curtains and an array of potted geraniums scattered across its deck when she sees the man walking towards her.

He is a long way off, a hundred metres or so, but the sight of him – and the young boy loping at his side – is like a physical blow to her body. The air rushes from her lungs. Blood drains from her face and her pupils dilate with shock, like the aperture of a camera seeking light. All around sound fades as her brain zeros in on the two figures walking towards her.

They're still fifty metres away but she knows beyond all

doubt that it's him: whippet-thin with snake-like hips and long dark hair.

She knows it's the man from the beach.

She peers as they come closer. The boy trotting along next to him is dressed in school uniform. He seems to be having trouble keeping up. An oversized satchel bounces on his back in time to his hurried steps. Dora cannot see the boy's face, he is too busy watching the path as it races beneath his feet, but the shock of his straw-like hair glinting in the sunshine is enough to make Dora feel dizzy. She reaches out and puts a steadying hand on the barge.

Thirty metres . . . twenty metres. She cannot take her eyes off them.

Fifteen metres away and the boy stumbles. The man yanks at his skinny arm, half in irritation, half to hold him up. He snarls something from the twisted corner of his mouth and Dora sees the boy's fair head droop lower still.

Ten metres and she remains fixed to the spot.

'Come on,' she hears the man urge, half dragging the scrap of a boy. 'I told you we'd be late. We don't have time for this.'

Dora ignores the man now. She only has eyes for the boy. She is willing him to look up at her. Pale freckled skin, wide mouth, her father's clear blue eyes; she can see it so clearly in her mind's eye. She already knows what she will see, but she needs to see his face all the same. She stands stock still, barely daring to breathe until finally the man spots her. He eyes her warily as they close the gap and moves one protective hand onto the boy's shoulder.

'My shoes hurt,' the boy whines.

Dora's heart misses a beat at the sound of the plaintive little-boy wail. She is back there on the beach. *Too fast. I'm thirsty. Can we stop?* She hears the echoes of Alfie and feels her heart split in two. It's definitely him.

Without thinking she steps in front of them, blocking the path. She doesn't know what will happen next. She doesn't think to worry whether the man is dangerous. All she cares about is seeing the boy's eyes. She needs to know that it's really him.

'What do you want?' asks the man. He is aggressive, irritated.

Look at me. Alfie, look at me, she wills.

And finally, he does. As the man pulls on the boy's arm, trying to move him onto the grass verge and around her physical blockade, the boy lifts his eyes and stares up at her.

She sees a narrow, heart-shaped face, a pointed chin . . . and watery-brown eyes filled with uncertainty and fear.

Dora peers at him hungrily, and then her heart sinks.

'Dad?' the boy asks hesitantly, his eyes darting from Dora to the man and then back again.

'Come on, son,' the man says roughly. He turns to Dora. 'You should watch where you're going, lady!'

'I'm . . . I'm sorry,' she stammers, 'I thought . . . I thought . . .'

'Silly cow,' the man mutters under his breath and as they disappear around the bend in the towpath Dora sinks to the still-damp ground, the breath leaving her body in great shuddering gasps.

She thinks about it the rest of the way home on the bus. Did she really think it would be Alfie? Ten years have passed. He wouldn't be a little boy any more and the fact that she'd managed to convince herself so wholeheartedly, even for just a moment, that the young boy walking along the canal could be Alfie shows her just how mad she is. That boy couldn't have been more than eight or nine and Alfie, if he were alive, would be fourteen now.

She rests her head against the graffitied interior of the bus and watches as the kebab shops and convenience stores of the Kingsland Road swim past. Is that what she wants, she asks herself? Does she really still want Alfie to be alive after all this time? Could he really have spent the last decade living some shadowy, alternate life, one far removed from the sheltered bosom of their family? It's something she has never been able to give voice to, to anyone. But if she's honest with herself, it's never far from her thoughts, lurking there in the darkest corners of her mind, filed next to the unbearable tabloid stories of paedophiles and child smuggling rings too shocking to contemplate.

She knows the police pursued every line of enquiry. She knows that the inquest, based on the best possible evidence, declared Alfie to be dead. They were confident enough to issue them with a death certificate so that the funeral could go ahead. So why can't she let it go? Why the nightmares? The panic attacks? The desperate searching for his face? Dora knows if she is to hang on to her sanity she must try to push the possibility of her brother still being alive from her mind. But it's easier said than done when her mind is capable of playing such agonising tricks on her.

She sighs and rubs one finger across a tiny matchstick man someone has taken the trouble to carve into the seat back in front of her. The day has taken it out of her: first the presentation, then the sickness, and finally the awful encounter on the towpath. As her stop comes into view she reaches for the bell and then steps down off the bus like an elderly lady, creeping her way along the pavement until she reaches the button factory. She climbs the three flights of stairs slowly and, relieved to find that Dan is still out, draws the curtains in their bedroom, shrugs off her work clothes, and crawls under the covers of the bed. She wills sleep to come, but she is still awake nearly two hours later when Dan's key eventually rattles in the front door.

They drive to Chichester after breakfast on Sunday morning. The roads are surprisingly clear and they arrive at the house just after eleven. Dora sees movement at one of the upstairs windows as they pull into the driveway.

'We're early,' proclaims Dan.

'Yes, and I think we've just been spotted too.'

Dan takes the key out of the ignition. 'Ready?'

Dora takes a deep breath. She's not sure she is ready for what lies within. Violet is lovely, and there is no denying she makes her father happy – at least as happy as she's seen him since Alfie – she just finds it strange still, seeing them together. 'Yes,' she says. 'I think so.'

Dan reads her mind. 'It still feels weird, huh?'

She nods her head. 'She's just so different to Mum. So . . . bubbly. But I do like her . . . and I suppose Dad would be very lonely without her.'

Dan holds up his hands in mock protest. 'You don't have to convince me. I know she's good for him. She's sexy too . . . in a Mrs Robinson sort of way.'

'She's old enough to be your mother!'

'I'm just saying . . . your dad's done well for himself, that's all. She'll help keep him young, after all, she seems very *energetic* for a lady of her age.'

He places a little too much emphasis on the word 'energetic' for Dora's liking and she grimaces. 'OK, enough already. I really don't want to think about this right now; not when we're about to sit down and eat lunch with them both. I'm already feeling nauseous as it is . . .'

Dan takes Dora's hand in his, his eyes suddenly serious. 'It'll be OK, you know. What I mean is, *we'll* be OK.' He reaches out and tucks a loose strand of hair behind her ear. 'It's good that we've come here, together. This trip is long overdue.'

She thinks about her father, and about how long ago her last visit to his home with Violet was, and realises that Dan is right. They've hidden from each other for too long. Sitting there in the car, looking across at Dan, his handsome face full of concern and kindness, she can't help but smile back. 'Yes. It is,' she agrees. 'It's long overdue.'

Suddenly Dan breaks into a toothy grin. 'Now, all we have to do is plan our escape route.' The mischievous twinkle has returned to his eyes. 'You know, in case it all kicks off when you tell your father about the baby. I've seen that old hunting rifle hanging above the fireplace in Dorset. He'll probably have us down the aisle and married quicker than you can say "shotgun wedding" if we're not prepared.'

This time she pulls him towards her. She is still laughing as their lips meet.

Violet opens the door. 'I thought that must be you. I heard your car from upstairs. Come in, come in, both of you,' she urges. 'Don't just stand there.'

She pulls Dora into a warm, fleshy embrace that fills her nostrils with the comforting scents of roasting meat and Violet's musky perfume. There is something about the feel and smell of her, something familiar and reminiscent of her long-lost childhood that makes Dora's head swim and her eyes well up suddenly. Bloody hormones, she thinks to herself and rubs discreetly at a tear in the corner of her eye.

Then it is Dan's turn.

'Come here, you lovely hunk of a man. Let me give you a hug too.'

Dan succumbs to Violet's bosomy embrace and leers suggestively at Dora over the top of her head. Dora turns into the hallway, masking her giggles with a cough.

'Come on in then,' Violet bustles. 'Make yourselves at home. Your father's in the living room.'

Dora and Dan step into the hallway, their shoes sinking deep into the luxurious cream carpet.

'Straight ahead, you know the way, don't you?' Violet ushers from behind.

'Yes thanks,' Dora calls out, making her way down the corridor towards the lounge at the back of the house.

It has always struck Dora, the few times she has visited her father in his new home, how peculiar it is that he has chosen to so completely leave his old life behind. Everything is different, and not just his wife, although that is, on the surface of things, the most obvious change. The two women have always seemed poles apart to Dora. Where Helen is tense and composed, Violet is all soft curves and perfumed sensuality; where Helen is guarded, Violet is relaxed and bubbly; and where Helen is highbrow and academic, Violet is bursting with small talk and gossip. She supposes that's why the two women were friends in the first place, drawn to each other's differences by the same fundamental alchemy that brings positive and negative ions together. But it isn't just in Violet where she can see the shift. Merely walking down the hallway of the house Richard now lives in is testament to everything he has left behind in Dorset.

The place still smells new. She guesses it is only a few years old; one of seven identikit mock-Tudor mansions built on a recent cul-de-sac development just outside Chichester. It is all deep pile carpets, double height ceilings, magnolia walls and designer taps, the epitome of small town suburban chic and the sort of bland interior design that saturates any number of week-night property programmes. But here and there are splashes of Violet's own personal taste amidst the beige surrounds. Down the hall Dora sees a series of canvases hung along the wall, silhouettes of voluptuous female forms which send Dan's eyebrows shooting skyward and leave Dora smothering yet more giggles. There are scented candles burning on almost every surface and, of course, vases of flowers everywhere. The arrangements are bold and bright and the house swims with their pungent aroma. It's all a little too staged for Dora's own personal taste, and a world away from the history and shambolic romance of Clifftops. Dora tries not to think about it too much. It makes her angry, for the irony is not lost on her that it is Helen who now lives in the Tide family house; Helen, who had been so reluctant to move there in the first place who now presides over the Tide family home, while her father has retreated to a life of chic, show home suburbia. She honestly can't understand why he has just walked away from it all; but each time she comes back to the conclusion that he must have wanted it that way. It had been Richard, after all, who had left Helen, and while she has not been privy to the ins and outs of their divorce negotiations, Dora has the sense that Richard willingly handed the Dorset house over to Helen. She supposes he just can't bear to be there any more – not after Alfie.

Violet guides them through open double doors and into the lounge. Dora can see her father seated in a leather armchair at the far end of the room. The Sunday papers are spread before him and the television is on, the glossy green vistas of a golf course filling the screen.

'Look who's here!' Violet exclaims theatrically, as if Dora and Dan have just dropped by, unannounced.

Richard looks up, peers at them both through steel-rimmed reading glasses before leaping to his feet. 'Aha! Here you are! I didn't hear you arrive.' He lunges forwards and gives Dora a hug. 'Hello, Panda, how are you?'

'I'm fine, Dad. How are you?'

'Splendid, splendid. And Dan,' he turns to him with outstretched hands, 'how are you, young man?' He pumps Dan's hand up and down warmly.

'Very good, thank you, Richard. Sorry we're a bit early. The roads were much clearer than we expected.'

'No trouble, no trouble at all,' Richard reassures them, switching off the television and tidying the papers quickly. 'Just pleased you made the journey. We've been looking forward to seeing you both, haven't we, Vi?'

'Yes, we have.' Violet grins. 'Your father's talked of nothing else all week.'

'Oh shush, woman, don't tell them that!' Richard laughs. 'They'll think we've got nothing better to do with our lives than sit here and talk about them.'

'Well, here we are,' Dora confirms with an awkward smile.

'Yes. Here you are,' Violet agrees.

The four of them stand looking at each other for a moment. The weight of expectation hangs over them and Dora suddenly feels suffocated by the burden of a thousand unspoken words bursting to break free. Luckily Dan steps in and breaks the silence. He turns to survey the scene outside the window.

'Wow, look at what you've done with the place. The garden looks so different.'

He is lying. Dora can see very little change in the manicured landscape since their last visit a couple of years ago but thankfully Violet leaps onto the subject with enthusiasm.

'Richard's been a busy bee out there. Those shrubs have really come along since we planted them last year and the climbing rose on that trellis will produce some lovely blooms next summer.'

'What an interesting feature you have there,' adds Dan, indicating a large structure in the centre of the lawn.

'Oh, do you think so? Richard was rather cross when I brought that home with me, but I just couldn't resist it.' They all stand and take in the large stone urn in the centre of the lawn spouting its constant and rather suggestive jet of water two or so feet into the air above the rim. Dora and Dan nod along politely while Violet continues with her monologue. 'I read somewhere it's good feng shui to have flowing water in your garden. It brings good luck . . . or good health . . . or wealth. Oh, I can't remember.' She laughs with a dismissive flap of her hands. 'It's good *something* anyway! And the greenhouse is being delivered next week,' she adds with excitement.

'Lovely!' exclaims Dan with over-enthusiastic cheer. 'Where will you put it?'

'Over there, in the far corner. Of course I'm more interested in flowers but your father's going to try his hand at growing veggies. Richard tells me your grandfather, Dora, was quite the green-fingered gardener so I'm expecting prize-winning courgettes and marrows by the end of the summer. As long as the rabbits don't eat them, of course. We're overrun from the fields out the back.'

'I keep offering to shoot them but she won't hear of it,' jokes Richard.

Violet gives Richard a friendly whack on the arm. 'Isn't he awful? Anyway, perhaps we'll have room in the garden for one of your sculptures, Dan – if we can afford you, that is! I hear you are the toast of the London art scene at the moment.' Dan smiles and shifts awkwardly, uncomfortable with the praise and unsure what to say but he needn't worry; she is off again before he can open his mouth.

'Of course, people ask me how on earth I have the energy to spend time out there in the garden when I'm so busy with work, but I just love it – and let's face it, arranging flowers and running a business isn't quite the same as digging down into the earth and planting things with your own hands – making something grow. Is it?'

'No I suppose not,' agrees Richard, smiling down at Violet indulgently. He turns to Dora and Dan. 'Did you know Violet has three stores now? Quite the floristry empire.' The pride in his voice is evident.

Dora wonders privately if that's how their relationship works. Richard has always been a quiet man, more likely to be found with his head bent over his desk or with his nose in the papers than out at parties or lavish dinners. Violet's businesses must keep her busy and out of Richard's hair for most of the week until she returns to provide him with infrequent but much needed injections of cheerfulness. And no one can deny she is crazy about him; it's obvious from the way she bustles about him, gazing up at him adoringly or reaching out to touch his sleeve while she chatters on and on.

'But listen to me, babbling on when here you are probably gasping for a drink. Now, what can I get everyone? We have sherry, or wine, or perhaps you'd like a beer, Dan?'

They decline the offer of alcohol, agreeing instead on 'a nice cup of tea' and Violet sashays out of the room leaving Dora and Dan with Richard. Dora notices her father's eyes follow Violet all the way to the door.

'Well, sit yourselves down,' he says, turning back to them. 'Let's not stand on ceremony now. We're all family.'

'Quite,' agrees Dan.

'So,' says Richard, turning to Dan, 'I hear business is good.'

'Yes, it's going rather well, at last,' says Dan. He fills Richard in on his new commissions and the recent exhibition while Richard sits nodding and smiling his approval. Then he turns to Dora.

'And you, my dear? How is work at the agency?'

'It's fine. I've just taken on a couple of high profile accounts of my own.'

'That's wonderful news,' cheers Richard. 'You clever thing. We must have a drink at lunchtime to celebrate. And what about your home? Hackney, isn't it? Are you enjoying London?'

As Richard and Dan begin a convoluted conversation about London property prices and mortgage rates Dora takes the opportunity to observe her father more closely. He is not a young man, but neither can he be called old. His sandy blond hair has whitened and thinned dramatically and she can see a shiny bald spot on the top of his scalp that she doesn't remember from the last visit. The metallic reading glasses he wears perched at the end of his nose and the slippers encasing his feet lend him a grandfatherly look, and while he is still relatively trim, there is now a definite paunch visible beneath the blue wool of his sweater. On the surface he appears like any other middle-aged man struggling with his weight and his hair loss, but Dora can see other subtle changes that run deeper, changes that would only be visible to someone who has known him well over the years. The frown lines etched into his face are a little deeper, perhaps, than one would expect for a man his age; and there is a fleeting sadness in his eyes, barely noticeable as he jokes and laughs with Dan from the comfort of his armchair, but still evident to Dora, all the same.

Dan has just turned the conversation round to Richard's

architectural firm when Violet hurries back into the room with a tray of clinking teacups and a plate of biscuits.

'I didn't know whether you would want Earl Grey or English Breakfast so I made both. Shall I be mother?' She looks around the room at them all with a beatific smile. It is impossible not to smile back. Violet's irrepressible good nature spills out of her like the water gushing from the stone urn on the lawn.

'Never let it be said that Violet under-caters!' jokes Richard. 'I'm pretty sure I have her to thank for this,' he adds, patting at his portly waistline.

'So,' Violet asks as she passes around the teacups, 'have I missed all the news?'

'Not all of it,' says Dan with a knowing look in Dora's direction. She supposes this is her moment.

'We do have some news actually,' Dora confirms.

Richard looks up from his tea. 'Oh yes?'

'Yes. It's good news.' She has already decided to be more positive. 'I'm pregnant.'

There is a moment of startled silence.

'We're going to have a baby,' she tries again.

Dora sees her father's hand tremble slightly as he places his cup and saucer back onto the coffee table. He swallows hard and then looks up at her. She can't tell if it is the light playing tricks or if there are tears welling in his eyes, but they seem to shine a little too brightly behind the glass of his spectacles.

'Well, say something then,' she urges.

'Darling . . .' Richard chokes. 'Darling, that's . . . wonderful news. My goodness, a baby! My baby girl is going to have a baby!'

Dora laughs. 'Yes, I suppose that's one way of putting it!'

Violet is on her feet. She has grasped Dan's hands in hers and is dancing a funny little jig in front of him that seems to make every ounce of spare flesh on her body jiggle with excitement.

'Oh a baby! How wonderful. Congratulations.' She plants another kiss on Dan's cheek and leaves a ruby red imprint of her lipstick on his stubbly skin.

Dora turns back to her father with concern. He seems to be having trouble breathing and is fiddling with the collar of his shirt. 'I know this is probably a bit of a shock . . .'

'No. No, my dear, it's not that.' He takes a deep breath inwards, as if suddenly finding his lungs. 'I'm sorry. It's wonderful news, it really is. It's just a little . . . unexpected. I thought maybe an engagement?'

'Dad!' exclaims Dora. 'Don't tell me you're getting all conventional on me? Mum was pregnant before you got married, wasn't she?' She sees that it isn't a trick of the light. 'Oh Dad, please don't cry. We didn't mean to upset you. We hoped you'd be pleased.'

'I am pleased.' Richard removes his spectacles and dabs at his eyes with a handkerchief. 'Really, I am. Please excuse me, I'm just being a silly old fool.' He hugs Dora so hard that she struggles to breathe.

'Yes you are, Richard!' exclaims Violet vehemently. 'A baby is wonderful news. It's just what this family needs.'

Richard wipes his eyes again and then walks over to Dan and claps him on the back. 'Congratulations, young man. I hope you'll look after my daughter and my first born grandchild.'

'Of course I will, Richard. You needn't worry about that.'

'No, of course not. I know you will. You're a fine young man.' He slaps him on the back again and then looks around awkwardly. 'Well, I don't know about all of you, but I think I could do with something a little stronger than tea now. This calls for a celebration, don't you think?'

'I've got just the thing in the fridge.' Violet is up on her feet and halfway out of the door when she turns to Dan meaningfully. 'Oh, Dan, would you mind giving me a hand out here? I'm not sure I can reach the champagne flutes.' She nods suggestively at Dora and Richard.

'Of course.' Dan leaps to his feet, gives Dora an encouraging look and then follows Violet out of the room, leaving father and daughter alone.

Dora moves across and perches herself on the arm of Richard's chair. 'I'm sorry if this has come as a bit of a shock. I didn't mean to take you by surprise. It's very hard to know how to do these things . . .' She trails off, unsure what else to say.

Richard blinks, removes his spectacles again and begins to polish them on his sleeve. 'No, my dear, it's I who's sorry. I wasn't upset because of your news. It *is* a surprise, but a wonderful surprise.' He pauses, seeming unsure whether to continue or not. 'I always hoped for these big family moments; weddings, babies – all the happy times you strive for in life. I suppose I had imagined them slightly differently; you know, all of us together, at Clifftops.' He pauses again. 'Does your mother know?'

Dora nods. It is the first time Richard has mentioned Helen in a very long time.

'Is she pleased?'

Dora doesn't know how to answer that question, so she just nods again, this time somewhat vaguely.

'You know, you were right about your mother and me. We fell pregnant with Cassie by accident, not long after we first met. It's still the best mistake I've ever made. I don't regret it for a minute.'

'When you found out . . . when you knew you were going to be a father . . .' Dora pauses, and then continues in a rush, 'I mean, did you know it was what you wanted, immediately? Were you both happy about it?'

Richard gives a little laugh. 'It was a shock, of course it was. But once we'd decided to make a go of it we didn't look back. I remember we took the train to visit her parents first and broke the news. They were horrified, of course.' He gives a little wry laugh. 'Then we drove down to Clifftops and told my parents.' Richard stops abruptly. He seems lost in his thoughts.

'That must have been awkward,' Dora suggests.

'Well, everyone was a little more old-fashioned in those days. But we'd already decided to marry, so the drama soon blew over.' Richard falls silent again.

'Our news must bring back painful memories for you? Of Mum . . . and fatherhood and . . . well, everything else?'

'Yes, I suppose so. But this isn't about my memories, or me now. This is about your life, Dora. And I certainly hope Violet and I were more positive than your grandparents were when we told them Helen was pregnant with Cassie!' He gives another little laugh and then pauses to replace his glasses. 'What's that saying: history repeating itself?'

'Oh!' exclaims Dora sharply. 'I hope not.'

Richard seems to realise his error. 'No, of course not. I don't mean . . . I didn't mean, well, not Alfie. I never would have meant . . .' he trails off. 'Sorry, darling, I'm not very good at this, am I? I am thrilled for you, Dora. You will make a wonderful mother.'

'Do you think so?' Dora leaps on his words hungrily.

'Of course. And you're both happy?'

'Dan is delighted. He can't wait to become a dad. I've had a slightly harder time adjusting to the news . . .' Dora admits.

'Do you plan to marry?'

Dora sighs. 'I honestly don't know. It doesn't seem that important right now. I think we're both more focused on doing the right thing by this baby. And really, what difference does marriage make? So many don't seem to last the distance these days . . .' She stops, suddenly aware of what she has said.

'Well, I can't argue with you there.'

They sit together in silence for a moment. Somewhere outside a wood pigeon's call drifts on the breeze. It takes Dora straight back to afternoons on the lawn at Clifftops. She closes her eyes. She can almost smell the freshly cut grass and the salt breeze blowing through the sycamore trees.

Richard clears his throat, breaking her reverie. 'Dora, I would hate to think that mistakes your mother and I have made in the past might be making things harder for you right now. You do know that despite what's happened between us, I still love you very, very much, don't you?'

'I know.' Dora reaches out and takes her father's hand in hers.

'One of my biggest regrets is that your mother and I couldn't make our marriage work. I was so in love with her. Perhaps one of the cruellest things I did, unintentionally, was try to possess her by putting a ring on her finger. But then I suppose we were just kids really, and that's what you did in those days. But you and Dan are different. I can see that.'

'Are we? Are we really different, Dad? Because that's something I worry about. I know things were bad after Alfie died – really bad – but I always hoped you and Mum would make it through. It was a shock when you left,' she admits.

'Yes, I suppose it was, although Cassie had left us by then, and you weren't far behind her. There seemed to be very little point us both pretending, rattling around in that great big house, both of us miserable.'

'I can understand that,' agrees Dora.

'You know, after Alfie disappeared we were tortured with so many unanswered questions and grief. *So much grief*. We were shattered; too broken to heal. Whenever we did try to console one another, it only seemed to make things worse. We hadn't just lost the ability to communicate, we'd lost the respect too; the gulf between us was just too great. We were tearing each other apart.'

Dora is surprised to hear her father speaking so openly. They've never had a conversation like this. She stays silent, hoping he will continue.

'I blame myself. Your mother never wanted to move to Clifftops. I should have listened to her, but I was so selfish, so one-eyed about it all. I forgot to listen to her, to truly understand what it was she needed. The house took over. It began to consume me. I was so concerned about doing right by it. I wanted to look after it exactly how my parents had, to make it a focus, our pride and joy. But I got it so wrong. In the end it wasn't just the roof over our heads – it became the towering wall that stood between us as well. You must have felt it too, being there with us, towards the end?'

Dora nods. She remembers what it had been like.

'You know, it's been a relief to be free of it. Shrugging off the responsibility of it all was very liberating.' He looks around the living room, as if seeing his surroundings properly for the very first time. 'Oh I know this new house isn't what you all expect of me. Between you and me,' he adds conspiratorially, 'I could do without the smelly candles and the fluffy toilet seat warmer.'

Dora can't help but smile.

'But it's what makes Violet happy, and seeing her happy brings me pleasure now, in a way I hadn't thought possible after Alfie.'

'We all still miss him so much, don't we? Even after all this time.'

'Yes,' agrees Richard.

Dora takes a deep breath. 'There's something I have to ask you, Dad. I need you to be honest.'

'Of course, poppet.' His clear blue eyes stare straight back at her.

'Do you blame me, Dad? You know, for what happened that day?'

Richard looks at her. He blinks and then shakes his head vigorously. 'Oh my dear girl, you don't honestly think it was *your* fault, do you?'

Dora doesn't say anything. She doesn't want to influence whatever he is going to say next.

'Dora, it was an accident; a terrible, tragic accident. It wasn't anyone's fault. God knows, I've tried to place the blame over the years . . . on myself . . . on your mother . . . even, God forgive me, for one wild moment on Cassie, her being the eldest of you girls. I hated myself for that.' He stares her in the eye. 'But never you; I never blamed you.'

Dora shakes her head. 'I don't understand. It was as much my fault as Cassie's. Alfie must have followed me out of the Crag that day. I never saw him. I should have been more careful. I should have returned sooner.'

'No! The blame never lay with either of you girls. You were both just kids. Besides,' he adds quietly, 'I've learnt over the years that it's no good looking for someone to blame. It's not going to bring him back, is it?'

She shakes her head. It's obvious there's still something he won't share, something he still won't tell her, but she doesn't push and Richard remains silent. Eventually he looks up at her. 'There's more, isn't there?'

She shrugs. 'I'm feeling a bit lost, to be honest. I'm scared that Dan and I might not make it. And perhaps more than that, I'm scared of losing him – him or the baby. I don't believe I deserve this happiness in my life and I honestly can't go through it all again.'

Richard nods. 'I understand. I didn't believe I deserved happiness either, not after Alfie. The few times I found myself smiling, enjoying a meal, sharing a laugh with someone, it always left me wracked with guilt. But then Violet and I grew close. It was after I'd left your mother . . . a good while after. We bumped into each other in London. I'd just finished work and she was up in town on some mammoth shopping spree.' He gives a low chuckle. 'I remember it was in the food hall in Selfridges. I couldn't see who it was at first. She called out to me by the oyster bar and all I could see were these bright red shoes poking out from beneath a mountain of bags.'

Dora smiles. That sounds about right.

'We had a glass of wine . . . spent an hour or so chatting and I only realised as we were saying goodbye that I had smiled more in that one hour than in the whole time following

Alfie combined.' He pauses for a moment. 'I'm afraid there are no guarantees in life. It pains me to say it, but I can't promise you that life won't bring suffering your way again. But answer me this, Dora: what do we do, stop living, stop trying, because we're afraid of getting hurt? Yes, life doesn't always turn out how we think it's going to. Yes, it can hurt us – almost destroy us, but I know now that we can heal too. We can get stronger. We can find happiness from the most unexpected of places . . . with the most unexpected of people.'

Dora swallows and both father and daughter remain still for a moment, both obviously struggling with their emotions.

'It was Violet who helped me take a chance again,' he says eventually. 'She has been my saviour. She's such a warm, jolly soul. She doesn't let me take myself too seriously. And perhaps, most importantly, I've really learnt from my mistakes. I listen to her. I respect her. I love her passion for her work . . . her desire to enjoy the best in life . . . her ability to see the best in people. I've even learned to appreciate her love of towering high heels, no matter how many times she steps on my toes! I know how lucky I am to have a second chance. Perhaps Dan and this baby is your chance now, Dora?'

Dora nods and they sit together in silence a while longer, until Richard speaks again.

'You know, it's the distance between us all now that I blame myself for most.'

Dora looks up in surprise. 'What do you mean?'

'You. Cassie. Perhaps I could have held things together more after we lost Alfie. I was lost in my grief, but I see now I should have tried harder, for you girls. I certainly missed all the signs with Cassie.' He sighs and rubs the bridge of his nose. 'Then I got caught up with Violet and the last thing I wanted to do was force my relationship with her on you girls. To be honest, I wasn't sure how you would take it. I worried it would be yet another thing to cause upset for you both. Perhaps that was cowardly of me, but I chose to take a back seat for a while. I always hoped you might find your way back to me though . . . and to each other.' He thinks for a moment. 'You know, it saddens me to see you girls still so distant. Have you had any contact with Cass?'

Dora shakes her head. 'Not really.' How does she explain it to him? How can she tell him about the one time she tracked Cassie down? How she had stood outside a grotty north London café watching through the fogged-up windows as her sister flitted between the tables, delivering coffees and fry-ups to a crowd of hungry night-shifters; about how she had just been screwing up her courage to enter the café when she saw her sister smile at something one of the customers had said, a warm, easy smile that had stretched across her face and transformed her back to the Cassie she remembered of old. It had been the sight of her standing there amidst the tables and chairs, a steaming coffee pot in one hand, looking so at ease with the world, that had finally demolished any desire Dora had felt to confront her sister. Instead she had scuttled back to the Underground without so much as a backwards glance. It was clear Cassie didn't need her in her life. She wasn't the depressed, suicidal creature she'd been imagining in her dreams. For all the trauma and tragedy, it seemed as though Cassie had moved on just fine without her.

That had been the last time Dora had tried to make contact with Cassie, although her sister had reached out to her over the years. Every year on Dora's birthday a card would arrive – a bland floral tribute simply signed 'with love, Cassie'. There was never any message, never any kisses, until, just once, on Dora's twenty-first, the card arrived with a mobile phone number scrawled next to Cassie's name.

Dora had considered calling. She'd kept the card for several months, turning it over and over in her hands, wondering whether to take the plunge. But she never had. Even on those particularly lonely nights, the ones when she'd found herself home alone with nothing but a bottle of wine for company, when the nostalgia and grief had really set in, even then she'd managed to restrain herself. For she only had to recall the pain she'd felt after Cassie had run away, after she had tried to end her life, or conjure up the image of Cassie standing there in that café, her white teeth shining under the glare of the strip lights as if she didn't have a care in the world, to remind her that there really was no point. Cassie had made her choice a long time ago and they were travelling different paths now.

Dora swallows. She knows she doesn't have the words to tell her father how she feels about Cassie, but she is intrigued about her sister nonetheless. 'Have you seen her recently?' she asks.

Richard nods. 'Violet and I saw her about six months ago. She seemed good. She's in Oxford now . . . has landed on her feet with a job of sorts. It's an interesting set-up.' He pauses. 'I know she'd like to see you . . .' He leaves the suggestion hanging in the air, but he doesn't push it. 'Look, Dora,' he continues finally, 'I can understand your fears. I've spent enough of my life wishing I had protected you kids a little more, protected myself a little better. But then would I have had the happy times I enjoyed with you, and your mother . . . and now with Violet? I think you have to give of yourself. I think you have to take a few risks. What's that saying: "A life lived in fear is a life half lived"?'

Dora nods. It makes sense in the cold light of day.

'You know, Panda, I really don't have the answers, but what I do know is that you can spend far too much of your life on the unimportant things: the big house, the stressful job, the perfect family and all the traditions and expectations that go along with it. But when all is said and done, that isn't what's important. It's taken me a long time to learn it, but I know now that it's the people you hold in your heart, and how you treat them, that's what's most important. So you hold onto Dan, and your baby. Hold on tight, and whatever you do, don't let them go. Hold tight, my girl.'

Dora nods again. She can't reply; his words have affected her deeply. She thinks of all the things her father has unintentionally lost from his life: his son, his wife, his home – even she and Cassie are absent to an extent. They are all gone. And yet here is her father, sitting here in his unexpected new life, learning from his mistakes, appreciating Violet and the things he holds most dear.

She reaches out for his hand and squeezes it tightly and they sit there in the lounge like that; just sitting, silently; holding on tight.

Eventually Dan returns. He holds a tray of champagne flutes before him, and is laughing at something Violet has just said. He seems oblivious to the charged emotion in the room.

'Well, here we are, folks,' he announces. 'Champagne for us . . . and sparkling water for the one "with child".' He hands Dora her glass with a flourish.

Violet bustles in behind him with the open bottle of Champagne. 'We must have a toast. Richard, will you do the honours?'

'Of course.' Richard stands and raises his glass. He clears his throat and looks across at Dora before speaking. 'To a new life . . . and to full lives, lived without fear.'

Violet throws him a gentle smile and they all clink glasses and pretend not to notice Richard's watering eyes as they sip at their drinks.

'Now, there's a lovely roast in the kitchen that needs carving,' Violet chirrups. 'Which of these fine alpha males is going to do the honours? Dan?'

'It'd be my pleasure.'

'Wonderful. Why don't you and Dora go on ahead and I'll just tidy up in here a bit.'

They take the hint, and as they leave the room Dora turns to see Violet fussing over her father. She is adjusting his shirt collar and murmuring something intently in his ear until a mischievous smile breaks out across her father's face. He leans in to brush Violet's cheek with his lips, and then, seeing Dora watching them from the doorway, gives her the slightest of winks over the top of Violet's blond curls. Dora turns from the room, a smile upon her face.

It's a relief when the atmosphere over lunch grows lighter and more jovial. Violet sets about her combined roles of hostess and comedienne in earnest and they have soon left behind the heavy mood from earlier. Richard cracks a stream of corny jokes over dessert and Dan has them all in stitches as he re-enacts an awkward meeting with a famous artist he has long admired. It seems none of them want to dwell on gloomier matters.

They leave just as it is getting dark outside. As they pull out of the driveway Dora turns to give a final wave. She sees her father and Violet standing outside the house. Richard has his arm slung around Violet's shoulders as she gazes up into his eyes adoringly. Dora smiles and turns back to Dan, putting her hand over his on the gear stick. 'You were right, you know.'

Dan nods knowingly. 'I'm always right.' He pauses as he indicates left. 'But what specifically was I right about *this* time?'

'Violet. She's really good for Dad.'

He nods and Dora leans back into her seat and watches as a green blur of hedgerows passes outside her window. *A life half lived.* It resonates deeply. Since Alfie disappeared she knows they have all been guilty of living stilted, half-lives, in their own different ways. Her father hasn't given her all the answers, but it has made her realise where she needs to go next.

As the hedges turn to street lamps and her eyes finally close, succumbing to the hypnotic haze of a hundred orange cats' eyes speeding towards her out of the darkness, there is one face that continues to drift in and out of her consciousness.

Cassie.

It is time for her to see Cassie.

HELEN

Nine Years Earlier

Later, after the dust had settled, the irony would not escape Helen that her marriage had finally ended at the exact same moment the rest of the world prepared to turn the page on a shiny new chapter.

It was millennium eve. The whole country was in the final, frenzied preparations for the party of the century but as Helen woke that morning she could think of nothing more pressing than boiling the kettle for a cup of tea, throwing some muesli into a bowl and perhaps turning up the central heating a degree or two. Cassie was still an absent figure, closeted away in London, incommunicado. Dora was away for the weekend at a friend's house. She and Richard had no plans to celebrate and she knew their evening would pass quietly with a bottle of wine and the television volume on low as they watched the loud razzle-dazzle celebrations beamed from various destinations around the globe. It was fine by her.

She padded downstairs and across the draughty hall, pulling her dressing gown around her body as she moved towards the kitchen. It was as she passed the open door to the living room that something off-kilter nudged gently at the corners of her mind. She nearly didn't stop; but a sixth sense told her brain what her eyes had failed to process. Slowly, she retraced her steps and stood at the open doorway looking in.

Tobias's painting of the gloomy seascape still hung in its

usual place on the wall, housed within its gilt-edged frame. Everything was perfect – untouched – except for a series of violent slashes that had ripped the canvas apart and exposed the shocking whiteness of the wall behind. It looked as though someone had taken a Stanley knife and set to it with a fury.

Helen felt her legs start to give way.

She moved forwards and sat on an arm of the sofa, surveying the damage more closely. The remnants looked like some expensive installation piece. It wouldn't have looked out of place hanging on the walls of a modern gallery. She could almost hear the critics gushing in extravagant hyperbole about its symbolism and the artist's bold, ironic statement. Only this was no art gallery. And the only statement being made, while undeniably symbolic, was one of anger, not irony. There was only one possible explanation.

Richard knew.

He had discovered the affair.

Helen gripped at the arm of the sofa. It had been two years since the affair ended. Two years since Alfie's funeral when they'd lowered an empty coffin into the ground and they had said farewell to their son. She'd expected the guilt to fade with time, but she still woke every morning, unable to forgive herself for her failings as a wife and mother, unable to look at herself in the mirror with anything other than disgust and self-hatred reflected in her eyes.

She sat for a moment longer, surveying the damage to the painting, reluctant to move and unwilling to face the conflict she knew awaited her. But as she sat, and as the storm of emotion began to settle in her mind, she was surprised to find that amongst the guilt and fear lay the glimmer of something sweeter, the nub of something that she realised she could only call relief. She was about to be exposed; her sordid secrets were about to come tumbling out and once they were out there, spoken and made real, she wouldn't have to lie or hide again. Whatever the outcome, it was time to face it, all of it, head on.

God knows she'd thought about confessing to Richard plenty of times over the last two years. The words had sat on the tip of her tongue for days after Alfie's funeral, burning like salt in an ulcer until she had nearly screamed out in agony. But whatever her own private pain, she knew she couldn't burden Richard with more heartache.

She had ended the affair immediately after Alfie's disappearance, and while it might have allowed her some peace on a personal level to confess her sins to Richard, she realised it would be nothing short of barbaric to inflict yet more pain on a man already drowning in his grief. She had never been able to shake that fear since. Any time she had contemplated revealing her betrayal to her husband, she was wracked by a nagging suspicion that it would prove to be her most selfish act of all. For wouldn't she, by easing her own conscience and seeking his forgiveness, merely be transferring the weight of her adultery onto her husband? It would be his load to bear; to digest, process and live with in whatever form he felt able. And if she were honest, she wasn't sure he could take much more.

It was a strange, twilight time immediately after the funeral. Broken fragments of memories resurfaced. She remembered the leathery smell of the car that had driven them back to the house after the service, and the damp handkerchief she had clutched between her fingers all afternoon, that only later she had realised was embroidered with Alfred Tide's initials, the same initials as her missing son. Back at the house Richard had slumped in a corner of the kitchen gazing out of the window at the gardens, a glass of whisky cradled in his hand. David Chamberlain, his business partner, had shuffled around and patted him awkwardly on the shoulder and repeated how sorry he was for their *loss* until Helen felt like screaming and throwing him and his wife out of the house. Bill Dryden and his wife Betty, who had both been so active in assisting the local search parties, had also returned with them. Betty made tea and laid out plates of digestives while Bill sat at the kitchen table with Cassie and Dora, the three of them reminiscing on happier times. They'd remembered the previous summer when Alfie had gone out to 'help' Bill dig the flower beds. Bill had the girls in giggles as they remembered Alfie putting a big, fat wriggling worm to his lips with an innocent smile. 'Mmmm . . .' he had said, "bagetti.' The three of them had snickered until the realisation that Alfie would no longer be confusing worms for spaghetti had dawned on them all. Their giggles had trailed off into tearful silence, and not long after Bill and Betty had made their excuses and left.

That had just left Violet, who had bustled around the kitchen in her tight black dress and too-bright lipstick making cups of tea and beans on toast. None of them had had an appetite but at least it had been a diversion of some sorts from the profound and somewhat intimidating business of grieving.

'You're an angel,' Helen had sighed wearily up at Violet as she poured herself another glass of wine. 'Thank you for coming.'

'Rubbish,' Violet had said. 'You lot need a little TLC right now. And here I am. It's not as if I've got anything better to do . . .'

She remembered Richard had cleared his throat. 'If you'll all excuse me . . . I think . . . I'd quite like to . . .' His face was pale and he stumbled over his words. 'I think I need to have a little lie down.'

'Of course.' Violet patted him on the arm. 'You go, dear. I'll look after the girls here.'

Helen exchanged a worried glance with Violet. 'He's just tired,' she said, more to herself than anyone else. 'It's been a long day.' But the truth was it was only three in the afternoon.

Not long after Richard had left the kitchen the telephone had rung. Helen rushed at it, reaching the receiver seconds before Cassie. 'Hello?'

'Can you talk?' It was Tobias. They hadn't spoken for a couple of days.

'Yes. Hold on one moment please.' Her voice was all polite efficiency. She turned to the others. 'It's a friend from work. Do you mind?'

Violet nodded. 'Come on, girls, let's go and see what we can find on the telly. Maybe an old movie or something?' Cassie and Dora had trooped out of the kitchen, reluctantly following Violet and her swaying hips, leaving Helen to her call.

'Are you still there?'

'I'm here. How are you, my darling? I've been thinking of you all day. Was it dreadful?'

'Yes. Unbearable.' She closed her eyes. 'They said we might feel a little better once we'd held the service, but to be honest, I think I feel worse. The house just seems so empty without him. I keep expecting him to burst through the door any moment, demanding his tea or asking me to find some toy or other.'

'My poor love. I would have come to the church but I didn't think it appropriate somehow.'

'No,' agreed Helen.

'When can I see you? I'm dying to hold you, to put my arms around you and make it all better.'

Helen breathed quietly down the phone for a moment. 'Tobias, there is no making it better. My son is dead. He's gone.'

'I know. I'm sorry. I meant how can I make *you* feel a little better?'

'I don't know that you can.' She paused as her words sank in. It was the first time she'd admitted it, to him, and to herself, but she found the thought of being with Tobias repellent now.

'You could let me try?' he asked plaintively. 'I miss you.'

'It's not a good time. I need to be with my family.'

Tobias was silent for a moment. 'You know, I need you *too,* Helen.'

Helen shook her head. 'No, I need to be here, with Richard.'

There was a heavy silence at the other end of the phone. 'What are you saying, Helen?'

She sighed. She felt so tired. Too tired for this conversation.

'I don't know. I have to get my head together. I never should have come to meet you that day. It was a mistake . . . a terrible mistake.' Her voice had risen to a strange, hysterical pitch. 'Do you know how guilty I feel? I'm tormented by the fact that we were there, together, when Alfie went missing. Can you imagine what it's like to know that it's your fault your son is dead? I haven't been able to tell anyone and it's killing me inside. I feel so alone.' She let out a strangled sob of anguish.

'Darling, you're not alone. I'm here for you. Why don't we meet? We can talk about it. You'll feel better, I promise. I can make you feel better. Remember how good I can make you feel?'

Her stomach churned at his words. 'No, Tobias,' she said. 'I can't do this right now. My family needs me.'

'So I don't matter? Is that it?' There was an unattractive whine to his voice. Helen wondered how she could have never seen this childish, egocentric side to him before. She thought of their many stolen moments together, in hotel rooms and in the back of his car, snatched moments of sex and lust wrapped up in the heat and excitement of the forbidden, and felt her stomach heave again. Swept up in the romance of their affair, she had failed to see what a terrible, pathetic cliché it all was. She had played the misunderstood wife to a T, she'd painted Richard as the neglectful, distracted husband to perfection, and Tobias had admirably filled the role of the illicit suitor. She wanted to shake herself. How had she ended up here? How had she put everything she cared about on the line, for this? All those years with Richard, spent building a life and a family, and she'd risked it all for what? A meaningless fling.

An image of Richard standing outside the church suddenly filled her mind's eye. He'd stood there, his face pale and taut with grief, his eyes gazing out across the horizon, one arm wrapped around each of their daughters as they leaned in to the comfort of his body. Dora's face had been buried in his jacket and Richard's lips had been moving slowly, offering words of comfort to the girls, even though Helen could practically feel the anguish radiating from his core. Her good, strong husband. How foolish she had been.

'Right now I'm afraid you don't,' she replied. Suddenly she saw things more clearly than she had in a long, long while. She had already lost her son. She couldn't risk losing her daughters, or her husband too. 'I'm sorry. I don't mean to sound callous, but I think it's best if we don't see each other again. My family is most important right now.'

'If it's time and space that you need . . .'

'No. It's not.'

Tobias fell silent at the other end of the phone. When he next spoke there was an edge to his voice. 'Well, this is a turn up for the books . . . After weeks of "Tobias, I want you", "Tobias, I need you" you just want to call it a day?'

'I'm sorry. I can't do this any more.'

'So that's it? It's over, just like that?'

'Yes.'

'I see.'

They were both silent for a moment. She could hear him breathing at the other end of the phone and realised she felt nothing, absolutely nothing. Her infatuation with him had simply dissipated into thin air.

He spoke next. 'Well, I guess there's nothing left to say then . . .'

'No.'

He paused again. 'Goodbye, Helen.'

'Goodbye,' she said.

There was another pause, as if he were waiting for her to change her mind but Helen remained silent and when the click of the receiver came she felt only relief. She sat there for a minute or two listening to the shrill bleeping of the disconnect tone and let the familiar sounds of her home settle in around her.

Over the coming days she collapsed at intermittent and unexpected moments. She'd feel OK, almost normal sometimes, but then the sight of something would send waves of unbearable sadness bearing down upon her. It could be anything: a stray toy retrieved from under the sofa cushions, the pencil marks on the kitchen wall where they had charted Alfie's height, or an old half-eaten box of sultanas found at the bottom of her handbag. They were small things but they had the power to knock the wind out of her lungs and send her running to the bathroom where she would collapse and ride out the pain with great heaving sobs. Or sometimes at night, when her grief was at its most wild and raw, she would take herself up to Alfie's bedroom, close the door and lie upon the coolness of his bed, letting the last, precious scent of him invade her nostrils and her tears stain his pillow.

Richard, on the other hand, collapsed completely. Her husband, normally so strong, so dependable, had simply disintegrated. Up until the moment they had lowered the little empty coffin into the ground Richard had been with purpose. He had spent every waking hour searching for Alfie. Then, when hope had faded and the police had called off the hunt, he had transferred his energy into the funeral arrangements. But once they'd held the service, Richard had fallen apart.

He stayed in bed for a week after the funeral. He just lay there, in the semi-darkness of the bedroom with his face turned to the wall, mourning his son. She had wanted to reach out to him; had been desperate to hold him, for him to hold her, to feel the reassuring solidity of his body against hers. After she'd wept her tears into Alfie's pillow, or screamed her pain in the privacy of the bathroom, she would go to him, driven by an overwhelming need for her husband. She would sit in the shadows and listen to the steady rise and fall of his breath, waiting for him to speak, wondering if she should tell him the truth about where she had been that day. But he hadn't spoken; and neither had she.

In the end it had been *her* words that broke the silence, but they weren't about the affair. Instead, she talked about Alfie. In halting, broken phrases she started to remember their son. She talked about his birth and about the precious moments she and Richard had shared standing over his cot watching him sleep. She remembered Alfie's desire to do everything in a hurry; how he'd cut his first tooth at six months, crawled around the living room floor after the girls at just seven months, and taken his first wobbly steps at eleven months. She reminded Richard of Alfie's first word: 'Dada'; how they had sat up all night with him when he had chicken pox, and the time he had run a dangerously high fever and covered every single item of bedding they owned with his watery vomit; how his hair had shone golden in the sun and how the old ladies of Bridport would stop and coo as she pushed him around in his pram. She remembered him repeatedly pulling all the books off the bookshelves until, exasperated, she had spent a morning wedging them all in tight as sardines. She'd recalled the time he had stood outside innocently one late summer's day and pelted rotting cherries, found at the foot of the cherry tree, one by one at the freshly painted exterior of the house; and the funny little dances he would do with the girls when they put their favourite CDs on and leapt and whirled around the living room. She relived a catalogue of memories from the end of the bed, sometimes laughing, sometimes sobbing, sometimes both, and all the while Richard had lain there, still and silent, his face turned away from hers into the darkness of the room.

And then once, in a moment of sheer need and loneliness,

she had padded upstairs, undressed silently and climbed into their bed, pushing her warm nakedness up against her husband's back. He was awake. She could tell from his breathing and she willed him to turn and put his arms around her. She wanted nothing more than to forget herself, to bury her pain in the familiarity of his scent and skin. But Richard just lay there, rigid and still under the sheet, until she had eventually turned away from him and fallen asleep.

Exasperated and out of ideas, she'd talked about it to Violet.

'I just don't know what to do any more. I'm so worried about him. He can't go on like this . . . he'll make himself sick . . . and I'm not sure I can handle things on my own.'

'Well, I'm here,' Violet offered. 'I've already told you I don't have anything pressing to rush back for and I really don't mind helping.' She paused, realising she'd missed Helen's point. 'But I see what you mean. It must be difficult for you. I suppose he's terribly sad right now. I think it might be harder for a man, in some ways.'

Helen had raised an eyebrow sceptically. 'Oh yes?'

'You know,' Violet had continued as Helen stared at her blankly, 'I'm not saying it's easy for you. You are Alfie's mother, after all. But Richard is the man. He's the provider – the provider and the protector of the family. I suppose he might feel a little as though he's failed you all, or failed Alfie. Not that he has, of course,' she rushed. 'I just think perhaps he's feeling terribly to blame. Poor chap.'

'But it's not Richard's fault!'

'Oh I know that! I'm so sorry, of course it's not anyone's fault,' Violet apologised. 'This is coming out all wrong. What I mean to say is that Richard is a very honourable man. I should think he's taking this very hard because he wishes there was something he could have done to save Alfie. Do you see what I mean?'

Helen nodded. No one understood that better than she. She woke every day and faced the guilt of her decision to spend that day with Tobias rather than care for her son. If she'd done things differently, if she'd made a different choice that morning, she had no doubt that Alfie would still be alive.

Violet interrupted her thoughts. 'You could call a doctor. There may be things they can do for him . . . antidepressants . . . counselling? I know there's all sorts of treatments available these days for breakdowns.'

Helen shook her head. 'Richard's not having a breakdown.' She paused. 'He's not. He's grieving. He's succumbed to his emotions. He was never one for really expressing himself, and this is what happens when you bottle everything up inside.'

Violet nodded.

'I don't know what to do, V.' Helen sagged at the table. 'Where do we go from here? How do we carry on with normal life when everything is so utterly destroyed? I don't think I can do this on my own.'

'I think you're probably all a long way away from a "normal life" right now. A little time will help. You'll see,' Violet said, patting her arm. 'Try and be patient.'

Helen had shrugged her shoulders. What else could she be?

In the end, and rather unexpectedly, it had been Violet who had got through to Richard. It had been her last day with the family and Helen had asked if she would mind taking Richard a tray of tea and toast before she left.

'Would you mind? You could say goodbye at the same time . . . not that he'll say anything back,' she added grimly, 'but maybe just let him know you're leaving?'

'Of course, however I can help, you know that.'

Violet had taken the tray and disappeared upstairs. When she hadn't returned a few minutes later Helen's curiosity was piqued. She'd crept up the stairs and stood outside their bedroom on the landing. The door to the room was ajar and she could see Violet sitting on her side of the bed. Richard lay with his back to her. Violet looked uncomfortable; she shifted her weight awkwardly on the mattress and played with the buttons on her shirtsleeves as she spoke to him in a low murmur. Helen could just make out what she was saying.

'It's so terribly sad, Richard. You all miss him and you each need to mourn Alfie in your own way. I can understand you wanting to stay up here, away from the world. I just don't want you to forget, in your grief, that you have two beautiful, vibrant daughters downstairs who need you an awful lot right now. And a wonderful wife who loves you very much.'

There was a small sigh from Richard's side of the bed.

'Helen is very worried about you. They all are. I know you'll be up and about when you're feeling ready to face everyone, and I'm not pressuring you. Truly I'm not. I just wanted to remind you that although Alfie has gone, there's a lot more life left in your home, for you to enjoy, when you're ready.' Violet paused and tucked her blond hair back behind her ears. 'Anyway, listen to me going on and on. I really just came up here to let you know that I'm leaving now. I have to return to Sussex. I need to go and check up on my shops. Autumn is a busy time for a florist; strange, isn't it? But if you ever need me, you or the girls, you just go right ahead and pick up that telephone. I'll be here like a shot, for any one of you.'

Violet leaned over and gently kissed the top of Richard's head and as she touched him, Richard jolted. He lurched up into a sitting position, reaching out for her hand and staring at her with wild, dark eyes.

'I can't do this,' he'd croaked at her. 'I can't carry on. I keep thinking of him, out there in the water . . . his little body battered and bruised from the waves, being pummelled against the rocks, or' – Richard's voice cracked – 'or dragged along the bottom of the ocean. I close my eyes and I see his skin being torn by the reef, his beautiful face all white and swollen. Fish nibbling at him . . . crabs tugging at his hands and feet . . .'

Helen shuddered. Her heart was in her mouth. She

couldn't bear to hear Richard's nightmares, but she couldn't tear herself away either.

'I can't talk to Helen about it. I don't want to upset her any more than she is already. It's not fair to her. Oh God,' Richard sobbed, 'I just want to hold him. I'd give anything to hold him one more time . . . to smell his skin . . . to touch his hair. My beautiful boy. My beautiful boy is gone.'

With that Richard had let out a cry and thrown himself at Violet. He put his arms around her, leaning his head onto the curve of her shoulder and let out loud, primitive sobs that made his whole body tremble with grief.

It was clear that Violet did not know what to do. She sat utterly still and helpless as Richard held onto her. Then, slowly, she raised a hand to Richard's head and began to stroke his head. As her hand moved, backwards and forwards, backwards and forwards, she murmured comforting shushing noises, over and over, until Richard's weeping subsided. The two of them sat like that for a while. Then, as if sensing Helen's presence, Violet looked up towards the door. The two women locked eyes over the top of Richard's head; they stared at each other, frozen in the moment, until Helen mouthed a silent 'thank you' and turned on her heel.

Violet left an hour later, and an hour or so after that Richard had wandered downstairs in his dressing gown. He'd walked into the kitchen and put the kettle on. 'Would you like a cup of tea?' he'd asked Helen, as if the last seven days of self-imposed isolation had been nothing more than a surreal dream.

She decided to follow his cue and pretend that this was nothing out of the ordinary. 'Yes. Yes, that would be lovely. Thank you.'

'I think I'll go back to work on Monday,' he'd added as he rummaged in the crockery cupboard for mugs.

'Oh, OK, if you're sure?'

'Yes,' was all he'd said.

And that had been that.

*

Helen shook herself. The memories were still fresh more than two years on. Just like her grief, just like her guilt. She glanced once more at the devastated painting hanging on the wall, sighed and then lifted herself wearily from the arm of the sofa. It was cold outside and her joints were stiff and sore. She felt tired, old and tired. Pulling her dressing gown around her body protectively, she walked through the chilly hallway, bracing herself for the confrontation she now knew was coming.

As she walked through the dining room, she averted her gaze, as usual, from the framed family photos spread across the sideboard, memories of a happier time. They hadn't thought to capture any moments on film since Alfie's disappearance. It was as if life had stood still in the Tide family; as if life now held nothing worth celebrating; a sad state of affairs but she hadn't had the energy to put things right. She'd been trying her hardest just to keep herself functioning, on some basic level.

After Richard had returned to work, Helen hoped things might settle down. The girls had gone back to school and Helen had steeled herself and returned to campus for a new term. It was as if some strange force, some inevitable momentum pushed her onwards. She woke. She dressed. She went to work. She bought groceries. She made dinner. She brushed her teeth. She went to bed. She felt like an actress playing her part on a vast, empty stage, day after aching day.

She did her best to avoid him, but Tobias pursued her. He arrived at her office unannounced and begged her in urgent, hushed undertones to return to him. He would leave flowers and notes on her desk, and messages on her voicemail, but Helen ignored them all. She simply couldn't face him, or the thought of the destruction their affair had wreaked. Each scribbled word he left her, every wilting bloom he plucked and presented as a symbol of his affection now served as nothing more than a painful reminder of her raging guilt.

Alfie's death had sucked every ounce of passion from their relationship, just as a raging fire sucks oxygen from the air, and losing Alfie only served to highlight an inevitable truth, one she had been too foolish to see: it was Richard she wanted. Only Richard. Only now did she realise his dependability, his fierce principles about family and duty and his fundamental goodness weren't signs of weakness or things to irritate and annoy, rather they were qualities to be admired, qualities to cling to.

Yet Richard was strangely absent. Business trips kept him away for longer and longer periods, and when he did return, he would drift about the house aimlessly, or take long solitary walks up onto the Cap, returning hours later mud-spattered and windswept yet with the same distracted look in his eyes. And at night, after they had completed their familiar round of locking doors and turning off lights, they would retreat to their bedroom, only to dress chastely in nightwear before turning off bedside lamps and slipping silently under the covers.

'Goodnight, dear,' he would say primly, the words and tone of a man much older than his forty-odd years.

'Goodnight,' she'd reply, turning away from him and pulling the sheets up underneath her chin, all the while silently yearning for the warmth of his touch. She couldn't remember the last time they had made love. She had spent nineteen years in a marriage she had convinced herself did nothing but stifle her, only to find that she now longed for its security, its safe dependability. It was more than ironic; it was perverse. But she knew it was nothing short of what she deserved. With Cassie, troubled and in hiding up in London, and Dora closeted away in her bedroom or out of the house at every seeming opportunity, Helen found herself wandering around Clifftops like a ghostly, lost soul. The echoing, empty house was her cross to bear, her punishment, and she knew it was being meted out in full force: purgatory.

Yet, through all the pain, and all the sadness they had

inflicted and endured, she still dared to hope that Richard loved her. She just needed to give him time, she told herself; time to let go of his grief, time to heal, and time to find her once again, this time, waiting for him.

She paused outside the kitchen. Perhaps now the affair was out in the open they could begin the necessary steps to healing their marriage. There didn't need to be any more secrets or lies. Perhaps this was the fire they needed to walk through to cleanse their marriage. It had been the worst two years of her life yet she could still hope there was a future for them; for really, what else did she have left?

She braced herself. Then, with a deep breath, she pushed open the door and walked in.

Richard was seated at the kitchen table. He had his back to her but she saw him stiffen as she entered the room and he spoke before she had a chance to address him.

'How long, Helen?' He didn't look at her. His voice was gravelly, like sandpaper, as though he'd been crying. 'How long has it been going on?'

She swallowed. 'Two months . . . maybe three, but it's over; it has been for a long time. It was nothing, Richard, it meant nothing.' Her words sounded clichéd, even to her ears. She moved around the side of the table to look at him but he avoided her gaze, turning his head to look out of the window instead. There was a scrap of paper on the table in front of him. She peered down at it, and sensing her interest, he pushed it across at her.

'You'll probably want this little memento.'

She looked at the scrap of paper lying in front of him. It was a simple sketch, drawn in charcoal, of a naked woman reclining under the shade of a tree. She had been captured in a blush-inducing pose by the artist's expert pencil. He had even taken the trouble to sign and date the piece, in the bottom right-hand corner. Helen stared at the image with horror.

'You look lovely,' Richard said.

'I . . . I had no idea . . .' she stammered.

'Don't try to deny it, Helen. It's clearly you. As you told me yourself all those years ago when you brought that hideous painting home, he's a "genius artist". The likeness is uncanny, don't you think?'

Helen swallowed again. Discussing the affair was one thing, but coming face to face with such graphic evidence was both unexpected and wholly mortifying. Poor Richard.

'How . . . where did you find this? Did *he* give it to you?' Helen's mind was racing.

Richard gave a little snort. 'Someone took pity on me and decided to post it to me at work. I received it yesterday. I should think his wife took it upon herself to inform me; poor cuckold that I am! I imagine she's sick to death of her husband's philandering and decided to take matters into her own hands.'

Helen bit the inside of her cheek. She couldn't bear to think of Richard opening an envelope containing the crude sketch, and in the office of all places. 'I don't know what to say . . . it's over. You have to believe me. It's been over for a long time. Since the funeral. There was no way I could . . .' Her words trailed off as Richard looked up at her. There was a genuine disgust in his eyes.

'No way you could sleep in another man's bed, a married man at that, when your own son was out there, lost? Dead? How very decent of you, Helen.' His voice dripped with sarcasm. 'How very noble.'

'I'm not proud of myself, Richard. I've lived with the guilt these last couple of years. I wanted to tell you – I really did.'

'Then why didn't you?'

'I didn't want to add to your burden, Richard. We were grieving for our son. The affair was over. I thought it was best . . .' Again, her words faded away.

They sat across the table from each other. Richard gazed at her blankly, and then shook his head with incomprehension.

All the while, the little scrap of white paper sat between them, staring up at them like a glaring reminder of all that had gone wrong for them over the years.

'Do you love him?' Richard asked finally.

'No!' she exclaimed. 'God, no! He was a mistake; a fling.'

'When did it start? I want to know everything. Don't spare me the details. I don't want any more lies, do you understand?' His voice was grim.

Helen nodded. 'It was a flirtation at first. We met that first time in Bridport, when I visited his gallery and bought the painting.'

Richard nodded.

'We flirted with each other, but it was nothing more at that point. We hadn't been in Dorset that long. It was a difficult time. Remember?'

Richard gave another little nod and turned to look out the window again. She could see tears welling at the corners of his eyes. She longed to move across the table and hold him, but she held herself back. She owed him an explanation.

'Then I got pregnant with Alfie. Tobias just . . . he just faded away; it was one of those things that never happened. It wasn't meant to be. You and I, we were happy. You must remember?' There was desperation in her voice. It was important he remember what they had, what they could be.

'So when did you first sleep with him then? What changed?'

'It was my second year lecturing at Exeter. He'd been appointed as Artist in Residence at the university.'

Richard nodded, 'Go on,' he said.

'We'd occasionally bump into each other on campus. Then at the end of the summer term he invited me out to lunch.'

'So you went for lunch and just happened to fall into bed with each other, is that it?'

'No! It wasn't like that. We were friends for a while before.'

Richard eyed her suspiciously. 'No lies, remember?'

'OK, we were more than friends. We flirted with each

other, for a few months. I liked the attention,' she sighed. She knew it was better if she were completely honest. 'I was lonely and bored. I was sick of only being seen as a wife and mother; I was sick of small-town life. You and I, we never talked about anything except the kids, about school runs and packed lunches, bills and laundry. Tobias made me feel special; he made me feel attractive, and desirable. I liked that. I liked him.'

'So it was my fault, is that it?' Richard asked with scorn. 'I didn't make you feel like enough of a *woman*? I didn't pay you enough attention?'

'No! It wasn't your fault; of course I'm not saying that. I'm just trying to explain how I was feeling. And you have to admit, we *were* going through a rough patch back then. There was the move . . . adjusting to this house . . .'

'Oh yes . . . this *dreadful* house . . . of course.' There was a flatness to his voice, but something else too, a hint of bitterness.

Helen ignored it. There was no point rehashing that old argument, not now. 'We started sleeping together just before the summer break, just before the holidays; you know, the summer Alfie died. And I ended the affair as soon as we lost him. It was a matter of weeks, two or so months at the most. It was a horrible mistake. We had lost Alfie. I couldn't bear the thought of losing you or the girls as well. I still can't.' Helen's voice cracked and she struggled to keep her composure.

Richard heard the emotion in her voice and turned to look at her for the first time. Their eyes locked across the table. She could see a tornado of emotion behind the clear blue of his eyes. She reached out her hand, desperate to make physical contact with him. Richard looked down at it for a moment but didn't move. Instead he continued with his questions.

'Why him? Why Tobias?'

She shook her head. 'I don't know. He was there. He wanted me.'

'Were you attracted to him – from the beginning?'

'Yes,' she confirmed. There was no point lying about it now.

'How many times did you meet up? How many times did you sleep together?'

'I don't know . . . eight, ten maybe?' She couldn't remember exactly.

'Did you meet him here? Did you ever sleep with him in our bed?'

'No!'

'Did the kids know about him?'

'No!' she said again. 'I was very careful; I would never have wanted them to find out.'

'Did you ever think of leaving me?'

Helen paused. She thought for a moment and realised that she never had. No matter how intense things had been between her and Tobias, no matter how many silly daydreams he had concocted while they were together, she had never once truly considered leaving Richard for him. 'No.'

'And it's really over?' he continued. 'You haven't been with him since you ended the affair?'

'No. I swear. I couldn't bear it. It's over. Losing Alfie made me realise how much our marriage means to me. Richard?' She gazed at him. 'Richard, look at me!' He glanced up and she stared him straight in the eye. 'Richard, I love you. I've made some terrible mistakes. I've caused a lot of pain. Truly, I don't know what the future holds for us, but I do know that I don't want to lose you. I couldn't bear it. Our marriage may not have started well. We may have had some rocky patches . . . and some downright miserable times . . . but the one thing I am absolutely certain of, more than anything, is that I *do* want to be with you.'

She meant every word she said. After nineteen years together they stood staring at each other across a great chasm of misunderstanding and pain, and Helen knew now the part she had played in creating the divide. She'd always privately blamed Richard for *talking her* into a marriage she'd since convinced herself she didn't want. She'd railed against his decision to move them from London and cloister them away in a small seaside town. She'd grown to resent his sense of duty to Clifftops and to the memory of his parents, and believed he had put these first, before her needs and those of their children. And yet she knew now it was she who had been wrong. She had forgotten to see how good he was, how strong and true and kind. She'd been determined to resent him and all the things he stood for in order to justify her infidelity; and later, in the storm of their grief, she had allowed the chasm to crack wider and wider. She realised now that she wanted a man who respected his family heritage and felt his responsibilities deep in his being, a man who could hold his two daughters up while inside he collapsed with grief, a man who spread his butter carefully on his toast each morning and turned off all the lights at night and locked the doors and kissed her goodnight in bed each night with a gentle dependability. Because that was *who* Richard was. And when all was said and done, when all the dust had settled on the remnants of their life together, it was Richard she still wanted most of all.

'Let's try again,' she pleaded. 'All this time that we've been locked in our own private pain, feeling so isolated, so at sea . . . and yet here you are, the only other person in the world who can understand what I've been through with Alfie and everything that came after. And I am that same person for you.' She shook her head sadly. 'It *could* have made us stronger, not torn us apart like this.' She held up her hands in protest. 'I know, I blame myself. But is it really too late for us, Richard? Is it *really* too late to turn this around and try to find something good and decent hidden beneath the wreckage of it all?'

Richard held her gaze, staring deep into her eyes for a very long time. Then slowly, inch by inch, his hand stretched across the table to clasp her outstretched fingers. They sat together, for a moment, in complete silence; their fingers entwined.

'I just don't know how we move forwards any more,' he said quietly. 'I don't think I can take any more punches.'

Helen nodded, tears welling in her eyes.

'But I don't want to do this on my own.'

Helen's breath caught in her throat.

Richard swallowed. 'Perhaps if we take it slowly . . .' he said finally, squeezing her fingers and closing his eyes.

Helen could have wept. She knew it was more than she deserved. She had imagined this moment many times, and it had never ended in anything other than total and utter devastation. To be given a second chance by Richard, to have a hope of saving their marriage, was more than she had dreamed of.

'You won't regret this, Richard. I promise. I love you. I'm going to prove it to you. If I have to spend the next nineteen years making it up to you, I will.'

Richard nodded again and opened his eyes. He took a breath. 'We've both got a lot of making up to do, haven't we? I guess I'm not totally blameless in this whole thing. I might have been a better husband, more attentive to you. I didn't always listen to what you wanted . . . to what you needed. Let's wipe the slate clean, shall we? Start again? Let's you and I start from the beginning. Let's do it for us . . . and for the girls. I'm sure they could both use us right now.'

Helen nodded sadly and as she thought of their daughters, and all the pain she had brought upon her family, she began to weep silent tears. Richard reached out and brushed them from her face with his fingers, and grateful for the compassion in his touch, she leaned her face into the palm of his hand, resting it there for just a moment. As she did, a teardrop ran down her chin and fell onto the scrap paper lying between them. It landed on the charcoal lines of the sketch, blurring the edges of the woman into a fuzzy grey mist, erasing them for ever. Helen looked down at the page and winced.

'Let's burn it,' she suggested, sniffing and wiping her nose. 'Let's get rid of it, once and for all. I can't bear to look at it.'

Richard nodded. 'Good idea; a fresh start.'

He reached out a hand to pick up the piece of paper but as he did so he caught sight of something on the page and froze, mid-stretch.

'What's wrong?' Helen asked, seeing him hesitate. 'What is it?'

He didn't respond, he just continued to stare at the piece of paper as the colour drained slowly from his face.

She looked down again, unsure what his eyes had fixed upon. He seemed to be staring at Tobias's signature in the bottom corner of the page, the area where he had scrawled his name and scratched the date. Suddenly, the pit of Helen's stomach gave way.

The date. There it was in black and white.

It was the day Alfie had gone missing.

Helen could see the cogs whirring in Richard's mind; she could feel a maelstrom of emotion suddenly flood the room. Richard looked up at her at last, but his blue eyes were no longer filled with forgiveness. They were on fire with rage.

'You were with him *that* day?' It was barely a whisper.

Helen couldn't reply.

'You were with Tobias Grey on the day Alfie went missing?'

She opened her mouth, but no words came out.

'You and *that man* were holed up in some cheap hotel conducting your sordid little affair while our son roamed by himself on the beach? You and your lover were screwing each other while our boy, our beautiful boy . . .' Richard's voice cracked with emotion, but he continued, spitting out the last words with venom, ' . . . was lost in the waves . . . drowning?'

She stared at him in horror. The look in his eyes was devastating.

'You said you were at work that day. You said you had

been called onto campus. It was *unavoidable.*' His words came fast. 'My God.' He shook his head. 'All this time, you've kept the truth from me. All this time you've let me believe it was some terrible, tragic accident. And yet all along you've known that if it hadn't been for your sleazy little affair, our boy might still be alive. You killed him.'

'No!' Helen cried.

Richard shook his head. 'Look at this, go on, look at it!' He waved the piece of paper in her face. 'How can you deny it when the evidence is right here in front of us? You are a murderer. You murdered our son. You should be locked up! And to think you nearly had me convinced. I was this close . . .' He held up his thumb and forefinger. 'This close. My God! How could you?'

'Richard, you don't understand . . .'

'What don't I understand, Helen?' He was roaring now. It was terrifying. Richard never raised his voice. She had never seen him so angry. 'What can you possibly say that will redeem you from this disgusting, sordid mess?'

She looked up at him. He was right. There was nothing she could say. She had no defence. She was guilty of everything he accused her of. It was her fault Alfie was dead. It was all her fault.

'Richard, please . . .'

'Please . . . please . . . please what, Helen?' he spat. 'Please don't leave me?' he mimicked in a high-pitched whine.

'Yes,' she said in a small voice.

'You know, I always knew, right from the start, that you didn't really love me.'

Helen looked at him in shock, unsure what he was saying.

'Yes, that's right,' he continued, 'I know you think I'm stupid, but I always knew. I was prepared to gamble. I was prepared to wait. I thought I could show you what real love was all about. I thought I could make you love me. But I was wrong.'

'No,' shouted Helen desperately. 'I do love you, Richard.'

'Ha!' He gave a sour little laugh. 'Love? You don't know the meaning of the word, Helen. I'm sick of it. I'm sick of this diseased marriage. I don't want to be a part of it any more, do you hear me? I can't bear to be around you. I can't bear to be near you. You disgust me.' Richard stood from the kitchen table. He moved with such force the chair he had been sitting on tipped and fell to the floor behind him with a crash. He didn't seem to notice. 'I'm going upstairs but I really don't think you want to be around me right now, Helen.' He was wringing his hands violently. 'I don't trust myself right now. Just stay away.'

'Richard,' she sobbed. She had no more words but she looked up at him imploringly, tears now streaming down her face.

'What? You want me to feel sorry for you? Is that it? Forget it, Helen. Just stay away from me. I mean it.'

He turned and stalked out of the room. The door swung shut heavily behind him and Helen was left standing alone in the kitchen next to the overturned chair and the little piece of paper that had brought their whole house of cards tumbling down around her. She sank to the kitchen floor and gave in to her tears.

Richard left an hour later. He packed a bag, made a couple of quick phone calls and then fled down the stairs towards his car, spitting his final words to her.

'I'll call you – in a couple of days. I'll let you know where I am, in case the *girls* need me,' he added pointedly. It was clear he couldn't care less about Helen's needs any more.

She merely nodded and bit her lip, terrified that if she opened her mouth she might start to plead and wail all over again.

It was over. There was nothing left to say.

Moments later Richard's car hurtled down the driveway and Helen was left with nothing but the eerie silence of the vast, empty house echoing all around her.

DORA

Present Day

Dora pulls the car up onto a scruffy verge and stares at the crumbling old manor house ahead. She glances back down at the address she holds in her hand, scrawled across the back of a tatty envelope: Swan House, Little Oxington. It's definitely the right place, but the old ruin standing at the end of the drive is not what she's expecting. It is in stark contrast to the crusty boarding house she has imagined over the past few years. Passing comments her parents have made about Cassie and her location have made her think of some sort of commune for pot-smoking hippies and hemp-clad drop-outs, but this place looks anything but. It is a glorious country estate.

A decade is a long time. It's a long time to pretend that a once-idolised sister no longer exists, and Dora has done a good job of it. When she looks back now, her memories of Cassie are a strange jumble; a series of glossy childhood snapshots mixed up with darker scenes and images from a troubled past. Yes, among the happier times lurk the tantrums and door slamming, the black moods and impulsive behaviour, the long periods of self-imposed isolation. It's a confusing swirl, but above all, Dora remembers the overwhelming sense of rejection at being left by a sister who had the world at her feet and still chose to send herself into exile.

Yes, ten years is a long time and Dora believes she's mastered her anger now. She's not the same person any more; long gone is the naive, daydreaming teenager, always eager to please, always eager to keep the peace. She has a career, a boyfriend, a home . . . and now, a baby on the way. But if ten years can bring about such dramatic changes for Dora, she can't help but feel nervous about whom she will greet inside the house. It's terrifying but Dora knows the time for hiding is over now. She needs to confront Cassie, if only to try to put the past finally to rest.

She shifts uncomfortably, remembering it all as she navigates her car around a huge stone fountain standing in the centre of the driveway, its pale young nymphs staring back at her with dead eyes. She turns away from the white stone faces, uncomfortable under their gaze, and pulls up outside the elegant manor, switching off the car engine and breathing deeply as a fresh surge of guilt washes over her. She should have visited before now. She should have made the effort.

She sits there, rooted to the spot, flooded with guilt and nerves. Fighting the overwhelming urge to turn the key in the ignition and speed off down the driveway, Dora grabs her handbag and steps out into the heat of the day.

It is glorious; the warm air wraps itself around her like a blanket, carrying with it the heady scent of summer and the distant call of a blackbird high up in the trees above her. Her shoes crunch on the gravel, and as she reaches the grand colonnaded entrance of the old house she pauses to look up. The doorway stands before her, dark and forbidding, a gaping black mouth in stark contrast to the lightness of the day around her. She shivers, and then summoning a final burst of courage, takes the steps two at a time, suddenly eager to confront whatever lies inside. She's come this far. All she has to do now is get it over with as quickly as possible, and then get the hell out of there. She takes another step forward and, before she can change her mind, presses decisively on the doorbell.

A very tall man with braided hair and drooping spaniel eyes opens the door. He peers out at her suspiciously. 'Can I help you?' he asks, his eyes flitting nervously up the driveway behind her. It's almost as if he expects Dora to jam her foot in the frame and barge her way inside, uninvited.

'Is Cassie here?'

'Who's asking?'

'I'm her sister, Dora.'

The man seems to relax slightly and looks her up and down. 'You don't look much like her.'

'No,' she agrees. She waits a moment longer, hoping to be invited inside, but the man remains where he is, solidly blocking the entrance until another voice booms out loudly behind him.

'Who is it, Jacob?'

The ponytailed man jumps. 'It's someone for Cassie. She *says* she's her sister.'

The door is suddenly wrenched open and Dora comes face to face with another man, attractive with smooth, nut-brown skin, unruly curled hair and high Slavic cheekbones. He is grinning at her. 'You must be Dora,' he says, offering her his hand. 'I'm Felix. Felix Reveley-Jones. Good to meet you. Sorry about Jacob here, he's our resident conspiracy theorist. He thinks everyone who shows up on the doorstep is either a spy or a journalist, ready to put the kibosh on our little Secret Garden project.'

Dora smiles politely and shakes his outstretched hand, not quite sure what he is talking about.

'Cassie's expecting you,' Felix continues. 'Come on in. She's probably out the back. Did you find us OK? You drove out from London, didn't you?'

Dora nods again and looks about surreptitiously as the man called Felix leads her into a grand entrance hall, her heels clicking noisily on the marble floor. There is nothing much in the room: a few muddy boots lined up by the door and an old oak table housing a landslide of unopened post, over which hangs a gilt-framed portrait of a severe young man dressed in black, the whiteness of his dog collar shining in stark contrast to the faded colours of the painting – the man seems to peer into the middle distance, as though contemplating a bleak and unpalatable future. There are grey shadow marks on the walls around, marking where other paintings presumably once hung, but the rest of the hall is empty besides an elegant wooden staircase that spirals away into the upper levels of the house and which is missing a few balusters here and there.

'Jacob, go and find Cassie, will you? I'll look after Dora.'

The ponytailed man throws Dora another suspicious glance before disappearing wordlessly through a doorway.

'Don't worry about him,' Felix continues, 'he's really very nice when you get to know him.'

Dora smiles and shuffles awkwardly, hoping her sister won't be too long. Her nerves are jangling. She glances again at the portrait on the wall. The man really does look quite miserable.

'My great-grandfather,' says Felix, following the direction of her gaze. 'The Reverend Robert Reveley-Jones, quite the comedian, apparently.'

Dora smiles despite her nerves.

'God knows how he wooed my great-grandmother, Lady Catherine Swan, but thank goodness he did, because, well, here we are.' Felix throws his hands out wide to indicate the enormous manor surrounding them.

'It's been a while since you and Cassie caught up, hasn't it?' Felix asks, staring at her with open interest.

It is Dora's turn to be suspicious. She wonders if he's Cassie's boyfriend and how much he knows about their past. She blushes at the thought. 'Yes,' she says, clearing her throat, 'it has been a while. A few years.'

'Well I know she's looking forward to seeing you and showing you our little outfit here. The Secret Garden is pretty much all thanks to her, I have to say.'

'So you work here too then?' Dora asks, still unsure what exactly this 'Secret Garden' is that he keeps going on about.

'Yes, I suppose I do. This is my house. I own the building and the estate. I'm your typical trustafarian, I'm afraid: spoilt little rich kid living the dream off his inheritance. I just don't have the crusty dreadlocks to prove it.'

'It's a beautiful house,' Dora says.

'Yes, isn't it? Of course it was far more beautiful in its heyday, but it suits us fine for now.'

As they are chatting two women wander through the vestibule. They are carrying large boxes of vegetables in their arms and throw shy smiles at Dora and Felix as they walk by.

'Hello!' greets Felix, before turning back to Dora. 'That's Scarlett and Sophie, our resident cooks. You should stay for dinner, if you can. You'd be very welcome.'

'Thank you,' murmurs Dora, wishing Cassie would hurry up, 'but I should probably get back.'

'No trouble, another time perhaps?'

Thankfully Jacob is back, sidling into the room with his hangdog expression. There is someone else behind him.

'Here she is,' says Felix.

'Hey, Dora, long time no see,' Cassie says, appearing from behind Jacob. She moves across to Dora, a smile playing on her lips and pulls her into a hug.

Dora submits herself to her sister's arms, but she feels stiff and awkward in the embrace.

'So, what took you so long?' Cassie asks.

'Sorry,' says Dora, breaking free to try and get a better look at Cassie. 'The M25 was a nightmare . . . terrible traffic.' The words are out of her mouth before she realises Cassie isn't referring to her lateness that morning, but rather her glaring absence over the past few years. She blushes and gazes around the empty hallway in panic. It's going wrong already. She should never have come.

'God, lighten up, will you? It was just a joke!' Cassie lets out a sharp bark of laughter, reminiscent of their father, and the sound of it takes Dora straight back to Clifftops; to sitting around in each other's bedrooms, trawling through magazines for new hairstyles and clothes, gossiping about some new supermodel or another washed-up pop star. She relaxes slightly. She is still Cassie, no matter what has passed these last few years.

'Sorry, I'm a bit nervous,' Dora admits.

Felix clears his throat. 'Well, we'll leave you ladies to it. It was nice to meet you, Dora. See you again, I hope.'

Dora nods. 'Yes, thank you. Nice to meet you too.' She turns back to Cassie. 'You look good,' she blurts. It's true. Cassie is not the pale recluse Dora has imagined on the drive down, but rather she looks fit and tanned, as though she has just returned from a Mediterranean holiday or an expensive spa break. Dora is surprised to feel a tiny tinge of jealousy well up within her. Cassie has always been the beautiful one.

Her sister, however, doesn't seem to register the compliment. 'I thought we could go for a walk, if you fancy it?' she suggests. 'You know, get out of the house and get some air, if you don't mind?'

Dora nods. 'That sounds great. I'd like to stretch my legs and it's a beautiful day.'

'Good. Come on then.'

Dora follows Cassie out of the marbled entrance hall and back into the daylight. Her sister walks fast, her long legs striding down the steps and across the drive, before turning down a gravel path running along one side of the house. As Dora races to keep up she notes Cassie is taller than she remembers and she wears her hair pulled back into a single, thick plait that hangs down the centre of her back and glints golden in the sunlight. She is dressed in a white T-shirt, trainers and an old pair of Levi's; a simple outfit that makes Dora regret her own careful choice of summer dress and kitten heels. She'd thought she'd feel poised and in control but instead she feels fussy and formal by comparison.

They round the side of the building and emerge onto an ornate carved terrace that runs along the back of the house. From its elevated position she can see across beautiful landscaped gardens flowing away down the hillside. Dora makes out the distant glint of water through the trees but instead of heading down towards the lawns, as she thinks they might, Cassie continues her gallop straight across the terrace and down a few more steps before passing through a discreet wooden door set into a brick wall. Dora has to bend slightly to fit through it and she follows her sister blindly, taking three or four more steps forward before stopping dead in her tracks. She shields her eyes from the fierce glare of the sun and looks around in wonder.

They have entered a secluded garden, hidden from the house by high stone walls. It is startling not so much for its unexpected appearance, but for the flood of colour and scent that suddenly assaults Dora from every direction. The garden is in full bloom. Vivid jewel-like shades of ruby and amber, amethyst and jade swim before her. She sees red-hot pokers, tangled fuchsias, roses, sunflowers and the pinkest of asters. Helianthus and the sturdy stalks of sedum and globe thistle stand proudly alongside vivid red dahlias. Along one wall a bold hedge of blue hydrangeas nod heavy flowers sleepily in the sun. At her feet a bank of lavender thrusts its lilac flowers up towards the sky and fills her nostrils with their heady scent. She turns in amazement and glimpses flourishing bushes of rosemary, basil and mint and the blue-green leaves of sage and thyme. Beyond the herbs stands a neat vegetable patch. It bears cane towers laden with twisting bean plants and rows of sprouting green tufts that give away the secret location of onions and leeks and carrots, all carefully tucked away in their soil beds. And beyond these, against one wall leans a ramshackle greenhouse, glinting silver in the late morning sun.

It is beautiful; a picturesque kitchen garden and a tiny, private oasis where, it seems, time stands still. Dora half expects a scullery maid to bustle past her at any moment with a wide basket and scissors readied to select herbs and vegetables for the evening meal up at the house. She is reminded of the secret garden she has read about as a child; the whole landscape seems to hum with life, with colour and sound and scent. Turning in amazement she drinks more and more of it in. She sees fat bees drowsy with pollen wafting past on the breeze; butterflies dancing daintily across the flower beds and somewhere, just below the chatter and hum of insect life, lies the low, steady bubble of running water. This final enchanting sound she is able to trace to a small water lily pond set into the centre of the garden. Beside this stands an archway covered in trailing pink clematis and hidden in its shade is a low wooden bench. It is towards this seat that Cassie moves. She brushes at something invisible on the seat, and then sits herself down, patting the empty space next to her. 'Come, sit with me.'

Dora moves across to the archway, revelling in the heady perfume of lilac blossom and basil as she goes.

'So, what do you think of our Secret Garden then?' Cassie asks. As she speaks she turns back to survey the garden, eyeing the rows of plants before her critically. 'It's my little project.'

Dora follows her line of sight. '*Your* little project?' she asks.

'Yes, the garden here, what do you think?' Cassie seems amused at Dora's disbelief.

'It's . . . gorgeous . . . beautiful.' Dora struggles to find the right words to sum up something so tear-inducingly lovely. 'Did *you* do this?' Dora indicates it all with a sweep of her arm.

'Not on my own, but yes, I did. It's kept me pretty busy over the last few years.'

Dora is amazed. 'Since when did you become so green-fingered?'

'I don't know really.' Cassie shrugs her shoulders. 'I just came out here one day and started digging around. It was a wreck. The whole place was covered in weeds and brambles, not to mention all the old junk from the house that had been heaped up over there.' She points to one corner, near the greenhouse. 'But as I started to clear a small patch, or dig out a flower bed, it became clear that underneath it all lay the bones of something really special, just waiting to take shape again. Most of the plants were still there, drowning under everything else. They were just hidden, waiting for someone to bring them to life again.'

Dora sits next to her sister on the low wooden bench and takes in the enchanting surroundings. It is hard to imagine the garden in any state other than the one of near perfection she looks at now.

'It was Bill's idea, actually,' Cassie continues.

'Bill?' Dora is confused.

'Yeah, old Bill Dryden. Remember, the gardener from Mum and Dad's place?'

Of course she remembers him. 'Bill was here?' Dora is still confused.

'Yes. I know. I was surprised when he turned up here. It was a bit of a shock. He said he was visiting an old friend in Oxford and wanted to look me up. Apparently Mum gave him the address here.'

'Bill Dryden came to visit you *here*?' Dora shakes her head.

'Yes. I didn't know what we'd talk about, to be honest. It was awkward at first. But then we just chatted about Dorset and the house and Mum and Dad, and you, and Alfie . . .'

'You talked about me? And Alfie?' Dora can't keep up.

'Yeah, nothing special. Just stuff like when we used to badger him for wheelbarrow rides; and that time we nicked all his flowerpots and canes to make jumps for our imaginary horses; and when Alfie hid in the pile of lawn cuttings and Mum went ballistic at him for traipsing grass all through the house.' Cassie pauses. 'Do you remember Bill showing us how to take a geranium cutting? I'd forgotten all about that, but he remembered. Such a sweet man. He died, you know?'

'Yeah, I saw Mum a few weeks ago. She told me.'

Cassie looks at Dora with interest. 'You saw Mum? How was that?'

'Oh, you know. Difficult.'

Cassie is staring at her searchingly with her clear blue eyes but Dora doesn't feel ready to expand just yet.

Cassie shrugs. 'Anyway, you wanted to know about the garden, right? I was working as a waitress in London, just killing time really, when I met Felix. We got friendly and he invited me down here to stay. He'd just inherited the old place and didn't really know what to do with it. I came to stay for the weekend and, to my shame, never left. Swan House became my home.'

Dora nods and wonders privately again if her sister and Felix are together.

'Anyway, Bill came to see me, God, it must have been about five years ago now. We took a little walk around the grounds. He was the one that spotted the door into the garden here. He went off when he saw what was in here. It was a mess, but he saw beyond all of that. It was all down to him really. He was the one that could see the promise of what lay underneath it all. He suggested I get my hands dirty. "Treat it like a little project," he said. "You look like you've got the time." Cheeky beggar.' Cassie laughs.

'I see,' says Dora. But she doesn't, not really. She can't control an unpleasant rush of bitterness that wells up inside her. While Dora has spent the last few years wrestling with guilt and grief, her sister, it appears, has been living like a character out of *The Good Life*; tucked away in some grand old love-nest with her hands in the soil and the sun on her hair. But then, she supposes, perhaps that's possible when you just up sticks and leave your family behind, mired in their pain and anxiety, while you dance off into the sunset without a care in the world.

'Anyway, it took me a few months to get up the nerve,' Cassie continues, seemingly unaware of Dora's surge of anger.

'Bill's idea kept bugging me, but I'd just walk past the gate there, and poke my nose in, but then get scared and back straight out again. Until one day I woke up and thought *today's the day*. I found some old gardening gloves in a store cupboard and I came down here and started clearing brambles that very afternoon. And after a week or two Felix got me some proper tools, just a spade and secateurs . . . a trowel, a wheelbarrow. It wasn't much, but it was enough to convince me to keep going. And the more I did, the more it sucked me in. It became my therapy, if you like.'

'So this is the Secret Garden Felix was talking about?' Dora asks, suddenly understanding.

'In part, yes,' says Cassie. 'The garden was the starting point. We began growing vegetables and flowers. A few more friends came and joined us, helped out in the grounds, until Felix realised we couldn't use everything ourselves. So rather than waste it we took the extra produce to the local farmers' markets. It's all organic, of course, and the posh old dears round here went crazy for it. Now it's not just fruit and veg. We make jams, soups, cakes – our own-brand muesli too! Felix came up with the name "Secret Garden". It works rather well, don't you think?'

Dora nods. She can see how their business taps into the current zeitgeist for all things home-grown and organic. 'But how did you know what to do with all of this?' she asks, still baffled at her sister's talents. 'I wouldn't know where to start.'

'I read books . . . lots of books, and Bill helped. I'd write to him about what I was doing and he'd send me letters full of information and advice about different plants. He sent me sketches of herb gardens and veggie patches and so I'd learn from him too.'

'Like a correspondence course,' Dora muses. 'But you're a natural. You have green fingers. You must have got them from Granddad.'

Cassie smiles. 'Yes. I suppose so. Now that the others help

out it's run like a cooperative, of sorts. We share the profits, and put some back into the house, for its upkeep. Felix is useless at managing the place, but we bully him into it. There's even a supermarket chain sniffing around. They want to distribute our produce in some of their local stores, but we're all a bit nervous about that. We don't want to lose the essence of what we do here. It's important to us all that we keep the business small, localised.'

'Is Felix your boyfriend?'

Cassie lets out a snort. 'Me and Felix? God no, he's just a friend.'

Dora nods, unsure why her question has been met with such derision; he seemed nice enough in the short time she'd met him.

There is a brief lull in their conversation and Dora closes her eyes and breathes deeply, trying to release the tension in her neck and shoulders. Her ears fill with the sounds of insects and birds and she realises, suddenly, that it feels good to be out of London. It has been the right decision to come, no matter what follows next. She turns back to her sister, eyeing her warily before asking her next question.

'So, you're . . . happy then?' Her question sounds more confrontational than she'd intended and Cassie studies her carefully for a moment, before answering.

'Yeah, I guess I am.' She leans back against the worn wooden slats of the bench and says with a faint smile, 'I like it here. I've got my friends, and the garden to keep me busy. It's enough for now.'

'Mmm . . .' says Dora. She tries to look pleased, but there it is again, that surge of bitterness churning in the pit of her stomach. She wants to know more. There are still so many things unspoken between them. Cassie, however, seems to have finished talking for the moment. She closes her eyes and turns her face to catch the sunlight and so they sit there, together on the bench in silence for a while longer before Dora summons the courage to ask her next question.

'Cassie?'

'Yes?'

'I need to know why you left. You know, not exactly why you *left*, but why you left in *that* way?' She pauses again. 'I mean, one moment you're leaving for university and I'm stuck in Dorset with Mum and Dad, then the next thing I know is you're in hospital, supposedly having tried to kill yourself. Then Dad leaves Mum and shacks up with Violet, and all the while I'm stuck at Clifftops, virtually on my own.' Dora is trying to control her emotions but an accusatory edge has entered her voice. 'Why didn't you tell me what you were going to do? Why didn't you talk to any of us? Didn't you realise what your leaving like that would do to us all?'

Cassie shakes her head. 'It must have been hard for you,' she says quietly. There is another silence, filled only by the flutter of wings as a bird takes off from a nearby pear tree. When the sound of its feathers beating the air has faded Cassie continues.

'To be honest, I wasn't really thinking about any of you. I'm sorry, but that's the truth. I know you might have felt shut out, like I didn't care, but I just couldn't stand being around you all then. When I was at Clifftops I felt surrounded by Alfie . . . and the emotion surrounding his death. I couldn't bear to look at you all and see the suffering. It was too painful. Deep down I knew Edinburgh wasn't an escape. I wanted to end it. I wanted to be free from it all . . . from all of Mum's and Dad's expectations, from all of the pain. I suppose I thought it might be a relief to you all if I just disappeared. I thought I was doing you a favour, but, looking back, I know I couldn't have been more wrong.' Cassie turns again to look at her sister with a sad sigh. 'It was pretty cruel, wasn't it?'

Dora nods and Cassie sighs deeply again, seemingly resolved. 'So I guess it's time we talked about it all; all of the secrets that have brought us to where we both sit today, if that's what you want?'

Dora doesn't say anything. She holds her breath, fearful

that if she speaks, Cassie will change her mind and the spell of intimate confession she appears to have cast over her sister will be broken. Cassie, however, doesn't waver. She continues in a slow and steady monologue.

'That day . . .' Cassie pauses. A shadow passes over her face. 'That day, when Alfie went missing, well, you know how it changed things for us all, for ever. I was pretty messed up after he died. We all were, in our own ways, but I really struggled. I couldn't eat. I couldn't sleep. I just knew Mum and Dad thought it was my fault. I knew they blamed me.'

'For Alfie?' Dora is shocked. Did Cassie blame herself as well?

'Why wouldn't they? After all, how could Alfie just disappear on a crowded beach when I was supposed to be looking after him?'

'We were *both* responsible that day, Cassie. If you are to blame, then I am too.' Dora feels sick; this is exactly what she has been afraid of, but Cassie is shaking her head vigorously.

'No, Dora, you're wrong. Trust me, it wasn't your fault. Not at all. If there was one innocent in our family that summer it was you. You . . . and Alfie, of course. Poor Alfie.'

'Yes,' Dora sighs, 'poor Alfie.'

'You know they never said anything,' Cassie continues after a pause, 'but I could tell what Mum and Dad were thinking. At least, I thought I could. They'd fall silent whenever I walked into a room, or avert their gaze from me. I could have sworn Dad would leave the room when I entered. And it all just reinforced what I already knew: it was my fault!' Cassie scrapes at the earth with the toe of her trainer. 'I just couldn't take it. I was desperate to escape but there was nowhere for me to go. I had school and A levels coming up. Mum and Dad had such expectations . . . they seemed to know better than I did who I was supposed to be and what I was supposed to be doing. I was so confused. I didn't have a clue what I wanted. So I just tried to lose myself where I could; you know, parties, sex, drink and drugs. I think I was just trying to *feel* something, you know, anything but all that awful teenaged confusion and the overwhelming grief about Alfie.' Cassie rubs at a dirty mark on her jeans.

Dora swallows and wonders if she's brave enough to ask. 'Is that why . . . is that why you cut yourself?'

Cassie turns her wrists outwards so they can both see the thin, silver scars criss-crossing like cobwebs all the way up her tanned arms. Dora winces at the sight of them but Cassie just shrugs.

'It was another way of taking control, I suppose.'

Dora nods.

'You know, when I got my A level results I felt nothing but a deep, sweeping depression. It was all there, laid out for me, the exact future Mum and Dad had planned for me. But they didn't have a clue. They didn't know how far from the exalted prodigal daughter I really was. I wasn't who they thought I was. I felt suffocated . . . I had to run . . . I had to get away from you all. I couldn't face letting you all down again. That's why I went to London. That's why I tried to kill myself.'

Dora thinks she knows the rest but Cassie continues.

'I was hysterical when I woke up in hospital and realised I was still alive. I couldn't bear the thought of returning to Clifftops and even though Dad tried his best to persuade me I was adamant: I couldn't go home. I couldn't face any of you. In the end I found a job working as a waitress for a while, in some grotty café. It was pretty shit. The pay was awful and the customers were pigs . . . but then I met Felix. We got friendly and he invited me here, to his family house. I suppose the rest, as they say, is history. I've been healing ever since, slowly coming to terms with the past – and the grief and the guilt I felt about Alfie.'

'That sounds familiar. I know a thing or two about guilt.'

'I've told you, Dora,' Cassie says firmly, 'you've got nothing to feel guilty about. Nothing.'

'You say that, Cassie. Dan says it. Dad says it. But it still doesn't help. I was there with you on the beach that day. It was as much my fault as it was yours. If Mum or Dad thought, even for just one wild second, that you could have been held in some way responsible then I should shoulder some of that blame. It doesn't make sense otherwise.'

'Trust me, Dora, it's different.'

'But why? Why is it different? I'm only eighteen months younger than you. It's not that big a gap. Do those few extra months in age that you have over me make you somehow more responsible for Alfie's safety that day?' Dora shakes her head. 'I don't think so.'

Cassie eyes her sister carefully. 'This is why you're here, isn't it? You still haven't let him go, have you?'

Dora shakes her head again. 'No. I guess not.' She pauses, and then continues in a rush. 'That day, at the Crag; I still think about it all the time. Do you?'

'Some days, sure, but not every day. I think that's probably good, don't you?'

Dora nods, but she is even more confused now. She'd always imagined her sister to be the unstable one and yet here Cassie is, seemingly at peace with the world while Dora struggles to move forwards with her own life, paralysed by dreams and panic attacks.

'So why are you here, Dora? After all this time, it's not just a social visit, is it? You're looking for something? Am I right?'

Dora nods. 'Yes. Yes I am.'

'Well, come on then, out with it. I've told you a bit of my story. Isn't it time you told me yours?'

There is no point holding back any more, she decides. 'I'm pregnant, Cassie.'

'My God!' Cassie turns to Dora with an amazed smile. 'That's wonderful news. Why didn't you say something earlier, you dork!' She leans across and puts a warm hand on Dora's arm. 'Here I am prattling on about myself and all the while you're sitting there politely listening while you actually have something IMPORTANT to tell me! Congratulations. Wow, my baby sister is going to be a mum!'

Dora looks up at her sister hopefully. Her reaction isn't what she's expected, not after her parents' more muted responses. 'You're pleased?' she asks.

'Of course I'm bloody pleased. I'm going to be an auntie.' Cassie is grinning from ear to ear, but as she looks again at her sister her smile fades. 'Are *you* pleased? I guess that's the more important question here.'

'Yeah, I think so. I mean, I'm coming round to the idea. Dan's over the moon about it but I've realised over the last few weeks that I'm absolutely terrified. It's Alfie, you see. I feel paralysed. Stuck. How can I celebrate a new life when I'm still mourning Alfie's? And how can I even consider motherhood when I failed my baby brother so catastrophically? What kind of mother will I really be, Cassie? Can you tell me that?' Dora takes a deep breath before continuing. 'Motherhood terrifies me.' She swallows. 'I have dreams, Cassie; horrible dreams where I lose things, important things. What if I make the same mistakes again? Everything is so fragile, so easily broken. I don't think I can hurt again the way I did when we lost Alfie that summer. It would tear me apart. I'm not strong enough. Do you understand?' Her words spill out into the air, tripping over each other.

'You've got to get over this guilt-trip you're on, Dora. It's all wrong. *You* are so wrong.'

'How can you say that when you just implied that it was *your* guilt about Alfie that was the very thing that tipped *you* over the edge and made you want to end your life?'

Cassie flinches. 'That's different.'

'I don't see how. Why is it different?'

There is a pause before she answers. 'Because I had something *real* to feel guilty about . . . something you don't know.'

The sun is shining down on Dora, making her squint, but even with the glare in her eyes she can see the flicker of

together. We were going to go to the Crag and hang out, just the two of us. We were . . . we were kind of *into* each other. I fancied her rotten.' She looks up at Dora meaningfully. 'We wanted to be alone. Looking after Alfie with you was the last thing I'd planned on that day.'

Dora's eyes widen in the eerie green light of the tree. 'You're gay?'

Cassie shrugs. 'Yeah.'

Dora nods slowly as a series of small cogs fall into place. *I wasn't who they thought I was . . . Felix and me? No chance!'*

'Do you have a girlfriend?' Dora is curious.

Cassie blushes slightly, a rosy glow flooding her cheeks. 'There is someone. It's early days . . . but she's nice . . . really nice. We're taking it slow.'

Dora smiles. She realises she's pleased for Cassie.

'Anyway, my current love life aside, that's why I was so sulky that morning,' Cassie continues. 'You know, Mum dumping Alfie on us and running off to "work" for the day, which of course was nothing but a blatant lie.'

'A lie?' Dora's head snaps up. 'What do you mean?'

'Are you kidding me?' Cassie looks at Dora in amazement. 'You mean you still don't know?'

Dora shakes her head. 'Know what?'

'About the affair?'

Dora looks at Cassie with confusion. 'What affair?'

'Mum's affair with Tobias Grey? You know,' she continues, seeing Dora's puzzled look, 'the artist. He's the one that painted that ugly picture Mum hung over the mantelpiece at Clifftops. Remember?'

Dora's brain whirs and dredges up a forgotten image of a fierce, brooding seascape painted in oils. She shakes her head. 'Mum had an affair with an artist? Are you sure?'

'Yeah, I heard it from the horse's mouth. He phoned the house once . . . a long time ago. He thought he was speaking to her. I didn't know who *he* was for a long time, but eventually things fell into place. I pretended I knew more than I did and in the end Dad spilled the beans. It turns out she had been with Tobias on the day Alfie disappeared. I think that's why Dad eventually left her.'

'My God!' Dora is shocked. It is too much to take in. Her mother had been with another man on the very day Alfie disappeared. She'd been having an *affair*. She thinks back to her encounter with Helen a few weeks ago, to her mother's brittle demeanour. She remembers Alfie's bedroom, like a time capsule, perfectly untouched with everything exactly as it had been the day he had gone missing and a glimmer of understanding suddenly registers. She's always thought her mother kept the room unaltered in order to punish her, to remind Dora of her own failings that day. But now she sees it in a new light. Helen is punishing *herself* every day. Just by staying in Dorset, by living at Clifftops and surrounding herself with memories of Alfie, she is suffering. She has created her own private prison for her failings as a mother. She must have looked wildly for others to blame because the pain of knowing that she had been with Tobias when Alfie had gone missing would be almost too much to bear. Dora shakes her head in disbelief. All this time. Her mind is whirling with the startling revelation when Cassie speaks again.

'But you see, in the end, Dora, it really doesn't matter where Mum was that day.' Cassie's voice cracks and Dora looks up in surprise. 'It was me. *I* killed him.'

The words are barely a whisper but they slice cleanly through the jumble of Dora's thoughts and seem to suck the air right out of her lungs. She is shocked to see tears welling in Cassie's eyes. 'What are you talking about?'

'That day at the Crag, you don't know what *really* happened. None of you do.'

Dora suddenly wonders if Cassie is OK. She's seemed so normal, but maybe it is a charade after all.

'What are you talking about, Cass? I'm not sure I understand what you're saying. You're scaring me.'

Cassie hangs her head, suddenly unable to meet her eye. 'After you left the Crag that first time, when you went to buy ice creams, Alfie, he . . . he came over to us. He was bored, you see. He wanted us to play with him.'

'Hang on. You mean he *was* with you and Sam in the cave?' Dora frowns, confused.

Cassie gives a small nod. 'He kept going on and on about collecting sticks and looking for crabs. He wanted us to collect sticks with him. I don't really know why.'

Dora remembers the pile of driftwood they had been building. Alfie *had* been in the cave with Cassie. It didn't make sense. Why had she lied about it?

'He kept going on and on at us,' Cassie says with a sad little smile. 'You know what he got like, really whiney and cross. He was angry that Sam and I wouldn't play with him. He stood there banging his stick against the cave wall and stamping his little feet, over and over. Bang, bang, bang. Over and over. It echoed horribly. The noise was horrible.'

Dora can see her brother in her mind's eye, his little fists clenched and his red galoshes pounding up and down on the gritty cave floor.

'Sam and I were really stoned; we just wanted to lie on the sand and be together. I was desperate . . . Sam was going home the next day. When you left the cave I knew it was our last chance. But then Alfie kept whining and banging, whining and banging. On and on. He was driving me mad.'

Dora can just imagine it: little Alfie stamping and complaining and Cassie desperate, her temper on a knife-edge, ready to explode.

'I tried to be patient. I told him to go and find more crabs at the other end of the cave but he said that was boring. So I told him to find somewhere to hide. To count to a hundred, and then we would come and find him.'

'He just wanted to play with someone,' says Dora sadly.

'Well, Alfie said he couldn't count to a hundred yet. He said hide and seek was boring. And that's when I really lost my temper. I told him if it was so boring in the cave, why didn't he leave. We hadn't asked him to come with us.'

Dora looks at her sister with disbelief.

'I told him . . . I told him to leave us alone. I told him to go and find you, wherever you were. I told him to go for a walk, to look for shells. He kept on whining and whining. *No. No. No.* On and on. Banging his stick, over and over. And so that's when I said it.'

'Said what?' Dora's heart thuds loudly in her chest.

Cassie puts her hand to her mouth, as if unable to continue, but then speaks the final words in a rush. 'I told him if he was so bored in the cave maybe he should go for a swim.'

Dora swallows. 'But you knew—'

'Yes. I knew he couldn't swim. He told me, too. He said, "Cassie, I can't swim. I'm too little." And do you know what I said back?'

Dora is frozen. She doesn't think she wants to hear the rest, but she doesn't want Cassie to stop either.

'I said, "But Alfie, you're a superhero. You can do anything, right? Of course you can swim."' Cassie is staring into the distance as a single tear rolls down her cheek.

Dora sits in stunned silence for a moment. She can't believe what she is hearing. All this time, all these years, Cassie has never breathed a word of this to anyone.

'I know it was cruel. I know it was a sick, twisted thing to say and I still don't really know why I said it. All I do know is that he just shrugged his little shoulders, turned his back on us, and began to clamber up and out of the Crag. And do you want to know how I felt as I watched him go?'

Dora doesn't move. She isn't sure she can take any more.

'I felt relief. Pure, sweet relief that he was finally going and that Sam and I would be alone, at last.'

Dora swallows back the bitter taste in her mouth.

'We . . . Dora, I'm not proud of this . . . we . . . well, you know. And then you came back with your friend. It seemed like only moments earlier that Alfie had left the Crag, but instantly I knew something was wrong. I knew what I had done. When you asked where he was, I just blurted out that I hadn't seen him, that I thought he had gone with you.' She shakes her head. 'I still don't know why I did that. The cave was so quiet . . . eerily so . . . I had this horrible image in my head of him. I saw him tottering out across the rocky outcrop, all the while blissfully unaware of the changing tides and the splash and spray of the waves as they dumped onto the promontory. I could see him standing on the edge, peering over into the waves as they splashed up over the tops of his little boots. I knew then . . . I just knew.'

'You knew he might have left the cave . . . gone to the rock pools?'

Cassie nods. She isn't meeting her eyes. 'I never meant to hurt him. I never meant to hurt Alfie.'

'But why did you lie? Why didn't you just tell the truth? We might have . . . we might have found him, you know . . .' Dora's voice drops to a soft whisper, '. . . in time.'

'I don't know . . .' Cassie shakes her head and another teardrop runs down her cheek and drips onto her jeans, turning the faded blue a dark navy where it lands. 'I was stoned. I couldn't think straight. I was so scared. I knew I would get into trouble, so I just blurted out the lie to protect me and Sam.'

'Why didn't Sam say anything? The police questioned her too, didn't they?'

'She just went along with what I said. After we all split up to search for Alfie I warned her that we'd need to stick to my story. I knew you didn't send a little boy out onto the beach by himself. I knew you didn't tell a toddler to go swimming! I told Sam we'd both be in trouble with the police if they ever found out what I'd said, what we'd done that day in the cave . . . the spliffs, the stuff we did . . . they'd find out all about it. I told her we'd be arrested for drugs. She was scared and she didn't like it, but she went along with it, for me.'

Dora suddenly saw a collection of blue paper envelopes

spilling out across Cassie's teenaged bed. Letters from Sam. No wonder Cassie had been so cagey about them. She shakes her head, piecing things together like a complex jigsaw. 'But all that time we spent in the Crag looking for Alfie . . . all that time we wasted when you *knew* . . . you knew that he was out there?' She is struggling to comprehend the enormity of Cassie's confession. 'You even told Mum later that you thought he had left with me? That's why she . . . why she blamed me so much.' Dora chokes on her final words.

Cassie hangs her head. 'I know. I'm so sorry.'

'But why lie?'

'When I saw Mum's face that day, I looked into her eyes and I knew she would never be able to forgive me. I couldn't bear it. So I told her that I hadn't seen him. I didn't realise it at the time, but it was probably the worst lie I could have told though, wasn't it? For you?'

Dora thinks about the blame and reproach she has felt in her mother's angry glances ever since Alfie's disappearance. She thinks about the heavy guilt she has borne these last few years and the hours and hours of agonising she has suffered, trying to fit the pieces of the puzzle together, to understand why Alfie had left the cave, and where he might have gone. All this time she has berated herself for leaving the cave; for being the most plausible reason Alfie had taken it upon himself to head out of the safety of the Crag on his own. She's imagined him following her out into the bright sunshine of the day, peering up the beach for a sign of her, before turning, for some reason, to head out across the treacherous rock pools. She's always thought it was her fault. Hers alone.

'So you see, Dora,' Cassie says, breaking through her painful memories, 'we each bear our scars and carry our guilt, but I am the guiltiest of us all. I live every day with the knowledge that I sent him out onto the rocks. And if I had told the truth straight away, there might have been a chance we'd find Alfie, alive. I live now with the suffering I've inflicted on you all, not just poor Alfie.'

Cassie runs her hands through her hair, smoothing her plait down the side of her neck and twisting the loose ends below the band nervously between her fingers. 'So now you know that I failed you. I betrayed you. I hate myself for that, for hurting you. And you, Dora, you did *nothing* wrong.' Her voice was rising insistently. 'Do you see? Do you understand?'

Dora closes her eyes.

It is too much to hear.

Cassie is weeping quietly next to her on the grass, but Dora can't bring herself to comfort her. Her head rings with her sister's words and her stomach twists with nausea.

Fragments of the day whirl frantically around her mind. Helen speeding off down the drive to be with Tobias. Cassie and Sam dropping down out of sight into the Crag. Alfie poking at crabs with a long, gnarled stick. A ball of ice cream disappearing into the oncoming breakers. The sight of Alfie's sodden cape in Cassie's arms. Her mother's disbelieving stare as she learns that Alfie is missing.

The images crowd her brain until she feels dizzy with it all. She presses her fingers to her temples to try to slow things down. She knows now. She knows it all. Each of them has played some part in the tragic events leading to Alfie's death and they have each paid, day after day, for their choices, their failings and their secrets. All of them, Cassie, Helen, herself, even Richard have lived a lifetime of guilt and regret. Cassie's hidden desires, her cruel suggestion and lies, Helen's affair, they are new pieces of the puzzle that fit together to form the whole sorry picture of that one day when Alfie was taken from them. But really, Dora realises, the only thing she can still be certain of amidst the swirl of emotion surrounding her, is that none of it, no tears, no recriminations, no confessions or self-inflicted punishment or pain is going to bring Alfie back.

'Do you hate me?' Cassie's words break through her thoughts. 'I'd understand if you do. I've found it hard enough to forgive myself these past years so there's no reason why *you* should.' She speaks fast, the words tumbling out of her mouth.

Dora sits utterly still under the shimmering boughs of the tree. She can't answer. She feels sick at the thought of what Cassie did. She is shocked by the news of her mother's infidelity. The revelations swirl wildly in her head. She needs some time.

As the silence deepens she notices her sister wilt a little. Cassie sits slumped in the shade of the willow, a river of tears drying on her face and the white criss-cross scars on her wrists glinting like delicate silver bracelets in the strange green light, and Dora knows. She's not sure if she can forgive her, but she knows she doesn't hate her.

'I don't hate you, Cassie. You've hated yourself enough for one lifetime.'

Cassie lets a small sigh leave her lips and then clasps her hands together in a prayer-like gesture, turning her wrists inwards so that the scars on her arms no longer show. They sit together in silence for a moment longer before Cassie speaks again in a small voice. 'You know if I could turn the clock back and do things differently that day, I would? I would give my own life, gladly, to protect Alfie.'

Dora nods. 'I think we all would.'

Cassie looks up from intently studying her hands. 'Look, Dora, there's no reason you should listen to me now. I wouldn't blame you if you got back into your car, drove away from here and never contacted me again. But while you are here you might as well know that I've had a lot of time to reflect on things in this place. I know all of us, if we could, would go back to that day and do things differently if it would mean a different outcome. But we can't, and nothing we do now will bring our little brother back, will it?'

Dora nods again, the tears welling in her eyes. She recognises that her sister's words echo her own thoughts just moments ago.

'So don't you think the best thing we can do for Alfie now is to look forwards and live our lives as best we can, for him?'

Dora wipes at her eyes as her sister continues.

'It might be too soon for you to let me back in your life again. What I did that day . . . and the way I left . . . well, I wouldn't blame you.'

Dora swallows. She doesn't know how to answer that.

'But let me just say this one last thing,' continues Cassie. 'For all the talking and analysing I've done, it was probably Bill Dryden who helped me to see it best of all.' She opens her arms expansively. 'The restoration of the garden . . . it's all for Alfie. I did it for him; it is my shot at redemption, if you like. I've brought it back to life; a way of healing.' Cassie reaches over and puts her hand on Dora's arm. 'And now you have a life growing inside you.' She looks at her meaningfully. 'It's time for you to let go too, Dora. It's time for you to move on. We can't bring him back but we can remember him through the things we do in our own lives.'

Dora nods. Suddenly it makes sense. Everything she's been fighting and everything she has feared is suddenly melting away. She doesn't need to be afraid. She doesn't need to feel guilty. The only thing she owes Alfie, her family and Dan is that she lives her life to the fullest possible. *A life half lived.* Her father's words echo in her ears. They have all been so busy with death they have forgotten there is still a world of life out there.

They sit together in silence for a while, both of them listening to the hum of insects and birds taking flight outside the shadowy green chamber. A shaft of sunlight penetrates the boughs of the willow and shines down in Dora's lap, warm as a cat and, as she sits there, next to her sister, she feels a sudden and immense peace wash over her, a sense of calm she hasn't felt for a long, long while. She imagines her mother in the kitchen at Clifftops arranging long-stemmed roses into one of Daphne's crystal vases, and Richard with his sensible slippered feet reading the paper in his beige living room as

Violet fusses around him; she thinks of her sister kneeling over the soil around them coaxing plants and seeds to life, and of Dan in his studio working clay and wax into a beautiful new creation. And then she thinks of the baby, a tiny, curled being nestled deep inside her with its own perfect heartbeat. She thinks of them all and as she does, she feels another wave of peace wash over her.

HELEN

Present Day

Helen is in the garden pulling thistles and bindweed from the flower beds outside the kitchen window when she hears the shrill cry of the telephone. She stands quickly, removes her gardening gloves and walks into the house, hoping to make it before the caller rings off. She is in luck.

'Hello?'

'Mum, is that you?'

Helen's breath catches in her throat. 'Dora?'

'Yes.'

There is a pause at the other end of the phone and in the silence Helen's mind fills with a jumble of questions and thoughts. Why is Dora calling? They haven't spoken since her visit earlier in the year. Is something wrong? Is the baby OK?

'What's happened?' she asks.

'Nothing, everything's fine.'

'The baby's all right?'

'Yes,' says Dora, sounding surprised. 'The baby's fine. We're all fine,' she adds.

'Oh, good.' Helen relaxes slightly.

'I was wondering . . . I thought maybe . . . would you fancy a daytrip to London?' Dora blurts the question and Helen feels her heart swell with sudden emotion.

'A visit? To see you?'

'Yes.'

'When?'

'I was thinking next weekend – but if you can't make it then we could—'

'No,' says Helen quickly. 'Next weekend is fine.' She mentally runs through her calendar. She can rearrange a few things; it won't be a problem.

'If you're sure?'

'Yes.'

'OK.'

There is another long silence and Helen can hear her daughter's quiet breathing at the other end of the phone. 'And you're all right, nothing's wrong?'

'No, Mum, everything's fine.' Dora gives Helen the name and address of a café in Primrose Hill, a tearoom called Rosie Lee's tucked away off the main drag.

'It will be nice to revisit an old stomping ground. I'll call you if I have trouble finding the place.'

'Great. See you there next Saturday at eleven?'

'Yes, see you there.'

'OK.' There is another pause. 'Bye, Mum.'

'Bye, Dora.'

Helen hears the click of the handset at the other end of the line. She stands in the kitchen holding the buzzing receiver against her chest, feeling an unexpected warmth seep through to her heart.

She catches the train up to London early the following Saturday morning and arrives at Waterloo station just before ten. Within minutes she is sitting on the Northern Line hurtling towards Chalk Farm. The tube carriage is virtually empty, but it still holds the residual smells of the thousands of bodies that have passed through its doors all week. She breathes in the warm reek of it and is taken straight back to the time she and Richard lived in north London as young newly-weds and nervy first-time parents. It seems like a lifetime ago now. So much has happened since then.

There is a young woman about Dora's age sitting opposite her. She wears a diamond stud in her nose that glints boldly under the artificial lighting and she nods along to music emanating from tiny white headphones. Helen catches her eye and smiles. The girl curls the corners of her lips in the slightest of acknowledgements, before turning her gaze politely to the adverts above Helen's head. Of course, she realises, it has been too long; she is out of practice when it comes to Underground etiquette.

Helen averts her eyes and begins to fiddle with her tube ticket, letting her mind wander back to Dora's phone call. It was strange; Dora had given no indication as to why she should suddenly invite her up to London. The last time they had seen each other was at Clifftops, when Dora had announced her pregnancy and they had spoken, albeit awkwardly, about Alfie. Since then Helen has tortured herself over the way she handled things. Dora had reached out to her and she had pushed her away. Once again, she had failed her family. She is haunted by their encounter and angry with herself for being too afraid to speak the truth to her daughter, when it is clear it was what she had needed to hear.

Helen has thought about calling her since, but every time she moved towards the phone, every time she stood in the kitchen with her hand hovering over the handset, aching to speak to her, she heard a soft, insistent voice in the back of her head saying *Don't do it. She doesn't need you. Leave her alone.* And it had proved easier to walk away and distract herself with everyday life, to carry on with her quiet routine down by the coast, than to pick up the phone and face her daughter.

That was the funny thing about Clifftops. From the moment they had moved there she had considered it her prison, a place she had only ever really wanted to escape from. Then, after Alfie, it became her punishment; and when Richard had finally left her she'd known with absolute clarity that it was her personal cross to bear. Richard hadn't wanted to live there; he'd made that perfectly clear during their strained divorce negotiations, and so she'd stayed on, treating the rambling old house as her penance. And it had proved a weighty cross, steeped as it was with the painful memories of losing Alfie.

Yet, over the years, something unexpected had happened. It was as though the house had slowly infiltrated her bones and had wrapped its heavy stone walls around her, pulling her into its comforting embrace. Perhaps it was the other memories the house held, memories of happier times with Richard and the children that she occasionally now felt strong enough to dwell upon. Or maybe it was the garden she had taken to pottering around, the simple tasks of dead-heading roses, weeding thistles or collecting apples from the orchard reminding her of the natural order of the world, the ebb and flow of a life force both timeless and inevitable. Even the things she had detested at first, like the great clanking Aga, the dusty clutter of antiques and paintings, or the draughty old window frames that rattled and moaned in the brisk sea breezes, had begun to feel like old friends. She realises now that she has assumed the role of custodian; she has become a sort of caretaker for the sprawling estate. It is as if she is keeping it safe – for the next generation perhaps? It surprises no one more than her that she should have come to this, but if she has learnt anything over the last ten years or so, it is that life is full of unexpected twists and turns, both good and bad.

And now Dora has called *her*. She has made the next move and invited her to London, and she can't help but wonder if this, at last, is a sign that they can finally get things back on track. Perhaps it isn't so ridiculous to imagine being a part of her daughter's life again, to look forward to sharing in the joy of a first grandchild. She knows it is more than she deserves but she can't help the tiny well of hope that bubbles up inside her. This feels like her last chance to bridge the divide.

*

It is a mild day for September, much warmer in the capital than down on the Dorset coast, and as Helen leaves the tube station and begins to walk down the busy road, past noisy cars with stinking exhausts and screeching brakes, she finds herself shrugging off her coat and rolling up her sleeves. She wanders past a shabby-looking dry-cleaners, a greengrocers with its sad array of wizened fruit and vegetables out on display, and blocks of red-brick council flats until she turns left onto Primrose Hill Road. The green grass of the park sprawls away invitingly to her right, but she carries on down the road, eager to get to the café on time.

Rosie Lee's Tearoom is tucked away at the end of a quiet, residential street lined with genteel Victorian homes. The shop front itself is decorated with a pretty rose-covered awning and Helen sees several tables and chairs outside on the pavement, covered in patterned tablecloths and cushions, already occupied by patrons soaking up the sunshine. She pushes her way through the front door and into the cosy interior.

The café's discreet exterior belies the buzz and hum of the crowds inside. Tables are bustling with confident young professionals chattering into mobile phones, sipping on lattes and reading the weekend papers. Helen looks around for a space, despairing at the lack of seats, until a frantically waving arm catches her eye.

'Mum! Over here.' It is Dora. She is sitting in the far corner at a table for two, a pot of tea already in front of her. It seems Helen isn't the only one who has arrived early. She gives her daughter a little wave, before squeezing her way through the cluttered tables to reach her.

'Hello.' Dora stands and Helen gives her a peck on the cheek and a little squeeze on the arm, noting with private delight the gentle swell of Dora's belly underneath her T-shirt. 'You look great,' she compliments. 'You're glowing.'

'Thanks, Mum. I like the new "do".'

Helen pats at her hair self-consciously. 'It's a bit shorter than I was expecting, but I'm getting used to it.'

Dora smiles. 'It suits you.'

'Thank you.'

She sits down opposite her daughter and folds her coat onto her lap, smoothing the fabric with trembling hands. She is suddenly overwhelmed with nerves. 'How are you feeling?' she asks. 'Is the morning sickness still bad?'

'No, it eased up a few weeks ago. I'm feeling good now.'

'Great. That's great.' She looks at Dora and can see it is true. Her cheeks are a little rounder, her breasts a little fuller, and her skin and hair shine with life. She looks beautiful.

A waitress in a floral apron appears at Helen's side, hovering politely with pen poised over pad.

'Do you want anything else?' Helen asks.

'No, I'm fine with my tea thanks.'

'Just a black coffee please,' says Helen, addressing the girl in the apron, who fades away with a scribble and a nod, leaving the two women alone again.

'Thanks for coming,' says Dora finally. 'I wasn't sure you would.'

Helen gives a start of surprise. Did Dora really think she wouldn't come? Is there really such a great divide between them? It makes her ache to realise how far she's let things slide. 'I was pleased you called,' she admits, finally. 'I wanted to call you. I really did. So many times I nearly picked up the phone, but something always stopped me. I guess I wasn't sure you would want to hear from *me*?'

Her last sentence has ended in a question but Dora just responds with a little shrug of her shoulders. 'Of course I would have,' she says, eventually.

'Really?'

'Yeah.'

'But things were so difficult . . . at your last visit.'

Dora nods.

'I handled it badly.'

Dora nods again.

I deserve that, thinks Helen.

Just then the waitress returns with the coffee. Helen distracts herself for a moment with the sugar, tearing carefully at the paper packet and stirring the granules into her mug, watching the silver spoon shift the dark liquid vortex round and round and round. It's like our relationship, thinks Helen suddenly, dark and deep and bittersweet. She stops stirring, tapping the spoon against her mug and placing it carefully back onto the saucer.

'So,' she says, 'here we are.' She gives Dora a nervous smile and Dora seems to be about to say something, but then stops, busying herself instead with the laminated menu in front of her. She flexes it back and forth in her hands, making a funny *whumph-whumph* sound with the air. Somewhere behind them a man breaks into a loud, braying laugh. Only as the sound of it dies away does Dora finally begin to speak.

'I went to see Cassie a few weeks ago.'

Helen starts. 'Oh yes? Was she OK?'

'Yes. She seemed great.'

Helen feels a surge of relief. 'She seems to have found her calling, doesn't she?'

It is Dora's turn to nod. 'Yes, it certainly seems so.'

They fall silent for another moment.

'We talked about the day Alfie went missing.'

'Yes?' Helen's voice sounds calm but she can feel her mouth suddenly go dry and reaches across for her coffee with trembling hands.

'Cassie told me some things I didn't know; some things about the day; things about her . . . and things about you.'

Helen takes a gulp of coffee. It is too hot but she forces it down, scalding her tongue and throat as she swallows. Here it comes. She steels herself, preparing for the juggernaut of Dora's accusations and recriminations but is surprised by what Dora says next.

'I don't honestly want to get into it all. I've done a lot of soul searching and I've come to the conclusion that how it happened . . . all the individual decisions we made that day that led to us losing Alfie aren't what's important. He's gone. We'll always live with that. So perhaps it's time to stop torturing ourselves with regret?'

Helen looks at Dora, confused. 'You know about the . . . you know about Tobias?'

Dora nods, slowly.

Helen feels herself blush. The shame is still fresh. 'You know, I wanted to tell you on your last visit. I really did, I just still find it hard to say out loud. I still feel so horrified about the choices I made.'

Dora nods. 'It doesn't matter, Mum. I've come to terms with a few things now. Between the four of us we've lived too many painful years of guilt and grief, haven't we? For all the yearning, and longing, for all the sorrow and pain we feel, none of that emotion can bring him back. It won't change a single moment from that day . . . it won't shift a single pebble on that beach.'

It is Helen's turn to nod. She looks down at her lap. She doesn't want to cry, not now.

'I just needed to tell you that I understand things a little more clearly now. And I wanted to let you know that you were right; it is time to let it go.'

From out of the corner of her eye Helen sees Dora gently rub the tiny swell of her stomach. It is such an unselfconscious, intimate gesture that it makes the tears Helen has been fighting suddenly flow freely. She sits, with her head hanging down, crying silent tears until she feels Dora press a paper napkin into her hand.

'Here.'

'Sorry,' Helen sniffs, dabbing the napkin at her eyes. She takes a moment to compose herself and then looks up at Dora.

'I really didn't want to fall apart in front of you. I actually wanted to apologise to you today.' She sees Dora tilt her head slightly. 'You know, for the terrible way I behaved when you last came to visit. I know I didn't seem it when you told me, but I am thrilled about your pregnancy. It's wonderful news. You and Dan will make great parents, I have no doubt.'

It is Dora's turn to look away now.

'Dora, please look at me. I have to tell you this. It's important.'

Dora raises her head and Helen can see the tears welling in her daughter's eyes.

'It pains me to say it, but a tiny part of me was jealous when I heard your news, you know, Dora. I know that sounds silly. I'm your mother. I want this for you more than anything. But I couldn't help but feel a stab of envy for the fresh start you have been given. It's a new life; a new adventure.' Helen pauses, runs her fingers through her hair. 'It's hard getting older, looking in the mirror and seeing time marching on.'

'You don't have to explain if you don't want to, Mum. I don't want to dredge everything up again.'

'No, Dora, I need to say this. I'm not angling for sympathy. I've made my mistakes – so many of them. And now I live with my regrets. I didn't realise what I had until it was gone: your father, Alfie, you girls. But maybe something good will come out of this; maybe my mistakes can help you in some way.'

Dora gives another slow nod.

'When Alfie went missing I couldn't face the reality of what I had done. I looked for anyone to blame but myself and I'm so sorry that you took the brunt of that. I was horribly unfair to you, Dora. I'm so sorry.'

As Helen stares into Dora's eyes she sees something else behind the tears, a look of something – perhaps relief – dart across her daughter's face.

'I failed Cassie too,' she continues, keen to lay it all out now. 'I didn't see what she needed. I pushed her according to my own agenda, heaped all kinds of pressure on her. And of course, perhaps most of all, I failed Alfie. I wasn't there to protect him when he needed me most. I would do anything to turn the clock back and make everything right again. But I can't. All I can do is sit here in front of you and tell you that I'm sorry. I'm sorry I hurt you, all of you.'

Dora gives another slow nod. 'It's OK, Mum. We've each made our mistakes. I'm sure you had your reasons for the choices you made. We don't need to thrash it through again and again. It was just important for me to tell you that we can leave it behind us. It's water under the bridge to me. I'm OK now.'

Helen drops her gaze again. Her coat is bunched up in her lap and she smooths it with the flat of her hand. She desperately wants to ask Dora if she can forgive her, if she will let her try to make amends, somehow. She wants to know if she can share a tiny part of her life again, but it still seems too much to ask.

There is another loud, braying laugh from the man behind them. Dora looks round and then back at Helen, rolling her eyes. 'Shall we get out of here?'

Helen nods and Dora waves at the waitress, leaving Helen to discreetly wipe her eyes and tidy the mascara smudges with the damp napkin she still clutches in her hand.

After they have paid the bill Helen suggests they take a walk up onto Primrose Hill. She doesn't feel ready to leave Dora just yet and there is nothing waiting for her at Clifftops. The sun is shining and she could do with stretching her legs before the long train journey home.

'I haven't been up here for years,' she confesses as they wander up one of the pathways leading to the top. 'Not since you and Cassie were little girls. Your father and I brought you both here one spring day when all the daffodils were out. I remember Cassie wanted to do roly-polys all the way to the bottom but she had to stop halfway down. She made herself sick.' Helen gives a little laugh and she sees Dora smile next to her. 'The London Eye and the Gherkin didn't exist then, of course. Gosh, it must have been over twenty years ago.'

'Yes,' agrees Dora quietly.

They walk on a little further until they reach an empty bench positioned perfectly for gazing out across the urban vista.

'Shall we sit for a minute?' Helen asks.

Dora nods and they perch next to each other, taking in the bustling city below. Helen can see tall towers of concrete and glass winking at them in the sunlight, and the spaceship-like thrust of the BT Tower from across the treetops of Regent's Park. It is all so familiar, like a painting she has gazed upon for half of her life. In some ways she realises she feels no different to the young woman she was all those years ago when she had first moved to London with Richard. And yet so much has happened since then. She takes a deep breath and then reaches out and puts a hand on Dora's arm, looking intently into her daughter's sea-green eyes.

'I know I've not always been a good mother.'

'Mum—' Dora puts up her hand to interrupt but Helen stops her.

'No, let me say this. I *need* to say it.'

Dora's hand falls to her side again.

'I've not been good to you. I've let you down.'

'Mum, you really don't—'

'Yes I do.'

Dora is silent again.

'I should never have let you carry one ounce of blame for Alfie's disappearance, or wear one moment's guilt. A good mother would have protected you from all of that.'

Helen sees a tear trickle slowly down her daughter's lovely face. She reaches out and brushes it away with her hand.

'I'm so sorry I failed you. I'm so sorry that I hurt you. Will you forgive me?'

Dora reaches for Helen's hand.

'Being a mother is a wonderful job, but isn't easy. You'll

find that out soon enough. But I know you will be a good mother to your baby. And if you'll give me a second chance, I'd like to try and be a better one to you?' Helen feels her own tears falling again now. They land like late summer raindrops on the coat lying across her lap. She feels Dora's hand in her own and squeezes it tight, both of them too choked to speak, until Dora finally finds her voice.

'Let's take it slow. Small steps, OK?'

Helen nods.

'After all,' adds Dora, 'this little one's going to need its grandmother, right?' She indicates the swell of her stomach.

Helen feels her heart skip. 'Perhaps we could do this again sometime?' she asks. 'Before the baby comes?' She holds her breath, waiting for her daughter's response.

Dora nods slowly. 'I'd like that.'

The two women sit a while longer on the bench, quietly watching the progress of others as they navigate their way up the steep hill towards them. Some walk fast, others slow; some jog, and one or two creep very slowly, stopping every few moments to catch their breath; but no matter what pace they manage, Helen notices everyone carries onwards up the hill, putting one foot in front of the other, climbing ever closer towards the top.

DORA

Present Day

The builders are already clambering about on the roof of the old factory as she lets herself out of the heavy metal door and makes her way down the stairwell and out onto the street. They've been there since seven a.m., pulling up flashing and gutters and dropping large pieces of felt and asphalt down the chute into the skip below.

'Cheerio,' one of them shouts, giving her a wave as she steps out onto the pavement.

She smiles up at them. 'See you.'

They're a cheery bunch; they've been working the kettle overtime since they arrived on the job yesterday, but they're hard-working and polite and Dora doesn't mind their easy banter. It feels good to be finally doing something about the leaking roof, especially now the fleeting warmth of summer has faded and they're back to the familiar grey drizzle of autumn. Thankfully it's another dry day, brisk and breezy, and as Dora makes her way along the road she sees curled brown leaves and crisp packets racing along beside her on the pavement. She's in luck: a half-empty number 38 pulls up as she reaches the stop. She clambers on and takes a seat near the back.

She's still a bit annoyed with Dan that he hasn't been able to rearrange his interview with the local paper. She knows it's a great opportunity to raise his profile and that the feature might bring in a few private commissions, but the scan's been booked for weeks now. She's sad he won't be there to share the experience with her and see the baby for himself.

'Just make sure it hasn't got my nose . . . or my teeth. We can't afford the dentist's bills,' he'd joked.

'I don't think they'll be looking for teeth, Dan! Have you even looked at those books I got you?'

'Sure I have.' But she could tell by the playful glint in his eyes that he hadn't, not yet.

'And you're sure you don't want to know the sex?'

Dan had shrugged. 'I don't think so . . . do you?'

'No, I think I'd like the surprise.'

'Good, me too.' He'd pulled her close. 'Try and get one of those photos, if you can, you know, the black and white ones that looks like a giant space prawn. I'll call you as soon as I'm finished with the journalist. Let's meet up later.' He'd kissed her hard on the mouth, patted her growing tummy and headed off to meet his contact in some East End café.

Giant prawn indeed, she muses, watching from the grimy bus window as the shops and cafés of the Essex Road trundle past. She's excited about the scan. This will be the second time she's seen the baby, and she feels so differently about the pregnancy now. It's not just because the dreadful fog of morning sickness has finally lifted, but because of how things are between her and Dan now. Ever since her visit to see Cassie at Swan House she's felt different. Lighter somehow, brighter and more buoyant in herself, which is ridiculous because she doesn't have to get on the bathroom scales to know that she's nearly two stone heavier already.

The truth is that both she and Dan know the visit to see her sister has offered some form of release. She still feels Alfie's absence, she still misses him and wishes things were different, but she doesn't agonise over the details of his absence quite so much, she doesn't berate herself with guilt, or search every crowd for his face; and perhaps most tellingly, she hasn't had one of her nightmares or panic attacks since. It will never be

OK that Alfie was taken from them, but Dora feels as though she is moving forwards, on the right track at last.

She places a hand on her growing stomach and strokes the firm, taut bulge of her belly. It's hard and warm and she enjoys the feel of it under her fingertips; it's so solid, so real.

There is a flurry of activity at the front of the bus as a group of kids push their way onto the vehicle, skimming their Oyster cards on the electronic reader by the driver with loud jeers and shouts; boys playing truant from school, she assumes. The barrage of noise and motion is an assault on her senses. She sees the wind whipping hair and scarves and suit jackets on people passing by on the pavement and suddenly longs to be blown along beside them. She jumps up and makes it through the beeping doors, just in time. It's only two more stops; she can walk the rest of the way to the clinic.

It's a treat not to be in the office. Most people, she knows, will be safely stashed at their desks by now, beginning the daily grind, staring at computer screens, talking into telephones, doing their deals, making decisions. She doesn't get to experience this side of London very often, the hours when elderly people creep out onto the streets and young parents push prams towards parks. She can hear the buzz of bike couriers weaving through the traffic and sees a group of tourists sitting in a café window, squabbling over a map and guidebook. She sidesteps a wan-faced nurse, still in uniform, returning home from her nightshift, and declines the advances of an enthusiastic charity worker wielding a clipboard and accosting unsuspecting people as they pass by. It's the same city – still home – but it feels different somehow, as if suddenly steeped in a different light, imbued with a different pace. She supposes it's a side she might see a little more of, when the baby comes.

Everyone at the agency has been great. She'd been worried about telling Dominic about her pregnancy but he'd simply given her a big bear hug and told her to discuss her maternity-leave terms with HR. The job would still be waiting for her when she returned. If he was annoyed to be losing a newly promoted Account Manager for a few months he'd hidden his frustration well. Gradually, as the news had spread, the girls in the office had crowded around her desk, everyone wanting to know how she was feeling, when the baby was due, if she had picked out any names yet or knew what sex it would be. It had suddenly made it all dauntingly real to be talking so openly about the pregnancy. Thank God for straight-talking Leela, who had just looked her up and down and said, 'Damn, I was going to ask where you'd got that amazing new bra from. Your tits look fantastic!'

The hospital isn't far from the bus stop and she arrives early, making her way through the maze of corridors and wards until she finds the ultrasound clinic. Dora gives the receptionist her name and then settles into the waiting room with a tatty magazine. It looks as though she might be there a while; several women are already seated. She hopes it won't be too long; she'd been told to arrive with a full bladder and she is already bursting for the loo.

With the magazine spread across her lap she pretends to read an article about how to get the perfect bikini body while actually sneaking surreptitious glances at the other women waiting in the clinic. They are mostly of a certain age, twenties and thirties she assumes, although one woman looks older; she carries a serious-looking briefcase and sits tapping urgently into her BlackBerry. There are partners there too, men shuffling around, some awkward and embarrassed, speaking quietly in hushed tones, others loud and proud, their hands placed with ownership on their wives' swelling bellies. She sees a harried-looking man race past after a manic, giggling toddler while his partner looks on with indulgent smiles, and in the furthest corner a woman pale and miserable, breathing deeply through her mouth as she clutches desperately at an emergency paper bag. Dora recognises the symptoms of morning sickness and throws her a shy, sympathetic smile.

She tries not to stare at them all but she can't help it; it is their bumps she is most fascinated by. She tries to compare her own growing stomach with those around her, sizing herself up next to them, but it's too hard. They are all different sizes and shapes – some non-existent, some tiny, and some downright enormous. It seems extraordinary suddenly, to be sitting there, surrounded by so much hope and expectation, so much burgeoning new life.

A woman in a sari is ushered out of one of the examination rooms, her partner following behind looking proud and triumphant. While he settles up with the receptionist Dora watches the woman stare at a small black and white photo in her hand. She can't seem to take her eyes off it. Dora thinks of Dan's 'space prawn' and smiles. The couple thank the receptionist and leave the clinic, and as they exit through the swinging door two more women enter the room. They sport matching hairstyles – artfully razored bobs – and are holding hands; one of them is obviously pregnant. Seeing them, Dora is reminded of Cassie.

She has thought about her sister a lot over the last few weeks. It's been hard not to. It makes no difference to her that her sister is gay. It makes no difference to her who her sister loves. She's glad she has told her; she's glad that Cassie can be open about her sexuality. Keeping an important part of herself hidden away like that . . . well, it can't have been easy . . . and for all Cassie's tough talk and bravado, Dora knows that her sister would have been scared to tell them, never really knowing how they would all react. But she's glad she knows and she's glad that Cassie might have someone in her life that makes her happy.

It's the other secrets that Cassie laid bare that day in the gardens of Swan House, the secrets that shifted the very foundations of Dora's own long-held guilt, those are the ones Dora has wrestled with. She meant what she told her mother last month up on Primrose Hill: she does believe it is time to move on and to leave the past behind them, and yet, whenever it comes to Cassie and the things she told her about that day, Dora's struggled.

She's lain awake at night staring at the ceiling, playing the scene over and over in her head, pressing pause, rewind and play over and over, until the new images Cassie has given her are intertwined with her own memories of the day. The pieces have fallen into place like a giant jigsaw puzzle; she can stand back now and see the whole sorry picture laid out before her eyes, the sum of all the various parts they each played, and while it has been a relief to understand the full picture at last, it has brought with it a new and troubling emotion.

It's anger that she's felt. Anger that Cassie could have been so cruel . . . so selfish . . . to push Alfie away like that and then to cover up her mistakes for so long and with such painful, enduring consequences. And yet she knows they *were* mistakes . . . selfish, teenaged mistakes, but mistakes nonetheless. Dora knows in her heart Cassie didn't want Alfie to drown that day . . . she didn't want him to die. There was nothing premeditated in her actions, nothing purposefully malicious or evil about what she did; and Dora knows, better than most, that if her own agonising guilt over the last decade is anything to go by, her sister will have paid in full. She will have suffered.

Yet something has held her back from contacting Cassie. She knows that if she can't forgive her sister for her part in the day, then she can't truly leave it behind and move forwards from the tragedy of their shared past. She knows that if she can't do this the only person she will be fooling will be herself, and yet she just doesn't know if she is ready to let go of the anger she has been feeling inside. It's still there, hot and real, and she simply doesn't know how to release it.

*

'Dora? . . . Is Dora Tide here?'

The nurse calling her name pulls Dora from her thoughts. She reaches for her handbag, rises stiffly from the chair and makes her way through to the examination room. She is greeted by a smiley technician who ushers her up onto the bed and then turns to fiddle with the high-tech equipment beside them.

'I'm Maria. This will feel a little cold, I'm afraid,' she says, as she squirts a cold jelly onto Dora's abdomen. 'Do you have a full bladder today?'

'Oh yes,' groans Dora.

'Good, don't worry, this shouldn't take too long. Is this your first baby?'

Dora nods.

'Lovely, well, let's take a look, shall we?'

Dora nods again, suddenly nervous, and stares expectantly up at the large screen angled above her. Up until now this scan has only ever seemed like routine, a chance to get another glimpse at her baby, but now, lying here surrounded by medical equipment and beeping machines, she feels terrified. What if something is wrong? What if something has happened to the baby and she hasn't even realised? She wishes Dan were there.

The woman called Maria presses the probe against her skin and moves it up and down and around until, suddenly, the screen is filled with grey and white lines and strange swirls. Dora peers at the image carefully, the woman moves the probe lower across her belly, and then there it is: the shape of a tiny human being nestled deep within her. She can see a head in profile, a tiny button nose and the curve of a spine before the image shifts and Dora loses the outline.

'It looks like we've got a wriggly one here. Your baby's just turned over. I'll try to get the image back. Come on, little one.' The technician presses the probe deeper still against her skin.

Dora seizes onto her words hungrily. *A wriggly one.* That

sounds good. That sounds healthy. Dan will like that. She ignores the discomfort in her bladder now; the technician can push as hard as she likes for all Dora cares, anything for another glimpse of that tiny person inside her body. And then suddenly there it is again, definitely a baby, not a prawn. Dora's eyes brim uncontrollably with tears as she watches the tiny being wriggling and kicking.

'A good strong heartbeat,' says Maria as they listen to the galloping hoof beats of the baby's heart.

'It sounds fast, is that OK?'

'Yes, perfectly normal.' She fiddles with her equipment and marks up some indeterminable black blobs on the screen. 'There are the four chambers of the heart.' There's another pause. 'And there's the blood flow. Everything looks good.'

Dora swallows.

'And look, there's a hand,' Maria says. She adjusts the probe slightly and zooms in on one fuzzy section of the image. 'Five digits on the left hand.' She repeats the process. 'And five on the right. All good.'

As the scan progresses, Maria checks off a scarily long list of body parts and functions, things Dora hadn't even known to worry about, like bone length, head size and blood flow through the cord and kidneys. Dora realises she's barely breathing. She's spent so long wondering whether to even keep this baby, she hasn't even thought of all the terrifying things that could be wrong with it. Thankfully her nerves are short-lived; the baby passes every test with flying colours.

'Ah, do you see that?' Maria asks as the scan draws to a close. 'Your baby's sucking its thumb. I'll see if I can get a picture of that for you.'

And then, all too soon, it is over. Dora leaves the clinic, clutching the black and white photo of her baby protectively to her. She can't wait to show Dan.

She doesn't need to be back at the office for another hour, so she queues in a tiny sandwich bar for a cheese toastie and then sits on a bench in a tiny garden square, watching the jet stream of an aeroplane thread across a tiny patch of blue high up in the sky. The sun might be making a rare autumn cameo but it's still cold. She pulls her jacket around her, noting that it doesn't quite meet in the middle any more. Then she pulls the image of the baby out of her bag and sits for a moment, marvelling at its perfection. She can't see evidence of her or Dan in the image, it just looks like a fuzzy line drawing of a tiny little person, but she can't stop staring at it. Their baby. She and Dan have created a whole new life. It's a cliché, she knows, but it seems nothing short of a miracle. Happiness bubbles up inside her and she realises, for the very first time, that she cannot wait to meet their child.

Dan's mobile is still switched off. The interview is presumably going well, but Dora is frustrated. She wants to share her excitement with someone. She wants to talk about the scan. She wants to laugh about the butterflies she can feel fluttering inside which are, Maria reassured her, the sensation of her baby moving about, and marvel at the fact she is growing a person inside her body, a real, living baby who wriggles and kicks and sucks its thumb.

She turns her phone over in her hands and then tries Dan's number again. It goes straight to voicemail. Frustrated, she begins to scroll through her contacts. The sight of one name makes her pause. She stares at it until the letters begin to blur. Her finger hesitates over the little green button on the keypad. She thinks for a moment and then, straightening her shoulders, she presses the button, holding the handset to her ear for what feels like an eternity until she hears the familiar voice answer at the other end.

'Cassie, it's me . . . it's Dora. How are you?' She smiles. 'Me? I'm good. I'm great, actually. I've just been for a scan.' She listens for a moment and then shakes her head. 'No, everything's fine. The baby's great. Everything's in the right place, thank goodness.' She laughs at her sister's response and then settles back onto the bench. 'How are things going?'

Dora listens to her sister's answer until a silence descends over the phone line. She knows it's now or never, so, with a deep breath, she speaks. 'Listen, I was wondering . . . if you might like to . . . I don't know, come for dinner one night? . . . Yes, we're in north London. It's not too far.' Cassie speaks again and Dora smiles. 'Great, bring your girlfriend, if you like? You can meet Dan. I know he'd love to meet you too.' Dora listens for another moment and then nods. 'I'd like that too.'

As the two sisters begin to make the arrangements, Dora watches as golden leaves spiral down from the branches of the tall elm tree overhead, landing like small blessings at her feet.

CASSIE

Present Day

Early on Christmas Eve morning Cassie gently extracts herself from Scarlett's warm embrace, scampers across the draughty bedroom and stands under a warm trickle of water in the shower. She dresses quickly and then, picking up her small weekend bag and a large bouquet of white roses, holly and winter jasmine, she quietly lets herself out of Swan House.

It is one of those blissfully crisp winter days that fills her heart with joy. Already it's been a gruelling winter, the days dark and dreary, but today the sky is eggshell blue and the sun glints pale silver through the bare trees. A local taxi is waiting for her, as promised, on the driveway.

'Where to?' asks the driver as she clambers into the back of the cab.

'The station please.'

'Right you are, love.' He eyes her through his rear-view mirror. 'Nice flowers,' he comments as she closes the door behind her with a slam.

'Thanks, they're for my mum.'

'Going home for the holidays?'

'Yes,' says Cassie with a shy smile. 'I'm going home.'

It is Helen's idea: Christmas at Clifftops. Everyone back together, just like the old days. Cassie is nervous; she hasn't been back since she left all those years ago and she is full of trepidation about returning to her family and to the memories that live on in the old house. But Helen has been persuasive. It's obvious she wants to host the day, to gather them all together, to rebuild the bridges and perhaps finally make peace with the past; and who is she to get in the way of that? It might be difficult heading back there after all this time, but it is only a couple of days, after all, and if Richard and Violet are adult enough to join in with the celebrations, well then, why can't she?

Even so, she'd called Dora beforehand, just to check.

'Yes,' Dora confirmed. 'Dan and I will be there too. And the bump, which I might add is growing rapidly by the day. I shan't be able to go near the sea for fear of being mistaken for a beached whale.'

Cassie had laughed. 'I bet you look amazing.'

'Hmmm . . .' replied Dora sceptically. 'Amazingly huge.'

Silence fell across the line. 'It's going to be strange, isn't it? Going back . . .'

'Yes,' agreed Dora. 'Yes it will, but I think it's time.'

'Yes,' agreed Cassie.

The two sisters had chatted for a while longer, both of them skirting around more sensitive subjects, but Christmas, it seemed, had been decided.

It is dark outside by the time her train pulls into Weymouth station, but Richard is waiting for her as arranged, his coat collar pulled up around his ears against the cold.

'Come on,' he urges, taking her bag and embracing her with his free arm, 'let's get you into the warm. Everyone's up at the house. They're all waiting for you. And your mother's cooking one of her special meals.'

Cassie raises one sceptical eyebrow.

'Don't worry,' Richard says as he starts the car engine, 'the chippie's open until nine. Dora's already checked.'

Richard's Volvo purrs through the streets of Weymouth and then on through twisting country lanes. Every so often a cottage or house emerges from the darkness, lit up from within with lights blazing. Cassie sees families sitting around dining tables, eating and laughing, log fires roaring in hearths, Christmas trees decked with baubles and lights, excited children playing games and pleading for just a few more minutes before bed.

'It's like an advert for Christmas,' she muses as they pass yet another brightly lit cottage.

'Yes,' agrees Richard. 'I suppose it is.' There is a pause before he speaks again. 'I'm glad you decided to tell us what happened out there, you know . . . with Alfie. It can't have been easy.'

'No.' She doesn't know what else to say.

Richard clears his throat. 'And, er . . . well, you know Scarlett would have been very welcome for Christmas too, if you'd wanted to bring her. I hope you don't think . . .'

Even in the darkness Cassie can feel the hot flush of her father's cheeks. She puts him out of his misery. 'Thanks, Dad. I did ask her but she already had plans. Maybe we could all do something in the New Year?'

'Yes,' says Richard, 'that would be lovely.' He pauses, indicating another turn. 'Anyway, we're all really glad *you* decided to come.'

'Well, I can't stay away for ever, can I?'

'No, I suppose not. But I know it means a lot to your mother. And to me, of course.' For a split second his eyes leave the road in front of them and they look at one another. Even in the darkness of the car Cassie can see the emotion in his eyes.

'I'm glad I'm here too,' she says.

They fall into silence until Richard clears his throat. 'How are things going at Swan House? Are you going to let us in on that secret muesli recipe yet?'

Cassie smiles. 'It's not mine, it's Scarlett's and my life wouldn't be worth living if I told you.'

Richard laughs. 'Fair enough. But you got the distribution deal you wanted?'

Cassie nods. 'Yes, it worked out really well in the end. We're starting small with some of the more upmarket, independent grocers but it will give us a chance to build our customer base and manage our stock while we expand. Everyone's really excited.' It's true. Felix and the others are thrilled with the direction the Secret Garden business is heading in. They are not only covering their living costs now, but also even starting to turn over a profit, which is being carefully channelled back into the business and Swan House. They have plans to restore a second huge greenhouse and the orangery next spring, new recipes and products to trial, as well as a 'pick your own' field of summer berries to plant and harvest. It's going to be a busy time.

But that is next year. For now, it is simply enough to be returning home. She feels butterflies when she thinks of Clifftops and the people already there, waiting for her arrival. She has come a long way in the last few years, yet the one place she has never revisited is Summertown. She has never been back to the place where it all began to fall apart. She knows it's time, but she can't help feeling a little scared. It is the last step.

Richard seems to sense her nerves. 'Not far now. Are you OK?'

'Uh-huh.' She nods and then realises with a start that she might not be the only one feeling strange about the holiday. 'Is it OK . . . being back at Clifftops, after all this time? It must feel a little weird for you too, and for Violet?'

Richard smiles. 'If you'd told me at the beginning of the year that we'd all be here celebrating Christmas together, well, you could have knocked me down with a feather. I wasn't sure how I'd feel returning to the old place after all this time, but it's rather nice to be here and not have the burden of it weighing on my shoulders. I didn't realise how much I felt it. Funny how time changes things, isn't it?'

Cassie looks across at her father and sees a definite lightness in his face.

'We're all just muddling through, I suppose,' he continues. 'Your mother is being very gracious, and Violet, well, Violet has such a big heart I don't think she'd see all of this as anything other than a wonderful excuse for a party.'

Cassie smiles. 'It will be good to see Dora and Dan,' she adds. 'Dora invited me for dinner last month. I met Dan and got to check out the bump. It was very neat then, but she says she's huge now.'

Richard laughed. 'She is. Hard to believe she still has a few weeks to go. She looks great, but if you ask me she looks ready to pop!'

Cassie looks out of the car window and sees a sign for Summertown illuminated in the car headlights. Three quarters of a mile. They are nearly there.

It is Helen who greets her at the front door. She looks nervous, hovering on the top step with her long cardigan pulled around her body as Richard's car sweeps up the driveway. Cassie grabs her bag and the bouquet of flowers off the back seat and then crunches her way up the gravel to the front door. They study each other for just a moment before Cassie walks into Helen's open arms.

'It's lovely to have you home, Cassie.' Her mother's embrace feels warm and tight.

'Thanks, Mum, it's good to be back.' She pulls away from her for a moment and lets Helen smooth her hair and squeeze her shoulder.

'Don't cry,' Cassie adds, 'it is Christmas after all.'

Helen nods and bites her lip. 'I know. I'm not sad. I'm happy. It's just so good to see you. It's wonderful to have *both* of you girls back home, together.'

As if on cue Dora appears in the hallway behind them. 'I thought I heard a car! And just in time for dinner as well, *lucky you.*' She pulls a funny face behind Helen's back leaving Cassie struggling to control her giggles. The two sisters embrace and Cassie feels the hard bulge of Dora's tummy push against her.

'You weren't kidding,' Cassie says, pulling back to regard her sister, 'you're enormous!'

'I know.' Dora beams and pats her stomach. 'How was the trip? Train OK?'

'Oh, you know. Delayed, crowded, smelly . . . but I'm here now. Oh,' she says, remembering the flowers, 'these are for you, Mum.' She hands Helen the bouquet.

'They're beautiful. Are these from your garden?'

Cassie nods. 'We grow the roses in the greenhouse.'

'Clever you.' Helen bends her head to smell the flowers. 'Thank you. Let's go into the kitchen. I'll find a vase and you can tell me how things are going.'

She follows her mother down the hallway. The house appears exactly as she left it all those years ago. The same faded wallpaper and heavy oak panels, the same scuffed skirting boards and carpets, even the same photographs on the sideboard as she walks past. It is strangely comforting to see that things, in some ways, have remained the same at Clifftops.

Helen pushes open the swing door into the kitchen, releasing a glorious smell of roast lamb, garlic and rosemary. It makes Cassie's stomach rumble and her mouth water. She realises she hasn't eaten anything since lunchtime and she is starving.

'I hope you're hungry,' Helen says, as if reading her mind. 'I've cooked a huge roast – far too much for the seven of us. But we can always have cold cuts on Boxing Day.'

'It smells so good!' Cassie exclaims. 'What's going on?'

Helen gives a little laugh. 'OK, OK,' she holds up her hands, 'I admit it. I've been taking lessons.'

Cassie takes another gulp of the delicious warm air filling the kitchen. 'It certainly smells as though you've found an excellent teacher.'

'Oh, yes, probably the best. Betty Dryden offered to teach

me. I go down the road once a week to her house and we spend the day pottering around her kitchen. She takes me through her favourite recipes and teaches me all the tricks of the trade. This is one of hers: slow roasted garlic and rosemary lamb with sweet potato and honey-glazed vegetables.'

'Oh yum! That certainly makes the journey worthwhile.'

Helen smiles. 'I wasn't *that* bad at cooking, was I?'

'Don't answer that, Cassie. It's entrapment.' Dora has burst through the kitchen door and is wielding an empty tray. 'Dad's looking for the decanter and I need some more wine glasses.' She stops in her tracks. 'What's that amazing smell?' She looks from Helen to Cassie sceptically. 'Is that . . . *dinner*?' she asks in disbelief.

Cassie nods. 'Mum's been taking cooking lessons from Betty Dryden.'

'Well, well,' says Dora. 'Wait until I tell Dan we can call off the fish and chip run.'

Helen gives a wry smile. 'The glasses and the decanter are in the sideboard in the dining room. Use the good ones. It's a special occasion, after all.'

Dora nods. 'Cassie, why don't you come with me? You can help me with the glasses.'

'You go,' Helen agrees, 'I just want to finish off in here. I'll join you all in a moment.'

Cassie follows Dora into the dining room. She watches her sister with interest as she moves ahead of her. There is a new, unmistakable waddle to her walk, a tilting of her pelvis and a fresh swing to her hips. It is fascinating to see her so physically changed, so plump and bursting with life. Dora turns and catches her staring.

'Weird isn't it? I catch sight of myself in the mirror and have to do a double take. I mean, I know I'm pregnant. I can feel the baby booting me from the inside out, but it's all this.' She gestures to her swollen belly. 'It's so . . . big!'

'I think you look great,' Cassie says. It is the truth. 'So you can feel the baby move?'

'Yes. It's really squirmy. Do you want to feel?'

Cassie isn't sure, but Dora has already grabbed her hand and placed it onto her belly.

'Wait for it . . . any minute now . . .' Cassie holds her breath. She isn't sure she'll be able to feel anything but then out of nowhere comes a definite jolt against the palm of her hand, the insistent little punch of a flailing limb.

'Oh my God!' laughs Cassie. 'That's so weird. Nice, but weird.'

'Tell me about it! You should try feeling it from the inside.'

Cassie smiles. She's not sure if she'll ever experience the sensation of growing a baby. It's not something she's sure she wants, but she's happy for Dora. 'Wow, so that's my niece or nephew?' She leans in towards her sister's stomach, her hand still on her belly. 'Hello, little one, it's Aunty Cass. I can't wait to meet you.' There is another kick. Cassie laughs.

'I think that was "Hello".'

Cassie is still surprised at the transformation Dora has undergone since she came to visit her in Oxford in the summer. It isn't just the physical changes her sister's body's gone through, but more the calm serenity she now exudes. Dora, it seems, has finally resolved her inner turmoil and is at peace. Cassie is pleased to see her so content.

For just a moment the two sisters are silent. It's as if neither of them knows what to say next.

'Thanks again for dinner last month,' Cassie tries. 'I enjoyed meeting Dan. He seems great.'

Dora nods. 'He is. He likes you too.'

'I wasn't sure I'd hear from you after your visit to Swan House . . . you know . . . I guess what I'm trying to say, Dora . . . is that it meant a lot that you called.' She manages to get the words out eventually.

Dora smiles. 'That's OK. I figured it's hard to move on if we don't at least give things a chance, right? After all, I've only got the one sister.'

It's Cassie's turn to smile. 'Wow, you really lucked out with me then.'

She realises they don't need to say anything else. It will take time, but it feels as though the roots of a friendship are forming slowly again between them.

'So, have Mum and Violet come to blows yet? I haven't missed any Dynasty-style scraps, have I?' she jokes.

Dora smirks. 'Everyone's been *very* well behaved, so far.'

'Just you wait till they've all had a few drinks . . .'

Dora laughs. 'God, don't say that!'

'Come on,' says Cassie picking up the tray of glasses, 'we'd better get to it. They'll be dying of thirst in there.'

'About time!' cries Dan as they enter the living room moments later. 'Hello, Cassie! Lovely to see you. You look well.' He pulls her into a bear hug and Cassie submits herself to the feel of strong arms and his warm, soapy smell. She likes Dan. He is kind and genuine and obviously madly in love with her sister. She is glad Dora has finally realised how lucky she is. As Dan releases her she feels Gormley brushing up against her, whacking her with his enthusiastic tail-wagging.

'Hello again, Gormley,' she smiles, patting the dog on his rump. 'Nice to see you too!'

'My turn!' pipes up a female voice from beside them. 'I want to say hello too.' It is Violet, resplendent in a silk magenta dress that shows just a little too much cleavage and rather a lot of leg.

'Hello, Violet, how are you?' The two women embrace warmly.

'I'm wonderful, thank you. It's so lovely to be here. Isn't it kind of your mum to host Christmas this year? I was just saying to Betty here that it's such a lot of work catering for us all like this.'

Cassie nods. Dora was right. Despite the obvious tensions

and awkwardness, everyone is trying very hard to make it feel as normal as possible. Richard is standing behind her, beaming as he fills glasses with mulled wine. She turns and sees Betty Dryden settled on one of the deep sofas.

'Don't get up, Betty,' she says as the elderly lady struggles to pull herself off the seat. 'I'll come to you.' She goes over and gives her a kiss on her cheek. Her skin is thin like tissue paper, but soft, with the floral scent of talcum powder.

'Cassie, it's wonderful to see you.'

'Thanks, Betty. How are you?'

'Oh, bearing up. I'm getting a bit doddery these days, and I miss my Bill. But I mustn't complain. Between you and me some of the old dears in the village are much worse off than me.'

Cassie smiles. Betty is nearly ninety years old herself. She takes the woman's wrinkly hand in hers and gives it a little squeeze. 'I miss Bill too.'

Betty's eyes water slightly. 'He was very proud of you, you know. He loved receiving your letters and photos. He'd read them to me in the evenings.'

'It's him I have to thank for my job,' said Cassie. 'If it hadn't been for him . . .'

'Oh tsk!' shushes Betty with a spirited wave of her hands. 'It's your own hard work that's got you where you are right now. Bill might have given you a jump start, but you've earned your success.'

Cassie shrugs. 'I still have a lot to thank him for.'

'OK, everyone,' says Helen, entering the room, 'dinner is served. Will you all come through to the dining room, please? And bring your drinks. Richard, will you bring the wine?'

Dora and Dan go first, Dan putting a protective hand on her sister's back as he guides her out of the room, the Labrador trotting at their heels. At the doorway Dan leans in towards Dora and whispers something in her ear; her sister smiles up at him in return and touches his cheek. Violet follows, swaying on her high heels while Richard helps Betty up off the sofa. Cassie collects their wine glasses and carries them through to the dining room. The curtains have been drawn and candles lit on the sideboard and table so that the room is filled with a soft amber glow. Helen has laid the table with white linen, silver cutlery and placed tiny arrangements of holly and winter berries at each setting.

'It looks gorgeous, Mum!'

'Thank you,' says Helen, standing back to survey her work. 'It does look nice and festive, doesn't it? Violet did the flowers.' She throws the other woman a small smile and Violet beams back at her.

'Well, Helen, I must say, something smells delicious,' adds Violet, returning the compliment.

Cassie winks at her sister and watches as Dora struggles to control her giggles.

'Don't just stand there, everyone,' urges Helen. 'Take your seats.'

The room is suddenly filled with chatting and the clinking of glasses and cutlery as they all find their place settings and take their seats. Richard wanders round the table topping up glasses until they are all poised expectantly for a toast.

'I think it's only right, don't you,' he says clearing his throat, 'that we remember our absent friends and family on this happy night? Our dearly departed.'

Cassie sees her mother look across at Richard and give a little nod. There is a pause, while everyone thinks of those absent from around the table. Daphne and Alfred, Bill . . . and Alfie, of course. Betty gives a quiet sniff and Cassie reaches across to squeeze the old woman's hand.

'Our dearly departed,' repeats Richard. He raises his glass and they all drink to his toast in silence.

'If you don't mind, Richard,' Dan pipes up, just as they are all returning wine glasses to the table and looking expectantly to the steaming dishes in the centre of the table, 'I also have a little announcement to make.'

Cassie looks from Dan to her sister. Dora's eyes are shining and there is a definite flush to her cheeks.

'It's twins!' shouts Cassie, making them all laugh.

'No,' says Dan, 'as far as we know there's just the one baby in there.' He pats Dora's stomach protectively.

'Though you'd be forgiven for thinking it was octuplets, judging by the size of me!' chips in Dora, causing further laughter around the table.

'No, seriously, there is something else we would like to share with you all.'

There is an expectant hush around the table, before Dora suddenly stands up next to Dan and takes his hand. 'We just wanted to let you all know,' she starts with a smile, 'that we were married this morning in London.'

There is a stunned silence.

Cassie looks from Dora to Dan and then back to Dora. Her sister is grinning from ear to ear like a Cheshire cat. She glances quickly across at their mother, who is sitting open-mouthed, staring up at Dora with undisguised surprise. Momentarily Cassie sees the shadow of a frown pass across Helen's face, but as soon as it appears, it is gone again. She seems to gather herself, and smiles benevolently up at her daughter. And then, the room is filled with a sudden rush of noise. Violet gives a piercing but delighted shriek. Richard leaps up off his chair and starts wildly pumping Dan's arm up and down with excited congratulations. Helen reaches for Dora and pulls her into an embrace, while Cassie sits quietly beaming at them all, waiting for her turn to congratulate the happy couple amidst all the laughter and the joking and the tears.

'You dark horses!' cries Richard. 'So you just sneaked off this morning and tied the knot, did you? Thought you could avoid all the fuss, eh?'

Cassie sees Helen release Dora and look searchingly into her eyes. She knows their mother is disappointed, probably feeling shut out from Dora's big day, but she is, at least, trying to hide it.

'Didn't you want a party? We would have thrown you a wonderful wedding if you'd wanted one, you know. I'd always thought you might get married here at the little church in Summertown. We could have put a marquee up in the garden—'

'I know, Mum,' says Dora, cutting her off. 'I'm sorry if you feel we cheated you out of a big family day, but we only decided earlier this week to do it. It was a spur of the moment thing and we really didn't want a big fuss. It just seemed right this way. I'm not sure I could have faced that church. You know?'

Helen gives a little nod of understanding.

'I thought it was about time I made an honest woman out of her,' adds Dan with a smile, throwing an arm around his wife's shoulders.

'You're not *too* disappointed, are you? It really seemed like the best way, for us.'

Helen shakes her head and smiles. 'No, darling, if you're happy then I'm happy.'

Cassie sees the tension leave her mother's shoulders.

'Well I'm peeved!' exclaims Violet theatrically. 'There goes another excuse for a posh new frock. Thanks, Dora!'

Richard rolls his eyes and they all burst out laughing around the table.

'So it looks like we have another toast then,' he adds. 'To the happy couple . . . and happy Christmas!'

'Happy Christmas!' they all chime.

As the hullabaloo eventually dies down Betty Dryden leans across to Cassie. 'What was that, dear?' she whispers. 'Are they having twins?'

It is agreed by everyone that Helen's meal is a triumph. The seven of them sit around the old mahogany dining table talking and laughing and feasting on roast lamb and a perfect

Cabernet Sauvignon that Richard produces from the cellar with a flourish. Cassie eats heartily and watches the proceedings with interest. It seems her mother and father have become friends in recent months. There is a lightness to their exchanges and laughter that she doesn't remember from years gone by. All of the brittle tension, all the thinly veiled insults and sniping criticisms have disappeared. In their place remains a genuine, good-natured banter and a warm affection for each other. It seems her mother and father have found each other at last, as just good friends.

After dinner the group retires to the sitting room. Helen makes coffee and produces a plate of delicate, home-made petits fours that Betty has baked earlier that day. Then Violet, tipsy on red wine and cognac instigates a riotous game of charades that pits the competitive spirits of Dora and Richard against each other and keeps them all up drinking and laughing until gone eleven.

'Oh goodness, is that really the time?' Betty exclaims, peering at her watch. 'I clean forgot about Midnight Mass!'

Much kissing and hugging ensues as the party breaks up and they all begin to bid each other goodnight. It is decided that Richard, Violet, Betty and Dan will head out to the village church. Cassie and Dora want to stay back. There is clearing up to do and Dora is tired. The sisters stand on the doorstep waving the merry party off into the night.

'I'm knackered!' exclaims Dora as the last torch beams disappear down the driveway. 'I'll just help with the washing up and then I think I'd better turn in otherwise I'll be a total waste of space tomorrow.'

'Yes, and you might miss Father Christmas too, if you don't go up soon!' teases Cassie.

'Ha ha!' laughs Dora. 'So are you sleeping in your old room tonight?'

'I guess so. I just kind of assumed . . .'

'Yes, I've put you in your old room, Cass,' interrupts Helen, coming down the hall with the last of the glasses. 'Do you mind? Richard and Violet are in the guest room. Dora and Dan are in Dora's room. So I've put you back in your old room too. It seemed like the right thing . . .' Helen trails off with a worried frown, suddenly unsure.

'It's fine, Mum,' reassures Cassie.

'Oh good,' says Helen. She seems to want to say something else. The three of them stand awkwardly, waiting, until finally, she speaks. 'Look, girls, I know you're tired. Let's leave all of this mess until the morning. There's something I wouldn't mind showing you both now. Will you come upstairs with me?'

The girls nod, intrigued, and follow Helen up the back staircase, exchanging glances as they go. It seems Dora is in the dark too. They pass the girls' bedroom doors and carry on past the bathroom until they come to a stop outside Alfie's old bedroom. Helen turns to them both with a deep breath. 'I've been thinking it's time I cleared out Alfie's room.'

Dora puts her hand on her mother's arm. 'Mum, that's a great idea. Truly. It's definitely time.'

Helen fiddles with one of the rings on her finger, twisting it around and around nervously. 'I wasn't sure if you would be upset?'

Cassie shakes her head. 'No, it's time we all moved on.'

'So you don't mind?'

'No!' they both exclaim again in unison.

'Seriously, Mum,' Dora says, 'it's the right thing to do. It must be awful living in this house with this . . . this shrine still here, exactly as it was the day Alfie died.'

Helen nods. 'I think it would be a relief to clear some things away. I thought you might be upset if I changed it, but it does feel like the right time.'

Cassie reaches out and takes her other hand. 'We can help you, Mum, OK? You shouldn't have to do this all by yourself.'

'Thanks, girls. I started with a few small things earlier this week, but there are so many memories in there.' She squeezes

Cassie's hand back tightly. 'I thought you both might like to keep some of his things as well.' She turns to look at Dora too. 'You know, for you both to remember him by . . . and for the baby of course.'

'Thanks, Mum,' says Dora. 'I'd like that.'

'Well, then. I guess we should go in?' Helen asks.

'Yes,' agrees Cassie with a deep breath. 'Let's go in.'

Helen pushes open the door and the two women follow her silently into the quietness of the little boy's room.

It is early when Cassie wakes the next morning, not yet six and still dark outside. She lies under the down duvet for a moment, luxuriating in its warmth and listening to the utter stillness of the house around her. Then slowly, as her eyes adjust to the gloom, she looks around at the posters and magazine pull-outs, tacked like trophies onto her bedroom walls, the memorabilia of a long-lost childhood. It is as though she's boarded a Tardis and stepped back in time ten or so years. She stares with detachment at the emaciated models, the moody pouts and the sulky, dark-kohled eyes of the rock stars surrounding her: heroes of a bygone era. There is no denying she had been experimenting with a grunge phase back then.

Suddenly Cassie knows exactly where she wants to be. She looks at her watch. There is plenty of time before anyone will notice she has slipped out and she can be there well before breakfast if she hurries. Leaping out of bed she hops around the room pulling on an old pair of jeans, two pairs of thick socks, a T-shirt and a fleece jumper. It is cold outside and she'll need to wrap up to stay warm.

Down in the kitchen only the hum of the refrigerator and Gormley's gentle snores break the deep silence of the house. The dog opens one eye as she passes, thumps his tail in greeting, yawns and sinks back into sleep once more. In the cloakroom she is faced with a huge array of coats and boots to choose from. Most of them look as though they haven't been worn in years, probably remnants from her grandparents' era. It really doesn't matter what she looks like, so she chooses a large Barbour jacket. It smells of damp earth and tobacco and swamps her slight frame but it makes her feel cosy and safe so she puts it on and does up the poppers. Then she slips her feet into old wellington boots and lets herself quietly out the back door.

It is freezing. Cold air bites at her cheeks and fights to infiltrate the gaps in her clothing, but she turns the collar of her coat up and pushes her hands deeper into the wool-lined pockets, hunching her shoulders and turning determinedly towards the Cap. There is just the faintest glimmer of steely grey light on the horizon as she stomps out across the garden and down into the orchard below.

Cassie walks and walks and gradually the grey first light gives way to a washed-out pastel-coloured dawn. As her body begins to warm up and her muscles relax she lowers her shoulders, raises her head and begins to take in the vista around her. Just like her bedroom, the local landscape is relatively unchanged. Winter has scrubbed the countryside to a dull, earthy palette, but as she tramps down muddy laneways and stamps across fields, familiar landmarks and views greet her like old friends. There is the gnarly old yew tree standing, solitary and alone, in Farmer Plummer's wheat field. It has been sculpted over the years by an unforgiving sea breeze into an exaggerated arch, its branch tips virtually sweeping the ground as it leans into its yogic pose. She walks beside hedgerows, now muted in their winter hues, guiding her on a familiar course. She smooths the scratchy bark of an old stile with the palm of her hand before hoisting herself up and over, reassured to feel it tilt and groan in its customary fashion. And there is the constant, soothing sound of water babbling companionably beside her as she walks along the banks of the meandering stream they had played poohsticks in all those summers ago. The steady splosh and squelch of her wellingtons makes her feel like a young girl again. It is disconcerting, and yet, Cassie realises, also strangely comforting. She is home.

It is the sight of the sea though, that brings her to a halt. As she rounds the top of the Cap, there it is suddenly laid out before her, an asphalt wash of ocean. In the early morning light it looks ominous and challenging; a cold, deep engine of water roiling and buffeting against the shore below. She stands for a moment and inhales its salty breath, suddenly unsure whether she wants to continue down the slope. But she has come this far; with fresh resolve she puts one foot in front of the other and continues down the walking track towards the beach.

The sun has risen by the time she reaches the pebbled beach below but it is an overcast morning and its light is nothing more than a pallid glow behind a blanket of heavy grey clouds. Now that she is closer she can hear the roar of breakers dumping onto the shore before sucking the water back through the shingle like an old man straining tea through his teeth. Across the pebbles, at the far end of the beach she can just make out a colony of stiff-legged seagulls huddled in a cluster, their feathers bristling in the raw winter breeze. And beyond them, in the far distance, is the splash and spray of salt water rising up off the rock pools. Cassie turns and begins her determined march across the pebbles.

It is the first time Cassie has visited the Crag since the search for Alfie had been called off; the first time she has entered its gloomy depths in over ten years. She is surprised to find her hands and feet remember the old holds and crevices and she pulls herself up over the rocky ledge with ease, dropping down into the cavernous space below, her feet landing with a crunch on the sandy floor. She blinks several times, trying to erase the inky blackness before her eyes and gradually it clears a little, allowing her to look around in the half-light and observe her surroundings. She can make out the graffiti scrawls on the stone walls, a huge pile of bottles and cans at one end of the cave and a faded red T-shirt hanging off a long branch of driftwood that has been hoisted like the bedraggled flag of an army of lost youth.

Cassie shivers. Now that she is still the cold seeps quickly into her bones.

The low stone boulder that has always sat in the centre remains; even more so now it reminds her of a strange ceremonial table; a sacrificial altar. She moves towards it, remembering with sudden clarity a series of images from *that* day: the flash of Sam's white teeth as she laughed a throaty laugh at one of her jokes; the high-pitched squeal of Alfie as he hunted for bats in the darkest corners; the steady drip, drip, drip of moisture falling off lichen as she and Sam kissed and kissed until her head spun and she had to stop; Dora, standing at the entrance to the cave, her hands on her hips, looking hot and cross. She closes her eyes and breathes deeply. There are goose pimples on her arms and if she didn't know better, she could have sworn she could still smell the smoke from Sam's heady spliffs hanging in the air. Standing there, in the darkness of the cave, it is as if ten whole years have simply been erased. Time has played a cruel trick; she is back in the shadows of that one, tragic day.

Cassie walks to the centre of the cave. The flat stone lying in the middle is cold and damp under her fingers. She rubs at its rough edges and blows a thin layer of sand from its surface, just as she remembers Sam had done. As her breath leaves her body it fogs white against the blackness. It is deathly cold, colder even than outside on the beach, but she ignores her discomfort. Looking around at the daubed walls of the cave she suddenly knows why she has come. She knows what she has to do.

It only takes a few minutes to find a rusty shard of metal half buried in the ground, and twenty more or so to complete her task, but she is trembling violently by the time she throws down the blade and stands back to survey her work.

The words gleam back at her, carved white into the grey of the stone.

Alfie Tide: beloved son and brother

The blunt metal instrument has been surprisingly effective. It isn't much of a memorial, nothing compared to the garden she has brought back to life, but it feels right. It is the right place; and it is indelible; it will stand for ever, a monument to her brother's short life.

'Goodbye, Alfie,' she whispers. 'I'm sorry.'

From somewhere far behind her there comes the faintest of sighs, a soft, sad whisper that floats away into the darkness almost as soon as she has heard it.

Cassie turns and peers into the darkness.

'Hello?' She knows it's silly but she calls out anyway.

'Hello-ello-ello,' echoes back at her off the high stone walls, her voice reverberating spookily around her.

She holds her breath.

Nothing.

Just her imagination, or a seagull perhaps, nestled in the Crag's steep walls. She shivers and turns for the exit, suddenly keen to leave. The Crag will remain here, its dark, gloomy walls standing forever still and silent but she wants the daylight now, and her family, who will be waiting for her up at the house.

As she moves a slither of rocks and gravel falls suddenly behind her, tumbling from one of the rocky ledges high up and landing on the sandy ground at her feet. She jumps around again, wide-eyed and afraid. 'Is someone there?'

'There-ere-ere.' The echo taunts her again.

Then silence.

She shivers. She is being paranoid. The cave is starting to spook her out. It is nothing but a little subsidence. Her presence has probably shifted the air in the cavernous space around her and dislodged a precariously balanced rock. It is definitely time to leave.

With a purposeful stride Cassie moves to the opening of the cave and pulls herself up and out onto the cliff face. The sun has risen higher in the sky now and she lifts her face to it and lets the bitter breeze whip across her skin.

She is about to jump down onto the beach below when she stops, startled.

There it is again.

That sad little sigh, barely more than a puff of air on the back of her neck, but definitely there. She feels the goose pimples prickle across her arms and spins around, looking down into the darkness again.

Nothing. There is nothing there. She is being silly.

It is just her mind playing tricks on her. She needs to get back to the house.

Cassie jumps quickly down onto the beach with a loud crunch. She stumbles, rights herself, and then begins to make her way back along the shore, and as she wades across the stones she begins to pick up speed.

Crunch, crunch, crunch.

She keeps her gaze resolutely fixed on the horizon and thinks about the house up on the cliffs starting to come to life.

Crunch, crunch, crunch.

She thinks of Dora, Helen, Richard and the rest of them stirring in their beds and waking to the daylight and the promise of Christmas Day morning.

Crunch, crunch, crunch.

As her feet stomp across the shingle she imagines them all, an imperfect family muddling through, making the best of the life and the love they share.

It is all she needs to accept the echo of Alfie's little wellington boots as his memory trails her home along the shore.

EPILOGUE

'Is she breathing?'

'Yes.'

'Are you sure? I can't see her chest moving.'

'She's breathing, Dan. Trust me.'

'She looks so sweet. Isn't she sweet?'

Dora smiles down at their sleeping baby. 'She's perfect.' She reaches out to brush a dark curl of hair from her daughter's forehead.

'Don't wake her!' Dan whispers.

'I won't.'

'What do you think she's dreaming about?'

'I don't know. I'm not sure four-week-old babies dream, do they?'

'Good point.'

They stand there for a moment longer, drinking in the sight of their daughter swaddled safely in her Moses basket before Dan takes her hand in his and pulls her quietly out of the room. As he shuts the door behind them he turns to her with a smile. 'Come on, there's something I want to show you.'

His hand is warm as he leads her through the flat towards his studio. She can feel the excitement rolling off him in waves. The room has been off limits to her for several months, but Dora realises he is now ready to show her what lies within. He pushes on the heavy door and pulls her through into the brightly lit room. She looks around with curiosity.

It's obvious he's been tidying. The studio is clear of its usual chaotic detritus. The mess of clay and wax, stained sheets, tools and chemicals has been pushed to one side of the room or piled underneath the trestle table in the far corner. In fact, the room is virtually empty. All that remains is one large object standing alone in the centre of the room, mysteriously shrouded beneath a pristine white sheet. Suspicious, Dora leans in to take a closer look.

'Hey, isn't that one of the new bed sheets I bought last week?'

Dan holds up his hands in mock innocence. 'Is it? I just grabbed it out of the cupboard this morning.'

Dora smiles in spite of herself. It is hard to resist Dan's cheeky grin.

'Anyway,' he shrugs, 'it's not the sheet I brought you down here to look at. It's what's underneath it that's important.'

Dora looks closely at her husband. She can see a range of emotions dancing across his face. There is nervous excitement, impatience and pride, and underneath it all, an obvious anxiety. 'I really hope you like it, you see, I made this one for you. You were my inspiration; you and the journey you've been on.'

Dan reaches out and tugs at the closest corner of the sheet. It floats to the floor with a soft *whoomph*, revealing a large bronze statue around one and a half times taller than Dora herself. It takes a moment for her eyes to adjust to the scale of the object. It is dazzling in its size and substance. The metal glows like dark treacle under the studio lights. It is golden brown in hue, but here and there she can see a flecked patina, greeny-blue in colour, running across the surface, emphasising the graceful curve of a leg here or the sharp jut of a collarbone. Gradually, she is able to see the figure as a whole, as the sum of all its parts. She turns to him in wonder.

'Oh, Dan,' she says, barely a whisper, 'she's exquisite. Simply exquisite.'

'She's called *Pandora*.'

The sculpture is of a woman seated on a low bench. Her legs are tucked underneath her and her head is slightly cocked, as though deep in thought. One of her arms is curled protectively around the obvious swell of her pregnant belly while the other rests lightly on the arm of the seat; her palm is outstretched and open. The woman gazes with a quiet intensity at an object sitting in her open hand.

Dora wanders around the figure, taking it in from all angles. She traces the smooth, polished lines and the gentle curves with her fingers, marvelling at the beautiful craftsmanship. The metal feels strangely warm beneath her touch, most likely generated by the glare of the studio lights and the blast from the electric heater in the corner, but nevertheless it gives the statue an eerie, lifelike quality. Dan has said she is called *Pandora*, her namesake then, and yet she can see clearly that the woman is not an exact likeness of her. There are obvious differences in their facial features, their hair and their build. But she can see *something* there, in the subtle lean of her body, the curve of her back, the ripeness of her belly, and the way her hair is pulled back off her face, that echoes her own image. It is as though Dan had captured an essence of who she is and cast her in bronze. She moves closer and studies the woman's face again, gazing at her for a long, long moment. There is such peace and contentment in her expression that Dora wants to weep.

'What's she looking at?' she asks, barely aware she is whispering.

'Take a closer look,' says Dan.

Dora moves towards the woman's outstretched hand. There is a tiny jewel-encrusted box on the flat of her palm. The lid is open and Dora leans in to take a closer look. She can see the swirl of a delicate chain, a necklace, or perhaps a charm bracelet, off which hangs a series of letters. Dora looks at them in confusion. O. H. P. E. She looks back at Dan searchingly.

'Rearrange them. What do you get?'

She thinks a moment, and then smiles. 'HOPE. She's holding hope. It's Pandora's box.'

Dan nods. 'Do you like her?' he asks.

She can't speak. The words stick in her throat. It is too much. Using his immense talent and a lot of patience Dan has fashioned something beautiful and utterly poignant out of the basest of materials, clay, wax and metal. The sculpture is perfect; it is the perfect symbol for their future together. Pandora's box is open. All of life's evils have already flown out into the world, released to cause their inevitable mischief and pain, but Dora knows it doesn't matter any more. She knows that now. Hope remains. While she and Dan are together, the two of them with their beautiful baby girl, and Cassie and Helen, and Richard and Violet, all of them living their large, messy, mixed up lives, she knows they will always have hope. Hope and love. And after all, what more is there to want in life?

Dora seizes Dan's hand and raises it to her lips. 'She's absolutely perfect.'

Then grinning, she pulls him out of the studio and back into their apartment and their life together, the sound of their laughter trailing behind them all the way.

ACKNOWLEDGEMENTS

My heartfelt thanks to uber agent Sarah Lutyens and the wonderful team at Lutyens & Rubinstein; Kate Mills, Lisa Milton, Susan Lamb, Jade Chandler, Gaby Young, Vanessa Radnidge, Fiona Hazard, Matt Hoy, Jaki Arthur and all the other many talented people at both Orion and Hachette Australia who have worked on this book.

I owe special thanks to my sister Jessica for reading the manuscript more times than any sane person should have to and for always finding the gentlest and funniest ways to point out its flaws, Mari Evans for her early encouragement and advice, and Ilde Naismith-Beeley for the frequent injections of coffee and positivity.

I never would have begun writing without the support and patience of my family and friends, both near and far, and in particular Matt, Jude and Gracie. Thank you. This book is dedicated to you, with love.

The Landscape of
SECRETS of the TIDES

One of the places I felt most comfortable as a child was out in the countryside, rambling across fields and through forests with our two dogs bounding at my side. It was the perfect time for daydreaming. This photograph sums up so many of those childhood walks I took. I can almost hear my wellies squelching up the muddy path and the wooden stile's creak of protest as I pull myself over into the meadow on the other side. I love stiles. They are so quintessentially English, and best of all, they are an open invitation: to keep walking, to explore and go further. (I only realised how many stiles I'd written into the novel when it came to the US edits of the manuscript – we struggled to find another suitable word that would translate to the American market!)

When Richard takes Helen to Clifftops for the very first time, he guides her on a blustery walk up to Golden Cap. Their route might have taken them past this very sign.

"'That cliff you can see ahead of us is the highest point on the south coast of England. It gets its name from the exposed yellow sandstone you can see at the summit. I've always thought of it like its golden crown.'

Helen gazed at the bald patch crowning the top of the cliff. In the gloom of the overcast skies it didn't look golden, more of a dirty mustard colour.

Richard read her mind. 'It's probably more impressive on a sunny day, but the views are great, it will be worth it, I promise.'"

Can you see it, there in the distance, cloaked in mist? That's Golden Cap. Every Dorset holiday I would walk to the summit with my family and although it always felt like a trek to reach the top, the views were spectacular. On a clear, sunny day the ocean sparkles cyan blue, the surrounding fields and cliffs are a dazzling green. You can see for miles and miles, all the way to Dartmoor. When it's overcast and windy and you're looking out across the water, you almost feel as though you could be up there in the sky, flying with the gulls.

This is the beach at Seatown, at its most wet and windswept, exactly how Helen would have experienced the fictional Summertown beach that very first time with Richard – empty but for two upturned fishing boats.

"Richard had been hoping for a romantic walk along the shore, but the lead-coloured sea lashed against the pebbles, and a bitter wind raged at them, tearing their coats. They stumbled and shivered their way along the shoreline until they both admitted defeat and hurried back to the car, heads bowed.

'Well that was a great success,' joked Richard, fiddling with the car heater. 'There's nowhere quite like England in the spring, is there?'"

In summer this scene would be transformed, of course, with families and holidaymakers, the narrow lane down to the shore choked with traffic and caravans; the backdrop of green fields filled with orderly lines of parked cars, their bonnets glinting in the sunshine.

It was the beach at Seatown that inspired the events of that tragic summer day when the lives of the Tide family are changed for ever. I always imagined the Crag to be located somewhere in the rocky cliffs at the far end of the beach.

These ancient church ruins at Stanton St. Gabriel, located on the blustery western slopes of Golden Cap inspired the scene where Dora unexpectedly visits her grandparents' graves. Legend has it that once the church was abandoned for ceremonies in the nineteenth century, it became a smugglers' warehouse. The site is now protected by the National Trust and is definitely worth a visit – it's an area that feels full of ghosts and history.

As a child, every day spent on the beach in Dorset felt like a treasure hunt. My grandfather encouraged us to comb the rock pools for shells, and my siblings and I lived in hope that we would be the ones to find a special fossil buried among all those millions of pebbles. When we weren't hunting for treasure we were often skimming pebbles or playing pooh sticks.

In Lyme Regis, even the lamp posts look like fossils and I'm sure that bench below, on a warmer day, would look very inviting – just made for sitting and enjoying hot, salty fish and chips eaten straight from the paper.

To me the Dorset coastline is like an ever-changing canvas. It offers such extremes, such contrast. On a sunny day it's awash with life and noise and vibrant colour. Under stormy skies it is stark and wild and unpredictable. Take these fishing boats, for example: normally they would be bobbing up and down on the ocean, hauling in catch, a lively hive of industry; but abandoned in a rainstorm they take on a more ghostly, melancholy feel. It was these shifting moods and colours that made Dorset the perfect coastal backdrop for the story of the Tides.

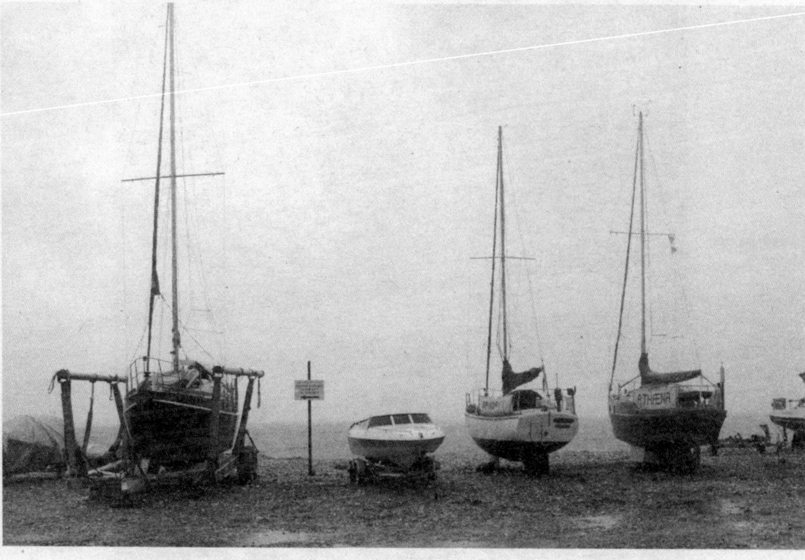

A rain-soaked cobbled alleyway, like this one in Bridport, was exactly where I imagined Tobias Grey's art studio and gallery to be located. Helen would have stumbled down here in a rage, seeking refuge from an unexpected downpour and instead found a whole new world of trouble.

I took this photo on a last pilgrimage to Dorset, just before I emigrated to Australia in 2005 with my boyfriend, Matt. The area meant so much to me that I wanted to share it with him before we left. On a sunny day down on the Dorset coastline the chalky cliffs gleam white and the sea goes on and on for miles, an endless blue merging with the sky.

Here I am revisiting memory lane in the pub garden of The Anchor Inn in Seatown in 2005. It was always such a treat; one of the few places, as kids, where we were allowed to drink Coke (always straight from the bottle) and eat packets of crisps, although they always came with the warning: *don't ruin your lunch!* I didn't have access to old family photographs at the time of writing *Secrets of the Tides*, so I would occasionally revisit these more recent photos when writing scenes for the novel – I think they helped me reconnect with the place and the emotions that landscape conjures in me. It's only now, as I watch my novel go out into the world and my own children grow and thrive, that I begin to understand just how powerful childhood memories can be.

Hannah Richell
July 2012